Blind to Love

She hopes his heart will decide...

Catherine George was born in Wales, and early on developed a passion for reading which eventually fuelled her compulsion to write. Marriage to an engineer led to nine years in Brazil, but on his later travels the education of her son and daughter kept her at home in the UK. And instead of constant reading to pass her lonely evenings she began to write the first of her romantic novels, which was published by Mills & Boon® in 1982. Since then, Catherine has written over forty novels and has currently sold over eighteen million copies of her books worldwide. When not writing and reading she loves to cook, listen to opera, browse in antique shops and walk the Labrador.

"Catherine George brings readers a delightful tale of falling in love."
—*Romantic Times*

Although born in England, **Sandra Field** has lived most of her life in Canada; she says the silence and emptiness of the north speaks to her particularly. While she enjoys travelling, and passing on her sense of a new place, she often chooses to write about the city which is now her home. She has been writing for Mills & Boon since 1974 and over fifteen million copies of her books have been sold worldwide, they have also been translated into more than fifteen languages. Sandra says, 'I write out of my experience, I have learned that love with its joys and its pains is all-important. I hope this knowledge enriches my writing, and touches a chord in you, the reader.'

"Sandra Field pens a phenomenal love story."
—*Romantic Times*

Blind to Love

LAIR OF THE DRAGON
by
CATHERINE GEORGE

LOVE AT FIRST SIGHT
by
SANDRA FIELD

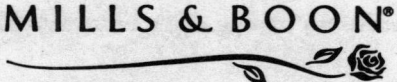

DID YOU PURCHASE THIS BOOK WITHOUT A COVER?
If you did, you should be aware it is **stolen property** as it was reported *unsold and destroyed* by a retailer. Neither the author nor the publisher has received any payment for this book.

All the characters in this book have no existence outside the imagination of the author, and have no relation whatsoever to anyone bearing the same name or names. They are not even distantly inspired by any individual known or unknown to the author, and all the incidents are pure invention.

All Rights Reserved including the right of reproduction in whole or in part in any form. This edition is published by arrangement with Harlequin Enterprises II B.V. The text of this publication or any part thereof may not be reproduced or transmitted in any form or by any means, electronic or mechanical, including photocopying, recording, storage in an information retrieval system, or otherwise, without the written permission of the publisher.

This book is sold subject to the condition that it shall not, by way of trade or otherwise, be lent, resold, hired out or otherwise circulated without the prior consent of the publisher in any form of binding or cover other than that in which it is published and without a similar condition including this condition being imposed on the subsequent purchaser.

MILLS & BOON and MILLS & BOON with the Rose Device
are registered trademarks of the publisher.
*Harlequin Mills & Boon Limited,
Eton House, 18-24 Paradise Road, Richmond, Surrey, TW9 1SR*

Lair of the Dragon and Love at First Sight were first published in
separate, single volumes by Mills & Boon Limited.
Lair of the Dragon in 1994 and Love at First Sight in 1990

Lair of the Dragon © Catherine George 1994
Love at First Sight © Sandra Field 1990

ISBN 0 263 80623 5

05-9710

*Printed and bound in Great Britain
by Caledonian Book Manufacturing Ltd, Glasgow*

LAIR OF THE DRAGON
by
CATHERINE GEORGE

CHAPTER ONE

THE crowded sales-room was so hot that Naomi yearned to leave once her part in the bidding was over. A ninety-piece ironstone dinner service was waiting for her to collect afterwards, along with a Minton dessert set and a pair of Chamberlain's Worcester vases, all the pieces acquired at a price which would delight her London employer. For this was Cardiff, where the truly phenomenal sums were reserved for Swansea and Nantgarw porcelain, and London buyers rarely competed against their Welsh colleagues. An almost cathedral-like hush had filled the sales-room as the bidding rose to its climax on the few such items on sale.

Up to now Naomi's interest had been professional and automatic as she noted prices alongside every lot, whether instructed to bid or not. As usual she'd taken pains to look inconspicuous, her jeans and jersey giving no hint of the large sums at her disposal. But now her bidding role was over and the part she'd been dreading was at hand. The auctioneer cast a bland smile over the assembly and announced a list of small individual items, starting with a Derby piece depicting two dancing figures. Naomi shot another apprehensive look round the crowded room, but the face she was searching for was still nowhere in sight. And if it had been she'd have known. She'd set eyes on Bran Llewellyn only once, but the experience had been more than enough to imprint his face on her memory for all time.

A month previously she had been sent to a similar

sale here in Cardiff. To her chagrin she'd been outbidden on every item her employer wanted, then afterwards the car had refused to start for the journey back to London. Naomi had found a garage to deal with the car by next day, rang her employer to tell him what was happening, then on Rupert Sinclair's advice took a room at the Park Hotel, a mere stone's throw from the New Theatre. All the irritations of the day were forgotten when she discovered the Welsh National Opera were giving a performance of *La Bohème* that very night. Naomi had ignored the 'sold out' signs and hurried to enquire for any returns. To her delight she'd been offered a seat in the circle, and she had gone off to the theatre very happily later, feeling like a child given an unexpected treat as she mounted the cream and gilt stairs from the theatre foyer to the attractive, serpentine circle bar. Glad she'd worn a suit for once, she had threaded through the crowd on her way to find her excellent second-row seat in the circle, then studied her programme as the orchestra tuned up, impressed to learn that the production was a new one by a rising young director, with sets designed by the celebrated Welsh artist, Bran Llewellyn.

A sharp tingle of anticipation had shot through Naomi as the curtain rose at the end of the overture to tumultous applause for the famous garret studio setting. The artist had stamped the scene with his own individual style and panache, even to providing the portrait Marcello, the baritone, was painting of the pretty, half-nude model, who was the only one on stage to stay mute as the opera began. All the frustrations of the day had melted away as Naomi lost herself in the music, and when the exquisite duet between Mimi and Rudolfo brought the house down at the end of the first act she'd made her way to the bar in a dream, with the melody still ringing in her head. Drinks were waiting on the numbered ledge all round the bar for those who'd ordered earlier, but Naomi had joined the throng for coffee, where disaster suddenly struck. As she turned away from the bar with her cup a tall, dark man in a dinner-jacket cannoned into her, almost knocking her over.

By some miracle of self-preservation Naomi had somehow managed to retain her balance and the coffee as the man grabbed her by the elbows, his handsome face aghast. He apologised profusely in a deep, musical, voice, offered to buy her another coffee, a drink, anything to make amends, but Naomi, scarlet and mute, had shaken her head to everything, and made her escape as fast as she could, overwhelmed by the fact that from the photograph in her programme her charismatic assailant was none other than Bran Llewellyn himself.

Naomi came to with a start as she realised the auctioneer was halfway through the list of miscellaneous items, her heart giving a great thump as she heard him announce a particularly fine piece of Leeds creamware.

'A subtle piece for the discerning taste,' said the auctioneer invitingly, and went on to extol the beauty of the clear rich tint of the creamware chestnut tureen, a lidded vessel perforated by hand in the late eighteenth century, with double twisted handles ending in flowers and foliage of exquisite subtlety.

This time Naomi deliberately turned round in her seat, craning her neck in all directions, but there was no sign of the unmistakable, flamboyant figure her sister had been so sure would be present. Unless Bran Llewellyn was disguised as an umbrella stand he hadn't turned up after all. Passionately grateful to him for his absence, Naomi relaxed and concentrated on the bidding, which was fast and furious, culminating in the sale of the tureen for an astronomical sum to a telephone bidder.

Since this was the only piece likely to have lured the famous artist to the sale, a great load rolled off Naomi's shoulders. The prospect of trying to ingratiate herself with the man on her sister's behalf had been hanging over her like the sword of Damocles.

Afterwards, after writing a large company cheque in the office, Naomi began on the endless task of wrapping every last individual dish of the services she'd acquired. When one of the porters, sympathetic with the small, toiling figure, offered to help her downstairs with the boxes, Naomi thanked him fervently, and after a minute or two managed to steer the conversation to the Leeds tureen.

'I was hoping to nab that,' she said untruthfully, swathing a Worcester vase in bubble-wrap. 'It went overseas, I suppose.'

The man shook his head, leaning close. 'Not supposed to say, mind, but just for the record it stays in Wales—went to Bran Llewellyn, the artist.'

Naomi's hands stilled. 'Really?'

The porter nodded importantly. 'He collects the stuff. Look,' he added, 'if you're parked in the multi-storey, nip out and get your car. Bring it to the door and I'll carry these boxes down for you. Too heavy for a little thing like you.'

Naomi did as he said with alacrity, and a few minutes later managed to find a parking space directly outside the building. When her genial helper had finished stowing the boxes in the back for her she smiled at him gratefully. 'How kind you are. Thank you so much. By the way,' she added casually, 'I'm disappointed Bran Llewellyn didn't turn up in person. I was hoping to get his autograph.'

He nodded. 'He usually does. But he had an accident last week, climbing on the Carmarthen Vans. I know a chap who delivers oil to his place up near Llanthony——' The porter stopped suddenly and shut the boot with a bang. 'I shouldn't be telling you this, love. Good thing you're not a reporter!'

Naomi winced. 'I won't say a word,' she assured him, and got in the car. She wound down the window. 'If he's an artist I hope the poor man didn't injure his hands.'

'That's a fact!' The man retreated quickly as one of his colleagues emerged from the building. 'Safe journey, then.'

Naomi, never the world's most courageous driver, was obliged to keep her mind firmly on what she was doing as she found her way out of Cardiff and back to the M4, with no thought to spare for Bran Llewellyn until she was chugging along in the slow lane on her way towards the Severn Bridge and London.

How on earth had her sister slipped up about the artist's accident? thought Naomi, baffled. Admittedly Diana worked in the features department of the *Chronicle*; nevertheless she rarely missed any hard news that came in. Naomi frowned, hoping the artist had suffered nothing too terrible in the way of injuries. At the same time she was deeply thankful he'd been prevented from attending the sale. After hearing about the incident at the theatre, Diana had been obsessed with the idea of an article about him. Her master plan had been for Naomi to buttonhole Bran Llewellyn at the sale, remind him about their accidental meeting, then persuade him to give an interview to her sister. The prospect had given Naomi nightmares. She not only quailed at the prospect of pushing herself at Bran Llewellyn, but knew only too well that he was famous for his scathing opinion of the Press, who tended to give him a hard time in the gossip columns.

Nevertheless, since bumping into Bran Llewellyn at the opera, Naomi was secretly as obsessed by him as Diana and had done a little private research of her own. She'd learned that he was hailed by some as the greatest Welsh artist since Augustus John, and was successful enough to be notoriously choosy about the commissions he accepted. He was skilled at both landscapes and portraits, and the latter were commissions he accepted these days only when the sitter's looks touched some chord in him. Consequently his studies of gnarled age were renowned, and lately even the simplest of his drawings fetched impressive prices. As if his formidable talent weren't enough, the Welsh artist possessed romantically wild good looks and a personality larger than life, with a charisma that drew women like bees to a honeypot, though to date he remained unmarried. And while women kept throwing themselves at him he'd probably stay that way, thought Naomi, annoyed with herself for a pang of illogical jealousy.

It was late in the evening by the time Naomi arrived in Kensington to report on the success of her day. Rupert Sinclair, fiftyish, sophisticated, lazy, and a highly respected authority in the field of ceramics, was waiting for her. Naomi had learnt a great deal from him since joining Sinclair Antiques. In return she'd gradually taken over the firm's bookkeeping from Rupert, who hated figures as much as Naomi liked them.

'What a clever girl,' he drawled, inspecting the contents of the boxes. 'Did you pack this lot yourself?'

'Who else?' said Naomi tartly. 'Though a nice Welsh porter did help me carry the stuff down to the car.'

Rupert, anxious to join his wife for dinner in the flat

LAIR OF THE DRAGON

above, patted Naomi's dark head. 'Take a taxi home, darling, you deserve it.'

The telephone was ringing as Naomi let herself into the poky flat she shared with a friend. Clare was away on holiday, which meant there was no meal waiting and the place felt very empty. Naomi sighed wearily as she picked up the receiver.

'Naomi?'

'Hello, Di.'

'You don't have to tell me. I know you didn't see him. The wretched man's had an accident, so it was a bit of a wild-goose chase for you after all——'

'It was nothing of the kind. I went to Cardiff to bid at the auction for Rupert, remember.'

Diana, a very single-minded lady when it came to her job, brushed that aside. 'Never mind Rupert. You'll never guess what I found out about our artist today! Crispin says Bran Llewellyn's been commissioned to write his autobiography.'

'And Crispin Dacre's never wrong!'

'As well as being my dear, faithful friend, Crispin's the best gossip columnist in the business; never misses a trick. He says Diadem's persuaded our artist to write his life story—bound to make number one first week on the list. Crispin was in school with one of the Diadem senior editors, so he was first to know our charismatic Celt had agreed.'

'Spiffing,' said Naomi, yawning. 'Now if you don't mind I'm off to take a shower, go to bed, and dream of doing nothing at all for three whole weeks. My holiday can't come soon enough.'

'I was just coming to that,' said Diana, something in her voice turning Naomi's blood cold. 'Listen, love, how about doing me the most wonderful favour?'

Before her conversation with Diana Naomi had been dog-tired. Afterwards she was so uptight that it took her until three in the morning to fall into a restless doze, haunted by dreams of a menacing figure which pursued her relentlessly, brandishing a giant paintbrush.

Diana Barry had joined the *Chronicle* straight from university, armed with an English degree and a personality like a Centurion tank. Now, several years on, she was a respected sub-editor on Features, her only weakness a consuming passion for Craig Anthony, the features editor. Diana had chestnut hair, flashing dark eyes, a tall, generously curved figure and lived in a constant state of frustration because Craig seemed immune to her charms. Her constant aim was some way to show him she was not only desirable, clever, and a good journalist, but the perfect soul-mate to share his life.

'All I need,' she had told Naomi, time and time again, 'is to bring off some *coup* big enough to peel the scales from his gorgeous blue eyes.'

And at last Diana felt she'd hit on the exact thing. Only she needed her sister's help to bring it off.

'Are you mad?' Naomi howled down the phone. 'I won't do it.'

Diana was undeterred, even when Naomi slammed down the phone. She promptly took a taxi round to the flat, installed herself in the one comfortable armchair and talked at her sister until Naomi was at screaming point.

The plan, in theory, was simple. Via Crispin Dacre Diana had learned that the famous Welsh artist would have no truck with a biographer. He would write his own life story or Diadem could push off.

'Only I don't suppose he said "push" off!'

Naomi glared at her sister. 'I don't care what he said. I'm not *doing* it.'

Diadem, went on Diana, unmoved, were providing

Bran Llewellyn with a secretary to work on the book with him in Wales for a couple of weeks, and Crispin had persuaded his editor chum to give Diana the job. The artist, it seemed, could spare only a short time for the project, the end product of which was to be a glossy affair, with coloured plates of the artist's work and the biographical details kept to a minimum.

'It's so maddening!' said Diana, jumping up to pace up and down. 'Just think of the article I could write if I actually stayed in the man's house, but Naomi, I *can't*.'

'Why not?'

'I've had every scrap of leave coming to me, but apart from that I daren't take off from the *Chronicle* at the moment because Craig's deputy is leaving to work on the *Financial Times*, and I stand a fair chance of getting his job. If I pulled this article off I'd definitely get it.' She pulled a face. 'In any case Bran Llewellyn's notorious for being able to smell a journalist a mile off.' She turned to Naomi with a cajoling smile. 'While you, my pet, are very obviously nothing to do with the Press, type very efficiently, and, best of all, have three weeks' holiday coming to you.'

'Which I do *not* intend to spend working like a dog in the Black Mountains of Gwent,' snapped Naomi.

'How do you know where he lives?' pounced Diana.

'The porter from the auction house told me. Not that it matters where the man lives. I'm not going near the place.'

Diana fixed her with pleading brown eyes. 'Not even to help me gain my heart's desire?'

'Don't talk such tosh!'

'It's true. If I scoop an interview with Bran Llewellyn I just know Craig will——'

'What do you mean, *you* scoop an interview?' demanded Naomi hotly. 'I'd be doing that, if you have your way—which you're not. I'm going home to the bosom of our family for a week's spoiling, and then I'm going on a nice little drive around the Lake District in the fresh air, all by myself...' She trailed into silence. 'Why are you looking at me like that?' she asked suspiciously.

'I hate having to resort to this,' said Diana miserably. 'But think back to the time when Greg walked out on you. Who picked up the pieces and put you back together again?'

'You did,' muttered Naomi, deflating like a pricked balloon.

'Exactly. And I was happy to do it, because you needed me.' Diana's eyes filled with entreaty. 'Well now, little sister, I need you. I know it smacks of emotional blackmail, but say you'll do it for me, Naomi. *Please*! It's only for a couple of weeks. My happiness—my whole future could depend on it.'

Naomi stared at her sister despairingly. 'I wish I'd never told you about bumping into Bran Llewellyn that night in Cardiff. You've been obsessed with the idea of an exclusive on him ever since.' She groaned, turning away from the pleading in Diana's eyes. 'Yes—of course I'll do it. If it means so much to you, what choice do I have?'

Diana threw her arms round Naomi and hugged the life out of her. 'You angel—I knew you wouldn't let me down. Now all you have to do is record brief details of your c.v. on tape and send it off to Diadem. Miles Hay—Crispin's chum—will forward it to Bran Llewellyn.'

'A *tape*?' exploded Naomi, pulling free. 'Are you kidding?'

Diana shrugged. 'Not my fault if the wretched man is cranky. Apparently our artist has a thing about voices—probably because he's Welsh. He prefers a tape to a letter of application. Don't scowl like that,' she added, sighing, then gave Naomi a look straight from the heart. 'I've never asked your help before, love.'

Which was such an incontrovertible truth that Naomi made the recording next day, feeling utterly ridiculous, then sent it off to Miles Hay, certain Bran Llewellyn would take an instant dislike to her voice. But only three days later the editor wrote that Mr Llewellyn was pleased to confirm the temporary secretarial post, and mentioned a fixed sum which took her breath away. Would she please report to Gwal-y-Ddraig by the following Wednesday at the latest?

'Bran Llewellyn must have liked my voice,' she told Diana tersely on the phone.

There was silence on the line for a moment. 'It's fate,' said her sister, sounding awed. 'Naomi, I'll never forget this.'

'I don't suppose I shall either,' retorted Naomi. 'My one consolation is the money I'm getting, which is quite fantastic compared with the peanuts Rupert pays me.' Her voice softened with affection. 'Besides, *you* were there for *me* when I needed you, heaven knows. But you owe me a holiday for this.'

'If this comes off I'll stand you a fortnight in the Bahamas,' promised Diana rashly, '*and* bully Rupert into giving you the time off.'

'After a spell in the lair of the dragon I'm likely to need it!'

'*Where*?'

'Home of Bran Llewellyn. I looked it up. That's the name of his house—Gwal-y-Ddraig, lair of the dragon.'

'I don't like the sound of that. As soon as you get there, give me the phone number,' ordered Diana, sounding alarmed. 'And make sure you keep the man at arm's length.'

'Don't be silly!' said Naomi, laughing. 'He probably won't even notice I'm there.'

'Now you're being silly. I wonder if he'll remember you?'

'I very much doubt it. By the way, does Craig know I'm going there?'

'Absolutely not! Have *you* told anyone?'

'No fear. Rupert would probably sack me on the spot. And everyone else of my acquaintance would think I'm mad.'

Naomi was tense with nerves by the end of her car journey from London, though the drive down the motorway had been pleasant enough in the spring sunshine. After crossing the Severn Bridge the journey was swift and uneventful along dual carriageways and major roads which took her past Abergavenny on the road for Hereford for a few miles until she reached the signpost—so suddenly she almost missed the turn—for Llanfihangel Crucorney. And suddenly, with no transition, Naomi found herself transported back in time, as by the simple expedient of leaving a modern highway she found herself deep in the Welsh Marches. Unspoilt and ravishingly beautiful in the spring sunlight as the area was, the blood-soaked drama of its past was hard to believe as the quiet road wound towards the next landmark on her route, the Skirrid Inn, the oldest public house in the Principality of Wales.

Naomi suddenly yearned for tea, or lemonade, or anything to quench a thirst which was sudden and overwhelming. But, recognising the longing as a subconscious attempt to postpone the meeting with Bran Llewellyn, she passed the inn and turned left again at a signpost for Cwmyoy and Llanthony, down a narrow steep road which levelled out after a short distance to meander on its convoluted way through the Vale of Ewyas.

It was impossible to drive at any speed, since the twisting, turning road was narrow, with passing places for cars to edge past each other when absolutely necessary. Much to Naomi's relief she met virtually no traffic, and despite her mounting tension was able to enjoy the beautiful scenery at leisure as she drove along a road edged by low, barbered hedges. Because her previous visits to Wales had been restricted to Cardiff and the windswept beaches of Pembrokeshire, she had visualised the Black Mountains as a bleak, austere place, inhospitable and hostile to intruders from beyond Offa's Dyke.

Nothing could have been further from the truth. Instead of great barren jagged peaks the mountains were sensuously rounded, as though a mythical race of giants had built a series of burial mounds for their kings along the bed of the Honddu, the small river which splashed companionably below, dictating the serpentine meanderings of the road.

The mountains, far from being black or bleak, wore bronze crowns of bracken above purple cloaks slashed with bright green, where decidous trees not yet in leaf grew cheek-by-jowl with feathery young conifers. And below the mantle of planted trees lay gentler slopes which bordered the road in a colourful patchwork of small, sheep-dotted fields edged by tidy hedgerows starred with daffodils.

The noise, to Naomi's delight and amusement, was quite extraordinary. She rolled down the window, amazed by the sheer volume of sound as she passed lambing sheds at the farms en route. The air, warm and spring-scented, fairly vibrated with the ovine chorus as she pulled over into one of the wider passing places to study the directions for the last lap of her journey.

Gwal-y-Ddraig, when she finally managed to find it, lay at the end of a steep drive which wound up through a forest of conifers to nowhere until the house swam into view like a mirage in an oasis of gardens backed by the mountain slope. Solid and four-square, built of rose-bronze sandstone, Bran Llewellyn's house came as a surprise. For one thing it was much smaller and less grand than she'd expected, with small, multi-paned windows and a plain oak door. But as Naomi got out of the car she could see another large building at the back, joined to the main house by a stone passageway. And, as confirmation that she'd found the right house, a weathervane on the roof flaunted a gleaming brass replica of the dragon on the Welsh national flag.

Suffering a bad attack of cold feet at the sight of Bran Llewellyn's home, Naomi stiffened her backbone, reminding herself that the money was fabulous and, whatever happened, the time would soon pass. She lifted her suitcases from the car and put them down in front of the main door, then rang the old-fashioned iron bell.

After a short interval the door opened wide to reveal, not the great artist himself, to Naomi's relief, but a thin, friendly woman in a neat navy dress. She beamed as she stretched out a hand in greeting.

'Welcome to Gwal-y-Ddraig. You'll be Miss Barry. Come in, come in, you must be tired after driving so far. London, isn't it? Follow me and I'll take you straight up to your room, then you can come down and meet Bran. He's in his studio at the moment, but while you tidy up I'll tell him you're here and he'll see you in the garden-room——' She stopped suddenly.

'There's silly of me, I forgot to say who I am. Megan Griffiths, housekeeper.'

'How do you do?' said Naomi, much cheered by the warmth of her welcome as she followed the bustling figure up the stairs leading from the small, square hall.

Megan opened a door on the landing and ushered Naomi into a sunny bedroom with a tester bed and flower-sprigged curtains at windows which gave breathtaking views of the garden and the valley below.

'I hope you'll be comfortable.' She opened another door. 'Here's your own bathroom, and there's a tray with kettle and china on the chest. You can help yourself to a cup of tea whenever you fancy one.'

'You're very kind. It's a charming room, Mrs Griffiths.' Naomi smiled warmly.

'Megan, please. And Tal will fetch your things. Tal's my husband,' Megan explained.

'Thank you. If you give me a minute or two to tidy up I'll be ready to meet Mr Llewellyn.' Naomi quailed inwardly at the prospect. 'Shall I find my own way to the garden-room?'

'Yes, if you like. It's to the right of the front door.'

No point in putting off the evil hour, thought Naomi when she was alone. In the small, beautifully appointed bathroom she washed her face, tidied her hair, then carefully applied a touch of discreet war-paint before setting out to confront the master of Gwal-y-Ddraig.

Naomi walked slowly down the stairs, running her hand over the carved wood banister, then halted halfway down, her attention caught by the dramatic landscape on the wall below. Even without the 'LL' of the initial in the corner it was instantly recognisable as the artist's work. Naomi gazed at it with a shiver, suddenly conscious of the enormity of what she was doing as she went down the remaining stairs to tap on the door of the garden-room.

When a deep, peremptory voice called, 'Come,' Naomi opened the door on a low-ceilinged, uncluttered room which seemed to merit its name solely because the French windows in one wall opened out into the garden. Late sunshine streamed into the room casting yellow fingers of light over the carpet towards the feet of the man standing very still by the fireplace.

Naomi's previous glimpse of Bran Llewellyn had been brief in the extreme, allowing little time for details. Now she could see he was tall for a Welshman, and powerfully built. He stood with hands thrust in pockets, his head thrown back, the familiar shock of coal-black hair longer than when she'd seen him last. He wore a dark green sweatshirt tucked into khaki trousers, espadrilles on his bare brown feet. And now she was actually in his presence again she realised that the face she found so hard to forget was arresting rather than conventionally handsome. His forehead was domed and leonine and his eyebrows arched thick above heavy-lidded eyes set well apart above a long, prominent nose, but the face was expressionless other than a hint of the sensual in the curve of his wide, tightly closed mouth. As Naomi approached him she saw that stitches had recently been removed from one cheek, leaving a red scar.

She cleared her throat nervously, holding out her hand. 'Good evening. I'm Naomi Barry.'

'Welcome to Gwal-y-Ddraig,' he answered, ignoring the hand.

Naomi let it fall, mortified because in her heart of hearts she'd hoped he'd remember her. 'Thank you.'

Bran Llewellyn sat down in one of the tall-backed chairs flanking the fireplace, waving her towards the other. 'Tell me about yourself.'

'What would you like to know, Mr Llewellyn?'

'Begin at the beginning.'

'But I sent the tape you asked for——'

'Obviously,' he interrupted. 'Nevertheless, now you're here in person please be good enough to refresh my memory.'

Naomi forced herself to speak calmly as she told the still, attentive man that she'd been born in Cheltenham, received the usual secondary education and gone on to take an English degree at London University, and then a job as a business researcher with a management consultancy before her present employment.

'What made you change to work in a shop?' he asked.

She stiffened. 'Because I find the work interesting. I'm quite good with figures, I can type, and I enjoy dealing with the public, all necessary requirements for someone working at Sinclair Antiques. I occasionally attend sales at places like Sotheby's, something I find stimulating——' She stopped, her attention caught suddenly by the alcove at the far end of the room, where a familiar chestnut tureen formed a centrepiece to a magnificent display of porcelain and pottery.

'What is it?' the deep voice enquired.

'I was looking at your collection of porcelain—especially the Leeds creamware.' Naomi turned to him with a polite little smile.

'It's not to everyone's taste.'

'I can't imagine why it's not. Personally I adore that deep creamy tint——' She broke off, flushing. 'Sorry.'

'Don't apologise for enthusiasm!' His mouth turned down at the corners. 'If you must know, it was your experience with ceramics which influenced me to take you on. That, and the way you speak. My main requirement was a pleasing voice.' He shrugged. 'I felt

I could live with yours for however long it takes to commit my life to paper.'

'I hope it's no longer than three weeks, Mr Llewellyn,' she said at once.

'Why?'

'Because that's exactly how much leave I've got coming to me from my job. I made that clear on the tape. I was told you were in a hurry to complete the work in that time, otherwise I wouldn't have applied.'

'I'm aware of that,' he said impatiently. 'I've dictated most of it already, so if there's any hold-up it'll be on your part, not mine.'

Naomi tried not to bristle. 'There's no danger of that, Mr Llewellyn——'

'Good. A rough first draft is all that's necessary. One of the editors from Diadem will take over from there.'

'Then perhaps you'd tell me what routine you require, Mr Llewellyn——'

'My first requirement is use of first names,' he said sardonically. 'For both of us.'

Naomi inclined her head. 'Whatever you say. No doubt you'll want to read through my day's work each evening before——'

'No!' he said, with such force that she blinked, taken aback.

'I—I'm sorry?'

'Let me put you right about this "routine" of yours,' he went on. 'You start at nine each morning, with a suitable break for coffee, lunch and so on, and carry on working until five in the afternoon.'

'Of course. But I don't mind working longer hours than that if it means getting the job down, Mr—Bran.'

'Not *Mr*, just plain Bran.' His mouth curved in a cold, mirthless smile. 'And don't worry, Naomi Barry. You'll earn your money. You'll have homework to do every evening—which is where the pleasant voice bit comes in. You'll be obliged to read back the day's work to me every night after dinner.'

Naomi sat very still, cold with the sudden realisation that the eyes beneath Bran Llewellyn's lowered lids had never looked directly into hers from the moment she'd walked into the room. She swallowed, seized with a sharp pang of prescience.

'I sense by the pregnant pause that you've worked out the reason,' he said harshly. 'You've heard about my climbing accident?'

'Yes.' She cleared her throat nervously. 'It was in the Press.'

'I threw that to the gossip columns so I could keep the really juicy titbit secret for as long as possible.' The grooves either side of his mouth deepened. 'I fancy you know what I'm going to say. My bloody stupid accident, on a climb I've made dozens of times before, has left me with a somewhat inconvenient legacy for an artist. In short, I'm blind.'

CHAPTER TWO

NAOMI gazed in horror at the bitter, morose face, totally at a loss for something to say.

'Well?' he demanded irritably. 'Cat got your tongue? Surely you've got some comment to make.' He scowled. 'Don't tell me you're a sniveller!'

'Certainly not,' she said, stung into response. 'The news came as a shock, that's all. I had no idea——'

'Bloody good thing, too,' he snapped. 'It's not something I want broadcast, so keep it to yourself, please.'

'Of course. May I ask who *does* know?'

'Megan and Tal Griffiths, naturally. Fortunately my condition wasn't discovered immediately, so the rescue team didn't find out. I was taken to a private hospital, where a consultant diagnosed the blindness as temporary.' Bran turned his face until he seemed to be staring straight into Naomi's eyes. 'As you can see I've been lucky—no lasting damage to my face, apart from the scar, which is the least of my worries. Vanity isn't one of my failings. The eye man assures me that gradually, bit by bit, I'll begin to see again. I bloody well hope he's right. In the meantime, to avoid going stark, staring mad, I agreed to do this autobiography.' He smiled sardonically. 'Not merely to alleviate boredom, of course. Only an idiot would have refused the advance Diadem offered.'

Naomi gazed numbly into his eyes, which were deep-set and ringed with lashes as thick as one of his sable brushes. The shock of his blindness was forgotten for the moment as she saw that instead of being dark as she'd assumed, Bran Llewellyn's eyes were purest pale green, with a glitter which made the blindness hard to believe.

'You certainly don't talk much,' he said drily.

'I couldn't think of anything to say,' said Naomi, suppressing a shiver. Blindness in any form to anyone was terrible. But to an artist it was a disaster of cataclysmic proportions.

'You're honest, I'll say that for you!' His mouth twisted. 'Has my handicap lessened your enthusiasm for the job?'

Since she'd never had any enthusiasm for it in the first place Naomi felt it made very little difference, other than deepening her guilt about being in Bran Llewellyn's home under false pretences.

'Not at all. I shall be only too glad to help in any way,' she said neutrally. 'Perhaps you'd tell me where I'm to work——'

'You needn't get down to it right away—I'm not that much of a slavedriver!'

'As you wish. I just thought it would save time in the morning, when I do start.' Naomi got to her feet, wondering what she should do next, somewhat startled when Bran, sensing her indecision, told her to do what she liked before joining him for dinner.

'You've got until seven-thirty. Normally I eat later than that, but I thought we'd make it a rule to eat early, to allow for the reading session afterwards.'

'Thank you.' Inwardly Naomi was dismayed. She'd hoped for a tray in her room.

'Something's wrong again,' stated Bran. 'Odd, really. When I could see I rarely noticed people's reactions. Now they fairly vibrate in the air. Or maybe it's just your wavelength I'm tuned into, Naomi Barry. Are you pretty?' he added, startling her.

'No.'

'Modest! Describe yourself, then.' He turned his face in her direction, his mouth curved in a mocking smile.

She obeyed reluctantly. 'I'm smallish, hair and eyes brown; skin olive.'

'What are you wearing?'

'White shirt, yellow sweater, blue jeans.'

'How about your feet?'

Taken aback for a moment, Naomi reminded herself that he was an artist, that colour was his life. 'Yellow socks, navy deck-shoes, white laces and soles.'

'Good. You appreciate my need to see.' His nostrils twitched. 'You smell good, too.'

Colour flared, unseen, in Naomi's cheeks. 'I'm relieved.'

He shook his head impatiently. 'I meant your perfume. I detest heavy, musky scents. Yours is flowery, subtle.'

'Christmas present.'

'Do you always talk in shorthand?'

'I'm nervous.'

'What's making you nervous — apart from the obvious?' Bran paused, raising a sardonic eyebrow. 'Could it be you're worried about eating with me?'

'Not — not worried, exactly. I just assumed I'd have a tray in my room.'

This time the smile was bitter. 'Have no fear. Megan makes sure I get food I can cope with, so I don't slobber.'

Naomi could have kicked herself. 'That never occurred to me — honestly!'

'Then what the devil *is* bothering you?'

The fact that she was here at all was bothering her, she thought miserably. She'd hated the idea of infiltrating Bran Llewellyn's private retreat when she thought he was in full possession of his faculties. Now she felt like the lowest kind of criminal. But, knowing a confession would have him booting her out of Gwaly-Ddraig a lot faster than she'd entered it, Naomi braced herself to give him some acceptable reason for her uneasiness.

'I just hope I'll be able to do the work efficiently enough to suit you, that's all,' she said lamely.

'Which is not the real reason, but obviously the only one I'm likely to get.' He shrugged. 'Perhaps you feel my manner's too personal on such short acquaintance. If so, don't blame the blindness, Naomi. I'm like that anyway. I've never believed in wasting time where women are concerned.'

'So I've heard,' said Naomi before she could stop herself.

'Ah, my reputation's gone before me, as usual. In which case I'm surprised you had the temerity to apply for the job.'

'So am I,' she blurted, then blushed fierily as his mouth curved again in a smile which raised the hairs on the back of her neck.

'Have no fear, Naomi. You'll be perfectly safe with me — if you want to be.' He turned his head as a clock outside in the hall chimed six. 'Saved by the bell. Go for a walk or have a bath, or take a nap, do whatever you like until dinnertime. I'll see you at seven-thirty.'

'May I make a request, please?' she asked stiffly.

'By all means.'

'Could I make two phone calls? My parents and my sister would like to know I've arrived safely.' She smiled wryly, forgetting he couldn't see. 'Their faith in my driving isn't very strong.'

'Ring anyone you like at any time, Naomi. Most rooms here have an extension.'

Naomi thanked him politely, then went off to make a short, reassuring phone call to her parents. Afterwards she rang Diana, left a brief message on her sister's answering machine, then made a cup of tea from the tray while she took stock of her meagre wardrobe.

Diana, who'd suffered increasing pangs of conscience as the day for her sister's departure approached, had begged to pay for some new clothes, but Naomi wouldn't hear of it.

'I'm going to work, not socialise,' she'd said firmly. 'You can lend me one of your silk shirts, if you like, and maybe a sweater, but that's it.'

Consequently it took very little time to choose something suitable to wear down to dinner that first evening. Not, she thought with a pang, that it mattered how she looked. Bran could neither see her, nor had any idea that he ever had. Once. Naomi smiled ruefully. If he wanted a description of her clothes all the time he'd soon get bored. After the first few days there'd be nothing new to report. She grinned at herself in the mirror as she brushed her damp hair into shape, realising she was taking unusual care with her appearance just the same. Which only went to prove how charismatic the man was, sighted or not. Her first real look into those sea-green eyes had given her a jolt like an electric shock. No wonder he mowed the ladies down! Not, of course, that there was the slightest possibility of joining the ranks of the mown where she was concerned. If those green eyes were functioning normally he'd know she wasn't his type at all. On the other hand there was no one else for him to sharpen his sexual claws on at this particular moment in time, a fact which counselled caution. The man was everything she'd known he'd be, Naomi thought, depressed. His powerful sexual appeal would have been dangerous enough normally, but in some strange way the unexpected trauma of blindness, far from lessening it, only made it all the more lethal.

A knock on the door sent Naomi hurrying to find Megan outside on the landing.

'There's nice you look, Miss Barry,' said the housekeeper in admiration.

'Naomi, please!'

'Right you are.' Megan came into the room, looking apologetic. 'I hope you've made yourself some tea. I felt terrible not giving you some downstairs straight away, but Bran wanted to meet you as soon as possible, and wouldn't let me serve tea in the garden-room.' She sighed heavily. 'Didn't want you to watch him fumble with it, you see.'

'I quite understand,' Naomi assured her. 'I made myself tea up here, and couldn't resist those biscuits in the tin. You made them?'

'Yes indeed. Bran's favourites. Dinner in ten minutes, then. Bran will be waiting in the dining-room—the door on the left across the hall.' Megan hesitated, eyeing Naomi anxiously. 'Think you'll get on with him all right?'

'Perhaps it's more a case of will he get on with me?' said Naomi ruefully, then smiled. 'I'll do my best, anyway.'

Megan looked at her thoughtfully, then nodded. 'Yes. I'm sure you will. I worry about him, you see. Terrible thing to happen.' She sighed deeply. 'Now I'd better get back to that dinner. I hope you enjoy it.'

'I will. I'm not much of a cook myself, but I appreciate good food.'

'Plenty of that here,' Megan assured her, and hurried off to see to it.

Naomi waited until the ten minutes were up, leaning at the window to gaze down the valley at the effect of sunset on the rounded, multi-tinted mountains. When she finally left the room to go downstairs, it was with an air of Daniel making a second visit to the lion's den.

Bran Llewellyn's garden-room had been furnished with a leaning to austerity only slightly relieved by the odd opulent touch. But his dining-room was the exact opposite. Naomi paused on the threshold, her eyes widening at the exuberance of carved mahogany furniture and heavy velvet curtains held back by great silk ropes thick enough to secure an ocean liner. An old, dim mirror in a heavily gilded frame hung over the fireplace, a pair of similarly framed oils hung on walls the tint of the terracotta pot which housed a flourishing palm. On the polished boards of the floor lay a rug in faded tints of coral and blue and sand, so exquisite that Naomi hardly liked to set foot on it.

Bran Llewellyn was already seated at the head of the table, his back to one of the pair of windows which overlooked the view Naomi could see from her bedroom. By his side stood a small, wiry man who said a quiet word to his employer as Naomi hesitated on the threshold.

'Come in,' ordered Bran. He raised an eyebrow as her heels clicked on the polished boards before sinking into the carpet. 'Not deck-shoes tonight, then?'

'No,' said Naomi. 'Though I think they'd be kinder to this carpet than heels. Good evening.' She held out her hand to the man beside Bran. 'How do you do? I'm Naomi Barry.'

'And this is Taliesin Griffiths,' said Bran as the quiet, smiling man shook Naomi's hand. 'For the time being he's working overtime, doubling as my eyes as well as driving me about and overseeing the garden.'

'Pleased to meet you, miss,' said Tal, and held out a chair for Naomi before going quietly from the room.

'I didn't get up when you came in,' said Bran

brusquely. 'I'm not very clever at all this yet. I knock things over.'

Naomi looked at the place settings, surprised that no allowances had been made for his blindness. The wine glasses were tall goblets, and the array of silverware was formidable.

'You're very quiet,' commented Bran.

'I was just wondering if it wouldn't be easier for you if there were less glass and cutlery and so on.'

'Of course it would,' he said impatiently. 'But I categorically refuse to make concessions. It's taken me most of my life to aspire to any luxury, and I intend to enjoy it, blind or not. Do you find that bloody-minded?'

'Not in the least. I admire you for it.'

'I'm not seeking admiration,' he said shortly. 'Tal says there's a minute or two to go before the meal arrives so tell me what you're wearing.'

'Are you going to ask that every time we meet?' she enquired. 'If so you'll soon get bored. My wardrobe's very limited.'

His mouth tightened. 'You think I'm rude. But I do the same with Megan and Tal, until Megan tells me off because she invariably wears a navy dress in the afternoons and gets tired of saying so. It's just that I'm cursed with this hunger to *see* everyone in my mind.'

Naomi felt a sharp pang of sympathy as she tried to view her clothes with an artist's eye. 'I'm wearing a saffron-yellow silk shirt and a narrow, shortish linen skirt—black, with a narrow suede belt through the waist loops. My shoes are suede too, with heels, and my earrings are silver filigree and fake topaz, sort of pear-shaped. My ears are pierced,' she added.

'Well done. Thank you.' Bran raised his head in the gesture she was coming to recognise. 'Dinner approaches.'

Tal served the first course. In the middle of each green plate lay a small crystal bowl containing mayonnaise redolent with garlic, and ringed round it were shelled Dublin Bay prawns, palely pink and succulent. Tal shook out a folded linen napkin and put it across Bran's knees, poured pale gold wine into the glasses then left them to their meal.

'Description isn't necessary at this point,' said Bran, and dipped the first prawn into the sauce with care. 'I know exactly how Megan serves these, so I can see the food quite clearly, which heightens the pleasure of eating to an amazing extent. Incidentally,' he added, popping the prawn into his mouth, 'Megan's mayonnaise is pretty lively, so if you're not a garlic-lover, beware.'

'I adore the stuff,' said Naomi indistinctly, her mouth full. 'Mmm, wonderful.' She watched, her heart in her throat, as Bran's long, sinewy hand reached out for a goblet and conveyed wine to his mouth without spilling a drop. He drank deeply, returned the glass to its exact location, then went on eating in silence for a moment.

'No applause?' he said at last.

Naomi choked on a mouthful of prawn. She drank some wine hastily, less deft by far than Bran as she replaced her glass. 'Applause?' she queried, playing for time.

'Don't pretend you weren't riveted by my performance with the wine glass, Naomi!'

'All right, then, I was *deeply* impressed! Will that do?' she said tartly, then bit her lip.

'Now what's the matter?' he asked impatiently.

'I'm sorry——'

'That I'm blind?'

'No. For the familiarity. Normally I'd be more polite. I apologise.'

'By normally, you mean if I could see.'

She thought it over. 'Well, yes—yes, I suppose I do mean that.'

'Don't sound so guilty.' Bran despatched the last prawn, then wiped his fingers on his napkin and turned his face in her direction. 'Let's get one thing clear, Naomi. I'm paying you to do a job for me, but I don't expect deference, or allowances for my handicap. We'll be thrown together far more than if we'd met in the usual way, but because our time together will be brief it seems only practical to take a few short-cuts. Here endeth the lesson.' He raised his head. 'Our next course is on its way. Not only do I hear the faint rattle of dishes, I can smell Megan's special beef casserole.'

'Is your sense of smell more acute now?' asked Naomi matter-of-factly.

'It seems to be. My hearing, too. It'll be interesting to see if they remain as sharp when I can see again. If I ever can.'

This time Megan accompanied Tal, in charge of a heated trolley as her huband removed the plates from the first course. She beamed as Naomi complimented her on the food.

'Thank you. I hope you feel the same after this lot, too.' Deftly she served Bran with tiny potatoes and small whole carrots, along with a creamy, fragrant helping of beef casserole, then put the dishes in front of Naomi for her to help herself. Tal refilled Bran's wine glass, gave Naomi the mineral water she requested instead, made sure everything was in its exact place in front of his employer, then went off with his wife to the kitchen.

Naomi gave herself a modest portion of everything and fell to with enthusiasm. 'Heavenly flavour,' she said rapturously.

Bran's mouth twitched at the corners. 'You like your food!'

'Too much, unfortunately. If I eat like this all the time I'm here I'll be dieting all summer afterwards.'

'So you're not the type who picks daintily at a lettuce leaf and dismisses puddings as the work of the devil?'

'Far from it. I share a flat with a really good cook, too,' said Naomi sighing.

'Male or female?'

Naomi stiffened. 'Female, as it happens.'

'Ah, I trespassed!'

She made no attempt to deny it as she watched his efficient way with his meal for a moment in silence.

'Lost in admiration again?' he enquired.

'Yes,' she said simply.

He aimed an unsettling smile in her direction. 'You know, Naomi, I'm beginning to think it was a lucky day for me when you applied for the job.'

She put down her fork, her appetite suddenly gone. 'You don't know that for certain.'

'Nothing's for certain,' he said with sudden bitterness. 'I can't even push my plate away in a temper, in case I knock something over, dammit.'

'Won't you have some more?'

He shook his head. 'Megan makes great puddings, I'll save myself for that, but you go ahead.'

'No, thanks. I'd like some pudding too.' Glad he couldn't see how much of her meal she'd left, Naomi rose to take their plates, careful not to disarrange anything in Bran's vicinity.

'Shall I ring that little bell?' she asked.

'No. Not yet. Let's just sit a little before Megan comes. You didn't eat much after all,' he added, startling her.

'I—I left some room for pudding. Clare and I make

do with a one-dish supper as a rule. We eat a lot of pasta. Which accounts for the unwanted bulges.'

'You don't sound like a girl who bulges.'

'So far I don't, too much. And I don't qualify for the term "girl" exactly, either. I'm twenty-seven.'

'I know. I learned that from your tape.'

'I thought you couldn't remember.'

'I lied. I wanted to hear you say it all again.' He shrugged. 'Twenty-seven sounds pretty young to someone of my advanced years.'

'Not all that advanced! It's common knowledge that you're a mere ten years older than me.'

His smile was bitter. 'Only in fact. In experience I'm probably twice your age.'

Naomi flashed a look at him, forgetting he couldn't see. 'My voice is obviously misleading. No one gets to my age completely unscathed!'

'I stand rebuked.' Bran's head went up. 'Our pudding's on the way.'

Megan came into the room with a tray, casting a disapproving look at the half-empty plates on the trolley. 'Wasn't it nice, then?'

'It was wonderful,' said Naomi hastily, 'but I was greedy with the first course, and I'm told you make irresistible puddings.'

Mollified, Megan set plates in front of them. 'Well, this coconut parfait's nice and light, and the passion-fruit sauce is good. Bran will vouch for that.'

'Very true,' he agreed, and reached unerringly for a dessertspoon. 'Normally, of course, I'd be posh and use a fork, but——'

'But if you did you'd waste that sauce!' said Megan. 'I'll put coffee in the garden-room.'

'Thank you, Megan.' Bran blew a kiss in her general direction and the cheerful woman laughed as she trundled the trolley from the room. He went on talking easily as they finished the exquisite parfait, then at last he laid down the spoon and turned his head in Naomi's direction. 'Now for the awkward bit. Shall I call Tal, or are you up to navigating me back to the garden-room?'

'I'll do my best,' she assured him, her heart in her mouth as he pushed back the carver chair and stood upright, using the arms for guides. When Bran was erect he held out his hand and Naomi hurried to take it, the impact of his hard, warm fingers touching off an unwelcome chain reaction along her nerve-endings as she steered him round the table and across the carpet to the door.

'At this point,' he remarked, 'much as I like holding your hand, I can manage the rest of the journey alone. I don't deal in false pretences.'

Naomi's stomach muscles contracted as though he'd hit her. She swallowed hard, and excused herself on the pretext of needing something from her room. She left the tall, slow-moving man to find his own way, and escaped to her bedroom to stare in the mirror, breathing rapidly as she met her hunted eyes in despair. This was going to be so *hard*. It had been bad enough to learn Bran was blind, without discovering that one touch of his hand was enough to turn her to jelly. She waited until she'd pulled herself together, then smoothed her hair and went from the room to join her new employer.

Bran was sitting in his usual chair beside the fireplace in the garden-room. He turned his head as she knocked and went in.

'You were a long time.'

'I'm sorry. How do you like your coffee?'

'Black, strong and sweet.'

In silence Naomi half filled a large breakfast cup,

stirred in the sugar and handed cup and saucer to Bran, then poured coffee for herself and sat down.

'I know one should drink it from a *demi-tasse*,' he went on casually, 'but this size is easier for me. Thank you for not overfilling it.'

Naomi nodded, then bit her lip. 'I keep forgetting you can't see. I nodded.'

'You'll have to learn to say yes — when the question merits it, of course,' he added, smiling crookedly.

'I'll try to remember.'

'I sense a feeling of unease, Naomi. Is socialising with me a strain?'

'No! Not in the least.' Naomi cast about in her mind hurriedly for some way of convincing him she meant it. 'In fact I was just thinking I wouldn't be coping nearly as well if I were you.'

The lines on his face deepened abruptly. 'Ah, but I'm not always like this. Tonight I'm on my best behaviour, with a guest to show off for. But other times the darkness drives me mad. I get claustrophobic, desperate to see the light again——' He stopped abruptly, shrugging. 'A touch of Celtic melodrama to gain sympathy.'

'What do you miss most?' she asked, getting up to take his cup.

He laughed shortly. 'I'd probably shock you if I told you.'

'I doubt it.'

'I shan't try, then.' He relaxed a little, leaning his head back against the chair. 'Apart from the obvious lack of my work, I miss reading. If I was sure I'd never see again I suppose I'd start learning Braille, get a guide dog. But the way things are I can't settle to anything therapeutic. In any case all this is relatively recent. I've just about mastered crossing a room without blundering into the furniture.' He paused.

'That's a point. Don't move anything. I've got a rough plan of the downstairs rooms in my mind, and I can get up the stairs in the studio to my own bed, but my proficiency depends on everything remaining exactly as it is. So for the time being there are no vases of flowers about, and no small scatter rugs to trip me up.'

Naomi eyed the strong, brooding profile for a moment. 'Would it be any help,' she asked tentatively, 'if I read to you? Or wouldn't that be the same?'

Bran turned his face in her direction, frowning. 'Are you sure you want to do that?'

'Yes. I could make a start with the morning paper, read a headline or two, then you could choose which item you wanted read in detail. Unless you prefer the radio, of course.'

'Up to now I've had no choice,' he said thoughtfully. 'Maybe I'll take you up on your offer. We could give it a try in the morning and see how it goes. If it's too much for you I can always revert to Radio Four.'

Naomi put her cup back on the tray, wondering if this was the moment to withdraw discreetly and spend the rest of the evening in her room. Once again Bran read her mind.

'Now you don't know whether to stay, or to go to bed,' he observed.

'Yes.'

'Ah! You learn quickly.' He shrugged indifferently. 'If you're tired, by all means go to bed.'

'I'm not in the least tired.' She hesitated. 'What I'd really like is a look at where I'm going to work tomorrow and, if it's not asking too much, a visit to your studio.'

Bran rose with care. 'Come with me, then.' He led the way from the room slowly, but with a sureness which made it hard to believe he couldn't see his way. Naomi followed him across the hall, past the dining-room and through a doorway into a narrow corridor with a pair of double doors at the far end.

'This used to be a barn back in the past, when Gwal-y-Ddraig was a farm,' he said, when they reached the doors. He opened one, fumbled for light switches on the wall, and Naomi gasped as he revealed a room with a thirty-foot ceiling. The north wall and the portion of ceiling which sloped to meet it consisted entirely of windows, with a dais in front of them, and near by an easel with a half-finished portrait of a young woman. Canvases were everywhere, some piled on the floor, others hung, framed, on the stone walls, along with drawings and sketches Naomi itched to examine. At the back of the room a spiral stair led to a gallery furnished with a bed, and in the niche below it a Chinese screen painted with flying storks sheltered an old brocade sofa draped with a length of figured russet velvet. Several large, battered tables stood in the central portion of the room, littered with every item of paraphernalia an artist could possibly need.

'Well?' demanded Bran, moving closer to her. 'What's the verdict?'

'It's like the first act of *La Bohème*,' said Naomi without thinking. 'The only thing missing is a stove for Rudolfo to burn his play.'

'Clever girl. I based my designs for the recent Welsh National Opera production on it. You like opera?'

Naomi bit her lip, glad he couldn't see her scarlet cheeks. 'Some of them. The more tuneful ones.'

'You must listen to some of my recordings, then. Music, as you can imagine, is a godsend under my present circumstances.'

'Would you mind if I looked round?' she asked shyly. 'I've only seen reproductions of your work up to now.'

'Feel free.' Bran moved between the tables without

once touching anything, and sat down on the sofa while Naomi explored the spectacular room. She moved slowly between the four canvases hung on the walls. Two of them were landscapes, both of them menacing with approaching storm, in contrast to a seascape which conveyed warmth and high summer, with golden cliffs and a transparent aquamarine sea. But the fourth canvas brought Naomi to a standstill, her eyes wide as they met those in the self-portrait of the artist.

It was a head and shoulders study of a younger Bran Llewellyn, the bare torso depicted with a skill which paid full homage to every nerve, sinew and muscle beneath the skin. The eyes, green and watchful as a Welsh mountain cat, stared from beneath slightly frowning brows, the mouth set as though the artist's teeth were clenched tightly in concentration.

'You haven't moved for the last few minutes,' commented Bran. 'What are you looking at?'

'Your self-portrait,' she said quietly, turning in his direction. 'I've seen photographs of some of your other work, but not of that.'

'For the simple reason that no one in the art world knows it exists.' His mouth turned down at the corners. 'Rembrandt painted himself so often because it was cheaper than hiring models, but I feel no urge to reproduce my own face. I painted myself just once because my mother asked me to. When she died the portrait came back here. And here it stays. I prefer models with rather more interesting faces.'

Naomi, privately of the opinion that no face she'd seen in her entire life was more interesting than Bran Llewellyn's, said nothing as she moved towards the painting on the easel. Unlike his celebrated studies of gnarled and battered age, the woman in the portrait was young and flawlessly beautiful. Even in its half-finished state the work was magnificent. Pale gold hair and fair translucent skin were saved from insipidity by dark, slate-blue eyes which looked out on the world with supreme confidence. This girl, thought Naomi, never had a self-doubt in her life.

'I assume you're looking at Allegra,' said Bran. 'What do you think of her?'

'Very lovely.'

'Your tone suggests reservations.'

'Not about your skill. I just wish I had half her glittering self-confidence.'

'I was successful in capturing her, then. Allegra's nothing if not confident.'

'What woman wouldn't be with looks like hers?'

'Are yours so unsatisfactory to you?'

'My face wouldn't launch a thousand ships, certainly. Why is the portrait unfinished?' she added, changing the subject.

'I was about to complete it when the accident happened. My just desserts, I suppose. I took off on a climbing weekend instead of finishing the job.'

'She came here to sit for you?'

'No — to my studio in London. Daddy commissioned the painting. Daughter fell in love with the artist — and vice versa. Artist blinded, Allegra no longer interested. End of story.'

'But surely she knows it's only a temporary condition?'

'She's convinced it's permanent.' Bran's face set in bitter lines. 'I should be grateful. Allegra's shortcomings are much easier to see now I'm blind. Not that I blame her too much. I find it hard to believe in the temporary bit myself.'

'But you must believe in it,' said Naomi quickly.

'Then of course I will!' He rose to his feet. 'Let's move back to the study. Which is a rather grand name for the cubbyhole which houses the word processor.' He waited until Naomi joined him. 'I assume you can use one?'

She laughed a little. 'I nodded again. I keep forgetting.'

'Gratifying! Will you put the lights out?'

She complied, then stood still with her eyes closed before opening the door.

'What are you doing?' he asked curiously.

'Standing with my eyes shut, trying to imagine what it's like for you.'

There was silence for a moment. 'You're a strange girl, Naomi Barry,' he said slowly, the lilt in his voice very much in evidence.

'Not really.' She opened the doors into the dimly lit corridor. 'In normal circumstances I wouldn't be so—so informal.'

'But because I'm blind and you're temporary we've bypassed several of the preliminaries which inhibit newly acquainted people.'

'Exactly.'

He sent a wry, sardonic smile her way, then preceded her along the corridor towards a door Naomi hadn't noticed earlier. Bran reached a hand inside and fumbled slightly for the light, revealing a small, very functional room.

'Until last week this was a sort of store cupboard. Now it's your new domain.'

Naomi sniffed at the smell of fresh paint as she inspected the word processor enthroned on a plain pine desk. Otherwise the room held only a couple of office chairs, a small side-table, and shelves containing typing paper, a thesaurus, a dictionary, and a cassette player. Bran informed her that the window looked out over the back garden and the small wing where the Griffithses lived in rooms above the kitchen.

LAIR OF THE DRAGON   45

'No one's likely to disturb you here,' he added. 'Will it do?'

'Admirably.'

'Good. Have a nightcap before you go to bed.'

'If you don't mind I'll just go straight up.' Naomi gave a rueful little chuckle. 'For the record, I'm giving you an apologetic smile.'

Bran stopped so suddenly that Naomi bumped into him. His hands shot out to steady her, but dropped the moment she regained her balance. 'Sorry. I didn't realise you were so close. I just wanted to say how much I appreciate your attitude. People tend to treat me like part of my porcelain collection.'

'Anything less like a piece of china would be hard to imagine,' she assured him.

Bran leaned in the doorway, blocking her way. 'Naomi, would you do something for me?'

She eyed him warily. 'If I can.'

'Just this once, would you let me touch your face? Your bone-structure will give me some idea of the way you look.'

'If you wish,' she said reluctantly.

Naomi did her best to stand still as Bran reached out to touch her. His long, spatulate artist's fingers moved with delicacy over her brow and nose and along her cheekbones, exploring the lines of her jaw and the length of her nose, light and fleeting on the curve of her mouth, but trailing a line of fire along her nerves in their wake. Her relief was intense when he moved his hand to her hair, running a tress of it through his fingers before he stood back.

'Thank you. I'd pictured you with shorter, straighter hair.'

'It just waves a bit at the ends.' Naomi stayed where she was, hoping he couldn't tell how much his exploration had disturbed her.

'You're embarrassed,' he said, standing aside for her to pass. 'Don't worry, Naomi, I won't repeat the exercise. But I can't believe you're not pretty. Your bones are beautiful.'

She eyed him uncertainly as they arrived in the hall. 'That's an odd sort of compliment.'

'From me it's the highest possible praise!' He held out his hand, and with some misgiving she grasped it with her own. 'So, Naomi.' He smiled enigmatically. 'You've come safely to the end of your first day at Gwal-y-Ddraig. Do you think you'll survive "amid the alien corn"?'

CHAPTER THREE

DESPITE the rigours of the drive from London and the testing evening in the company of Bran Llewellyn, Naomi found it hard to sleep that first night at Gwal-y-Ddraig. Guilt at the deception she was practising, worse than ever now she'd met Bran, battled with another emotion as disturbing as it was unexpected. Aghast at her own response to Bran Llewellyn's famous attraction, she lay awake for hours, knowing that she should make some excuse to leave this beautiful place right away. She tried to soothe her conscience by assuring it she was obliged to stay to help Diana, that she was committed now to helping Bran, too. But the truth was more basic. Now she'd met Bran she had no wish to leave a moment before she had to, a fact which kept sleep at bay almost until dawn. When Naomi woke again, only an hour or two later, she found rain sheeting down outside and the Black Mountains of Gwent living up to their description.

Afraid that seven in the morning was on the early side to go in search of breakfast, she had a leisurely bath, dressed in the same jeans and sweater as the day before, and took time in choosing socks to match her blue chambray shirt. She smiled crookedly. Bran's thirst for pictorial detail was affecting her already. She made her bed, tidied the room, then went downstairs, drawn by the scent of bacon towards a door in the alcove under the staircase. She knocked and entered the kitchen, smiling apologetically when she found Tal and Megan seated at one end of a large scrubbed table, finishing what looked like a very substantial breakfast.

They both sprang up, but Naomi waved them back to their seats, embarrassed.

'Good morning—please don't let me interrupt. I wasn't sure what I was supposed to do.'

'Come in, come in,' said Megan, smiling, her husband quieter but no less welcoming as he returned Naomi's greeting and began to clear away. 'There's early you are. I was just going to bring you a tray.'

Naomi shook her head vigorously. 'No, indeed! Couldn't I just eat in here?'

The other two exchanged looks doubtfully. 'Bran said you were to have a tray in your room,' said Tal. 'That's what he does, you see, miss. He's not at his best in the mornings.'

'I'd much rather come down,' said Naomi firmly.

Megan jumped up and began clearing dishes. 'If you're sure, then. I'll just put some bacon on for you.'

'I never eat a cooked breakfast——' began Naomi, then stopped. 'On the other hand it does smell wonderful. Could I just have some in a sandwich?'

The kitchen was big, and even on a dull, rainy morning it was welcoming and warm, with plants on the windowsills, and herbs hanging from hooks ranged along the central beam of the ceiling. Naomi was soon provided with a sandwich made from wholemeal bread and crisp, flavoursome bacon, and ate with appreciation, as Tal laid a tray and made toast to accompany the scrambled eggs Megan crowned with a silver cover.

'You've forgotten the paper——' Megan stopped, biting her lip, and Tal patted her shoulder.

'There, there, love. None of us is used to it yet, Bran most of all. I'll go up and see to him.'

Megan brought over the pot of tea Naomi had asked for, and sat down at the table to share it with her. 'It's terrible, terrible,' she said tearfully, and swiped at her eyes with a corner of her apron. 'Thank the lord his poor mother's not alive to see him like this.'

Naomi leaned over and touched her hand sympathetically. 'But the blindness is only temporary, Megan. Mr Llewellyn said so.'

Megan nodded, sniffing. 'Yes, I know. And if praying will make his sight come back he'll soon be all right, believe me. Not *his* prayers, of course. Mine.' She shot a searching look at Naomi. 'Are you wondering why Tal and I are on such familiar terms with him?'

Naomi smiled. 'I imagine you've known him a long time.'

'All his life! We knew his family well, you see, came from the same village in the Rhondda. His dad was a collier, like Tal, but had to come up the pit with dust.'

'Dust?' queried Naomi, frowning.

'Pneumoconiosis — coaldust in the lungs,' explained Megan. 'Mrs Llewellyn taught in the infants' school. Lovely woman she was. But they weren't young when Bran was born. Brangwyn he was christened, after Sir Frank, the man who painted the panels in the Brangwyn Hall in Swansea. But the boy had such a shock of dark hair when he was born his Dad said he looked like a little black crow — *bran* in Welsh — and that's what he's been ever since.'

Naomi listened, rapt, making a mental note of it for Diana. 'Was he the only child?'

'Yes, indeed. His mother was forty when Bran was born, caused quite a stir in the village!' Megan's face shadowed. 'But Huw Llewellyn died when Bran was a teenager and Olwen about ten years later. They didn't live to see their son's success. I think his dad was disappointed that Bran had no interest in teaching, or engineering. But all the boy ever wanted was to draw and paint, and in the end he showed everybody he was right, didn't he?'

'Has he lived in this house long?'

'No. Only a few years.' Megan smiled fondly. 'About the time he bought Gwal-y-Ddaig the colliery where Tal worked closed down, so Bran asked us if we'd like to come here and keep house for him.' She looked fierce suddenly. 'You don't want to believe all this rubbish they write about Bran in the papers—women and stuff, I mean. They throw themselves at him, that's the trouble. Bran can't help the looks God gave him.'

'For pity's sake, Megan,' said Tal, coming back into the room. 'Give it a rest.' He smiled apologetically at Naomi. 'She thinks the world of him.'

'And you don't!' scoffed Megan, unoffended, then eyed the tray with disapproval. 'He didn't eat much this morning.'

'Not one of his good days, love.' He turned to Naomi. 'He says he'll leave you in peace this morning, miss, so you can get used to the machine on your own. He gave me a tape for you. I've left it on your desk.'

Deeply grateful to Bran Llewellyn for leaving her alone for her first morning, Naomi quickly familiarised herself with the equipment, but found it difficult at first to coordinate her typing to the deep, musical voice on the tape. In time she managed to adjust the tape to a speed slow enough for her to work at a comfortable rate, and settled to the task. Naomi smiled when she heard that the title was to be *The Flight of the Crow*, wondering if she should tell him she knew the reason for his choice. Not that Bran Llewellyn could object to Megan's confidences, which were only a rather more colourful version of the facts Bran was telling her on the tape. For a time Naomi concentrated on just transposing the spoken word to the screen, but after a while her absorption in Bran's story was so intense that her fingers were soon flying over the keys of their own volition.

Naomi was so lost to the world that she jumped yards when a hard, warm hand descended on her shoulder, sending a shiver down her spine. She spun round to see Bran Llewellyn shaking his head at her.

'I know you're in a hurry to get the job done, Naomi Barry, but Megan tells me you've been at it for hours. It's time you knocked off for a bit.'

Naomi blinked owlishly, swallowing a yawn as she wished him good morning. 'I didn't realise it was so late.'

'Nice to have something to pass the time so quickly,' he said dourly. 'Come on. Megan's taken a tray of coffee to the studio.'

'But couldn't I just have it here?' she asked, looking longingly at the screen.

'*No*. Take a break.' Bran felt for the door and left, taking it for granted she was following behind, but Naomi paused to write the last page to disk, then made a hurried visit to the cloakroom in the hall.

'Right,' she said brightly, when she reached the studio. 'Coffee?'

'I can't pour it myself,' he said irritably.

Naomi's lips tightened as she handed him a cup of sweetened, strong black coffee. 'Biscuit?'

'No. Sit down. Relax. Your obvious yen to escape is bloody insulting!'

'You should be flattered,' said Naomi tartly.

'Why?'

'Because your story's so engrossing I can't wait to get back to it.'

Bran was silent for a moment, his head bowed over his cup as though it comforted him to feel the heat of the liquid on his face. He was dressed for the weather in moleskin trousers and a heavy fisherman's jersey, his feet in battered suede boots. 'How does it sound?' he asked morosely. 'Grammatically, and so on?'

'Good. Very good. But so far I've been too lost in what you're saying to worry about the way you're saying it. In any case I'll sort that out later before I print the first tape.'

'So you go for the rags-to-riches theme?' he asked sardonically, raising his head.

'Hardly that,' retorted Naomi, determined not to pander to his mood. 'You come from a highly respectable working-class background.'

'I was speaking metaphorically.'

'There's always appeal in the man of talent who works his way from obscurity to limelight, whatever field he specialises in.'

'Do you think the book will sell?'

'I've no idea. But your publisher must think so, otherwise you wouldn't have been offered a big advance,' she added bluntly.

Bran shrugged. 'I suppose you're right. But if they're expecting a kiss-and-tell epic, with lots of celebrity names peppered over the pages, they'll be disappointed. Besides, if I'd been to bed with half the women I've been accredited with I'd never have had the energy to lift a brush and there wouldn't be any story.'

Naomi's cheeks warmed. 'Perhaps you could limit yourself to those women who've provided inspiration—motivation, and so on.'

'Lately I've painted very few women at all—and then only when commissioned. I prefer to paint age, character, even suffering, morbid Celt that I am.'

Naomi turned swiftly to the painting on the easel.

'You're looking at Allegra,' he said at once.

'Yes. No age or suffering there.'

'I was — infatuated with Allegra.'

'It shows.'

'Nevertheless, go and look at that face more carefully, now you can see it in daylight.'

The weather had cleared by this time. A watery sun was breaking through the clouds, illuminating the portrait far more revealingly than the artificial light of the night before. The beautiful, assured face looked different. Naomi stood in front of the painting, hands behind her back, her eyes narrowed assessingly.

'Tell me what you see,' commanded Bran.

'The light makes a difference,' admitted Naomi. 'I took her to be younger than me. Now I'm not so sure.'

'Well done. Anything else?'

'Are you sure you want me to say more?'

'Yes. Be honest. Speak your mind.'

Naomi scrutinised the portrait closely. 'She looks — not spoilt exactly, but wilful, used to having her own way.'

'Go on.'

'I get the impression she's demanding, expects a lot.'

'Right on the button.' His mouth twisted bitterly. 'One of her demands being a lover with twenty-twenty vision.'

'Is it any good saying you're better off without someone like that?' said Naomi quietly.

'None whatsoever.'

She scowled, unseen. 'Time I got back to my desk.'

Bran waved a newspaper at her. 'First I thought I'd take you up on your offer to read. I heard an item in brief on the radio, and I'm curious.'

Naomi took hold of the paper as if it were red-hot, then sagged with relief as she found his taste ran to a more sober publication than the *Chronicle*. 'What do you want to know?'

'A Canaletto sold yesterday in London for a preposterously large sum. I'd like to hear the details.'

Naomi found the article and began to read, as interested as Bran Llewellyn in the sale. Afterwards they discussed it for a moment then Bran waved her off.

'All right, Naomi. I'll let you off any more until after dinner.'

'I'll have a chapter ready by then, maybe even two,' she promised as she made for the door.

'Just a minute,' said Bran peremptorily. 'What are you wearing today?'

'Nothing very different. Jeans, same yellow sweater, new blue shirt and socks.'

His mouth twisted. 'You must be cursing the day you answered my advertisement, Naomi.'

More than he knew, she thought, suppressing a shiver, glad he couldn't see her face. 'Whenever I flag I'll think of the money you're paying me,' she assured him, keeping her tone light.

'Is money important to you, then?'

'Only when I don't have any, which happens with monotonous regularity just before pay day.'

He frowned. 'Can't you find something more remunerative to do, for heaven's sake?'

'I like my job,' she said very precisely.

'And I should mind my own business!'

Naomi went back to her labours feeling that life at Gwal-y-Ddraig would prove even more wearing than anticipated if Bran Llewellyn was so quick to pick every nuance of her mood. It was something never encountered in a man before. Certainly not with Greg. She sat staring into space, praying that Bran's antennae weren't strong enough to detect this new, unwanted vulnerability on her part.

Lunch was served on a tray at her desk at her own

LAIR OF THE DRAGON

request. Bran, it seemed, would not be in evidence until dinnertime. Tal had taken him for a drive, as Megan said he did most days since the accident.

Naomi ate quickly, eager to edit and print the first chapter. It was well after five by the time she'd finished, after a reminder of the time from Megan. Bran, it seemed, had left instructions that Miss Barry wasn't to be allowed to work late.

'He said you're to go for a walk in the fresh air,' warned Megan. 'Oh, and by the way, your sister rang this afternoon, asking if you could call her back this evening. She wouldn't let me fetch you to the phone.'

Naomi was relieved Diana'd had the sense to wait until their talk was relatively private. Not that it would do to be careless, even so. The slightest suspicion of what she was up to, she knew, would have Bran packing her back where she came from at the speed of light.

In contrast to the morning the spring evening was so warm and sunny that Naomi enjoyed her stroll through the rambling gardens, which were on several levels, with retaining walls in the few places where the lawns were flat. Long ago in the past the owner who had first converted the farm to a private house had planted trees and laurel hedges to maximum effect. Now, in full maturity, they formed windbreaks and separate areas bounded by beech and conifer and horse-chestnuts, with the bright peachy pink of Japanese maple in accent here and there. The bare branches of a liriodendron, the tulip tree, towered above the shrubbery, marking the boundary of the largest lawn, which had stone seats either end for watching whatever game had once been played there. To her delight, beyond it Naomi discovered a wild, woodland portion dense with trees flourishing as nature intended among drifts of daffodils piercing a carpet of last year's leaves. Tal must have his work cut out, she thought in awe, as she took in the extent of the grounds in his care. Megan might well extol Bran Llewellyn's kindness, but the roles the Griffiths couple filled at Gwal-y-Ddraig were anything but sinecures.

Naomi had a bath and got ready for dinner before making the call to Diana.

'I got your message. I've been on pins waiting for you to call,' said her sister at once. 'Look, Naomi, I've changed my mind. I was a selfish pig to make you do this. I'm getting bad vibes about the whole thing, so make some excuse and come back right away.'

Naomi almost dropped the telephone. 'Now you tell me! Anyway, it's too late. I—I'm committed. Everyone here's very kind. I even have a telephone in my room like everyone else here,' she added significantly.

There was silence on the line for a moment. 'I see,' said Diana unhappily. 'Well, if you must stay, please take care.'

'You still have the same aim, I suppose?' asked Naomi guardedly.

'Well, yes. But only if it's feasible.'

'I'll do my best. See you when I get back to London.'

'Right. But, Naomi—please be careful.'

'Don't worry. I will.'

Naomi sat at the dressing-table when she'd put down the phone, jotting a few brief sentences in the notebook Diana had provided. Afterwards she locked it away in her suitcase, feeling like a criminal as she stowed the suitcase at the back of the wardrobe. She hadn't dared ask Diana exactly what was needed in case they were overheard, but one thing was certain. As no journalist had ever penetrated the environs of Gwal-y-Ddraig before, Diana could at least describe the house. But Bran Llewellyn's blindness was a secret Naomi had no intention of telling anyone.

When she went downstairs to join Bran in the dining-room he was slumped in his chair, a glass of whisky in front of him. His head rose as he heard her come in, his face morose as she seated herself at his right.

'Good evening,' said Naomi, eyeing him, aware at once that unlike his choice of clothes his mood was funereal.

Bran sat with long legs outstretched under the table, his fingers encircling the glass. He wore a corduroy jacket the colour of expensive claret, with a Prussian blue bandana knotted at the open collar of his cream linen shirt.

'Portrait of an artist,' he said with bitterness, sensing her scrutiny. 'One is expected to be colourful.'

Naomi leaned back in her seat. 'Are you in the habit of doing what's expected, then?'

His face relaxed slightly. 'No. Far from it. To be honest——'

'People usually follow that with a whopping big lie,' she said, hoping he could tell she was smiling.

'How right you are! Anyway, what I was about to say sounds like a plea for sympathy, so I won't say it.'

'Now I'm curious!'

He shrugged. 'It's just that I choose my clothes these days by the feel of them. Texture has suddenly assumed enormous proportions. I've had the clothes a long time, so I can picture the colours, but the real comfort comes from the smoothness of the silk scarf and the soft old corduroy. Can you understand that?'

'Very easily. I like the feel of good material against my skin myself.'

'I remember. You were wearing a silk shirt last night.'

'My sister lent it to me. And before you ask I'm

wearing it again tonight. The only variation is my earrings, which are ordinary pearl drops tonight.'

Bran's mood lightened visibly. He took a pull on his whisky, then turned to her. 'What would you like to drink?'

'There's some nice Welsh mineral water on the table. I'll help myself to that,' she said quickly. 'I don't drink much.'

'Because you can't afford it?'

'There is that, of course. But the main reason is a tendency to headaches if I drink more than one glass of wine.'

'Very inhibiting,' he said, amused, then raised his head. 'Dinner approaches. Good evening, Megan,' he called, 'what are you delighting us with tonight?'

Megan came into the room with a tray, chuckling. 'You love doing that, Bran Llewellyn. I was trying to be so quiet, too.'

'I'd know your fairy footsteps anywhere!' He sniffed as she put a dish down in front of him. 'What's this?'

'Melon in port wine. Nice little cubes—use your spoon.'

'Not too much port, I hope. Naomi has a low alcohol threshold.'

Naomi laughed. 'Not too low to manage this; it looks wonderful. Megan's very artistic with food,' she added once they were alone, then hesitated.

'What is it?' he asked instantly.

She must learn to be stricter with herself, she thought in dismay. 'Perhaps you should know that Megan told me one or two things about you this morning. She felt a stranger might wonder about her informality with you, so she told me how they came to work here.'

'It's not quite as philanthropic as it sounds. I could hardly manage here on my own.' His mouth twisted.

'I'd be lost without them at this particular juncture in my life, lord knows.'

For the rest of the meal he kept, very deliberately, to lighter, more impersonal topics of conversation, asking questions about Naomi's job, with particular interest in her knowledge of ceramics.

'You can bid for me at the next sale, Naomi. I always feel I'm getting fleeced over the phone.'

She assured him she'd be happy to bid for him, confident in the knowledge that when the next sale came up she'd be far away from Gwal-y-Ddraig, back where she belonged.

Later, in the garden-room, Naomi drank her coffee quickly so that she could begin reading the first chapter of *The Flight of the Crow*.

'I didn't finish two, after all,' she told Bran. 'I decided to go over this one thoroughly, then work on the next chapter tomorrow. With only forty thousand or so words of text it shouldn't take me long to finish anyway.'

'You're very eager to be up, up and away,' said Bran moodily. 'Is my company so wearing?'

'Not in the least,' said Naomi, not entirely truthfully. 'I'd merely like to spend a couple of days with my parents if I can before I get back to work in London.'

His face relaxed. 'Ah, I see. Right, then, Scheherazade. Read.'

Naomi took her time over the introduction to Bran Llewellyn's life-story, a red ballpoint at the ready for any alterations he might want. With a Welsh love of words as potent as his gift with the brush, Bran Llewellyn painted a very vivid picture of the small village where he was born, where the dominant factor was the colliery which had provided most of the inhabitants with their livelihood.

From its beginning in a slate-roofed, terraced household, Bran's childhood came through as one influenced by a respect for learning, with love and discipline in abundant supply. He received his first taste of education at the infants' school where his mother had taught for years before her late, unexpected marriage, though Olwen Llewellyn had made very sure her son could read and write long before his first lesson at a schooldesk. She also taught him to play the piano in the hope that music, in some form, would eventually be his career. 'Mam,' said Bran in his text, 'had high hopes of one day seeing me graduate as a doctor of music from Oxford.'

Not for Bran Llewellyn the artistic launchpad of grinding poverty and aggro from unsympathetic parents. Harmony in the Llewellyn household had been the stuff of everyday life, until the death of his father when Bran was in his teens. Abruptly the carefree, sunlit prologue to his life was over as the descent of his father's coffin into the grave had changed Bran Llewellyn from boy to adult in the space of one sombre, hymn-resonant afternoon.

'Well, what do you think?' asked Bran.

'I think it's excellent,' said Naomi. 'But is that how you want it to sound? I edited it a bit, but only to tighten it up in places. If you want to change anything, please say so.'

'I'm impressed. Whether it's my own literary style or your expertise I'm not quite sure, but it sounds pretty good so far.'

'*I* think it's very good. So is the next bit.' Naomi chuckled. 'Now you can see why I was so anxious to get back to it. I couldn't wait to see what happened next.' She glanced over at the grand piano in the corner of the room. 'Do you still play?'

Bran shrugged. 'Occasionally. I'm no virtuoso, but I play well enough to amuse. I was in great demand in college. My crowd hung out in a local with a piano, and the others used to stand me drinks as long as I made the night hideous with whatever was in the top ten. If they grew maudlin some of them would even settle for a bit of Debussy sometimes, but not often.'

'I'd settle for some Debussy, if you'd play for me,' said Naomi impulsively, then held her breath, expecting a snub.

To her surprise Bran got up. 'You're a glutton for punishment, Miss Scribe.'

He threaded his way expertly through the furniture to the open piano and sat down. He ran his fingers experimentally over the keys for a moment or two, then began to play.

Naomi sat still, hardly daring to breathe as the strains of 'Clair de Lune' crept softly through the room, then merged into 'The Girl with the Flaxen Hair', and on to Ravel and 'Pavane for a Dead Infanta'. Suddenly, with a great rippling *arpeggio* up and down the keys, Bran launched into a medley of Beatles songs, choosing the earlier, raucous tunes at first, then changing to the plaintive strains of 'She's Leaving Home'. The sad, subtle interpretation moved Naomi so deeply that she remained silent long after the last plangent note had died away.

'Still no applause, Naomi?' He returned to the sofa and leaned back, stretching his long legs out across the carpet. 'What a deflating creature you are, to be sure.'

'I didn't want to break the spell,' she said, clearing her throat. 'You play very well.'

'No. I play *quite* well. And that's as highbrow as I get. If you want Chopin and Liszt you'll have to resort to my record collection.'

'Was your mother very disappointed when you turned down music as a career option?'

'My mother was a very practical woman. When Dad

died it was obvious that I'd need a scholarship of some kind to get to college.' Bran shrugged his shoulders. 'When I got one to the Slade there were no more arguments. She couldn't see how I was going to make a living out of painting, but consoled herself with the fact that if necessary I could always teach, like her.' He turned in her direction, eyebrow raised. 'Naomi, pour me a whisky—please. Half and half with a lot of soda.'

She poured a generous measure of spirit into a tumbler, topped it up with soda, then took it back and put it in Bran's hand.

'Thank you. What *shall* I do without you when you leave?' he asked mockingly. 'You've only been here five minutes and already you're indispensable.'

'No one's indispensable.'

'Some more than others, Naomi.'

'By the time I leave you'll be able to see,' she said briskly. 'Now if you don't mind I'll say goodnight. I'm a little tired.'

'Not surprising. Working for me is no soft option, is it?'

'It makes a change from washing-up,' she said wryly.

Bran frowned blankly. 'Washing-up?'

'When my employer brings back a carload of china from a sale, who do you think washes the stuff?'

'Give me your hand.'

Bran's fingers moved over her palm, smoothing the skin.

'They don't feel like dishpan hands.'

'Rupert supplies us with handcream,' she said with difficulty, her entire body alight in response to his touch.

'Us?'

'His wife helps in the shop, with two part-timers at

weekends. The others do more washing than me, actually.'

'Why?'

'I keep the firm's books.'

'Capable creature! What else do you do with your life?'

'Not much. My life isn't really all that interesting,' she said, and pulled her hand away before his fingers could reach her racing pulse.

Bran gave a short, mirthless laugh. 'In my present state, Naomi, anything that breaks the monotony for me is interesting, even the brand of detergent you use to wash all this antique china!'

CHAPTER FOUR

NAOMI went up to her room that night a prey to several warring emotions. The sensible thing, she knew perfectly well, was to go back to London right away. The fact that she had no intention of doing so was nothing to do with helping Diana, either. She simply wanted to stay in Bran Llewellyn's vicinity for as long as it took to complete the book. It was useless to pretend she wasn't attracted to his abrasive, powerful personality, and had been from the moment she'd bumped into him at the opera. Even the shock of discovering he was blind had only added to the attraction, making him more accessible, somehow, more human. Naomi stood in the middle of her room and closed her eyes, trying hard to visualise what it was like to be condemned to darkness, when the very essence of life to Bran was colour and light and the gift to transfer what he saw to canvas.

She opened her eyes and came back to earth with a bump as she took the notebook from its hiding place. Dreams of Bran Llewellyn as anything but a temporary employer were pipedreams, whereas Diana was part of the fabric of her life, a loving supportive sister who for once needed help which Naomi could provide. If an inside story on the artist was what it took to get Diana her heart's desire, Naomi felt she owed it to her sister to help even if it risked bringing the wrath of Bran Llewellyn down on her own head in the process. Not that he need find out. He probably never read the *Chronicle*. Even if Diana did get the article printed he wouldn't see it. Nor would there be anything in it the least bit objectionable, Naomi consoled herself. She had no intention of passing on anything personal, other than a description of his house. The rest of it would soon be common knowledge in the autobiography, anyway, except for the blindness — and Allegra. And she had no intention of saying a word on either subject, to Diana or anyone else.

The next few days were very similar in routine; breakfast with Megan and Tal and an early start at the word processor, with a visit from Bran at coffee time, then no further meeting until their evening together.

Naomi's guilt diminished with surprising rapidity as she succumbed to the allure of life at Gwal-y-Ddraig, where the loudest noises came from the occasional swooping jet. Now lambing time was over even the sheep were less vocal. London receded into the background. Reality was life here with Bran Llewellyn in his remote, beautiful home in the Welsh Marches.

'Tomorrow is Saturday,' said Bran over dinner the following week. 'I vote we go out. You've been working without a break since you arrived and you need a day off. I'll get Tal to take us on a trip round the area. You can't go back to the city without a guided tour of the land of my fathers, Naomi Barry. We'll visit my favourite haunts and you shall describe them for me, let me see them through your eyes.'

'Oh, but——'

'But nothing. You can't do any more until I give you another tape, anyway, and I refuse to do that until Monday morning,' he said flatly, then his face darkened. 'You'll have Monday to yourself to work in peace. I'm off to the eye man for a check-up.'

Naomi's knife and fork clattered to her plate. 'Something wrong?'

'No. Just routine. Do I detect a note of sympathy?'

'Of course you do.'

His mouth twisted bitterly. 'Just make sure it's not pity, Naomi. That I object to—violently.'

'I'll try to remember,' she said tartly.

'Ah. Now I've annoyed you.'

'Yes, you have.'

'Which means you won't come tomorrow, I suppose.'

'Certainly not. I'd be silly to turn down an outing.'

'Such practicality!'

'A quality you admired in your mother.'

He snorted. 'True. You remind me of her. Often.'

'I'll take that as a compliment,' said Naomi, amused. 'Why do I remind you of your mother?'

'Like you, she had a tendency to cut me down to size.'

'I wouldn't dream of attempting any such thing!' Naomi folded her napkin. 'Now, if you've finished, I suggest we get on. I did more than usual today, so I'd like to make an early start on the reading.'

'Not before I finish my wine, woman!'

Naomi subsided. 'Oh, sorry. Shall I ask Megan to take the coffee to the garden-room?'

'No. I've a fancy to listen to you in the studio tonight.'

This prospect made Naomi uneasy. In the rest of the house she could forget what Bran's blindness meant to him. In the studio she was deeply conscious of his deprivation. Among the trappings of his craft the tragedy of his blindness was inescapable, honing her own conscience to the point where it cut deep with sudden, unwelcome reminders that however she felt about Bran she was, in essence, using him for her own ends. The fact that she was doing it to help Diana made it no better. In the end, thought Naomi cynically, as she went with Bran to the studio, what could one solitary article possibly do for her sister, anyway, other than boost her career a little? If Diana really believed it would make Craig Anthony fall in love with her she was deluding herself. Love just happened. Suddenly, sometimes. As she knew herself only too well. And just as suddenly it stopped and left you flat. Which brought her back full circle to Diana. Without her sister's love and support, thought Naomi bleakly, she'd have been in a sorry state after Greg walked out of her life.

'You seem distracted tonight,' remarked Bran, when they were sitting on the sofa together in the studio.

'I'm a bit tired, that's all. I worked a few minutes longer to finish a chapter.' Naomi leaned forward to pour coffee, careful, as always, as she handed a cup to Bran.

'I'll make sure Megan blows a whistle promptly at five if you persist in working overtime.' His mouth tightened. 'Your tearing hurry to escape is very bad for my ego, Naomi—what lure lies in London to make you so keen to get back there?'

'The lure of a steady job.'

'No possessive lover, lusting for your return?'

'My private life, Mr Llewellyn, is entirely my own business,' said Naomi quietly. 'Now can we get on, please?'

He replaced his cup on the coffee-tray with unerring accuracy, then sat back. 'In a minute. Tell me about this lover.'

Naomi got up. 'Since you're obviously in no mood for work——'

'Sit down!' He pointed an imperious finger in her direction. 'I decide when I'm not in the mood to listen, Naomi Barry, not you.'

She subsided, offended, and rustled the manuscript ostentatiously.

'All right, all right,' he said irritably. 'Stop bristling

and get on with the great work. If you must know, I'll be as glad to finish the blasted thing as you are.'

Naomi began to read, her delivery stilted at first because she was annoyed. But after a while she forgot to be offended, seduced, as always, by the fascination of Bran Llewellyn's struggle for fame. The autobiography had reached the stage where Bran was leading a hand-to-mouth existence in Camberwell, reluctantly dependent on subsidies from his mother to pay the rent for his draughty attic studio. From the text it was obvious that Bran Llewellyn had good reason to be thankful in those early, striving days for the charisma which persuaded more than one girl to model for him for love.

'I can tell by your tone you're looking down your nose,' he said challengingly.

'I'm not. You've already told me you never had to pay for a model — not in money, anyway.'

'If you mean I conferred sexual favours in return for a sitting, you're right.' He laughed. 'Though to be honest, Naomi, I never saw it like that at the time. All those romps with willing, generous young things were just part and parcel of life and the urge to transfer my inner vision to canvas, paper, anything I could lay my hands on.'

Fortunately for Bran Llewellyn, his work had excited interest even before he left college. His teachers were unanimous in pronouncing him an accomplished, even brilliant draughtsman, and an early series of pencil drawings of his mother and various inhabitants of the Welsh village of his birth had been sold before he left the Slade. Then a famous actor, impressed by the young Welshman's work, had asked Bran to try his hand at a portrait. This had proved so successful that it had brought in a flood of similar commissions, but Bran Llewellyn had refused to succumb entirely to what Gainsborough described as 'This curs'd Face Business'. Landscapes were his true metier, and while sensual drawings of youthful models earned his bread and butter in his Camberwell days their main function for Bran had been to allow him to get on with an exhibition of oil-paintings of his native Wales, the work of such consistently high standard that it had quickly brought him recognition as one of the most gifted landscape painters of his generation.

Next morning it seemed at first as though Bran's plans for an outing were doomed to disappointment. When Naomi arrived in the kitchen for breakfast the room was in a rare state of chaos, with no sign of Megan.

Wondering what was wrong, Naomi filled a kettle and cut slices of bread to put in the toaster, then began clearing away, much to Megan's distress when that lady rushed in shortly afterwards.

'You mustn't do that, love!' she remonstrated.

'Why not?' Naomi carried on serenely. 'Something wrong, Megan?'

'It's Tal. He's not well, touch of flu, I think. He's ever so cross with me because I rang the doctor!'

'The best thing you could do. Here, sit down. I've just made some tea.'

'I can't sit down, Naomi, there's Bran's breakfast to see to yet——'

'Not for a moment,' said Naomi, pressing Megan into a chair. 'Just tell me how I can help.'

'You're helping already!' Megan subsided gratefully. 'I get so worried about Tal. He's got this bad chest. He's got dust too, like Bran's dad, only not so bad, mind. When he catches cold he gets this terrible cough.' She glanced at the clock and shot to her feet. '*Duw*, that's never the time? Bran must be wondering what's happened——'

'You tell me what to give him and I'll take him a tray,' said Naomi firmly.

'I can't let you do that!'

'Megan, calm down. Of course I can. I'm not working today, Look, while I eat this toast you make Bran's breakfast then I'll pop it along to his studio while you go back and see to Tal.'

Only Megan's worry over her husband persuaded her to let Naomi take Bran's breakfast-tray along to the studio. Naomi knocked on one of the double doors at the end of the corridor, then opened it carefully and backed into the studio, balancing the tray.

'Tal?' called Bran from the floor above. 'You're late. Is anything wrong——?' He stopped as Naomi began mounting the spiral stair. 'Hallelujah, unless Tal has taken to using perfume, I do believe it's you, Naomi.'

'Full marks,' panted Naomi as she reached the gallery bedroom. She put the tray down on the rather large table beside the bed, alongside the radio Bran had switched off at her approach. She eyed him closely to gauge his mood. He was sitting up in bed, propped against pillows, his chin dark with overnight stubble and his chest bare above the quilt.

'Please don't think I'm unappreciative,' said Bran, looking astonished, 'but why are you deputising for Tal this morning?'

'He's ill——'

'Ill?' said Bran sharply. 'What's the matter?'

'Megan thinks it's flu, but what she's really worried about is his chest.'

'If you'd ever heard him cough you'd know why,' he said grimly. 'Tell her to call the doctor right away.'

'She's already done so.' Naomi hesitated. 'Megan's made you an omelette. Shall I cut it up a bit?'

'No, thanks. If you put the plate on my lap and hand

LAIR OF THE DRAGON 71

me a knife and fork I can manage. Just butter some toast and pour the coffee,' he instructed, and cursed under his breath. 'This puts the skids under our day out, blast it.'

Naomi added sugar to his coffee, stirring briskly. 'Not necessarily.'

He frowned. 'What do you mean?'

'If you weren't planning on going very far — or very fast — *I* could drive. As long as you'll put up with my Mini. I'm safer with the devil I know when it comes to cars.'

Bran chewed on some toast thoughtfully. 'You mean that?'

'I wouldn't have offered if I didn't,' she said with asperity. 'Look, if you're willing to trust yourself to my driving and my car we could leave Megan in peace to look after Tal — and I'll still get my outing.'

'Oh, in that case,' he said, grinning, 'I accept, with thanks.' He waited a moment. 'What's the matter?'

Something about an unshaven Bran, a smile gleaming in his remarkable eyes, was creating the now familiar havoc with Naomi's nervous system. Keeping her voice as businesslike as possible, she asked him if he needed any help with getting dressed.

'Why? Are you offering to wash my back?'

Naomi blushed fierily. 'Certainly not,' she snapped. 'I thought I could help you choose what you want to wear, that's all.'

He waved a hand in the direction of the bathroom. 'Thanks just the same, but Tal puts everything ready the night before in there. Sometimes I'm up and showered and dressed long before he gets here. Other times I laze around in bed until breakfast-time. It all depends on the mood I'm in.'

'I see.' Naomi took his plate and handed him a cup of coffee. 'Is the mood good or bad today?'

'Good, of course — can't you tell? The prospect of a day out in charming company like yours, Naomi, made the world seem bright this morning the moment I woke up.'

'Very flowery,' she said acidly. 'I'll leave you to drink your coffee and take the rest of the things down, then.'

'What time would you like to leave? It's sunny today, isn't it?'

'Yes. So far.' She thought for a moment. 'Give me a couple of hours, in case I can do anything for Megan before we go. Will that do?'

'Whatever you say; I'm in your hands. A happy thought!' he added, leering in her direction.

Naomi preserved a dignified silence as she went carefully down the spiral stair, amazed that Bran was too stubborn to use one of the other bedrooms in the house in the circumstances. In her opinion he was mad to insist on risking his neck on a stairway she found it hard enough to negotiate with two good eyes to see her way.

Megan was delighted to hear that Naomi had volunteered for the role of chauffeur.

'It was a lucky day for us when you came to work here,' she said fervently, fortunately too preoccupied with preparing a picnic lunch to notice the sudden shadow on Naomi's face.

The sun was shining with surprising warmth when Bran lowered himself carefully into Naomi's Mini. He looked relaxed, and even more attractive than usual to Naomi's eyes in an old suede jacket and yellow cashmere turtleneck, with a rather transatlantic air to his shining loafers and pale chinos.

'Where shall we go?' he asked, as Naomi got in beside him.

'If you don't mind I'd rather not venture too far

afield. My only view of this beautiful valley of yours was on the drive here the day I arrived. I'd like to explore it more fully.'

'Fine by me.' He turned his head towards her. 'Will you do something for me, Naomi?'

'If I can,' she said guardedly.

'All I want is a description from you as we drive. You can't drive fast along these roads, anyway, so you won't find it difficult.'

'But surely you know the Vale of Ewyas like the back of your hand!'

'True. But I'd like to see it through eyes new to it, like yours.'

It seemed little enough to ask. 'Fine,' she said, switching on the ignition. 'But in that case we're not likely to get very far. I don't drive fast at the best of times, but if I'm doing a commentary at the same time we'll be doing hours per mile instead of the other way round.'

He laughed and leaned back in his seat. 'Who cares when the air coming through the window is warm and spring-scented, and my guide has such a beguiling voice?'

'Which I'll be obliged to raise to shouting point if I'm to make myself heard if we pass any lambing sheds! Are your Welsh sheep a particularly noisy breed?'

'They probably like the sound of their own voices, like me and every other Welshman ever born.'

Naomi laughed. 'You said that, remember, not me!'

As she drove carefully down the steep, winding drive she felt a sudden lift of spirits. Today she would forget her guilt and her motive for coming to Gwal-y-Ddraig and the land of the Black Mountains. This was an outing, a pleasure trip, with a complex, attractive man for company, and sunshine to add the gilding on the gingerbread.

'There were showers early this morning,' she began, 'and I think there may be a few more lurking ahead, because directly over us there's a rainbow. It looks like a gleaming striped bridge spanning two of these amazing rounded mountain tops, with a thundery grey cloud beyond, a washed powder-blue sky above, and bright, wet green fields below.'

Bran nodded in appreciation. 'That's what I want to hear. Tal's a great driver and the best of men, but his description tends towards the terse.'

'I may run out of adjectives,' she warned.

'Before you do, tell me what you're wearing today.'

'You haven't asked me that for a while now.'

'Because every morning it was blue jeans, a shirt and sweater, and I could picture that much for myself. Is there any change today?'

'Oh, yes. It's my day off. I'm wearing navy leggings, a striped navy and white shirt and a thick, baggy red sweater. Bright red like a pillarbox. And today I've tied my hair back with a red ribbon, and I'm wearing shoes like yours, only navy blue leather instead of that lovely glossy chestnut shade.' She looked sideways at him curiously. 'Why the sigh?'

He shrugged, his mouth twisting in the way she'd come to know so well. 'I was just wishing I could see the face that goes with the clothes. The rest of you I can picture clearly enough, but not the face. It's bloody frustrating.'

'You're not missing much!'

'Stop putting yourself down! From my one respectful exploration I know there's nothing untoward about your face.'

'If you mean I don't have a nose like Concorde and

teeth like Bugs Bunny, you're right. I'm just not—pretty.'

'One day I'll find out for myself!'

Not, thought Naomi, if she could possibly help it. By the time Bran Llewellyn could see again, *if* he ever regained his sight, she would be back in London well out of his reach. In the meantime her task was to paint a picture for Bran. There was no lack of subject matter for description. Every bend in the road brought them to a different scene, each one as worthy of Bran's brush as the last.

After consulting with Bran Naomi eventually took the turning to Llanthony Priory, and parked the Mini in the small car park beyond the small, ancient church of St David.

'I won't get out,' said Bran quickly. 'You go ahead and explore. You can report on your findings when you get back. I've been here scores of times, so don't feel guilty. Is there a radio in your car?'

Naomi switched it on for him, left him with a Schubert symphony and hurried off to inspect the ruined priory. A tablet on one of the walls informed her she was on the site of the first Augustine foundation in Wales, and it was beautiful, even in its ruined state, with redstone arches graceful above a sward as green and smooth as a billiard table. Naomi cast a longing look at the small hotel cum pub built over what had once been the abbot's house. She would have liked to linger over coffee or a drink there with Bran, and felt a sudden sharp pang of sympathy with him for some of the simple pleasures in life he was missing.

Reluctant to leave him alone for long, she took a quick look round the tiny church of St David, impressed to find there had been a place of worship there since the sixth century, then on impulse she knelt and said a prayer before rejoining Bran.

'Well?' he asked. 'Were you pleased with what you found?'

'Who wouldn't be?' Naomi slid in beside him and leaned over to switch off the radio. She tensed as his long hand shot out to capture her wrist. 'What's the matter?'

'Several things. Your perfume, for one. It gave me a sudden urge to touch,' he said harshly, and released her.

Naomi subsided in her seat, heart thudding. 'Shall I drive on?'

'What time is it?'

'Just after twelve.'

He fumbled for the seatbelt. 'Where's the blasted socket for this thing?'

'Here.' Naomi leaned across and clipped the belt into place, her throat constricting as she sensed the tension in his body. 'Where shall we go now?'

He sighed explosively. 'I'd like to take you to a pub for lunch, but my face is too well known around here.'

'Oh, don't worry about lunch,' she said, deliberately cheerful as she started the car. 'I've got that organised — with Megan's help, of course. I'm going to drive back down the road until I find a spot where I can park the car again, and then we're going to have a picnic.'

CHAPTER FIVE

ACTING on instructions given earlier by Megan, Naomi rejoined the road through the valley and headed north along twists and bends which, Bran informed her, would bring them to the little whitewashed church of Capel-y-ffin if they went far enough.

Long before that point Naomi made for a turning and a farm gate where she could tuck the Mini out of harm's way. She undid her seatbelt and scanned the sky, but there was no sign of the earlier showers. 'It's quite warm,' she told Bran. 'I've brought a rug, and there's a rather inviting log out there. Would you like to sit outside in the sun? Or would you rather stay in here?'

'Is there anyone around?'

'Not a soul in sight.'

'Then lunch al fresco it is.'

Naomi jumped out of the car and went round to open the passenger door. Bran disdained her assistance until he was standing outside, but took her hand to gain the safety of the fallen tree-trunk. Naomi stooped inside the car for the rug, spread it on their impromptu couch, then lugged the picnic basket out on to the grass.

'How efficient you are,' remarked Bran from his perch. 'I feel loweringly superfluous.'

'Not at all,' contradicted Naomi cheerfully. 'You provide the company. No picnic worth its name is good if eaten on one's own.' She passed him a napkin and a plastic plate. 'What do you fancy?'

'If I told you it's ten to one you'd drive off and leave me here, at the mercy of passing strangers!'

Naomi glared at him, then laughed reluctantly. Icy glances of disapproval were pretty useless under the circumstances. She explained why she was laughing, then cast an eye over the contents of the basket.

'Megan's made sandwiches with some of the Wye salmon intended for your lunch at home, or you can have small crusty rolls filled with either liver pâté or the mustard-glazed ham we had roasted for dinner last night.'

'Lucullus himself couldn't ask for more,' declared Bran. 'I'll have something of everything, please, but only one thing at a time.'

Naomi was careful to anticipate Bran's every want as they made inroads on the picnic basket, listening raptly as he regaled her with snippets of local legend while they ate. To make up for not taking her to the nearby Skirrid Inn for lunch Bran told her something of its history instead, how the first recorded existence of the inn known as the Skirrid had been as early as fifty years after the Norman Conquest, when two brothers by the name of Crowther had been sentenced, James to nine months for robberies with violence, John to death by hanging from a beam in the inn for sheep stealing.

'In those days,' said Bran, deepening his voice deliberately, 'they believed the devil rode abroad, and the innkeeper kept a pot of "devil's brew" on the shelf above the fireplace, which gave rise to the saying "sip with the devil". And when the last of the customers had gone for the night a jug of *pwcca* was left on the inn doorstep to appease the spirits of darkness.'

'*Pwcca*?' queried Naomi, trying to get her tongue round the unfamiliar sound.

Bran spelt it for her. 'Shakespeare is rumoured to

LAIR OF THE DRAGON

have taken his idea for Puck of *Midsummer Night's Dream* from *y pwcca*.'

Naomi laughed. 'You Welsh take the credit for everything! And seem pretty preoccupied with the devil in these parts, too, by the sound of it.'

Bran gave her an enigmatic smile. 'The dragon, you may care to know, was believed to be a manifestation of the devil.'

Naomi shivered. 'So your house could just as well be called "Lair of the Devil", then.'

He grinned. 'I bet if you'd known that you'd have thought twice before setting foot in it, timorous Saxon!'

Sensibly, Megan had provided nothing more demanding for pudding from Bran's point of view than crisp green apples, and they munched in unison, until Naomi giggled suddenly and told Bran they bore a definite resemblance to the sheep grazing on the steep fields all round them.

'Do that again!' commanded Bran.

'Do what?'

'Giggle like a little girl.'

'Yuck! That sounds horrible—arch and coquettish.'

Bran shook his head. 'I can't see your face, Naomi. Yet. But I'm damn sure arch is the last word for you.'

'For which many thanks! Coffee?'

'No champagne?' he said, mock-aggrieved.

'Certainly not.' Naomi took his plate and napkin, but as she poured steaming coffee into beakers from a Thermos jug Bran turned to her suddenly and knocked the jug from her hand. Scalding coffee cascaded down Naomi's front, and she screamed involuntarily as the heat of the liquid penetrated right through the thick wool sweater and the shirt beneath.

'What is it?' demanded Bran wildly, stretching his hands towards her. But before he could make contact with her he tripped over a tree root and lost his balance. He grabbed at her instinctively and fell, taking her with him, swearing violently as he collapsed with her into an awkward heap on the grass behind the log. '*Naomi*,' he howled. 'Hell, what a clumsy swine I am. Are you all right?'

'A bit winded, but otherwise in one piece,' she said breathlessly, pinned by the muscular body sprawled awkwardly on top of her. 'Are *you* all right?'

He swore again under his breath. 'Not counting my dignity, yes.'

She waited, breathing unevenly, but he made no move to let her up. 'Do you need help to get on your feet, Bran? If you move over a bit I can——'

'I *can* get up, but I seem to have lost the will to do so.' Bran shifted slightly, easing his weight a little, but making no other move to let her go.

Colour rushed to her face. 'Bran—please!'

But Bran wasn't listening. Eyes closed, he slid his hands over her blazing cheeks, then thrust them into her hair and bent his head, his mouth searching over her cheek until it found hers. At the touch of his lips Naomi gasped involuntarily, her lips parting beneath his. Bran groaned, his kiss suddenly fierce and voracious. He shifted until he was directly above her, his arms encircling her like manacles as he kissed her over and over again until her senses reeled. He muttered something, the words muffled against her mouth as he freed a hand so that he could trace the outline of her jaw, moving his fingers down her throat and lower to caress her breasts. And encountered sodden wool still hot to the touch. He flinched away from her with a curse.

'Naomi, you're soaked! The blasted coffee must have burnt like hell—why didn't you say, you little fool?' he demanded hoarsely.

She drew in a deep, shaky breath. 'I—I'm not scalded, my sweater's too thick.'

'Is that the truth?'

'Yes.'

'Let me touch you,' he demanded, reaching for her, but she intercepted his hands and scrambled ungracefully to her feet.

'I'm fine. Really.' She made a valiant effort to pull herself together. 'If you reach out in front you'll be able to steady yourself on the log. Or would you like me to help you up?'

'No, I bloody well wouldn't,' he said with sudden savagery, and hauled himself to his feet, staggering a little as he stood upright. 'Just get me back to the car.'

In taut silence Naomi guided him to the Mini, then left him to settle himself into the seat. Swiftly she gathered up the detritus of their lunch and packed it away in the basket, then tipped back the front seat and stowed everything into the back of the car.

'I suppose you expect an apology,' he said bitterly, fighting to jam his seatbelt into the socket without her help.

'Of course I don't. It—just happened.' She got in beside him, determined to lighten the atmosphere. 'I've learnt one thing today, though. Whoever said "easy as falling off a log" hadn't a clue what they were talking about.'

'Spare me the bright chatter,' he said through his teeth. 'Let's get home so you can get your clothes off.' He ground his teeth audibly. 'I mean——'

'I know what you mean!' Red-cheeked, Naomi drove off down the winding road at uncharacteristically reckless speed, too distraught to be cautious for once. Even so it seemed hours before they reached Gwal-y-Ddraig, by which time the silence in the car was so intense she was ready to scream.

As they reached the house Megan emerged from the front door, her smile fading at the sight of Bran's grim, set face.

'Whatever's happened?' she asked sharply.

'Naomi can tell you,' snapped Bran, his mouth tightening as he was forced to accept her helping hand to get out of the car. 'I'm off to the studio.' He paused, suddenly remorseful. '*Sorry*, I forgot. How's Tal?'

'Only a cold, after all, the doctor said. Nothing a few hot drinks and a day's rest won't cure,' she assured him, and made to lead Bran indoors.

'I'll be all *right*. See to Naomi. I threw boiling water over her.' Bran shook off her hand and marched into the house, narrowly missing contact with the open door.

Megan flew to help Naomi, who was busy unloading the car. 'Never mind that, *bach*. Good gracious, just look at your jumper—come inside and take it off at once.'

Meekly Naomi let herself be fussed over, submitting to having her sweater and shirt stripped off in the kitchen, wincing as she heard Bran slam the studio doors shut behind him.

'My bra will probably never pass the whiteness test again,' said Naomi ruefully, looking down at herself. 'But I'm not burnt. My front's a tasteful shade of shrimp-pink, that's all. My sweater was thick enough to insulate me from the worst.'

'What a thing to happen,' said Megan, handing Naomi a towel. 'There, wrap yourself in that. I don't think you'll blister. I'll swill these things out for you before the stain sets.'

'Thank you, Megan.' Naomi swathed herself obediently then slumped down at the kitchen table. 'It was such a shame. Up to then we'd been having a really pleasant time.' She explained how the accident happened, but made no mention of the kisses. Those, she thought miserably, were best forgotten. By all concerned.

It took Naomi every last scrap of determination she possessed to go downstairs later that evening for dinner, only to be informed by Megan that Bran had refused anything to eat, and was barricaded in his studio. And since she was determined to keep Tal in bed for the day Megan suggested diffidently that Naomi might like to have her meal in the kitchen to keep her company.

'I would indeed,' said Naomi, secretly limp with relief.

'Bran's in a terrible mood tonight,' confided Megan, laying two places at the kitchen table.

Naomi, who knew precisely why, refrained from explaining. She felt that poor Megan had enough on her plate, without worrying because her beloved Bran was subject to the very normal frustrations of a man deprived of the sexual attentions he was used to. 'He'll be fine tomorrow,' she said cheerfully, and changed the subject.

Next morning Naomi woke early, and lay wondering what to do with her day off. From several points of view it seemed wise to take herself off out of the way for most of it. By the time she returned Bran might be back to normal. Although the black mood could well *be* normal for him for all she knew, she reminded herself. Yet he'd been the perfect companion yesterday until he'd begun to make love to her. Familiar heat enveloped her at the mere thought of it, and with a shiver she slid from the bed and went to stand at one of the windows, closing her mind to Bran's expert, hungry kisses as she gazed out on a day bright with sunshine. She would go out, she decided. If she was on stop until Bran gave her another tape she might just as well remove herself from his vicinity for a few hours and widen her knowledge of the hauntingly beautiful Welsh Marches.

'You're up and about early,' said Megan, when Naomi arrived in the kitchen. 'I thought you'd be having a nice lie-in.'

'Something I bet you don't indulge in very often, Megan,' said Naomi, smiling. 'The sunshine woke me early so I thought I'd take myself out for the day to do some more sightseeing. How's Tal?'

'Better this morning.' Megan's mouth tightened. 'Which is more than I can say for Bran. Like a bear with a sore head, he is.'

Naomi pulled a face. 'Still in a bad mood, then.'

'He gets moods, mind. Nothing to do with the blindness; he always did. What Welshman doesn't?' Megan laughed comfortably. 'Anyway, you eat your breakfast and I'll make you a nice picnic lunch.'

'You won't!' Naomi waved Megan to a chair. 'Come and have something with me, then I'll make my own picnic lunch, if you'll let me forage for myself.'

Megan subsided with a grateful sigh, and poured tea for them both. 'You take whatever you want, *bach*. And make sure you take plenty, mind, because it's only cold supper tonight. Tal's brother's coming to visit him this evening, so I'll leave you to see to Bran— that's if you don't mind,' she added anxiously.

Naomi, quailing secretly at the prospect, lied convincingly as she assured Megan she'd be glad to help out. Confronted with the prospect of a meal *à deux* with Bran later that evening, she found she badly needed a few hours away from the house and its owner; time to herself to get things in perspective.

All fingers and thumbs in her haste, Naomi packed her picnic in the Mini as quickly as she could, wrestling afterwards with the passenger door, which as usual was maddeningly difficult to close. At last she banged it shut impatiently, then looked up in dismay to see Bran approaching, his head raised at the familiar, questioning angle.

'Naomi?' he said peremptorily. 'Is that you?'

For a moment she contemplated diving into the car and taking off without talking to him, but common sense prevailed. Reluctantly she stayed put, her spirits plummeting at the grim set to his face. Bran Llewellyn's sightless, spectacular eyes were bloodshot and black-ringed as they turned in her direction.

'Were you just going to drive off without saying anything?' he demanded tersely.

'I didn't think you'd want to be disturbed.'

His face set in familiar, bitter lines. 'You mean it was just easier to take off without a word!'

'I didn't realise I had to clock in and out,' she cut back at him, suddenly out of patience. 'Do forgive me, Mr Llewellyn. I shall be out for a while, as it's Sunday and you've no work for me to do. I'm not sure how long, but if it's of any interest to you Megan's provided me with a picnic lunch, and unless I get hopelessly lost I'll be back in time for supper.'

He looked so thoroughly taken aback that Naomi's anger evaporated.

'My mistake,' he muttered dourly. 'I thought you were leaving for good.'

She sniffed. 'How could I? The job isn't finished yet.'

'I thought my sudden resort to basic male instincts had frightened you off.' He gritted his teeth. 'Is it any use saying I'm glad I was mistaken?'

'Yes. It is. Not,' added Naomi, 'that I'm idiot enough to turn tail and run over what happened yesterday.'

'I stand corrected,' he said sardonically. 'Tell me, *did* the coffee harm you?'

'No. My sweater is the heavy, oiled wool type—practically waterproof.' Naomi moved close enough to touch his hand with hers. 'It was just an accident, nothing to get het up about.'

'Unlike the lovemaking, which was no accident, and something I, at least, got very het up about,' he said, training his heavy tourmaline eyes on her with such accuracy that Naomi tensed.

'Something the matter?' he demanded.

'No. It's just that sometimes it's so hard to believe you can't see,' she said, her heart thumping.

His mouth twisted bitterly. 'While I, at the risk of sounding mawkish, find it bloody impossible to get used to it.'

'Yes,' she said, with sympathy. 'And since you've brought the subject up it's as good a time as any to say I quite understand.'

His brows flew together. 'Understand what?'

'Your reasons.'

'My reasons for what?'

'You know perfectly well what I mean,' she said tartly. 'Your reasons for—well, for making love to me.'

He raised a derisive eyebrow. 'I made love to you, Naomi, for one reason only. When I fell on top of you I went berserk. I could no more resist what followed than any other man in the same situation.'

'Oh.' Naomi swallowed, retreating a little. 'Well, I—I suppose it's quite natural, in the circumstances.'

Bran scowled. 'Circumstances?'

Naomi hesitated, trying to phrase it as tactfully as possible. 'The fact that you've had no contact with a woman for a while. I can understand you must be missing. . .' She trailed into silence at his expression.

'The love of a bad woman?' he enquired silkily.

'I was going to say feminine companionship,' she retorted, her colour high.

'But you've been providing that ever since you arrived, Naomi.' He smiled mirthlessly. 'What you really mean is that I've missed having someone to share my bed and slake my evil lust.'

'I wouldn't have put it quite like that,' she said huffily. 'But yes, that's more or less what I meant — perfectly understandable for a man like you.'

He folded his arms across his chest. 'What the hell do you mean by that?'

'Nothing derogatory. I meant you're obviously not the type of man used to sexual frustration.'

'If you believe that, I'm surprised you're not making your escape from the lair of the dragon right now, as fast as that old banger will take you, Naomi Barry!'

'Only when I've finished the work I came here to do,' she repeated, unruffled.

'Are you afraid a sharp exit might forfeit you the all-important money?'

Naomi, wanting badly to slap his face, ignored him. 'Time I was off, I think.'

'Naomi, wait. That was uncalled-for,' said Bran wearily. 'I've no right to inflict my bloody awful moods on you.'

Naomi's resentment lessened slightly. 'No, you haven't. But I don't mind. Well, not much, anyway.'

He laughed softly and put out a peremptory hand. 'Barring my mother and Megan, you're the only woman I've ever met who's so scrupulously truthful. Shall we shake and be friends?'

Praying he'd never discover how mistaken he was, Naomi put her hand gingerly into his. Bran squeezed it very gently.

'Off you go, then. And take note of what you see. I shall expect a full report over supper tonight.'

'Of course.' She hesitated. 'Perhaps you'd like me to read from the Sunday papers afterwards?'

He raised his eyebrows. 'What a magnanimous little soul you are, Naomi. I'd like that very much, as it happens. No doubt you've been informed that tonight we get pot luck. To give Megan a break I told her to leave a tray of bits and pieces in the studio for us.'

Naomi, not at all sure she cared for the hint of intimacy in the arrangement, couldn't steel herself to ask for a different venue for the meal. For one thing it sounded a lot easier for Megan. 'I'll see you later then.'

Naomi drove away from the house, feeling relieved that things were back to something approaching normal with Bran Llewellyn. As she negotiated the winding road down to the valley she frowned, trying to analyse what, exactly, *was* normal with Bran. Sometimes it was impossible to remember that she hadn't known him for years. She no longer thought of him as a famous artist. His blindness had cut through the usual formalities, and put them on a footing they would never have established under normal circumstances. Something she couldn't help feeling grateful for. It was new and oddly moving to have such a man dependent on her, because it was very obvious that Bran Llewellyn was a man normally dependent on no one — unless it was Tal and Megan.

Naomi drove slowly along the winding road, noting that bluebells were coming into flower to replace the departing daffodils. Her mouth drooped. By the time the bluebells were gone she'd be gone, too. Which would be a good thing. Her best course was to get the job over with and get the necessary information back to Diana as quickly as possible. But she'd be sorry to leave Gwal-y-Ddraig. She'd become very fond of Megan, Tal too. But the biggest wrench, she knew perfectly well, would be parting from Bran.

Her cheeks warmed as she remembered her own response to his kisses, how ravished she'd been by his urgency as his arms practically cracked her ribs. She sighed. Her sudden propulsion into Bran's arms might well have sent him momentarily berserk, as he said. She had all the curves and hollows of any normal female. But if he could have seen her as well it would never have happened. Naomi smiled bitterly. But if he'd been able to see there'd have been no fall and the incident would never have happened. Which, from her own point of view, would have been by far the best thing. Bran Llewellyn's lovemaking, brief though it had been, came into the unforgettable category.

As Naomi turned off on the sunlit, deserted road to Skenfrith she put Bran's kisses from her mind to pay full homage to the scenery. The rolling, rounded hills of this part of the Marches, so near to the Black Mountains of Llanthony, were subtly different in their green, inviting allure. It was hard to believe that once blood had been shed so copiously among these hills when the Normans fought to subdue the Welsh as they forced their harsh imprint on the border country.

Naomi made first for Whitecastle, the first of the Trilateral, the three castles which had once formed the main defence for the north-eastern corner of old Monmouthshire. Deeply impressed by the imposing, moated ruin, she took some photographs, then headed for Skenfrith, a few miles further on. She found little remained there of the original castle other than a ruined tower and some outer walls, but along with the mill and several beautiful houses it was built of the same rose-bronze sandstone as Gwal-y-Ddraig. Pierced by a sudden longing to share her delight in it all with Bran, she parked her car alongside the Bell Inn and walked through the tiny village to take a brief look at the castle before going on to the church, which possessed a tower topped by what looked remarkably like a dovecote, a form of church architecture Naomi had never seen before.

Inside the peaceful, welcoming St Brigid's she found the sixteenth-century tomb of one John Morgan and his family of Skenfrith, and in a glass case behind a curtain the Skenfrith Cope, an exquisite example of fifteenth-century embroidery on velvet, a miracle in its own right for having escaped destruction from two Cromwells, both Henry the Eighth's Thomas and the later Lord Protector himself. But the feature which impressed Naomi most of all was the impressive roll at the back of the church giving the names of the Lords of Skenfrith, among them William de Braose and John of Gaunt, Duke of Lancaster. Her eyes widened as she noted that the first on the list, one Bach, Son of Cadivor ap Gwaethvoed, Prince of Cardigan, pre-dated the Conquest by a year. What, she wondered, fascinated, had happened to Bach when the Norman Brientius de L'Isle had come on the scene in 1066?

It was so late by the time Naomi got back that she had to rush over her bath to get dressed in time for supper.

'You look as though you've had a good day, love,' commented Megan, as Naomi hurried into the kitchen.

'I did. What a beautiful part of the world you live in,' said Naomi fervently, as she hoisted the tray Megan had ready. 'I'll take this to the studio for you.'

'Can you manage? I've been spoilt today,' Megan declared, smiling. 'I had a nap this afternoon while Bran sat with Tal, and now you're fetching and carrying for me——'

'I should think so. It's little enough to do. I'll come

back for the coffee tray in a minute.' Naomi smiled cajolingly. 'Only can I have a pot of tea, Megan?'

'You can have anything you like, love,' promised Megan fondly. '*Duw*, but I'll miss you when you leave.'

Naomi went off with the tray hurriedly, trying to outrun the guilt which had dogged her permanently since her arrival. In the studio she found Bran stretched out on the sofa, listening to a recording of Sir Geraint Evans as Dr Dulcamara in the first act of *L'Elisir d'Amore*. The dramatic, wonderfully resonant voice filled the room, full justice done to its timbre, not only by Bran's state-of-the-art equipment, but by the acoustics of the high-ceilinged studio. Lost to the world as he listened, for once Bran failed to hear Naomi come in until she put the tray down on a table near his sofa. He shot upright, pressing the off button on the remote control.

'Naomi? You're back.'

'Yes, indeed—but don't switch the music off on my account. I've got to go back for the coffee, anyway.'

'I should be fetching it myself,' he said morosely. 'I wish to God my eyes would start behaving themselves.'

'Perhaps you'll have good news from the consultant tomorrow,' she said briskly. 'By the way, how will you get to see him? Will Tal be fit enough to drive?'

'Megan says he is.' Bran smiled wryly. 'And, believe me, she wouldn't let Tal out of the house if she thought he wasn't up to it. I've salved my conscience by insisting she comes along too. Can you cope on your own until we get back?'

'I'm sure I can manage a sandwich and a pot of tea for myself. In fact,' she added, 'I'm perfectly willing to have a shot at dinner for us all as well, given the go-ahead.'

'I can just see Megan's face if I——' He halted, grimacing. 'Which I can, you know. In my mind.'

'I'm sure you can,' said Naomi cheerfully. 'She's a very memorable lady. I'll just dash back for the coffee-tray. Won't be a moment.'

'Has Tal's brother arrived?' Bran asked when she rejoined him.

'Not yet. He's coming after chapel, according to Megan.' Glad there was no reversion to the tension of their morning encounter, Naomi began an animated account of her day's travels as she helped Bran choose from the array of delicacies.

'That's better,' he said eventually, as he accepted some luscious fruitcake to round off the meal.

'The fruitcake?'

'No, you. I'm obviously forgiven.'

'Look, Bran,' she said bluntly, 'there was nothing to forgive. Really.'

His head swivelled towards her. 'Does that mean you wouldn't object if it happened again?'

'I draw the line at libations of boiling coffee,' she parried, her pulse racing.

'That, as you know perfectly well, was not what I meant,' he said impatiently. '*Would* you object, Naomi?'

'If you mean the kisses I probably wouldn't in practice,' she said with complete truth. 'You must have noticed I wasn't exactly fighting you off. But in theory, which is what I'll keep to, I do object. I came here to help with your autobiography, not console you for what you're missing out on sexually.'

Bran's eyebrows met his hair for an instant. '*Diawl*—you don't pull your punches, Naomi, do you?'

'I believe in making things clear! Coffee?'

'If that's the only thing on offer, yes.'

'It's not. I'm perfectly willing to read the Sunday

papers to you as well,' she said lightly, as she handed him his cup.

'What a saint you are, Naomi.'

Her mouth tightened. 'No way. Sanctity is the last thing I lay claim to. Talking of which, I saw the most wonderful church today.' And with an enthusiasm designed to divert Bran she described St Brigid's to him, delighted when she found he was familiar with all three places she'd visited.

The dovecote tower, he told her, had once fulfilled a very practical purpose when the Welsh border was subject to sudden raids, which was the reason for walls five feet thick, and its surmounting 'dovecote', which could house pigeons and provisions for eating, as well as bells.

'Did you notice the great timber bolt on the west door?' Bran asked.

'I did, indeed.' Naomi touched his hand in lieu of the smile he couldn't see. 'At Skenfrith it was so easy to picture how things once were, where everything was so close together with the church as its nucleus. Grosmont was beautiful, too, but there the castle was more detached, and looked more sophisticated, somehow. Probably that tall, elegant chimney on the bit added by John of Gaunt had something to do with it.'

'Nevertheless Grosmont was a busy town in medieval times, hence the very large church.' Bran grinned. 'Unfortunately a fellow Welshman of mine, Owain Glyndwr, torched the place in 1405 and it never really recovered.'

Naomi laughed. 'Violent lot, you Celts.'

The evening passed quickly as Naomi read excerpts from the newspapers, which led to discussions on various news items until Bran decided Naomi needed a rest and aimed his remote control at the stereo system so that they could listen to the rest of the first act of *L'Elisir d'Amore*. When it was finished Bran went over to remove the disc from the machine, his fingers unerring as he replaced it in its case and returned it to the row of compact discs on a shelf fixed to the wall at the back of the alcove.

When Bran returned to the sofa Naomi laid a hand on his.

'Now I *am* impressed.'

'At last!' He held on to her hand.

Naomi let it stay, reluctant to disturb the mood. 'How do you know which disc is where?'

'Simple. Tal arranged them for me in alphabetical composer order, then together we numbered them off and I memorised the numbers. When I want *Otello* I simply count along the row until I find it.' He turned his head towards her, smiling a little. 'Putting the disc in the machine is relatively easy, of course. We inhabit a push-button world.'

'Which you cope with so well——'

'No, I don't,' he said swiftly, his fingers tightening on hers. 'You know exactly what a swine I can be at times. If I were really coping I wouldn't give in to these bloody awful moods.'

'Ah,' said Naomi slyly, 'but Megan tells me you've always had those. Your present affliction is nothing to do with it.'

'Megan,' said Bran forcefully, 'talks too much!'

'As far as I'm concerned,' warned Naomi, 'Megan can do no wrong.'

'She feels the same about you,' said Bran drily. 'She'll miss you when you leave.' His voice dropped half an octave. 'So will I.'

Naomi sat very still, her eyes bleak as she stared the length of the big room at the portrait on the easel. 'Only for a while. The moment you can see again your beautiful Allegra will come running back here.'

'I doubt it. She doesn't like Gwal-y-Ddraig. Too remote.' Eyes closed, Bran leaned his head against the velvet swathed across the back of the sofa. 'Allegra's an urban creature of nightclubs and theatres and endless lunches with girlfriends.'

'Where did you fit into all that?' asked Naomi curiously.

'I didn't. She posed for her portrait in my studio in London. Sometimes she'd coax me to take her to the theatre, or whatever restaurant was the latest craze among her set.'

'Do you still love her?'

'No. But then, I never did.' Bran stroked a long finger over the back of Naomi's hand. 'I was just hot to share her bed.' He turned his head and opened his eyes on hers so accurately that she tensed involuntarily. 'Something in your tone tells me you disapprove strongly of Allegra.'

'I don't know the lady—but I'd disapprove of anyone who behaved as she has.' Naomi scowled blackly at the portrait. 'If one loves someone it shouldn't make a scrap of difference if he's blind, injured, disfigured or—or anything else.'

Bran's eyebrows rose. 'Such passion, Naomi!'

She subsided, embarrassed. 'Sorry. I'll get off my soapbox.'

'Those were very heartfelt sentiments, Naomi. Were you speaking from experience?' he asked curiously.

'If you're asking if someone once left me for much the same reason, then the answer's yes.'

'But you've never been blind, surely?'

'No, of course not.' She tried, without success, to tug her hand away. 'My handicap was too trivial for words. I was just stupid enough to set up house with a man who said he loved me for my personality, my sense of humour, even my brain. Then he subjected me to a particularly public form of humiliation by leaving me for the new receptionist at the firm where we both worked. She's the cutest thing you ever saw: all errogenous zones and yards of hair. No brain. Probably no sense of humour. But not even Greg could expect everything — and I must be barking mad to tell you all this,' added Naomi shortly; 'enough to put anyone in a bad mood.'

'Of course it isn't,' he said impatiently. 'But I don't follow you. Where does a handicap come into this?'

'My looks, Mr Llewellyn! In the end it wasn't enough for Greg to have someone to love and laugh with. He wanted a beautiful face to look at as well.'

'Instead, you mean,' Bran snorted. 'By the sound of it you're well shot of the jerk.'

'That's what I said about Allegra,' Naomi reminded him. 'But you didn't agree, as I recall.'

'True. But since then I seem to have come round to your point of view.' His mouth curved in a sardonic smile. 'Perhaps we should introduce Allegra to your erstwhile swain. They'd make a great pair.'

Naomi forced a laugh. 'So they would. Sorry I sounded off like that. As a rule I find it impossible to discuss Greg at all.'

'Perhaps this is one time when my blindness is an advantage,' said Bran. 'The priest can't see the penitent in the confessional, remember.'

'You're nothing like my idea of a priest!'

'Good. In that case you won't be shocked.' And before Naomi realised what he meant she was in his arms and Bran's lips were testing the delicate skin beneath her eyes for tears before they moved lower to settle unerringly on her mouth.

CHAPTER SIX

NAOMI pushed fiercely at the arms encircling her, but Bran made nonsense of her struggles.

'Why not?' he demanded arrogantly.

'I gave you my reasons earlier on.'

'But I'm not trying to lure you to bed, Naomi.' He stifled her protests with a kiss so expert and victorious that she subsided against him, defeated, as his tongue caressed and invaded in a way which put paid to any last remaining shreds of resistance. It was a long time before he raised his head a little to move his cheek against hers. 'What harm is there in taking a little comfort from each other?' he said unevenly.

Naomi drew in a deep, shaky breath. 'Pure sophistry.'

'No. Plain common sense, *cariad*. Besides,' he added, laughing suddenly. 'Can you imagine the havoc if I tried to carry you up that staircase over there? I've only just mastered getting up there as a solo performance!'

Naomi giggled involuntarily, and made no further move to push him away. Sensing the change in her, Bran lifted her on his lap and leaned back in the corner of the sofa, cradling her against him.

'There, you see? Isn't that good?'

'I wouldn't have said good exactly — nor wise.'

'Miss Practical!'

'Not all the time, alas.'

Bran gave a deep sign of pleasure as he smoothed his cheek over her hair. 'This is very good for *me*, anyway, wise or not. And it's nothing to do with raging lust and this frustration you keep alluding to with such maidenly disapproval. I just want to touch. I *need* to touch, Naomi. The way I need to breathe and eat.'

'Does it make up a little for not being able to see?'

'Yes.' Bran moved his hand down over her temple and cheekbone. 'Though to match your honesty, Naomi, the blindness isn't my only reason for wanting to touch you.'

'I've told you before, you really wouldn't feel the same if you could see me.'

The hand moved to grasp her chin firmly. 'How can you possibly know that? I refuse to believe it. All right, so your self-esteem took a dive when this Greg of yours took off with someone else. But he's probably the type who can't stick to one woman anyway. I very much doubt it had anything to do with this face.' Bran's lips touched her forehead and moved down her nose and along her cheekbones until he reached her mouth, his lips gentle at first, then fierce as though he meant to underline his words. Naomi responded in kind, abandoning herself to the pleasure she discovered was mutual when Bran crushed her close against his thudding heartbeat.

'Maybe comfort wasn't quite the right word,' he panted. 'Perhaps we'd better stick to conversation after all. No, you don't!' He jerked Naomi back against him as she tried to sit up. 'I prefer to talk with you on my lap.'

'It's no aid to serious conversation,' she pointed out breathlessly.

'I disagree. I think it's the best possible way to hold a conversation. So let's talk about this man of yours.'

'No. Let's not.'

'All right.' Bran ran his fingers down her spine. 'Tell me, is this your sister's silk shirt again tonight?'

'No. This one's mine. Birthday present from my mother.'

'What colour is it?'

'Raspberry-red.'

'And the skirt?'

'Same one—black.'

'And short,' said Bran, his exploratory fingers finding her knee. She slapped them and he returned his hand to clasp the other one at her waist. 'Pax! Knees, I take it, are out of bounds.'

'You bet they are. Look, I really should go.' She tried to sit up but he tightened his grip. 'Bran, please, it's time I went to bed.'

'Not yet. Stay a little longer and tell me about this sister of yours. Does she look like you?'

'Not a bit,' said Naomi glumly. 'Diana's tall, red-haired and beautiful. You'd never know we were sisters.'

'And what does the beautiful Diana do for a living?' asked Bran curiously.

Naomi willed herself to stay relaxed. 'She works for a publisher.' Which was only a whiteish lie. The *Chronicle* was certainly published every day.

'And is she married?'

'No.'

'Too wrapped up in her career?'

'More or less.' Naomi freed herself determinedly and slid off his lap. 'I must take these things back to the kitchen.'

Bran rose to his feet carefully. 'I suppose it's useless to try and dissuade you.' He stood listening as she tidied the trays. 'But before you go, tell me something, Naomi.'

She stilled, her back to him. 'What do you want to know?'

'This man of yours. Did he stay with the queen of

the reception desk, or did he move on to pastures new?' Bran caught her by the hand and turned her towards him, alert to her urge to escape.

'I don't know,' Naomi drew in a deep breath. 'For ages I couldn't bear to hear his name. By the time I could it seemed pointless to make enquiries. By then I had a room-mate who'd never met him, and Diana's opinion of Greg discouraged any mention of him.'

'Try to find out,' advised Bran. 'I'd lay odds he's gone on to someone else by now, maybe more than one.'

'I doubt it. Susie was — is — a stunningly pretty girl.' Naomi paused, eyes narrowed. 'On the other hand, you've roused my curiosity. Maybe I will ask. Or get someone to do it for me.'

'Good girl.' Bran tugged on her hand, drawing her nearer. 'Stay, Naomi.'

'No — please, I must go.' Naomi pulled her hand away and seized the tray, rattling it ostentatiously, then blushed as his slow smile told her he knew exactly what she was about.

'Goodnight, then, Scheherazade.'

'Goodnight.' She hesitated. 'I hope all goes well tomorrow.'

'Say a little prayer for a miracle!'

Naomi was glad when the others had finally set off on their trip to Cardiff the following morning. Megan had been very uptight as Naomi ate her breakfast in the kitchen. Bran, it seemed, had sent his tray back virtually untouched, and when Naomi asked if she should pay a quick visit to the studio to wish him good luck Megan shook her head.

'I wouldn't, love. He's a bit tense. Can't blame him, mind, but if I were you I'd leave him be. He gave me two tapes to put on your desk, by the way.'

'Oh, right, I'll start work, then.' Naomi patted Megan on the shoulder. 'Chin up.'

Naomi found it hard to start work. She made a show of switching on the word processor and putting a tape in the cassette player, but it was hard to concentrate on Bran's voice for once. For the simple reason, she informed herself crossly, that the mere sound of it makes you want to run to put your arms round him and tell him everything will be all right.

She was on her feet and halfway across the room to do so when the door opened and she cannoned into Bran in the doorway.

He grasped her involuntarily, his fingers digging into her waist. 'Where are you off to in such a hurry?'

'I was coming to see you.'

'I gave Megan the tapes.'

'I know. I just—needed to see you.'

He pulled her against him, kissing her as though his life depended on it. 'And I needed that,' he muttered hoarsely as he let her go. 'A talisman against the day.'

Naomi grasped his hands hard. 'You won't need a talisman. Everything will be fine, I know it. What time will you be back?'

'Some time this afternoon.'

'I'll see you later, then.'

The grooves deepened alongside Bran's mouth. 'I wish I could say the same, Naomi.'

'You will see,' she said emphatically. 'Not today, maybe, but very definitely soon. I feel it in these famous bones of mine.'

'Bran!' called Megan, from the hall. 'Are you ready? Tal's in the car.'

'Coming.' Bran reached out a hand and Naomi put hers into it, grasping the long fingers.

'Good luck.'

Once everything was quiet Naomi settled down in

earnest to work, determined to finish both tapes before the day was over, and in the process keep her mind off what was happening in Cardiff. It was just a check-up, she assured herself. But despite her brave words to Bran she was afraid the consultant might give him bad news, tell him the condition was not temporary after all, that Bran must learn to live with his blindness for the rest of his life.

Naomi finished the first tape by noon, at which point it became obvious that only a little more work was necessary before the short, concise autobiography would be finished. She thrust the second tape into a drawer hastily, and went off to make tea. She drank it at the kitchen table, her eyes dark with depression at the thought of leaving Gwal-y-Ddraig—and Bran Llewellyn—in only a few days' time. Her spirits sank still lower as she went back through the hall to find a letter from Diana among the others left by the postman.

Diana, it seemed, had been afraid to trust her request to the telephone in case the conversation was overheard.

The thing is, Naomi, Craig took me out for a drink after work last night and I let slip about the article. He's really keen on the idea, so *please* post off anything you've got right away, love—about the house and lifestyle in his Welsh retreat, and so on.

Diana signed off with reiterated gratitude, love and kisses, leaving Naomi staring at the page in dismay.

She raced up to her room and grabbed the telephone to dial the *Chronicle*'s number.

'Diana?' she demanded when her sister came to the phone. 'It's me.'

'Naomi! I thought you couldn't talk——'

'Everyone's out. I must be quick before they get

back. Look, do I have to do this? You were the one who told me to come home!'

'I know, but since you hung on down there I assumed you'd come round to the idea, especially as it could do such a lot for me.' Diana sounded uptight. 'Jack Porter, Craig's deputy, is leaving on Friday. This story could be the decider as to whether I get the job or not.'

'Surely there's something else you could write about——'

'Nothing that someone else isn't writing about as well on some other paper! You know perfectly well your man never gives interviews. I'll be very careful, I promise. You *know* I wouldn't write anything libellous. In any case this isn't gossip, it's just a feature——' Diana halted, sighing. 'But if you can't, you can't. I won't press you, love.'

'Oh, all right,' said Naomi unhappily. 'But for heaven's sake make sure the article's not out until I get back. I'd hate anyone to find out before I leave. Everyone's so kind here.'

'Including him?'

'As it happens, yes.' Naomi gritted her teeth. 'But don't worry, I'll do it. Just for you. I'll drive down to the main road and post whatever I have off to you now before everyone gets back.'

'Where's he gone?'

'Cardiff.'

'Why?'

'How should I know? I'm only the hired help.'

'If you send me this information you'll be more like fairy godmother as far as I'm concerned, and believe me, I appreciate it. I haven't forgotten the Bahamas.'

'I don't need a trip to the Bahamas. But you can do something else for me.'

'Anything!'

'Can you find out what Greg's doing these days — and who he's doing it with?'

As Diana promised, her name was called in the background, and she rang off hastily with more fervent thanks. Quickly, before she could change her mind, Naomi took her notes from the wardrobe, stuffed them in an envelope and addressed it to Diana at the *Chronicle*, then ran downstairs to drive down to the postbox on the main road. By the time she got back to the house afterwards an old, familiar pounding had started up in one side of her head, and she felt hideously sick.

Frantic with pain, Naomi knew of old that there was nothing she could do except take to her bed and stay there until the migraine released its grip. Crime and punishment, she thought in misery, as she lay in her darkened bedroom, unable to read, or listen to the radio or do anything at all other than let the waves of pain wash over her. At one stage she staggered to the bathroom and threw up, and felt better for a while. But the pain soon began gripping her head again with pincer-like contractions, rising to a crescendo which sent her to the bathroom for another bout of nausea that left her shivering and wretched as she crawled feebly back to bed.

She had no idea what time it was when she heard the car draw up outside below her window. Soon afterwards Megan came looking for her, eyeing the drawn curtains in alarm as she hurried over to the huddled figure in the bed. 'I've been looking everywhere for you, *bach*. Whatever's the matter? Is it a cold, like Tal?'

'No,' croaked Naomi, 'migraine.'

Megan clicked her tongue in sympathy. 'There's nasty. Do you get them often?'

'Now and then, but never mind me.' Naomi struggled upright, clutching her head. 'How's Bran?'

'The specialist was very pleased with him. He's confident it won't be long before Bran's sight returns.' Megan piled pillows behind Naomi and straightened the covers. 'Now just lie still, there's a good girl. *Duw*, you're a terrible colour. Aren't there some pills you can take?'

'No use while I'm throwing up.'

'You've been sick as well? Poor girl, let me make you some tea——'

'No! No, thank you, Megan.' Naomi tried to smile. 'Tell Bran I'm sorry I couldn't work this afternoon.'

Megan snorted. 'I should think not, indeed; you have a good rest! I'll leave you in peace and come up later.'

Much to Naomi's relief the pain began to lessen slowly after Megan's visit, taking the nausea with it, and eventually she slept. When she woke it was almost dark. She switched on the lamp then slid cautiously out of bed on legs which wobbled precariously as she made for the bathroom. After washing her face and brushing her teeth Naomi tidied her hair gingerly and staggered back to bed to lie against the stacked pillows, washed out, but blissfully free from pain except for a slight soreness about the head and a familiar floating feeling. The migraine, as she knew from bitter experience, was stress-related; a direct result of sending the notes to Diana.

A few minutes later Megan appeared. 'I've been up before,' she told Naomi, 'but you were out for the count. How do you feel, my lovely?'

'Much better, thank you, Megan.' Naomi could smile by this time. 'A bit weak and feeble, but no headache any more.'

'That's good. I'll fetch you something to eat.'

'Oh, Megan, not at this time of night. Some tea will be fine — and I can make that up here.'

Megan looked shocked. 'Certainly not! I made some chicken soup for Bran's starter tonight, so I'll bring you some of that and some nice crisp toast to go with it. You can't sleep on an empty stomach, now, can you?'

Naomi gave in meekly, surprised to find that now food had been mentioned she was a little hungry, and when Megan arrived with the meal it was no real effort to eat everything provided.

After Megan had gone Naomi switched on her portable radio and lay listening to some music, wondering disconsolately if Bran had missed her company at dinner. She felt furious with herself for getting ill — one whole day of Bran's company wasted, when there were so few days left. By the weekend, however much she tried to spin out the work, she'd have no more excuse to stay. She tried to read, but when her eyes protested she tossed the book away impatiently, and lay back against the pillows, feeling suddenly caged by the pretty, comfortable room. She wanted to be down in the studio with Bran, reading to him or just talking to him. Or lying in his arms on the sofa, said a brutally candid voice inside her head.

Naomi lay with eyes closed and fists clenched, trying to block the thought out. But shutting out the light threw Bran's face into sharper focus in her mind; the thick, sable eyelashes and translucent green eyes, his shock of crow-black hair and the sensuous, irresistible curve to his bottom lip. She sat up, and tried to arrange the pillows in greater comfort behind her sore head, then stilled as she heard a quiet knock at the door.

'Come in,' she said warily, assuring herself it was only Megan.

But the door opened to reveal the tall, unmistakable figure of Bran Llewellyn. She gazed wide-eyed, convinced for a moment that her fevered imagination had conjured him up to torment her, until the reality of his deep, confident voice as he said her name won a smile of such radiant welcome from her it was as well he couldn't see.

'Bran—please come in.' She leapt out of bed and flew across the room to take his hand. 'Careful, there's a little chair beside the door, and another near the bed where Megan was sitting. Come and sit down. Are you all right? Did the consultant really say there's an improvement? Were you tired after the trip——?'

'Hey!' he said, laughing, and felt for the chair. 'Let me get a word in, chatterbox. I'm fine, you're the invalid.'

'No, I'm not. I had a migraine, that's all.'

'Then close the door and get back into bed,' he ordered.

Naomi did as he said, touching his hand fleetingly as she passed him to get under the covers. 'I'm sorry I missed dinner.'

'It was lonely without you, Naomi.'

She relaxed against the pillows, content just to look at him. Early that morning he'd been dressed in a formal dark suit for his consultation, but tonight he was wearing a blue chambray shirt and crimson sweater, his long legs encased in navy corduroy.

'Why are you so quiet?' he asked softly.

'I was just looking at you. You look different, somehow.'

'It must be the glow of optimism, *cariad*.' His smile dazzled her. 'It seemed like tempting providence to mention it before, but for the past few days I've noticed a greater degree of sensitivity to light, and the consultant confirmed it. He says my sight should be fully restored before long.'

Naomi leaned over impulsively to clasp his hand. 'That's wonderful news, Bran—I'm so glad.'

His hand closed over hers. 'You really are, too, aren't you?'

'Of course I am,' she said indignantly. 'Why shouldn't I be?'

'Because then I'll be able to see this face of yours. Something I'm looking forward to, because I refuse to believe that voice could possibly come from a face I didn't want to look at.'

'It doesn't matter, anyway,' she said forlornly. 'Unless your sight returns by the weekend you'll never know. I'll have finished the draft of your book by then.'

Bran's hand tightened on hers. 'What has that to do with it? If I can see I can drive. So what's to stop me coming to visit you in London?'

Naomi went cold. It had never occurred to her that he might want to see her again, once she'd left Gwal-y-Ddraig.

'By the deadly silence,' said Bran cuttingly, 'I take it the idea doesn't appeal.'

'It—it isn't that.'

'Then what's the problem?'

'It's pretty obvious, really. At the moment I'm the only woman around, except for Megan,' she began, trying to be reasonable. 'It's very flattering to have you enjoy my company, of course, but at the same time I don't kid myself that once you're back to normal you'll feel the same. Think of all the other woman you'll have falling over each other to welcome you back once you're in circulation again.'

'What a pretty picture you paint of my sex life, Naomi,' he said mockingly, 'and don't pull away, I've no intention of letting you have your hand back just yet. In fact,' he said, his voice deepening, 'your migraine is the only thing keeping me from holding a great deal more of you than your hand.'

'Then for once I'm grateful to the migraine,' she said tartly.

'Why? Is the idea such a turn-off?' he demanded.

Naomi sighed impatiently. 'You know very well it's not. It must have been quite obvious, both last night and this morning, that I like being in your arms far more than I should — or is wise.'

Bran got to his feet, still holding her hand, then felt for the bed and sat down on the edge of it, close enough to touch his free hand to her face. 'Naomi, we're both single and over age. Why shouldn't we take advantage of something that gives us both such pleasure?'

'You know perfectly well why,' she said irritably, trying to shrink into the pillows. 'I've got another life to return to next week, and I want to get back to it all in one piece, Bran Llewellyn.'

'"The lady",' said Bran very softly, '"doth protest too much, methinks".' And he bent close to kiss her, but when she turned her cheek to his seeking mouth he stiffened and got to his feet, breathing in deeply. 'All right, Naomi. I'll leave you to your chaste and lonely bed, and I'll go back to mine. Reluctant and unwilling, but I'll go.'

'Let me see you to the door,' she said quickly, sliding from the bed to take his hand.

'You don't make it any easier,' he said harshly, as she led him across the room. 'I may not be able to see you, but I can feel your pulse throbbing under my fingers, smell perfume and warm, flustered female. It's driving me crazy!' He stopped dead, tugging sharply on her hand so that she fell against him, and this time when he bent his head his mouth fastened unerringly on hers.

Naomi gave up. She slid her arms around him and held him close, her breasts hard and urgent against his chest through the thin cotton of her nightgown. He muttered something unintelligible against her mouth, then kissed her with a growling, starving insistence she responded to with such fervour that they were both breathing in agonised gasps when Bran tore his mouth from hers at last. He held her away a little to run his hand over her face and down her throat to the upper curves of her breasts, and Naomi's blood pounded in her ears, her eyes glazed as she stared up into the intent, passionate face above her. A great shiver ran through her as he slid the nightgown from her shoulders and cupped a breast in each hand, then bent his head to take each hardening nipple in his mouth in turn.

Naomi uttered a smothered, hoarse cry and clutched wildly at him for support, then Bran suddenly raised his head, listening.

'*Hell*, no—' He gave her an ungentle push. 'Back to bed. At the double.'

Naomi tugged at her nightgown and dived across the room to the bed. She pulled the covers up to her throat as Bran made for the door, thrusting his hand through his hair. As he reached it someone knocked quietly, and Bran took a deep breath, squared his shoulders then opened the door, smiling wryly.

'Hello, Megan.'

Megan, in a flowered dressing-gown with her hair neatly pinned beneath a bright pink hairnet, looked thunderstruck. 'Bran? What in the world are you doing here?'

'I came to ask after the invalid,' he said, with a composure much envied by Naomi.

Megan took his arm and made him sit down on the chair by the door. 'Just you wait there a minute, Bran Llewellyn. Before I go to my bed I'd like you safely back in the studio, if you don't mind.' She crossed the room to look at Naomi, frowning as she saw hectic colour in cheeks which had been ashen earlier on. 'Are you all right, love? You've got a temperature by the look of you.' She laid a hand on Naomi's forehead and clicked her tongue at its heat.

'I'm fine,' said Naomi, glad for once that Bran had no way of catching her eye. 'My headache's gone and I'll be fighting fit in the morning, I promise.'

'I hope so,' said Megan doubtfully, and glanced across at Bran, whose face was so rigidly expressionless that Naomi knew he was desperate to laugh. 'I just thought I'd come and see if Naomi wanted anything before I go to bed. Never thought I'd see you here, Bran.'

'I, too, wanted to see how Naomi was faring. Great minds think alike, Megan, *bach*.' He got to his feet and held out a hand in the direction of her voice. 'But I'll go quietly. Take me, I'm yours!'

'You just stop your old nonsense!' Megan laughed, shaking her head as she turned back to Naomi. 'And you get a good night's sleep, my girl. Goodnight.'

'Goodnight, Megan. Thank you for coming.' Naomi swallowed a laugh as Bran turned his face towards her with a bland, innocent smile.

'You haven't thanked *me* for coming, Naomi.'

'And thank you, too. You're all very kind.' Her eyes danced as she smiled and Megan sighed.

'There's a pity you can't see her, Bran. She's got a lovely smile.'

'Really? According to Naomi she's as ugly as sin.'

Naomi could have hit him as Megan stared at her in astonishment.

'Why ever did you tell him that?'

'I didn't say that, exactly!'

'I should hope not.' Megan crossed to Bran and took him by the arm. 'Naomi's got a dear little face, believe me.'

'Oh, I do,' Bran assured her. 'Far more easily than I believe Naomi on the subject.' He threw a smile over his shoulder as Megan drew him from the room. 'Until tomorrow then, Scheherazade. I missed my story tonight.'

'I'll make it up to you tomorrow,' she promised, then rather wished she hadn't when Bran's deepening smile won him a strange look from Megan as she hustled him from the room.

CHAPTER SEVEN

NAOMI had a very bad night after her visitors left. A combination of restlessness after Bran's lovemaking and guilt over Diana's article scotched all hope of a good night's rest.

'And how are you this morning?' said Megan, when Naomi arrived in the kitchen. 'Should you be up? I was sure you were coming down with a fever last night.'

'I feel a lot better than yesterday,' Naomi assured her, glad Megan had no idea of the exact nature of the 'fever'.

'Now you eat a good breakfast, my girl, and don't overdo it today. Bran won't mind if the book doesn't get finished dead on the dot, I'm sure.'

Naomi smiled wryly. 'But *I* will. I've got my proper job to get back to, remember.'

Despite her usual post-migraine fragility, Naomi worked with a will once she was back at the word processor. The time passed so quickly that she looked up in surprise when Megan came to say Bran had given orders for Naomi to join him for coffee.

'Is it that late already?' she said blankly.

'I told you not to overdo it,' scolded Megan. 'Off you go and have a break.'

'About time,' complained Bran when she arrived in the studio. 'Megan wouldn't let me interrupt you before.'

'I wanted to make up for lost time yesterday.' Naomi

crossed the room to touch his hand in her usual greeting. 'How are you this morning?'

'All the better for being with you.' He retained her hand, pulling her over to the sofa. 'Come and sit down and tell me how you feel today, and how you look, and what you're wearing and anything else you think will be of the slightest interest to me.'

Naomi chuckled. 'I feel fine and I look pretty much the same as usual in jeans, navy jersey and pink shirt. There. May I pour the coffee now, please? Now I've stopped I realise how much I've been looking forward to it.'

'To what?' he said instantly. 'The coffee, or being with me?'

'Both,' she said reluctantly, then caught her breath at the look of triumph on Bran's face.

'You've admitted it,' he crowed, then released her hand. 'All right, pour the blasted coffee if you must. Tell me how you felt last night.'

Naomi filled his cup with an unsteady hand. 'When, in particular?'

'When Megan interrupted us, woman! Lord knows I'm fond of her, but I could have wished her anywhere else at that particular juncture.'

Naomi stirred sugar into the coffee and handed him the mug. 'Perhaps it's just as well she arrived when she did.'

'Why? Were you afraid I'd overcome your objections and have my wicked way with you?' He turned in her direction, his eyes glittering a challenge which brought a hectic flush to her face.

'The thing that really frightened me was my lack of any objection at all,' Naomi told him with painful honesty.

Bran sat very still, the laughter fading from his face. 'Does that mean you'd have let me stay last night?'

She breathed in deeply. 'I don't know. I hope I'd have found the strength from somewhere to call a halt. So from now until I leave I've decided the best plan is to avoid situations like last night.'

'You mean you won't let me into your bedroom.'

'The question won't arise. I don't get migraines very often.'

'What makes you think I need an excuse?'

'Not what. Who.'

Bran gave her a twisted smile. 'Ah, I see. You think I wouldn't dare under Megan's eagle eye.'

'Exactly.' Naomi shivered audibly. 'If such an unlikely situation should arise—which it won't—she'd forgive you, but she'd never forgive me.'

'Why should she forgive *me*?'

'Because,' said Naomi very quietly, 'I'm sure that Megan, like all the other women you know, would forgive you anything.'

Bran reached out a peremptory hand. 'Does that go for you too?' he asked huskily.

Naomi put her hand in his. 'I don't know. And since I'm unlikely to be put to the test I never will.'

Bran's fingers tightened on hers. 'Something tells me I'd forgive *you*, Naomi, whatever your trespass.'

Blood flew to Naomi's face. Guilt and longing took her breath away as his hand tightened, pulling her towards him and into his arms. He rubbed his cheek against hers, eyes tightly closed as he registered the smooth heat of it against his own. He drew a deep, ragged breath as he felt her yield, then his seeking mouth slid along the line of her jaw to find her mouth and she trembled against him as their lips met and locked and parted only when neither could exist any longer without oxygen.

Naomi buried her head against his shoulder, her

entire body vibrating with their combined heartbeat as she fought with the urge to confess.

Bran smoothed a hand over her hair, breathing rapidly. 'I meant it, Naomi.'

She stiffened, and drew away to look up into his face. 'Meant what?'

'That I'd forgive you anything.'

From somewhere she managed to find the strength to stand up. 'I doubt that, somehow,' she said in a stifled voice. 'You're only human, Bran.'

'Isn't that the truth,' he said grimly.

'And I'm human, too, Bran.' She touched his shoulder fleetingly to take the sting from her words. 'So let's avoid passages like last night — and this morning — from now on.'

His face set. 'That's what you want?'

'No, it isn't,' she said honestly. 'But it's what I'm asking, just the same.'

Bran raised a sardonic eyebrow. 'I don't make promises I can't keep, Naomi.' He shrugged irritably. 'And now I suppose you're going to run away again, back to that bloody machine. You'd think it was human — and male — the way I'm getting to resent the damn thing.'

Naomi chuckled breathlessly. 'I'll see you at dinner.'

'I thought I'd stay in today and see you at lunch as well,' he said swiftly, his smile so persuasive she badly wanted to say yes.

'No way. I'm not stopping for lunch.'

'Cruel woman.'

'No, just sensible,' she said firmly, hoping Bran had no idea what a fight she had to be sensible where he was concerned.

Naomi won the battle for the next two days, while she finished off the draft of *The Flight of the Crow*. She dined with Bran as usual, read the day's work back to him afterwards, before going on to read excerpts from whatever book he wanted, though often all Bran really wanted to do was just talk, or listen to music, but always with his hand holding hers, as though the contact was necessary to his morale.

'You're my night-light in the dark, Naomi,' he told her.

'I'm glad I'm useful,' she countered, secretly touched to the heart.

'I'd like you to be more than that,' he sighed moodily, 'but you frighten me.'

'*Frighten* you? How can I possibly do that?'

'I'm afraid that if I demand more than just this small, comforting hand in mine you'll run away. And don't rabbit on about being sensible,' he added testily, 'or I won't be responsible for my actions.'

'Then I won't,' she said calmly. 'How about some music?'

'All right, as long as it's something lively and unromantic. A man can only stand so much, *cariad*!'

Time was flying by far too swiftly for Naomi. Soon, much too soon, it would be time to leave. The draft was almost finished, and, although Bran had asked her to stay to the weekend as originally planned, she knew her best course was to leave Gwal-y-Ddraig the moment there was no excuse to linger. Bran, with unconcealed reluctance, had refrained from actually making love to her as she asked, but there were more ways of making love, she discovered, than mere physical contact. Bran had a love for poetry that held an allure for her mind almost as powerful as the irresistible hint of dependency beneath his virility.

Naomi had gone to bed earlier than usual the following evening, worn out by the strain of hours alone with Bran in the studio. That he wanted to make love to her was an unspoken, living undercurrent between them the entire time they were together. Naomi knew that she had only to relax her guard for a moment and she would be in Bran's arms and that would be that. If he really set out to make love to her she had no illusion about her own opposition, either to him or to herself, which was more to the point. She could fight one of them, but not both.

Naomi was tossing and turning restlessly in bed, cursing herself for leaving Bran so early, when a knock on the door made her heart thump in her chest.

'Come in,' she called, her throat suddenly dry. Then she saw Megan's head pop round the door and disappointment swamped her in a cold, humiliating tide.

'Thank goodness you're still awake, love,' said Megan, looking so distraught that Naomi shot upright in bed, her eyes anxious.

'Something wrong, Megan?'

The other woman nodded, wiping tears from a face creased with worry. 'It's Haydn.'

Not Bran. Naomi fought to hide her relief. 'Tal's brother? What's the matter?'

'He's been in a car accident—some joyrider out in a stolen car went into him near Newport earlier this evening. They've taken him into the Gwent—the hospital there. Tal's his next of kin now, you see, which is why the hospital just rang him.' Tears ran suddenly down Megan's cheeks. 'They said Haydn's poorly. And you know what that means, in hospital terms.'

Naomi jumped out of bed and put her arm round Megan. 'I'm so sorry. Is there anything I can do? Anything at all?'

Megan sniffed hard. 'Well, there is, but it seems such a cheek to ask. I've just been to see Bran and he says it's all right if we both go, Tal and me, I mean. But I don't like leaving Bran on his own——'

'But he's not on his own,' said Naomi, pulse racing. 'I'm here. In any case Bran will be all right overnight. And I'll see to his breakfast if that's all that's worrying you.'

'There's good you are!'

Not good at all, thought Naomi, her cheeks hot. 'Nonsense. You can't let Tal go on his own. But please ring at some stage and let me know how things are.'

Megan, all at sea for once with worry, assured Naomi she'd keep her posted, then hurried off downstairs. Naomi jumped out of bed and pulled on her dressing-gown to follow her, to see if there was anything she could do to speed the grief-stricken pair on their way. She met Tal in the hall, obviously on his way back from the studio. He looked drawn and worried as he assured her that Bran needed nothing until next morning.

'It's funny, see, love,' he said, hurrying with her into the kitchen. 'I'm the one who's always under the weather, with this chest of mine. Haydn's usually fit as a fiddle. Salt of the earth, my brother—he didn't deserve this!'

There was no sign of Bran as Naomi helped Megan and Tal collect their things. She waved them off down the drive, then went back into the house and locked the door, casting a yearning look towards the corridor that led to the studio. But, she reminded herself stringently, she had been the one with all the high-minded objections. They might have the house unexpectedly to themselves, but it couldn't be allowed to make any difference.

Naomi went upstairs slowly, her eyes on the oblong of light coming from the corridor. But no tall, familiar figure materialised there to halt her progress. With a sigh she went back to her bedroom and closed the door, then got into bed. But before she could switch off the light the door opened and Bran stood there in silence, his hand against the lintel to orientate himself. He took two steps into the room, then closed the door behind him and walked slowly towards the bed. Naomi leapt out of bed to meet him halfway across the room, sliding her arms round his waist and laying her cheek against the gratifying thunder of his heartbeat as his arms locked her against him.

'I almost didn't come,' he said, his voice harsh with emotion as he leaned his cheek against the crown of her head.

'I almost came to you,' she told him, and felt him relax, shaking with sudden laughter against her.

'Such honesty, *cariad*!' He bent his head and she raised hers eagerly, meeting his mouth with her own. Her hands went up to encircle his neck and Bran stopped and lifted her in his arms. 'I couldn't carry you up that stair in the studio, Naomi, but I can manage it from here to your bed.' And, as sure-footed as though he could see, he walked to the bed and laid her down on it, then straightened and stood still.

She stared up at him uncertainly, and, sensitive as always to her mood, he smiled exultantly as he stripped off his dressing-gown before sliding into bed beside her to take her into his arms.

'Surely you didn't think I was about to turn tail and go back again,' he said mockingly.

'I did wonder for a moment,' she admitted in a stifled voice.

Bran pulled her closer, his lips warm against her cheek. 'Naomi, I know you have reservations about all this, but when Megan and Tal were sent for tonight, grief though it might mean for them, I took it as fate. That this was meant to be for you and me. As must be blindingly obvious right this minute, I want you, Naomi, so badly I'm going out of my mind.'

'It would be a pity for that to happen,' she said sedately. 'After all, it's such an *informed* mind.'

Bran laughed and rolled over to capture her beneath him. 'Ah, Naomi, what a delight you are!'

Having just been told that Bran was on fire with the urge to make love to her, Naomi tensed, expecting an onslaught designed to bring him relief as quickly as humanly possible. But Bran was no callow youth, at the mercy of his own senses. When he kissed her there was tenderness as well as urgency in the caress, so that she yielded to the desire flowering inside her, responding ardently to the persuasive caresses of his hands as they moved in a slow, relishing journey over her body.

'Ah, *cariad*,' he breathed against her lips. 'If you only knew how much I've yearned to do this, and this——' He moved his head lower, his lips searching for the pulse that throbbed at the base of her throat. When his descending mouth encountered the slight obstruction of her nightgown he made no move to push it aside, but returned his attention to her mouth, his lips and probing, subtle tongue winning him such rewards that Bran tensed and raised his head a fraction.

'I'm trying my hardest to take time over this, my lovely,' he said hoarsely. 'Having gone so long without such glorious solace, I'm determined to prolong the experience to the full.'

Naomi ran her fingertips over his shoulders and down his spine, at the same time embarking on a series of swift, feather-soft kisses along his hard jaw. 'Amen to that,' she agreed piously.

Bran's breath rasped in his chest. 'But there's a problem, *cariad*. Such flattering co-operation, welcome and delightful though it is, makes delay rather difficult.'

Naomi threw her hands wide instantly. 'Then I'll be good.'

'Not too good,' he whispered, and kissed her smiling mouth, at the same time running his hand down her ribs over the thin lawn which covered them, his fingertips lingering as they outlined her hips before moving down to slim bare thighs which tensed at his touch.

'Have you ever heard of Dafydd ap Gwilym?' he asked, surprising her.

Naomi gave a stifled laugh. 'No. Is he a delaying tactic?'

'By no means.' He clicked his tongue in disapproval. 'He's only the greatest poet of medieval Wales, I'd have you know.'

'Oh, *that* Dafydd ap Gwilym,' she said pertly, wriggling closer.

'Irreverent Saxon! Besides, medieval he might be, but his poetry's extraordinarily apt at this moment in time.' Bran's arms tightened round her, his deep voice seductively ragged, its lilt more pronounced than usual as he began to woo her with words composed centuries before, yet so tailored to the moment that he could have written them himself that very day.

'"Grant me, dear life, this lover's blessing",' began Bran slowly, in a tone which sent shivers down her spine, '"a conquering kiss, a swift undressing".' He dispensed with the nightgown deftly and moved his hands slowly over her body, as if memorising every curve of it.

'"A wild delight, a long caressing",' he went on hoarsely, '"and all to end in heart's possessing".'

Bran lay half beside and half over her naked, expectant body, his eyes tightly closed as his hands continued on their caressing journey. With a sinuous movement he slid lower in the bed, his lips roving over her lifting breasts, drawing a choked cry from her as his mouth closed over first one hard, erect tip and then the other. Her heart hammered as his exploring hands found the secret place which opened to his caresses with such abandon that he replaced his probing, insistent fingers with his lips and tongue and brought Naomi to sudden, throbbing fulfilment, taking her so much by storm that she gasped and cried out and arched her body in its throes.

Bran laughed exultantly and caught her close in his arms, kissing her with all the triumph of a conqueror who had stormed the citadel. Naomi clutched at him wildly.

'But it was *you* who wanted——'

'And intend to have,' he promised, and began his assault on her senses all over again, but this time she retaliated, instigating a counter-attack of her own with hands which stroked and teased, coming close to, but never quite touching, the part of him he wanted her to touch most.

'Little devil,' he panted, kissing her, then groaned as she wriggled close and captured him at last in a caress which brought a groan of such anguish from him that she thought he was hurt and threw her arms round him, at which point Bran Llewellyn could no longer face delay and entered, finally, the portal that opened to him with unrestrained welcome. Their bodies met and matched each other in quickly found harmony, all Bran's efforts to delay abandoned in triumph as he accepted Naomi's surrender as his right, taking her with him to heights of pleasure never imagined in her wildest dreams.

Afterwards the long, tranquil aftermath of their loving, held close in Bran's arms, was as beautiful and wonderful in its own way to Naomi as the heat and frenzy of the loving itself. She tightened her arm round his waist and Bran sighed with pleasure.

'If this were fiction,' he said, moving his lips over her face, 'the shock of such a superlative experience would have brought my sight back.'

Naomi hoisted herself up on an elbow to smooth back the black hair from his damp forehead. 'Oh, I see. That's why you were so hot to make love to me. You hoped I'd provide a miracle cure!'

He pulled her down to him again, threading one hand into her hair to draw her face against his throat. 'You know damn well it wasn't, witch! I made love to you because I was about to expire if I didn't. And don't tell me I'd have felt differently if I could see you because I flatly refuse to believe it.'

Naomi lay quietly against him, making no effort to contradict him for once, then she reached up and turned out the light. 'There. Now I can't see you either.' She moved her hand down his chest delicately. 'I'll let my fingers act for my eyes.'

'If you do,' said Bran in a constrained voice, 'I won't answer for the consequences.'

'Shall I stop, then?'

'No — *duw*, no!'

Naomi laughed with sudden, confident elation, and went on with her exploration, until suddenly he thrust her on her back and ran his hands down her spine to cup her and lift her and make love to her again. This time their quest was shorter and even more tumultuous, so glorious and overwhelming that afterwards when they lay quiet in each other's arms exhaustion overtook Naomi and she fell deeply asleep.

CHAPTER EIGHT

WAKING in Bran's arms at dawn was a new and dangerously blissful experience. Naomi lay very still, aware in every nerve of Bran's warmth, of the brush of his thick black hair on her shoulder, the weight of the imprisoning leg he'd thrown across hers in the night. She moved slightly, and he murmured, his arms tightening a fraction, and she lay motionless, abandoning all idea of getting up. Just this once she would allow herself the luxury of lying here with him, cut off from the rest of the world in an oasis of miraculous privacy.

Naomi lay looking at the light as it brightened the room, and relived the events of the night, suddenly mindful that her bliss was the direct result of Haydn Griffiths's accident. Remorsefully she wondered how he was faring, and when Megan would ring to let them know.

When the telephone rang at a few minutes past seven Naomi, even though expecting it, jumped out of her skin, disturbing Bran, who tightened his arms involuntarily. When Naomi placed a restraining finger on his lips he slackened his hold just enough to let her take the receiver from its cradle, then threatened her composure badly by planting a series of kisses on her bare back as she gave the Gwal-y-Ddraig number.

Megan sounded strained and tired as she reported that Haydn had been operated on in the night and was still unconscious, but by courtesy of a strong constitution had survived his ordeal better than expected.

'I hate to ask this, love,' she said anxiously, 'but could you cope if I stayed down here with Tal today?

He wants to be there when Haydn comes round, you see. It's a terrible cheek, I know, but if you could put up some food for Bran——'

'Megan, *please*. Of course I can, and you mustn't worry about anything here,' said Naomi firmly. 'I'll tell Bran you're staying there until you feel you can leave. Stay as long as you want, and don't worry. I'll take good care of Bran.'

Megan's gratitude was tearful and heartfelt. She sent her love to Bran, issued a stream of instructions, then rang off to hurry back to Tal.

Naomi put the phone down and tried to slide out of bed, but Bran pulled her back under the covers and kept her there by the simple expedient of lying on top of her.

'Stay where you are. How's Haydn?' he asked, and listened intently while Naomi gave him the details.

'Megan will ring later in the day,' she finished breathlessly.

Bran nuzzled his lips against her neck. 'Good—I'm glad Haydn came through all right. Now we can enjoy the day with a clear conscience.'

Naomi tried to wriggle free. 'You can,' she said tartly, 'but I've got work to do.'

'No, you haven't,' he contradicted, holding her still. 'Now we've got the bonus of an extra day to ourselves I'm damned if I'm going to let you waste it at that blasted machine.'

'But——'

'But nothing.' Bran kissed her protesting mouth into silence. 'Naomi,' he said at last, in a tone which sent shivers down her spine, 'did you mean what you said?'

'What did I say?' she whispered.

'You told Megan you'd take care of me.'

'Of course I meant it!' Naomi tried to push him away. 'Look, Bran, if you won't let me go I can't get your breakfast, which is what Megan means by taking care of you.'

'To hell with breakfast. Anyone can make a meal for me. But only you, *cariad*, can provide nourishment for my soul.'

Certain Bran was teasing, that she should laugh and treat his words as a joke, Naomi found herself blinking hard on sudden tears. Bran frowned, his hands sliding into her tangled hair as his lips found the tell-tale dampness on her cheeks, then he found her mouth and kissed her with such demand that all thought of food vanished from Naomi's mind as her body caught fire from his.

Making love in the morning, in the sunlight, when Naomi knew she should have been doing any one of several other things, was an experience which possessed its own individual form of magic. The illicit aura to it all added a new dimension to the experience as Naomi's body answered the thrusting urgency of his, her open, dazzled eyes on Bran's face, watching it mirror the sensations overwhelming him as his body convulsed in the throes of the climax he reached only seconds before her own blotted out everything other than the cataclysm of feeling which engulfed her.

'Stay with me,' he said hoarsely, holding her with arms that bruised, and Naomi kissed him, and clutched him closer, as reluctant as he to break apart.

'With you,' said Bran, a long time later, 'I feel whole. As though I'd found the vital part missing from my life.'

A shiver ran through Naomi and Bran held her closer.

'What is it?'

'Someone walked over my grave.' She detached herself with determination. 'And now I *must* get up,

Bran Llewellyn. I need a bath and breakfast and about a gallon of tea.'

'What an unromantic creature you are, to be sure,' he mocked, and got to his feet, stretching, totally unselfconscious of his splendid nudity.

'Someone has to be practical,' she muttered, cheeks hot as she thrust his towelling robe into his hand before scrambling into her own. 'If you'll give me a few minutes in the bath while you get back to the studio I'll cook breakfast afterwards and bring it in to you.'

'I'd much rather share your bath,' said Bran, fumbling with his belt. 'And don't look at me like that!'

'Like what?'

'I don't need sight to know there's disapproval in those long, dark eyes of yours.'

'How do you know my eyes are long?'

'By touch, of course. Just as I know your nose tilts a little and your mouth is wide, with lips so full and sweet I can't resist them.' He smiled, turning her bones to water. 'I know the size and delectable shape of your breasts, and the curve of your hips and the sleek, satin feel of your thighs——'

'Stop it!' said Naomi, her face burning. 'Go away, do. I'll be with you as soon as I can.'

'Hurry up, then!' He felt for the doorknob. 'Until Megan and Tal get back, time apart is time wasted.' He held out his hand. 'Come here.'

Naomi went to him and took the hand, only to be pulled into Bran's arms and kissed at length before she was finally released.

'Fifteen minutes,' he ordered.

'You'll be lucky!'

Naomi rushed through a shower and dressed at top speed, sprayed herself with perfume and tied up her damp hair with a ribbon, then flew downstairs.

In the kitchen she worked rapidly, making coffee for Bran and tea for herself, grilling bacon, slicing bread and breaking eggs into a bowl. Before she could start cooking them Bran came into the room and closed the door, standing against it.

'I'm nearly ready,' said Naomi, surprised. 'If you'll go along to the studio I'll bring your breakfast in a minute.'

'No, you won't! I refuse to let you carry trays when I can perfectly well eat in here. Megan won't allow it, but you will, *cariad*, won't you?'

'I suppose so. It would be easier, I'll admit. Come and sit at the table.'

Bran remained just inside the door, smiling wryly. 'I require a navigator. Megan hasn't let me in here since the accident—afraid I'll do myself lasting injury with her egg-whisk, or something.'

Naomi flew to him to take his hand. 'Allow me,' she said jauntily, and led him to the chair at the head of the table. 'There you are—chairman of the board. Now talk to me while I work.'

Bran lounged back, legs outstretched, his hands relaxed on the arms of the old Windsor carver. He looked rested and vital in denims and bulky green sweatshirt, his eyes following her movements as though he could see as well as hear her, as she quickly laid the table.

'First of all,' he said huskily, 'let's talk about last night.'

Naomi frowned, suddenly still. 'Last night?'

'Yes. The most wonderful, glorious, fulfilling night of my entire life,' said Bran with emphasis. 'I want you to know just how much it meant to me to have you welcome me into your arms like that.'

Naomi began to whip the eggs savagely. 'In contrast to Allegra's rejection, you mean.'

'Hell, no!' Bran looked thunderstruck. 'I never gave a thought to Allegra—nor any other woman. Last night there was just you and me and the incredible experience we shared. Or am I taking too much for granted?' His face suddenly darkened. 'Maybe it wasn't the same for you.'

'Of course it was,' said Naomi breathlessly. 'And you know it.' Her entire body hot at the mere recollection, she doggedly chopped hot bacon into the scrambled eggs and transferred them to hot plates. She put them down on the table, poured orange juice into their glasses, then sat down beside the man who sat with closed eyes, the lines evident again in his brooding face.

'How do I know you're telling the truth?' he demanded.

For answer Naomi leaned across and kissed him at length on the mouth. 'Does that convince you?' she enquired, straightening, but Bran reached up an unerring hand and brought her face down to his so that he could return the kiss with interest.

'Somewhat,' he said, releasing her. 'Indulge me in a little more convincing after breakfast.'

'Would you kindly start eating?' she said tartly, settling back into her place. 'I haven't gone to all this trouble just to watch the eggs grow cold.'

Bran grinned and did as she said, refusing Naomi's offer to turn on the radio. 'No—talk to me instead. After breakfast you can read bits from the papers if you would.'

'Certainly. Anything to oblige,' said Naomi demurely, surprised and secretly rather embarrassed to find she was ravenous once she'd begun on her own meal.

It was well into the morning before Bran agreed to

return to the studio, on condition that Naomi joined him there as soon as possible.

'I'll be an hour,' she said firmly.

'An hour! What the hell are you going to do?' he demanded wrathfully.

'Some tidying up. I couldn't face Megan if she came home to a messy house.'

Bran sighed, exasperated. 'If you must, you must — but get a move on. I need you a damn sight more than the house does.'

Deeply gratified, Naomi whisked through a few basic chores, then ran to her room to tidy herself. Her eyes gleamed as they studied her reflection. A life of illicit pleasure was definitely good for her looks, she thought satirically, not daring to imagine how she'd look once she'd returned to her old life. A life without Bran Llewellyn.

'At last!' growled Bran, when she joined him in the studio. 'What the devil have you been doing? Spring-cleaning the entire house?'

'Actually,' said Naomi severely, 'I'm ten minutes earlier than promised. What do I have to do to win your approval, may I ask?'

Bran held up his arms. 'You know very well. Come here.'

'Certainly not. I'm going to read to you from today's paper,' she said firmly, and sat down on the sofa beside him.

He flung away into the corner of the sofa and leaned his head back. 'Oh, very well.'

Peace reigned for several minutes while Naomi chose items she hoped would interest Bran. When it became obvious that he was waiting instead of listening she gave up.

'All right, you win. Shall I switch on the radio, or would you prefer one of your CDs?'

'Neither. I want you to sit on my knee.'

'Possibly,' she said, secretly elated by his open need of her.

'But you won't. All right, spoilsport, let's go for a walk, then,' he said, surprising her. 'There's a green, lush smell of spring coming through the windows, and I want out of here for a while. Come and be my guide. We can take the mobile phone in case Megan rings.'

Naomi was only too happy to stroll hand in hand with Bran in the gardens, quick to anticipate any pitfall for him, counting steps when they went down from the terrace past the bluebell wood to the lawn which Bran told her had once been a bowling green. They sat close together on one of the stone benches, beneath the green, spreading shelter of a giant beech tree, while Bran tried to identify all the different scents assailing his newly sensitive nostrils.

'I never realised before how many different components make up one particular smell,' he observed, 'or truly appreciated the pleasure of warm sun on my skin.'

'Mmm,' agreed Naomi contentedly, 'it's heavenly out here in the sun this morning. I've got my eyes closed, too, to keep you company.'

Bran's arm tightened round her waist. 'You know I could almost cope with the way things are on a permanent basis with you to make up the deficit, Naomi. Now don't go all shy and stiff on me, I don't intend remaining blind, believe me. But having you here with me this last couple of weeks has made a hell of a difference.'

'Probably you'd have felt the same whoever came to work for you,' said Naomi with constraint.

Bran said something brief, rude and explicit in contradiction. 'Last night, when I mentioned my soul,' he went on very quietly, 'I wasn't talking complete nonsense, Naomi. My father had quite a good voice, and one of my earliest recollections is hearing him sing a song about a blind man. I've been thinking about it a lot since you arrived on the scene, especially the last line, which said something about God taking away his eyes so his soul might see.'

Naomi gazed up into his open, glittering eyes, then turned away sharply, suppressing the urge to blurt out the confession which would wreck their newfound harmony.

'What I do see,' went on Bran, holding her closer, 'is that before the accident I was too materialistic. I wanted possessions like this house, and a flash car, and a high-profile lifestyle, so I accepted commissions to paint boring people because it earned me money. I took the easy way out.'

'But the portraits won recognition which lets you do what you want now, surely? Besides,' added Naomi, 'it was a commission that brought you Allegra, I seem to remember.'

'A good argument for never painting a portrait again!' Familiar, cynical lines replaced the visionary look on Bran's face, and impulsively Naomi reached up to kiss them away.

'Let's go back to the house,' he whispered, his hands sliding up beneath her sweater.

Naomi pushed him away firmly. 'No. Let's stay here in the fresh air a little longer, then I'll make you some lunch.'

There was an idyllic quality to their time together as the day wore on. Naomi made sandwiches in the kitchen, while Bran lounged at the head of the table. They talked incessantly, about Naomi's job and her friends, about some of the people Bran had painted, others he'd known in the village of his birth. Then after lunch Megan rang again. Tal's brother was recovering, but weak and full of tubes, she reported, then asked anxiously if Naomi could manage until after visiting time that evening.

Naomi told her emphatically that it was no problem at all, sent her good wishes to Tal, then handed the phone over to Bran, who added his assurances, teasing Megan to allay her anxiety, and telling her to stay at the hospital with Tal as long as she liked.

'Put up at a hotel and come back tomorrow, if you like,' he said casually, grinning in Naomi's direction at her sharp intake of breath. He listened intently for a moment or two, then smiled again, in triumph this time. 'Of course you can, Megan, *bach*. Everthing's fine here, Naomi's doing a yeoman job, and don't worry, I'll pay her some overtime. Take it easy now, buy Haydn some grapes from me, and we'll see you at lunchtime tomorrow.'

Naomi stood very still as Bran put down the phone. 'Megan's not coming back today?'

Bran leaned back in his chair, his eyes gleaming through his lowered lashes. 'No. Tal's got some cousins in Newport. They went to visit Haydn and suggested Megan and Tal stay with them overnight so they can call in at the hospital before coming back here tomorrow.'

Naomi sat down at the table abruptly. 'Bran, there's something I must tell you——'

'No need,' he interrupted, suddenly serious. 'All I ask is your company, Naomi. I'd be lying if I said I didn't want to make love to you, too. What man wouldn't? But just having you with me to talk to, to be near me, is enough if you want it that way.'

'Not to mention a shot at cooking your dinner,' said Naomi with difficulty.

'Not if it means hours spent in preparation! Open a tin of something—soup, beans, anything.' Bran stretched out a hand, and Naomi put hers into it. 'Come back to the studio and listen to some music, then we'll go out for a stroll in the garden again.'

Naomi, who'd been on the very brink of telling Bran all about Diana and her article, cast confession to the winds. It would be madness to spoil the unexpected gift of an extra day alone with Bran. There would be time enough for sackcloth and ashes. Afterwards.

The dreamlike quality of the day persisted. Afterwards Naomi could never remember what music they listened to, or what books and films they discussed. There was only her pleasure in Bran's company, and his, openly displayed, in hers. Throughout the long warm afternoon Bran made no move to touch her other than to hold her hand. But always there was an underlying *frisson* of excitement, the memory of their night vivid and unforgettable beneath the badinage and laughter.

Dinner was a lamb and leek pie from Megan's freezer, accompanied by tiny potatoes in their jackets. They ate it informally at the kitchen table, with seedless grapes and a wedge of Caerphilly cheese to round it off.

'I'm not much of a cook, I'm afraid,' confessed Naomi, as she helped Bran to cheese. 'I was relieved when Megan told me to raid the freezer. She's got enough in there for an army.'

'She's manic about emergencies,' said Bran. 'I keep telling her this place is off-limits to visitors, but she keeps the place stocked with food just the same, convinced people will find it and drop in.'

'She'd be shocked to see us here like this at the kitchen table,' said Naomi, getting up to clear away. 'She probably expected me to serve the meal in state in the dining-room.'

Bran laughed, and leaned back in the chair, stretching luxuriously. 'What Megan doesn't know can't hurt her.'

'Isn't that the truth!'

Suddenly the atmosphere was different.

'You mean she wouldn't approve of the way we spent last night—and this morning?' asked Bran bluntly.

'Since I don't intend to ask, I'll never know.' Naomi began loading the dishwasher rather noisily.

Bran said nothing more for a while, until there was a lull in the activity. 'Have you finished?' he asked.

'Yes. I'll just make some coffee——'

'To hell with the coffee. Let's just go back to the studio and listen to some soothing music, and talk for a while. I've got something to ask.'

Naomi put her hand into the one Bran held out towards her as he got up from the table, her eyes troubled as they searched his face, which was as informative as a wooden mask as they went along the corridor to the studio. They found the big room filled with an eerie green twilight. Gathering clouds had replaced the sunshine of the afternoon, imparting an air of menace which sent Naomi hurrying to switch on lamps, shivering as she described it to Bran.

'Are you cold?' he asked.

'Not really.'

'Same person tramping on your grave again?'

'Something like that.'

'Come here, then.' Bran reached out a seeking arm and hooked her close. 'What's wrong, Naomi?'

'You said that you had something to ask.'

'Is that all? It's just that I realise you'll be finished on the book tomorrow. I want you to stay on for a while afterwards instead of running away the minute you've handed over the draft.'

'I promised to stay with my parents——' she began, but he interrupted her swiftly.

LAIR OF THE DRAGON 137

'Visit them the following weekend. You can drive back to London early Monday morning.'

'I can't do that,' she said reluctantly. 'If I stay — *if* I stay until then I'll have to leave on Sunday evening at the latest.'

'Better than nothing,' he said grudgingly, and caught her chin in his hand, turning her face up to his seeking mouth. 'Now,' he said against her lips, 'no more talking, just kiss me!'

Naomi obeyed without question, locking her hands behind his neck as his mouth met hers, suddenly as desperate as Bran for the touch of his mouth and his hands and the feel of his body against her as he swung her up on to his lap and held her hard against his chest.

His breathing quickened as he moved his mouth over face and down her throat, his fingers skilful as he flicked open her shirt and searched for the small clasp between her shoulder blades. As her breasts filled his hands he gave a groan and buried his face against her, his tongue flicking her nipples into erect, quivering response and Naomi gasped and clutched his head closer.

Suddenly Bran set her on her feet and stood up, his hand holding hers in an iron grip as he drew her towards the stair leading to his bedroom.

Naomi hesitated, pulling back for a moment, but he jerked her into his arms and kissed her again, then laughed against her open, protesting mouth.

'I'll carry you up if you prefer——'

'Bran, no——'

'I agree, better on your own two feet, my lovely.'

'That's not what I meant,' she said desperately. 'I don't know that I want this.'

Bran stood stock-still, all the heat and anticipation draining from his face as he released her. 'You're lying, Naomi. I may not be able to see, but I could feel your response.'

'It's nothing to do with that.' She tidied herself with shaking hands, willing him to understand. 'Last night was an accident, unpremeditated, something we hadn't planned or expected to happen. Tonight it's — well, it's different.'

Bran thrust a hand through his hair, looking distraught. 'Naomi, what possible harm can it do to anyone if we share a bed tonight? Or any other night, if it comes to that?'

'It's not something I do,' she muttered doggedly.

'You think I don't know that?' He turned away, feeling his way to the sofa. He slumped down, his face set in the familiar bitter lines. 'I thought we'd found something very special together. Or were you just taking pity on a blind man last night?' he added, in a voice that slashed at her like a razor.

'No, Bran, no!' she said in horror, and flew to him, sitting on his lap and wreathing her arms round his neck all in one movement. She kissed him in an agony of reassurance, oblivious of the pain when his arms closed round her like a vice.

'Then come with me. Now.' Bran got to his feet, still holding her in his arms. He set her on her feet and hauled her with him across the room, pushing her up the stair ahead of him. Beside his bed Bran halted, his breath hot on her face as he bent to take her in his arms. 'Surely you can tell this isn't just sex, *cariad*?' he demanded, in a voice so harsh with emotion that she threw her arms round his waist and hugged him close, nodding violently, unable to trust her voice.

Bran rubbed his cheek against hers. 'I need you, Naomi. Before you came I was wallowing in despair, sorry for myself, Now I know I can cope with life whether my sight comes back or not.'

CHAPTER NINE

NAOMI, glad that Bran couldn't see her heavy eyes, insisted on starting work next morning immediately breakfast was over, determined to restore some kind of normality to life before Megan got back.

'That won't be for hours yet. Let's just go back to bed,' Bran suggested as she steered him through the kitchen door.

Naomi paused, eyeing his rested, confident face narrowly. 'Why? Is it an urge to make up for lost time — because you've been sex-starved for longer than usual?'

Bran scowled. 'No, it bloody well isn't. I thought I made that clear last night. And,' he added softly, 'you may like to know that just having you in my arms, curled up against me in the night, was almost as much pleasure as having you writhing beneath me like a wild thing as I made love to you.'

Naomi breathed in sharply, her colour high. 'If you're going to say things like that, I'm off to the study.'

Bran turned, holding out his arms. 'Can't I persuade you to stay?'

'All too easily.'

'Tell me how and I will.'

'You know exactly how,' she said tartly. 'Anyway, Megan said she'll be home by twelve. I want to get an hour in before she does. I've liberated one of her cartons of soup from the freezer, and made some sandwiches so she won't have to get lunch the minute she comes through the door.'

'A very paragon of virtue!'

'Hardly!' Naomi reached up and give him a swift kiss, then dodged out of the way quickly. 'See you later.'

'Read me something from the papers first,' he said imperiously.

'Afterwards. Listen to the radio instead.'

'I'd much rather listen to you, *cariad*.' His smile flipped her heart over in her chest, but Naomi struck doggedly to her guns.

'I've only got an hour's work to do and I'll be finished! Do whatever you used to do before I came here.'

Bran's face turned bleak suddenly. 'And, presumably, what I shall have to do again. When you go.'

'Well, I'm not going yet,' she said briskly, secretly devastated at the very thought.

Once at her desk, Naomi worked hard, fighting her way through a fog of heavy lassitude after the long, unforgettable night in Bran's bed. The aftermath had left her depressed and anticlimactic, harrowed by the knowledge that tonight, and every other night for the foreseeable future, she would sleep alone.

To keep her brain occupied Naomi worked doggedly through until the last of the tapes was typed, edited and printed, managing to finish just as Megan and Tal returned. She stacked the manuscript neatly together when she heard the car, and ran through the kitchen to the yard at the back to welcome the couple home.

In a flurry of greetings, Megan gave the latest news on Haydn's progress, while Tal went straight off to find Bran.

Megan was full of questions as she parked her bags in the kitchen and took her coat off. She reached for the striped apron hanging behind the door almost in one movement as Naomi assured her Bran had been well taken care of in her absence.

'I know that, love,' said Megan, looking Naomi in the eye. 'Otherwise I wouldn't have stayed in Newport so long.'

Naomi flushed a little as she waved a hand at the refrigerator. 'I made some sandwiches earlier on and left them in there, and I took some of your soup from the freezer and put it in a pan. And there's some pie left from last night. I thought I'd save you having to cook lunch, at least. You must be very tired.'

'That's lovely of you, Naomi—though we had quite a good night's rest last night in Gwyneth's house in Newport.'

'Good. I'm glad Mr Griffiths is on the mend.'

'Aren't we all?' said Megan with a heartfelt sigh. 'How's the book going, then?'

Naomi told her she'd completed it only minutes before. 'One more bit to read back to Bran, then I've finished.'

'He's not going to be easy to live with once you're gone,' said Megan gloomily. 'No sign of his sight coming back, I suppose?'

Naomi shook her head. 'But it will, Megan, I'm sure of that.'

'*Duw*, I hope so!' Megan shook off her momentary depression. 'Right, I'll go and see Bran before doing a tray for you both.' She eyed Naomi closely. 'It's you who look tired, mind. Haven't you been sleeping well?'

'Not very,' said Naomi, with perfect truth, and escaped, pink-cheeked, to join Bran.

She found him sitting bolt upright at one end of the sofa, a still, waiting air about him whicn set her mental alarm bells ringing.

'Naomi,' he stated.

'Sorry I kept you waiting.' She sat beside him, poised to serve the meal. 'Did Megan think you'd survived satisfactorily without her?'

'I believe so. She told me you've finished the draft.'

'Yes. After lunch I'll read the last bit back to you, make any alterations you want, and that's it. The job's done. Sandwich?'

'I'm not hungry. Just coffee. Please.'

Naomi eyed him apprehensively as she handed it to him. 'Would you like me to read the last pages to you now?'

'Don't you want to eat first?' he said curtly.

'I'm not hungry either.'

'In that case by all means make a start. Afterwards perhaps you'd spare the time to read a few items from the paper.'

'Yes, of course.' Naomi eyed him despairingly as she reached for the manuscript. Something was horribly wrong. The lover of the night had vanished, replaced by the morose Bran Llewellyn of her first day or two at Gwal-y-Ddraig.

The reading took very little time to complete. Bran nodded afterwards without enthusiasm, brushing aside her offer to make any alterations he wanted. 'It'll do. Some editor from Diadem will probably chop the thing to bits, anyway. Send it off this afternoon.'

'Very well. Anything special you want me to say in the covering letter?'

'No.' Bran reached down beside him for a newspaper and handed it to her. 'Now read this. Tal tells me there's a very interesting article on page five.'

Naomi took the paper, then almost dropped it. Instead of his usual *Times* Bran had given her a copy of the *Chronicle*.

She cleared her throat. 'This isn't your usual paper.'

'No. But Tal gets it whenever he can. He bought one this morning in Newport.'

Naomi's heart thudded in her chest. She'd never thought to ask about the Griffithses' taste in daily papers. She stared at the *Chronicle* in her hand without hope. Diana had sworn her article wouldn't be published until the following week, but it was obvious from Bran's manner that Nemesis was at hand just the same. Nor was it difficult to find the article. Diana's headline hit her right between the eyes. LAIR OF THE DRAGON stood out in bold type above a photograph of the house shot from a distance with a zoom lens.

'You've found the piece?' said Bran.

'Yes,' whispered Naomi.

'Read, then.'

'"Bran Llewellyn,"' began Naomi, then stopped, forced to clear her throat and start again. '"Bran Llewellyn, one of the best artists to come out of Wales since Augustus John, has for years found refuge in the Welsh Marches, where his picturesque country retreat is a far cry from the terraced house in the Rhondda coal-mining village of his birth."'

'A little florid, but so far reasonably accurate,' commented Bran. 'Read on.'

The rest of the article described the exterior of the house and the spiral stair and great north windows of the studio, where the walls displayed some of the artist's work, including a self-portrait never exhibited to the general public. Diana went on to the wild charm of the terraced gardens, mentioned the loyal Welsh couple who looked after Bran, and commiserated on his climbing accident. His social popularity was glossed over rather cleverly, before the article finished with a brief chronicle of the artist's various exhibitions, and the famous faces he'd recorded for posterity, then gave a plug to the forthcoming autobiography 'The Flight of the Crow' to round things off.

The silence in the room was a tangible thing afterwards as Naomi sat shivering and speechless. There was nothing untrue or libellous in the article, but one look at Bran's face was enough to see he was seething with icy rage.

'So,' he said at last, his voice grating, 'I'm getting guilty vibrations, loud and clear, Scheherazade.'

'I—I don't know what you mean.'

'Oh, come on, darling,' he said derisively. 'Let's not play games. When Tal read me the article it didn't take much to identify the source of the reporter's information. If you'd stuck to exteriors and the garden all would have been well. But no one's been inside my studio since it was completed—apart from Megan and Tal, of course. No one else has ever seen the self-portrait, Naomi. And not even the editor at Diadem knows the title I've chosen for the book. The only thing missing is the hottest item of all—my blindness! Why did you spare me that, I wonder?' He clenched his fists, his face a mask of fury. 'Tell me, did *you* take the photograph?'

'No!'

'So someone came trespassing. But it was you who supplied the rest!'

'Yes.'

'I hope they paid you well for it.'

Naomi gasped. 'I didn't do it for money!'

'Why, then?'

'I can't tell you that.'

'You don't need to.' Bran's teeth showed in a tigerish smile. 'I got Tal to put a call through to the *Chronicle* to ask who'd written the article.'

Naomi's shoulders sagged. 'I see.'

'I'm sure you do. Even a blind man like me can

see—now. Miss Diana Barry's lucky to have a sister willing to do a little insider trading.'

Naomi sat with bowed head, unable to say a word.

'Why the hell did you do it?' he demanded.

'Because Diana needed the information,' she said flatly.

'It isn't the article itself that sticks in my throat.' His face set in menacing lines. 'It's the fact that you lied your way in here to get the information. *You*, Naomi—the one person I would have bet my last cent on as honest.'

'Normally I am,' she said bleakly, 'not that I expect you to believe it now. But if I'm in the witness box you may as well know it all. A friend of Diana's arranged for her to do the work for you, but she couldn't take the time off from the *Chronicle*, so she begged me to take her place.'

Bran thrust a hand through his hair convulsively. 'And you agreed?'

'Yes.'

'Willingly?'

'Of course I wasn't willing!'

Bran's mouth tightened. 'Then *why*?'

'Diana believes the article will help her get the promotion she's after,' said Naomi brokenly. 'She—she was a tower of strength to me in the past when I needed help, so I couldn't refuse mine the only time she's ever asked for it. I had three weeks' holiday due so in the end I gave in and agreed to come here and work for you, and at the same time provide her with copy for the article she's convinced is a matter of life and death to her career.'

'So now I know how you come to be here,' Bran said after a protracted, simmering silence. His face was mask-like, the eyes tightly closed. 'And now you've explained I suppose it's just about possible to understand your motives. At least you didn't sell the bloody information for money.' His eyes flew open. 'But what I can't understand,' he said with sudden savagery, 'is why the *hell* you let me make love to you.'

Because I'm madly in love with you and knew I'd regret it forever if I didn't, thought Naomi despairingly. If I'd had any sense I'd have shut the door in your face the other night, blindness or no blindness. It would have made things a lot simpler, one way and another.

'Wasn't it obvious?' she said unsteadily.

'At the time I was fool enough to think so. But I don't any more. Was your idea to soften the blow when I found out? Or was it some strange quixotic idea of paying for the information you'd leaked to your sister?'

'It was neither,' she said, her voice barely above a whisper. 'I know an apology's useless, but I am sorry, Bran. Desperately sorry.'

'So am I,' he said bitterly. 'And not about the publicity—I'm used to that! There's nothing objectionable in the article. Compared with some of the garbage written about me in the past it's bloody flattering.' He flung out a clenched, white-knuckled hand. 'What burns me up is the fact that you were responsible for it. You *used* me, Naomi, infiltrated my house, my confidence, even my bloody bed—and all just to get a story for your sister!'

'No—*please*, it wasn't like that, Bran! What can I do to convince you?'

'Do? I'll tell you exactly what you can do, Miss Judas.' Bran leapt to his feet, putting out a hand to steady himself. 'You can get out of my sight——'

He gave a sudden, wild laugh at the word, and Naomi flinched as though he'd struck her, then backed away before he found out she was crying. Letting the tears run silently down her face, she snatched up the finished manuscript and fled from the studio to sanctuary in the study, where she huddled against the closed door, thrusting her clenched fists against her mouth to stifle her sobs. It was a long time before she was calm enough to mop herself up and sit down to type a brief covering letter to Diadem. Afterwards she scribbled her own initials above Bran's name, then sealed the manuscript in a padded envelope and tidied the desk.

Half an hour later she was ready to leave. She took her suitcases down to the hall then went along to the kitchen to seek out Megan, who was in the throes of preparing dinner.

'There's some tea in the pot, love,' said Megan, her eyes on the sauce she was making. 'Bran's gone out for a drive with Tal.'

Naomi cleared her throat. 'I'm leaving now, Megan.'

'*Leaving*?' The other woman spun round, her eyes like saucers. 'Naomi! You look dreadful. Whatever's the matter?'

'The article in the paper,' said Naomi unsteadily. 'It's my fault. My sister wrote it, but — but I gave her the information.'

Megan nodded impatiently. 'I know that. Bran told Tal. But there's no real harm done. There was nothing very terrible in it, for goodness' sake. Bran likes to keep this place private, of course, but anyone could find out he lived here if they tried.'

'But it wasn't *anyone*.' Naomi choked on a sob. 'It was me — and Bran told me to get out of his sight.'

'That's just his temper!' Megan pushed her down in a chair at the table. 'Now just you sit yourself down and drink some nice hot tea.'

Naomi took in a deep, steadying breath. 'Megan, I

just want you to know that I didn't gain by it. Money, I mean.' She blinked hard. 'I just did it for love.'

Megan nodded. 'For your sister.' She handed Naomi a cup. 'Now you drink that, there's a good girl.'

Naomi swallowed the tea, oblivious to its heat, then got to her feet. 'Thank you. I'd better be on my way.'

Megan did her utmost to dissuade her, but Naomi was adamant, desperate to be as far away as possible by the time Bran returned. She gave Megan a quick hug, implored her not to come outside to see her off, then collected her luggage and went out to the car. She gave a last, melancholy look at Gwal-y-Ddraig, then slid behind the wheel and drove as fast as she dared down the steep, winding drive to the road, feeling as if she'd left the vital, living half of her behind.

Naomi returned to London after a few quiet days with her sympathetic but blessedly tactful parents in Cheltenham, to find that Diana had, indeed, been offered the job she was so desperate for; not, ironically enough, because of the article, but because the editor of the *Chronicle* had intended offering her the job all along.

The news came as the last straw. Naomi had spent a long, hot Monday wrestling with the chaos Rupert always managed to create among the accounts while she was away. By the time she saw Diana later that evening she was depressed, irritable and tired, and in no mood to pull her punches when Diana, looking the picture of guilt, told her about the job.

Naomi glared at her sister, incensed. 'Are you telling me that my trip to Wales wasn't even *necessary*?'

Diana nodded, shame-faced. 'Not that the article didn't do me a lot of good—Craig was delighted with it. Plenty of articles have been written about Bran

LAIR OF THE DRAGON 149

Llewellyn before, but never about his lair in the Black Mountains. The house gave me a fantastic headline!'

'But why on earth was it published a week earlier than you said? You didn't tell me you were sending a photographer, either,' said Naomi furiously.

Diana gave her a pleading look. 'Sorry. I knew you wouldn't like it, but Phil didn't do any trespassing to get the picture, I promise, and when I showed the article to Craig he wouldn't hear of keeping it back a week. I'm ashamed to say I was too much of a coward to let you know. Besides, you said Bran Llewellyn didn't take the *Chronicle*—I counted on his not seeing it.' She paused, eyeing Naomi's haggard face with concern. 'Good grief, Naomi, you look like death. Was Bran Llewellyn a pig to work for? I *told* you to come away from there, remember.'

'But then you wouldn't have had your precious article,' said Naomi savagely. 'And Bran Llewellyn, just for the record, was fine to work for. Everything was fine until he chanced on the article. He rang the *Chronicle*, found that you wrote the wretched thing, wiped the floor with me and threw me out of his house.'

Diana looked horrified. 'Lord, Naomi—how ghastly for you! Honestly, love, I tried my best to keep the piece back until you were home and dry.'

Naomi made a sharp, dismissive gesture. 'Well, it's done now. I don't want the subject mentioned again. Ever. But next time you want some dirty work done, Miss Hotshot Journalist, you can do it yourself!'

'I'll never ask you to do anything like that again, believe me!' Diana hugged the small, unyielding figure penitently, then stood back, looking down into Naomi's face. 'If you felt that badly about leaking the information why didn't you come back straight away? You could have made some excuse.'

Naomi blushed to the roots of her hair, and pulled away. 'By that time,' she said stiffly, 'I was committed to helping Bran with his manuscript.'

'Bran,' repeated Diana thoughtfully. 'Are you sure you didn't fall head over heels in love with the man?'

'Certainly not,' snapped Naomi.

Diana, obviously unconvinced, had the grace to leave the subject alone. 'I found out about Greg, by the way.'

'Greg.' Naomi looked blank for a moment. 'Oh—right. You needn't have bothered. I don't know why I asked.'

Diana looked deeply relieved. 'I must say it worried me a bit. Why did you want to know?'

'Just curiosity.'

'Good. I'd hate to think you were still hankering after him. Greg, it seems, ditched sexy Susie after only a couple of months in favour of a colleague's bride, then, after making a pig's breakfast of said marriage, flitted off after another Lolita-type even younger than Susie.'

'Busy old Greg,' said Naomi, yawning.

Diana stared at her in wonder. 'It really doesn't matter to you any more, does it?'

'Not a bit. Though I suppose in a way it's some comfort to know it wasn't just me he couldn't stick to.' Naomi yawned again. 'Right. Off you go. And congratulations about the job. I just wish you'd got it sooner. Like three weeks sooner.'

'So do I,' said Diana penitently.

'How about Craig, by the way? Any progress there?'

To Naomi's surprise Diana blushed vividly. 'Actually, yes. He took me out to dinner last night. That's why I wasn't around when you got back.'

Naomi's smile was bitter. 'Nice to know my sacrifice wasn't in vain.'

'Was it such a sacrifice, then?' said Diana swiftly.

'If you mean did I feel like a burnt offering by the time I left, yes!' Naomi pushed her sister towards the door. 'Now let me get to bed before Clare comes home and keeps me up half the night!'

Diana paused on the landing. 'Did Bran Llewellyn pay up, by the way?'

'On the nail. I received a cheque only today, via Diadem.'

The cheque, for twice the sum originally agreed, had been sent with a card inscribed 'Bran Llewellyn' in bold black typeface. On the back of the card, in what Naomi took to be Tal's handwriting, were the words, 'Enclosed your thirty pieces of silver'.

CHAPTER TEN

SUMMER came early that year. By the end of May London was sweltering in an early heatwave, ablaze with chestnut trees in blossom, and the scent of lilac was heavy in the quiet tree-lined road where Naomi shared an attic flat with Clare. When the sun shone Naomi learned to avoid Hyde Park, where she normally took her picnic lunch, unable to bear the sight of couples walking hand in hand, or lying entangled on the grass. She took to eating her chainstore sandwich at the desk in the little office in the basement, and assured herself that someday she'd get over Bran Llewellyn, just as she'd got over Greg. In theory it ought to be easier this time. She'd spent a whole year of her life with Greg, while all she'd been allowed with Bran were eighteen brief, unforgettable days in Wales.

'Naomi,' said Rupert one day, 'far be it from me to intrude on your private life, but Laura and I feel there's something wrong. That foxy little face of yours is growing thinner by the day. You're all eyes and bones, you know. Can we help?'

'I'm afraid not.' Naomi smiled gratefully. 'But it's very sweet of you, Rupert. Sorry I'm such a misery lately.'

'Man trouble?'

'You could say that.'

'Find another chap, Naomi.' Rupert's eyes twinkled. 'Laura says we're all alike, so a replacement should be easy enough.'

Naomi smiled wryly. 'Not for this one. But don't worry, I'll get over it. Eventually.'

'Of course you will. And as part of your recovery programme I suggest you stop incarcerating yourself in here day after day and go to a couple of sales.'

'Anything you say.'

Rupert patted her hand. 'Good girl. Sotheby's this week, then, and Cardiff next Tuesday.'

Naomi made a face. 'Sotheby's, fine, but not Cardiff, please, Rupert.'

Rupert's eyebrows rose. 'Ah! Right. I'll do that one, you do Lewes.'

Naomi nodded gratefully. 'Anywhere.'

'Bar Cardiff!' Rupert raised a hand. 'And don't worry. Discreet, tactful fellow that I am, I shan't ask why.'

'Thank you, Rupert. What price do you want on these Bristol vases?'

One evening, three interminable weeks after her return from Wales, Naomi gave in to Diana's coaxing and met her after work for a meal in an Italian restaurant near Sinclair Antiques.

'You look terrible,' said Diana.

'It's the heat,' said Naomi shortly, and changed the subject. 'How are things with you and Craig?'

'Fine.' There was a pause while Diana applied herself to an artistic plate of monkfish salad. 'In fact,' she went on, 'he's asked me away for the weekend.'

'Dear me, things are hotting up!'

Diana sighed. 'We had everything arranged for next week, to go to a literary festival, but now Craig's doubtful he can make it.'

'Pity—can't you go away some other time?'

'Yes, of course. But I really fancied the literary festival. Craig booked for a couple of lectures.' Diana smiled persuasively. 'Look, why don't you come instead?'

Naomi shook her head regretfully. 'Can't afford it.'

'Of course you can. Craig's paid for the tickets, and I'll treat you to a room—come *on*. A break will do you good.'

Naomi thought about it. As an alternative to a weekend spent sweltering alone in a London heatwave it was certainly tempting. 'Who's giving the lectures?'

'A man by the name of Benedict Carver's doing one,' said Diana smugly. 'How does a talk on eighteenth-century ceramics grab you?'

Naomi's eyes brightened. 'Why didn't you say that before? In that case I will come. Where's the festival?'

'Somewhere near Hereford,' said Diana vaguely. 'Fancy some pudding?'

With something to look forward to for a change, Naomi's mood lightened a little during the following week. She gave in to Clare's persuasion and went out to the cinema for the first time since coming back, and even enjoyed the film. The rawness of her agony over Bran began to lessen slightly, and when the shop was busy she even managed to go for minutes at a time without thinking of him, something which had been totally beyond her up to now. Every day since her flight from Wales she'd picked up the phone to apologise, longing to hear his voice, but her courage had failed her every time and she'd replaced the receiver without dialling, afraid he'd refuse to speak to her. And letters of apology were out of the question. Naomi had no intention of baring her soul for someone else, even Megan, to relay second-hand to Bran.

By the time Diana collected her early the following Saturday morning Naomi felt better than at any time since her return from Gwal-y-Ddraig. Diana's smart new Cabriolet ate the miles very comfortably as they bowled along the M4 towards their goal in the early morning sunshine, and for the first time in weeks

Naomi felt her spirits lift. Diana was a careful, smooth driver, and after a while Naomi grew drowsy, her run of wakeful nights taking their toll as she slid lower in the seat and gave way to the sleep her system craved.

When Naomi woke she found herself staring down at the wide waters of a familiar estuary as the car crossed the Severn Bridge. 'Hold on—what on earth are we doing here, Diana?' she demanded, sitting bolt upright.

'Craig planned the route for me,' said her sister as she turned off the bridge and made for Chepstow. 'He said this is the prettiest way.'

'And the longest,' retorted Naomi, her stomach churning at the discovery that she was in Wales again, breathing the same air as Bran Llewellyn. 'Surely this isn't the easiest way to Hereford?'

'Search me,' said Diana casually. 'Anyway the place we're heading for is quite a few miles from Hereford.'

'Diana,' said Naomi sharply. 'Where exactly *are* we heading for?'

'Hay-on-Wye, darling. Where all the bookshops are. You'll love it.'

Naomi gazed at her sister in horror. 'But Di, that's in Wales. Hay's not far from Llanthony! I'd never have stirred from London if I'd known.'

'That's why I didn't tell you,' said Diana, unrepentant. 'Now keep quiet while I look for signs. Apparently we don't go into Chepstow itself. We make for the racecourse roundabout where Craig says I take a left turning for Itton and Devauden, and keep straight on until I see a sign for Llansoy and Raglan. Now you're awake, do some navigating.'

Naomi subsided in her seat, simmering, but after a while her common sense reasserted itself. Hay was far enough from Llanthony to make an accidental meeting with Bran one chance in a million. And with his present handicap a town crowded with culture-seekers was the last place he was likely to visit, even with the faithful Tal in attendance. She forced her mind away from Bran, concentrating hard on the scenery instead as they drove along a quiet road edged in some places with walls, but mainly with hedgerows and green, hilly fields. At last she spotted the roadsign they were looking for and directed Diana to take a left turning for Llansoy, both girls exclaiming in unison at the beauty of the Vale of Usk spread out in panorama below as the narrow road swooped downward on its steep scenic way to Raglan and the bypass to Abergavenny. Naomi felt a sharp pang of pain as they sped along the faster, familiar road, but ignored it sternly as she pointed out the Sugar Loaf to Diana, making no mention of the fact that Bran's home was just beyond the mountains looming closer with every mile. Once Abergavenny was behind them she felt better. There were no reminders of Bran Llewellyn on the route which led past Crickhowell and on to Talgarth and Hay. Not that she needed any, thought Naomi bleakly. He was with her constantly, wherever she went.

They arrived in Hay-on-Wye in time for much needed coffee before a browse round the famous bookshops lining the streets of the town. Hay, they discovered, was not only a paradise for bibliophiles, but a delightful place of terraced stone cottages and steep streets, a covered marketplace and a cinema now crammed with books for sale instead of showing films.

'What time's the first lecture?' asked Naomi.

'Not until three. We'll have loads of time to find the chapel where your ceramics man is talking, so we'll have an early lunch,' said Diana.

'Fine. In the meantime let's go into that shop over

there. Fancy going halves on an antique map for Dad's birthday?'

Over lunch in the garden of a busy little café Naomi and Diana pored over a guide book which informed them that to the Normans Hay had been the gate to Mid-Wales.

'All that past blood and turbulence is hard to believe now,' said Naomi, shaking her head. 'It says here that nowadays the main excitements are the sheep sales and the literary festival.'

'Eat some of that salad,' ordered Diana.

'Not hungry.' Naomi glanced at her sister's plate. 'You haven't eaten much either — in fact you're very fidgety today.'

'Hay fever, I think,' said Diana, looking flushed, 'must be all the green fields everywhere. Come on, let's make a move. If the chapel's small you'd better be early to get a front seat.'

'Frankly I'm surprised Craig was interested in a ceramics lecture,' said Naomi as they strolled through the crowded town. 'Not his cup of tea, surely?'

Diana looked sheepish. 'Actually he booked that once he knew you were going. His interest was in the lecture by the BBC foreign news reporter in the main auditorium tonight.'

Naomi grinned. 'Yours too, no doubt! Does this mean you'd rather go back to the bookshops than listen to Benedict Carver?'

'Would you mind very much?' Diana smiled guiltily. 'I know you're riveted by bits of ancient china, but frankly they leave me cold.'

Naomi laughed, assuring her sister she'd enjoy the lecture far more on her own than with a companion bored to tears by the entire thing.

'I'll just see you inside, then,' said Diana, as they arrived at the chapel. 'Here's your ticket. I'll meet you back at the café at four-thirty.' She gave Naomi a hug. 'Take care.'

Assuring Diana she could hardly come to harm in a ceramics lecture delivered in a respectable Welsh chapel, Naomi settled herself in a place on the end of the front row. The building filled up rapidly, soon so warm that she was glad she'd given in to Diana on the subject of clothes. Instead of the inevitable jeans and jersey she was wearing a loose yellow T-shirt and a flowing green cotton skirt printed with lemons. Even so once the chapel was full it was so hot that she found it hard to breathe, and felt glad when Benedict Carver arrived dead on time to begin his lecture.

Naomi took notes as the ceramics expert began to talk, knowing Rupert would expect chapter and verse when she got back to work. She soon forgot the heat as the lecture progressed. Benedict Carver, she found, was not only an expert in his field, but such a witty, accomplished speaker that she was sorry when his talk was over and it was time to go looking for Diana.

As she moved towards the door in the rear of the crowd Naomi stooped to pick up her fallen notebook, and almost fell over as she was jostled. When a hand caught her by the elbow to haul her upright she looked up with a smile of thanks which changed to shock as she gazed up in disbelief into the intent face of Bran Llewellyn. Heat rushed into her cheeks, then receded with sickening speed, leaving her breathless and dizzy. Cold perspiration broke out on her forehead, the walls of the chapel spun round her and she crumpled into strong arms which shot out to catch her. When she came to she was sitting on one of the seats in the front row, supported against an all too familiar shoulder while a sympathetic woman held a glass of water for her to drink.

'Feeling better, dear?' enquired the woman with

sympathy. 'It was very hot in here today. Will you be all right now? I'm on duty at the auditorium soon.'

Naomi nodded dumbly, almost convinced she was hallucinating as she listened to Bran's assurances that he would take care of the invalid. When they were alone in the deserted chapel he slid a finger under Naomi's chin and forced her to look into the handsome, scarred face which haunted her dreams.

'So,' said Bran softly, his eyes bright with recognition, and something else less easy to define. 'We meet again. What cultural venues we choose for our accidental meetings, to be sure. First the opera, now an obscure lecture on eighteenth-century ceramics. But this time, I swear, I'm not the one who knocked you over.'

Naomi gazed at him in despair, realising that, while the miracle had happened and Bran could see again, he had no idea who she was other than the girl he'd bumped into in the bar of the New Theatre in Cardiff.

Belatedly she tried to free herself, but Bran kept a firm, impersonal arm round her waist. 'I shouldn't try to stand yet. Lean against me. You look distinctly seedy.'

Seedy! thought Naomi wildly. Frantic was more like it. This was a Catch-22 situation with a vengeance. If she opened her mouth to speak Bran would know who she was, but if she remained dumb he'd think she was a total idiot. Which, one way and another, wasn't far wrong.

'I can't get over my luck in running into you again,' said Bran, astonishing her. 'From the moment I saw you that night I've yearned to draw that face of yours. Your bone-structure had me itching for a pencil.' He smiled, his eyes dancing with a light which made Naomi dizzy again.

She gave him a dazed, speechless smile and scrambled to her feet, desperate to escape, but a long arm shot out to bar her way. 'No you don't, Cinderella,' he said sharply. 'You won't run away from me a second time——' He looked up with a wry, unsurprised smile as Diana came hurrying into the deserted chapel. 'Ah! The cavalry's arrived.'

'Hello,' said Diana, smiling guiltily.

'My fellow conspirator, I assume,' said Bran, holding out his hand. 'Good to meet you, Diana.'

Naomi looked wildly from one to another, dawning comprehension in her eyes. She heaved a deep, shaky breath. 'So. You knew who I was all the time, Bran Llewellyn. You were just playing with me,' she said bitterly.

Diana looked desperately uncomfortable. 'I sent him the snap Dad took of us on the lawn last year.'

'You sent Bran a photograph? How—why——?' Naomi's eyes filled with weak, angry tears and she bit hard on her lower lip.

Bran moved in closer, the eyes holding Naomi's as green and unreadable as bottle glass in the shadowed chapel. 'I contacted Diana to ask for a picture of you.'

Naomi eyed her sister in bitter reproach. 'Why didn't you *tell* me?'

'You'll never know the struggle I had to keep quiet about it!' Diana took her hand, squeezing it remorsefully. 'But Bran swore me to silence. He wanted to speak to you himself first. Don't be angry, love. At least it gave me the chance to tell him I was to blame for what happened.'

Naomi shook her head. 'Not entirely. You were the one who ordered me home the moment I got to Gwal-y-Ddraig, remember.'

'Is that true?' said Bran softly, his eyes gleaming.

Naomi's pallid face coloured painfully. 'Yes.'

'So why didn't you go?'

'I—I was committed to doing the job by that time. Once I found out—I mean once I——' She floundered at the look in his eyes.

'Discovered I was blind,' he finished for her, then smiled at her look of dismay. 'It's all right—Diana knows.'

Diana dropped Naomi's hand, frowning. 'Don't look like that—I won't rush straight back to the *Chronicle* with the news! Bran told me that in confidence.'

Naomi pulled herself together, and turned back to Bran. 'How long have you been able to see?'

'I was beginning to distinguish shapes before you ran away——'

'You *sent* me away!'

'Do you blame me?' he demanded.

She shook her head miserably. 'No.'

They stared at each other in tense silence, forgetting Diana, who was obliged to cough loudly at last to remind them she was still there.

'Look,' she said awkwardly, 'I imagine you two have a lot to talk about. In any case I'm meeting Craig at a hotel called the Swan at Hay soon so I'll go back there and wait for him.'

Naomi blinked in astonishment. 'Craig? But I thought——'

'Bran will explain,' said Diana hastily, and gave her sister a hug. 'Lord, you look peaky. Are you all right?'

'She'll be fine,' said Bran firmly. 'I'll take care of her.'

Diana gave him a long look. 'You'd better. See you later, then.'

By this time Naomi had given up asking questions. The whole day had taken on such an air of unreality that she wouldn't have been surprised to wake up in her bedroom in London and find she'd been dreaming.

'Are you feeling better?' asked Bran.

'I don't know how I feel,' she said, watching her sister hurry away. She turned to him shyly. 'I should have said so before—I'm very glad you can see again, Bran. Is your vision as good as before?'

'It is now.' He took her hand and led her to a chair. 'In the beginning it was grainy and indistinct, like an old black and white film. But bit by bit it grew clearer until the definition was back and I was seeing in Technicolor again.' He smiled quizzically. 'Though now you know I can see I'm surprised there's one question you haven't asked. Aren't you wondering why I haven't contacted you before?'

'I assumed you didn't want to,' she muttered, looking down at her tightly clasped hands.

Bran loosened them and took one small, clammy paw in his. 'Let's get one thing clear, Naomi Barry. When I told you to get out of my sight that day, I meant out of the way for a while until I'd recovered my temper, not out of my life! When I got back I went berserk when I found you'd taken off. I was so mad with you I made Tal post off that cheque—the one you sent straight back, incidentally. When Megan heard about it she wiped the floor with me!'

There was a long, tense silence.

'That was some time ago,' Naomi pointed out at last.

Bran let out a deep breath. 'I know. But I needed my eyes back in full working order before I could go racing off after you to London to drag you back by the hair. Then I realised I had no idea where you lived. I rang up Diadem and demanded your address, but all they could give me was the address of Sinclair Antiques, which you'd put on your application. Then it dawned on me that I had no idea what you looked like, either. It would have been bloody embarrassing to charge into a shop and grab the wrong girl!'

Naomi smiled a little. 'Bad for Rupert, too. Seeing me dragged by the hair through his shelves of priceless porcelain would have given him a heart attack.'

Bran grinned. 'True. Fortunately for him I abandoned this melodramatic scenario and contacted Diana via the *Chronicle* instead. I introduced myself, made one or two points crystal-clear, and then listened with great interest when she told me how worried she was about you.'

Colour flooded Naomi's face, then receded again, and Bran reached for her involuntarily.

She evaded his hands, shaking her head. 'I won't faint again. I'm merely suffering from embarrassment at having my private life made public. Diana's not usually so forthcoming to strangers.'

Bran raised a sardonic black eyebrow. 'I'm hardly a stranger where you're concerned, *cariad*. Nor do I ever intend to be. A point I had to make very clear before your sister would talk about you at all. Though it was my sob-story about the blindness that finally persuaded her to lure you here today.'

Naomi frowned. 'Why didn't you just ring me?'

'I wanted to meet you in person, not to talk to a voice.' He smiled wryly. 'But I needed a photograph to recognise you.'

Naomi stared at him woodenly. 'And so you saw my face at last.'

'Again, Naomi, not at last.' He smiled triumphantly. 'I'd seen your face before, remember. I could hardly believe my luck when I realised you were the girl at the opera.'

'Luck?' Naomi stared at him in disbelief, her heart thumping.

Bran grasped her by the shoulders, his eyes locked with hers. 'Yes. Luck. Good fortune, or whatever else you choose to call it. When I saw the photograph I offered up a prayer to the god of coincidence!'

She shook her head. 'There was no coincidence about it. From the moment I told Diana about bumping into you at the opera all she could think of was wangling an interview with you—the one you refused to every other member of the Press. Originally, heaven help me, I was supposed to buttonhole you at the Cardiff sale and trade on our chance meeting to get you to talk to her.'

'Only I didn't turn up.'

'Much to my relief.' Naomi pulled a face. 'Which was short-lived when Diana outlined the new gameplan she had waiting!'

They looked at each other in silence, Naomi still beset by so many emotions that she found it hard to sit still under the searching green gaze.

'I want you to sit for me, Naomi,' said Bran abruptly.

She swallowed, still finding it hard to believe that he wanted to paint her. 'Are you working again, then?' she hedged.

He nodded casually. 'Once the consultant gave the go-ahead I decided to get my hand in by finishing off Allegra's portrait.'

The news damped her down like a wet sponge. 'Ah, yes, Allegra. Did she come running back, just as I forecast?'

'She wanted to. Why? Are you jealous?'

'Certainly not!'

'Then why the hell ask?'

Naomi shrugged. 'Idle curiosity.'

Bran's eyes glittered coldly. 'I was quite happy to see her again, as it happens. Purely because, like the Greeks, she came bearing gifts. She was so keen to have the portrait I let her drive down to collect it, with Daddy's cheque in her hot little hand.'

'Was she pleased to know you can see again?' asked Naomi tonelessly.

Bran scowled at her. 'Yes. A bloody sight more than you seem to be, as a matter of fact.'

'That's not true!' said Naomi hotly. 'How can you say that? I know it's the most important thing in your life!'

He shook his head. 'One of the *two* most important things in my life.'

She waited, tense, and he smiled slowly.

'The other being the entry into my life of Naomi Barry, who turned out to be the girl at the opera — the girl whose bones made me itch to draw them. Don't look at me like that,' he added swiftly. 'I'm telling the exact truth. Afterwards, I had a clear view of you across the circle.'

Naomi stared at him, her mind going round in circles. 'I didn't see *you*.'

'I was at the back of a box, free to gaze at that face of yours as much as I liked, which was a damn sight more than my companion liked, believe me. She got very stroppy over it.'

'I can see why if it was Allegra. With a face like hers she must have found it hard to understand why you were fascinated by mine!'

Bran looked at her for a moment in silence. 'Naomi, why are you so paranoid about your looks? All right, so you're not conventionally pretty. Not in the way Allegra is, or your sister. But your bones are beautiful, and the way they contrast with that wide, full-lipped mouth of yours makes you a damn sight more interesting to draw than most women——' He looked up suddenly, at the sound of voices. 'We'd better get out of here, or we'll be locked in for the night.'

He took the dark glasses from the top pocket of his jacket, then picked up a panama hat lying on a nearby chair.

'Disguise?' asked Naomi, as she slung her bag over her shoulder.

'No—protection. Now my sight is back I feel the urge to cherish it.'

They walked out into the bright afternoon, Naomi very conscious of the contrast they must present: Bran, tall and imposing in a fawn lightweight suit cut by some master Italian hand, the hat set at a rakish angle above the black lenses protecting his eyes, herself in her inexpensive chainstore clothes, her hair untidy after the rigours of the afternoon.

'I was to tell you,' said Bran, tucking her hand through his arm, 'that Craig Anthony will be escorting your sister to the lecture tonight, and then dining with her at the Swan at Hay, where they'll be staying overnight. Diana told me to say you're welcome to join them for all three if you prefer that to the alternative.'

Naomi looked up at him quizzically. 'Are *you* offering me the alternative?'

He gave her a glittering, assured smile. 'After all the cloak-and-dagger stuff with Diana to get you here in the first place, I should damn well hope so!'

'What do you have in mind?' she asked quietly, and Bran stopped dead in the middle of the pavement, obliging the flow of passers-by to part round them to get past. He looked down into her face for a long, searching moment, then began hauling her along at top speed.

'I'm taking you home,' he informed her, with a look which dared her to argue. 'The moment we've told Diana what's happened I'm driving you straight back to Gwal-y-Ddraig for as long as I can bully you into staying.'

For the rest of her life would do nicely, thought a dazed Naomi, hard put to it to keep up with the long, purposeful stride she'd always known must be characteristic of a Bran Llewellyn with twenty-twenty vision.

The meeting with Diana and Craig was convivial but brief, Bran so obviously impatient to have Naomi to himself that he would spare only the time it took for introductions and a few moments' conversation before spiriting her away.

'Did *you* tell Diana to have my overnight bag ready?' demanded Naomi, as Bran hurried her along to the car park.

He grinned. 'No. That was a dash of enterprise on her part.' He raised a challenging eyebrow as he unlocked the car. 'I could always drive you back later if you insist.'

Naomi slid into the passenger seat of a low-slung car in British racing green, impressed to recognise the Lotus Esprit Greg had always lusted after. 'Let's see how things go,' she murmured.

He smiled as he started the engine. 'Be warned. I'll do my damnedest to persuade you to stay.'

Naomi clenched her teeth against the wave of longing which swept through her, wrenching her mind from speculation about what form Bran's persuasion might take. Fortunately the route they were following was breathtaking enough to divert her attention very successfully, as he drove due south of Hay on a road which climbed gradually into the high country of the Black Mountains.

'They call this the Gospel Pass,' said Bran, as she gazed in awe at the panoramic views which appeared round every curve of the narrow, winding road. 'Legend has it that a daughter of Caractacus, the leader of the Silures in the revolt against the Romans, invited St Peter and St Paul to preach the Gospel to her fellow countrymen here. The road's been given a better surface since those days,' he added with a grin, 'though I imagine the views are much the same.'

'It's magnificent,' she said breathlessly, 'but a tiny bit on the narrow side.'

'Plenty of passing places, *cariad*. Don't worry, I know it well. Soon we'll climb to about eighteen hundred feet as we leave the lower slopes of Hay Bluff, then we dive down into the Vale of Ewyas past Capel-y-ffin, and you'll be back on familiar territory.'

The journey through the Gospel Pass was an unforgettable experience for Naomi, not only for the scenic qualities of the route, but for the inexorable rise of anticipation overtaking her as their destination grew nearer with every mile. When the powerful green car purred up the drive to Gwal-y-Ddraig at last Naomi ran a comb through her hair and touched some lipstick to her mouth, to Bran's amusement.

Noting his grin, she shrugged, smiling. 'Just making myself tidy to meet Megan.'

Bran switched off the ignition and leaned forward to release Naomi's seatbelt. 'Sorry to disappoint you, Naomi—Megan and Tal are enjoying their annual holiday on the Gower coast. They go off to the Mumbles every year at this time without fail.'

The news affected Naomi like an electric shock as Bran leapt from the car and came to help her out.

'I suppose that means I'm cook again,' she said, trying hard for flippancy as she gazed in joyful recognition at the summer beauty of the gardens, where the liriodendron was now in full leaf as it towered in domination over the main lawn.

'We're a touch remote here to send out for a Chinese,' he answered in kind, and unlocked the front door. '*Croeso*, Naomi,' he said as he ushered her inside.

'What does that mean?' she asked, breathless suddenly as he closed the door behind him.

'Just welcome, Naomi,' he said simply, and put her grip on the floor. 'I'll leave this here—for the time being.'

Naomi flushed. 'Perhaps I could just go up to my room—I mean the guest room, and have a wash.'

Bran smiled and touched a hand to her cheek, sending another jolt of electricity through her. 'My house is yours, as they say in Spain. Go up and do whatever you want, then come down to the kitchen. From the look of you some food might be a good idea. What have you eaten today?'

'Just coffee, really,' she muttered.

His mouth tightened. 'I thought so—get a move on, then. I can't have you fainting on me again.'

'It's not a habit of mine,' she protested.

'Then why did you do it today?'

'It was the heat, I suppose. And the shock,' she added tartly.

'At seeing me?'

Naomi's long dark eyes met his without wavering. 'Yes, Bran. Shock at seeing you. I thought you'd never want to lay eyes on me again after what I did to you.'

He moved closer, until they were only inches apart. 'You were wrong, *cariad*—utterly, totally wrong,' he said softly, his eyes darkening until they were almost black. He breathed in deeply, then stood back, shaking his head. 'Don't be long, Naomi. Or I come and get you.'

She smiled in sudden elation, the light in her eyes transforming her face. 'Is that a promise?' But before he could react to the challenge she'd snatched up her bag and was racing upstairs.

Upstairs in the pretty, familiar room, Naomi took a hasty shower, suddenly crazily, madly happy now she was back in the lair of the dragon, where she belonged. She stopped short, staring at her face in the steamy bathroom mirror. Belonged? She nodded in reassurance to her reflection. From the look in Bran's eyes in the hall, just now, not to mention the lengths he'd gone to to get her here again, surely he felt the same?

Naomi brushed her hair until it gleamed, added a few touches of make-up to a face which already bore little relationship to the one she'd first confronted in her mirror that morning, then slid on the pink linen shift Diana had insisted on buying her to celebrate the new job. She smiled, remembering how she'd expected to wear it for a meal with Diana, never dreaming that her dinner companion would be Bran instead. Thoughts of dinner had her scurrying to find the pink linen pumps bought to wear with the dress, then she sprayed herself with perfume, threaded pearl drops through her ears and hurried from the room to find Bran halfway up the stairs coming to fetch her.

'Sorry I'm late,' she said breathlessly. 'I had a shower.'

'So did I.' His eyes travelled over her with a relish which brought the colour to her cheeks. 'You look better. Good enough to eat, in fact.'

'Talking of which, you'd better find me an apron. This dress is new,' she informed him as they made for the kitchen. 'Present from Diana.'

'You won't need an apron. Supper's ready,' said Bran smugly, and opened the kitchen door with a flourish to point at an impressive array of cold dishes on the table.

'I suppose you just threw all this together after you had your shower,' said Naomi, with the first genuine laugh she'd managed since the shock of meeting Bran again.

'Not exactly,' admitted Bran. 'I just took the dishes from the fridge, whipped off the covers and there you are. Cold buffet, kind courtesy of Megan. She only left this morning.'

And suddenly they were back to the rapport of the time spent alone before Bran knew about Diana's article. Naomi's appetite returned with it, her enthusiasm for salmon mousse and game pie equal to Bran's as he questioned her about the weeeks they'd spent apart.

'I was sure you'd ring me,' he said accusingly.

'I picked up the phone so many times I lost count, but I always chickened out, afraid you'd refuse to speak to me—especially after I received your cheque and accompanying note,' she added darkly.

'I was in such a rage I needed to lash out.' His mouth tightened. 'I got my just deserts when you sent it back with no note and no return address.'

Naomi met his eyes very squarely. 'I couldn't bear the thought of someone else reading my letter to you. And to put my address would have seemed like begging for a reply I knew I didn't deserve.'

They regarded each other in silence. 'These weeks without you have been purgatory,' said Bran at last. 'The only ray of light was my returning sight. When it was certain I'd see again I lost no time in planning a campaign to lure you, unsuspecting, back to Wales. First I had to persuade Megan and Tal to take their holiday a week early to coincide with the Hay Festival——'

'Why?' demanded Naomi.

Bran's eyes lit with a gleam which turned her bones to water. 'Because, my lovely, I wanted this place to myself when I finally brought you home again. Which is why I didn't come dashing after you to London the moment I could see. It was a gut reaction at first, I admit, but when I'd simmered down a bit and thought it over I realised it wasn't the ideal way to go about things.'

'Why not?' asked Naomi wistfully, thinking of the misery it would have saved her.

'Because I needed to see you alone, not with a flatmate in attendance, nor at Sinclair Antiques under the eyes of your boss and lord knows who else.'

'Oh.'

'So I contacted Diana instead and persuaded her to lure you to the literary festival, for which I'm deeply in her debt.' Bran smiled suddenly. 'I've thought of the perfect present to give her by way of appreciation.'

Naomi eyed him curiously. 'What do you have in mind?'

'I'll tell you later,' he said mysteriously. 'Right now I suggest we have some cheese, then we'll take our coffee to the studio. I might even get in a sketch or two of you before the light goes.'

Naomi's eyes narrowed. 'You mean you were actually serious about doing a portrait of me?'

He frowned impatiently. 'Of course I was serious! I've got the usual quota of faults, *cariad*, but insincerity isn't one of them.'

She smiled radiantly. 'Let's go now, then. I'll pass on the cheese. It keeps me awake.'

Bran took her hand and drew her to her feet, holding her lightly by the shoulders as he smiled down into her eyes. 'It just so happens I know an infallible cure for insomnia, *cariad*.'

'Do you, now!' she said breathlessly, wriggling free. 'I'll clear away. Do you know how to make coffee?'

'Not a clue,' he said shamelessly, and perched on

the table, one leg swinging as he watched her put the kitchen to rights. 'Let's have champagne instead.'

'Have we something to celebrate?' she asked, as they made for the studio.

'Oh, yes, *cariad*, we most definitely do,' said Bran very deliberately, in a tone which made Naomi's toes curl in the new pink shoes. He threw open the double doors and drew her into the room she'd last seen through a haze of agonised tears.

'I never thought I'd see this place again,' she said in a low voice, and went hurrying to look at the pictures on the walls as though greeting old friends, darting from one to another before coming to rest in front of Bran's self-portrait. She stood looking at it for so long that Bran called her name impatiently.

She turned to him, looking at him across the room with her heart in her eyes.

He caught his breath, and stretched out his arms. 'Come here. Now!'

Naomi went. She flew across the room like a homing bird, her face upturned to meet Bran's kiss as his arms closed about her. He picked her up and sat down with her on the familiar sofa, kissing her with a passion that reassured her more than any words could have done.

'What the hell did you mean by running off like that?' he said at last, panting. 'You knew I loved you, woman!'

Naomi's eyes opened wide on his. 'You never said so,' she whispered.

He scowled. 'Of course I did—well, perhaps not in so many words, but surely my actions spoke loudly enough?'

'A woman needs the words as well,' she informed him tartly.

Bran smiled down into her flushed, heavy-eyed face. 'Then listen well, my lovely, because in the future there may be one or two days when I forget to tell you, and I don't want you running off again. I've never loved any woman before in my entire life, unless you count my mother and Megan. I've enjoyed the company of a fair number of your sex, but never the same one for long. You're different. Small as you are, you feel like my other half, the missing piece that makes the puzzle of life complete.' He smiled with a light in his eyes which fairly blinded her. 'Now it's your turn. Tell me you love me.'

Naomi heaved a great shaky sigh. 'Of course I love you. These past weeks without you I've been so miserable I couldn't sleep, couldn't eat—why do you think I'm such a bag of bones?'

'Exquisite bones,' he said huskily, and began kissing her again. She responded fiercely, her body trembling under his urgent caresses until suddenly Bran stood up, holding her in his arms, his eyes burning into hers. 'I want you,' he said hoarsely.

For answer Naomi buried her face against him, kissing the strong, taut column of his throat, and Bran strode with her towards the spiral stair, and mounted it rapidly, breathing heavily by the time he set her on her feet beside his bed.

'Don't worry,' he panted, grinning. 'It's your proximity, not your weight, that's taken my breath away.'

Naomi's eyes danced wickedly. 'Good. I'd rather get up here under my own steam than find you'd run out of yours now we've finally got here!'

Bran's eyes filled with an unholy light. 'That's rash, fighting talk, *cariad*!'

'Only I don't want to fight,' she said, holding up her arms.

He pulled her hard against him. 'Tell me what you want, then.'

'I just want that wild delight your Dafydd ap Gwilym talked about—the one that ends in heart's possessing.'

'You've got my heart already, in the palm of your hand!' He tipped her face up to his. 'Give me yours in exchange and I'll take good care of it, I promise, in sickness and health till death us do part.'

'Is that what you want?' she whispered, her heart thudding against his.

'More than anything I've ever wanted before.' Bran kissed her gently, then less gently, the desire flooding through them both in such swift, overwhelming spate that there were no more words other than breathless endearments as his urgent, disrobing hands revealed the slender body he could now caress with his eyes as well as his clever, coaxing hands. And in the end there was no time, nor need, for the poet's 'long caressing' as their bodies merged in a union so perfectly attuned that it transcended the mere physical to create a fusion of heart, mind and soul.

'I'll always be grateful to Diana,' said Bran huskily, a long time later.

'For conspiring with you to get me to Wales again?'

'No—for her brilliant idea of getting you to come here in the first place.'

Naomi drew away, and propped herself up on one elbow to look down into his brilliant sea-green eyes. 'Bran, I love Diana, and I owe her gratitude for her love and support during a bad patch in my life. But I didn't come here just because she coaxed me to.'

Bran's eyes narrowed. 'Why, then?'

Naomi smiled mischievously. 'Let's put it this way. If Diana had wanted an article about anyone else I'd have flatly refused. But I'd already met you, remember. At the risk of inflating your ego, Bran Llewellyn, one look was all it took. I couldn't get you out of my mind.'

Bran shot upright to take her in his arms. 'You mean——?'

'Exactly! After seeing you that night at the opera I couldn't resist the temptation of meeting you again even if the price was a spot of spying for Diana.'

He breathed in deeply as he looked down into her face. 'I never thought I'd have cause to be thankful for my accident, *cariad*, but if the blindness brought you to me it was worth those weeks of darkness.'

She clutched him to her in fierce appreciation of the greatest compliment he could have paid her. Bran returned the embrace with such fervour that they were quickly engulfed in another tide of delight as wild as anything the medieval poet had ever envisaged. Afterwards they slept in each other's arms, until Naomi stirred to the touch of Bran's fingers as they stroked her cheek.

'Wake up, sleepyhead,' he whispered. 'I want to ring Diana in Hay.'

Naomi shook with laughter against him. 'Darling—at this time of night?'

He chuckled. 'It's only just gone ten, *cariad*. We came to bed rather early.'

Naomi stretched, yawning, suddenly aware that it was still light. 'I still don't know why you want to ring Diana.'

'I thought we'd announce our forthcoming marriage.'

Naomi lay very still against him, her heart thudding at the mention of marriage. She breathed in deeply, then reached up to kiss Bran's smiling mouth. 'You're really going to trust Diana with the news? She's with Craig, remember, and they're both journalists.'

Bran hugged her, laughing. 'That's the whole point, my lovely. It's my present to her—my way of thanking

Diana for sending you to me in the first place. What better way to show my appreciation?'

'You mean you're going to give her the exclusive all the gossip columnists would murder for?'

Bran held her close, smiling smugly. 'Absolutely. I can just see it in the *Chronicle*. "Welsh Artist Marries Beautiful Ceramics Expert"——'

Naomi giggled. 'I'm no expert.' She pulled a face. 'I'm not beautiful either.'

Bran cupped her face in his hands, his eyes suddenly serious. 'Never say that again—much less think it. Always remember that I see you with the eyes of love, *cariad*. You'll never be anything but beautiful to me.'

Naomi smiled, her eyes incandescent through a haze of happy tears. 'Then in that case nothing else in the world matters!'

MILLS & BOON®

Enchanted™

Look out for
Catherine George's
new romance:

THE COURTING CAMPAIGN

Available in paperback in November 1997.

Patrick Hazard had a plan of action which took Hester by surprise. She hadn't intended on falling in love with anyone, but Patrick wasn't content just to be friends —he wined and dined Hester, pursued and wooed her, whatever it took to win her over...

Here's a preview!

THE COURTING CAMPAIGN

'Did you enjoy the concert last night?' asked Patrick as he drove her through the warm summer evening on the way to Bredecote Hall.

'I didn't go. Edward's down with this flu that's going round. I asked around, but no one fancied a night of culture so I left the tickets at the Assembly Rooms.' Hester smiled at him. 'Pity, though. I like Mozart.'

'Why didn't you go alone, then?'

The confident tones were more clipped than usual, and, thought Hester, frowning, held a sudden tinge of hostility. Why? She glanced at him curiously. Patrick looked rather wonderful in a fawn-coloured lightweight suit, his face dark against the white of his shirt collar. And she wasn't looking too bad herself, in the pink shantung dress which had caught his eye at Mrs Cowper's. Her hair was loose and shining, and she'd taken a long time to make up her face to look as natural as possible. But her escort was suddenly and all too obviously in a bad mood.

'I did some gardening instead.'

'I would have been happy to take you to the concert. I suppose it never occurred to you to offer *m* *e* the spare ticket?' said Patrick, overtaking a lorry with rather alarming panache.

'No,' said Hester breathlessly. 'It didn't—could you slow down a bit, please?'

'Why?'

'I scare easily—'

'I meant why didn't you ask me?'

Hester chose her words with care. 'You saw me last Saturday, and again on Monday, and we were due to go out again tonight. Even if I'd thought of it, which I didn't, it would have seemed like overkill.'

His jaw set ominously. 'I see.'

'Look,' said Hester angrily, 'if this is your mood for the entire evening I'd rather go back home right now.' She saw his hands clench on the steering wheel, the knuckles white for an instant, then the car slowed perceptibly and she sensed his efforts to relax.

'Sorry, Hester. I'm behaving like a schoolboy,' he said at last.

'Yes, you are,' she agreed, and to her relief he smiled reluctantly.

'I still think you couldn't face going out with me to such a public place,' he said bluntly.

'You're wrong. I never even thought of asking you.'

'That's supposed to make me feel better?'

She laughed. 'Sorry, Patrick—oh, how lovely!'

Their argument was forgotten as Patrick turned off the road down a long, formal drive where wildfowl strutted on the grass and more sailed on the large lake which came into view in front of a building more in the style of Queen Anne than the earlier architecture common to the Cotswolds. The sun set the water on fire as Patrick parked the Jeep among more elegant vehicles drawn up on the tree-fringed space near the pillared main doors.

'A good thing I didn't wear jeans tonight,' said Hester later, in the large conservatory which housed the bar.

Patrick moved a little closer on the sofa they were sharing. 'Not that you didn't look good in them, but tonight you look perfect for your surroundings,' he assured her.

'So do you.' She toasted him with the glass of Pimm's he'd insisted on. 'May the rest of the evening pass without—friction.'

'Amen to that.' He smiled, his eyes as green as the manicured grass of the lawns outside, and suddenly Hester felt absurdly happy—glad to be sitting in this beautiful place with attentive waiters and a lively buzz of conversation from the other diners. It was a beautiful summer evening, she knew she was looking good and her escort was easily one of the best-looking men in the room.

The feeling persisted as they ate exquisitely presented food in a room more like a library than a dining room, with books on floor-to-ceiling shelves on some walls, beautiful panelling on others and the only lighting—other than the sunset glow from the windows—coming from candles in silver holders. Enclosed with Patrick in such intimacy, with only the occasional intrusion from a waiter, Hester smiled at him in the candlelight, her pleasure in the occasion open on her face.

'This was an inspired choice, Patrick. Thank you for bringing me here.'

'I thought its distance from Chastlecombe might be the best thing going for it, but I was wrong.' Patrick glanced around him. 'I haven't come across better service or food anywhere, certainly not allied with surroundings like these. Jack was right.'

'He's brought your sister here?'

'Not yet. He came to a conference recently, and recommended it.'

The earlier clash was forgotten. The evening proceeded in complete harmony as Hester reported on her talk to the history society, and Patrick on his progress with the book. They had savoured the leisurely meal and repaired to the conservatory again, to drink coffee and watch the moon rise over the lake, before he reverted to their earlier disagreement.

'I'm sorry I was angry,' he said at last, taking her hand as they sat together near the windows to enjoy the view.

'Why did you mind so much?' she said curiously, watching his slim fingers as they smoothed the back of her hand.

'Because I'm vain, I suppose. It was a bit deflating to learn you never even thought of asking me to the concert, Hester. On the other hand I value truth. I would like us to be the kind of friends who are totally honest with each other, always.'

She eyed him wryly. 'I wouldn't have been asked to sit on the bench if I wasn't known to possess a certain amount of integrity, Patrick. But nobody's perfect.'

He smiled. 'True.'

'And are you always unfailingly honest? Do you never lie, Patrick?'

'I suppose if you asked me if I liked your dress, or the way you'd done your hair, I might possibly say yes even if I didn't mean it, to avoid upsetting you. But on important issues I try to deal in the unvarnished truth.'

'You were pretty blunt about the black dress!'

'But that was because of what it represented.'

Eventually they went outside into the moonlit night, where a rim of afterglow still lingered on the horizon. Stars were appearing and the evening was still, and Hester breathed in deeply as they wandered back to the car.

'This is an outrageously romantic place, Patrick.'

'I know,' he said smugly. 'Why do you think I brought you here?'

She looked at him and laughed. 'A softening-up process?'

'Yes, he said shamelessly. 'I'm doing all I can to

establish myself in your good books: buying furniture from you, ingratiating myself with your family—David, anyway. And,' he added, his voice deepening, 'I'm somehow managing to keep at arm's length when you know perfectly well my instincts urge me otherwise. In the interests of truth I'm warning you—it's all a plan of campaign.'

They stopped outside the car in the shadow of an overhanging tree.

'Campaigns usually mean battles,' she said thoughtfully. 'What, exactly, do you intend to gain?'

'Victory,' he said promptly, and took her in his arms and kissed her.

Hester stayed very still in his embrace, her mouth unresponsive. Then deep inside her she felt stirrings of long-dormant response. Of its own volition her body curved against his, her lips parted and she felt a shudder run through him. His chest rose and fell more rapidly, and her own breathing accelerated to match. He drew her closer, then a group of departing diners emerged from the hotel entrance and the spell was broken.

Patrick let out a deep, unsteady breath and released her with gratifying reluctance. He unlocked the car, lifted her into the passenger seat, then paused with his hands on either side of her waist as he looked deep into her eyes. 'I wish I hadn't kissed you, Hester.'

Her eyes opened wide. 'Why?'

'You know why. Now I shall never be able to rest until I've kissed you again.'

'That would be a pity,' she whispered, and leaned forward until her lips touched his. 'There. Is that better?'

'No,' he said with sudden violence. 'It's not.'

The drive home was accomplished in silence, Hester

taut with expectation of what might happen at the end of it. Patrick glanced at her from time to time, but the entire twenty miles passed without a word of conversation, until every nerve in Hester's body felt winched to snapping point. When they arrived at Pear Tree Cottage Patrick killed the engine, helped her out and walked with her to her front door, holding out his hand for her key. He unlocked the door, stood back for her to go inside, then followed her in and pulled her into his arms, his back against the door.

The kiss was an explosive mixture of desire and release from the tension which had built between them during the long drive. Patrick slid his hand down her back and splayed it at the bottom of her spine, moulding her against him, and Hester trembled at the contact as though she were a schoolgirl and this her first experience of the changes desire wrought in a man's body.

When he raised his head at last Patrick looked pale beneath his tan, as though the self-control he was so patently exerting was costing him dearly. 'I'm going home,' he said roughly, in a voice so hoarse and far removed from his normal, confident tones that Hester clenched suddenly chattering teeth.

'Would you like coffee?' she said with difficulty.

'No, I wouldn't,' he snapped. 'You know damn well what I want, so I'm taking myself off before you throw me out. The entire evening was one long, aphrodisiac experience from start to finish. If I'd known the effect that hotel would have on my libido I'd have given the place a wide berth. So goodnight, Hester.'

'Goodnight, Patrick.' She pulled herself together. 'Thank you for—for a beautiful evening.'

For a moment she was sure he was going to seize her in

his arms again, but instead he turned blindly and went out, slamming the door shut behind him.

Hester stood where she was until she heard him drive away. Then she went upstairs, stripped off the dress and took a shower, got into bed and lay looking at Richard's photograph in silence.

When the phone rang she realised she'd been waiting. She let it ring three times, then picked it up.

'Hello.'

'I thought I'd ring to say goodnight, Hester,' said Patrick in her ear.

'Thank you. I'm glad to know you're home safely.'

'Are you?'

'Yes.'

'Then I didn't blot my copybook irreparably?'

'No, Patrick.'

'Good. Sweet dreams, then.'

He rang off, with no mention of another meeting. Hester smiled a little in the dark.

Having roused a response in her, Patrick was unlikely to leave matters there. Nor, she realised, did she want him to.

© Catherine George 1997

LOVE AT FIRST SIGHT
by
SANDRA FIELD

My thanks to Meredith Ripley
of the Canadian National Institute
for the Blind,
Halifax, Nova Scotia.

A donation from the proceeds of this book
will be made to
Canadian Guide Dogs for the Blind,
Manotick, Ontario,
to whom I also express my appreciation.

PROLOGUE

'You'vE *what*?' Jenny Sibley demanded.

'I've rented the house out,' Bryden Moore repeated patiently.

'Whatever *for*?'

Before Bryden could reply, Jenny's husband interposed mildly, 'Jenny, darling, calm down.'

'I can't, I don't understand—what on *earth* are you renting the house out for, Bryden, you're not going anywhere, are you?' Unspoken in the air hung another question... how can you go anywhere now?

Bryden's hand tightened around his glass; the skin was pale, too pale considering the blazing sun that was knifing through the chinks in the bamboo blinds. But his voice, to all except those who knew him well, would have sounded normal and relaxed. 'Where do I always go in August?' he drawled. 'Got to get out of this Ottawa heat somehow.'

'You're going to the cottage?' Jenny squeaked. 'But——'

Her husband sent her a warning glance. 'Good idea,' he said. 'It's really been intolerable the last three weeks, hasn't it? The Oultons will be glad to leave as well, I'm sure.' The Oultons had looked after Bryden's house, which was next door to the Sibleys', for over five years.

Bryden carefully placed the glass on the solid teak coffee-table in front of him; it had been bought in Jenny's Scandinavian phase, while the bamboo blinds were a result of her trip to China. 'Look, let's not play games,' he said roughly. 'The Oultons aren't going. I'm going alone.'

For once Jenny was struck dumb. Matthew Sibley, after a perceptible pause, said with the licence of a long friendship, 'Do you think that's wise, Bryden?'

'Maybe not. But that's what I'm doing.'

Jenny had had time to recover. 'You only go to the cottage for a month—so why are you renting the house out?'

'I'm staying for the winter.'

'For the winter? What about your job?'

'I've taken a year's leave of absence.'

Staring at him as if he had taken leave of his senses, she gasped, 'Have you fired the Oultons?'

'They'll stay next door. Part of the rental package.'

Matthew ran his fingers through his salt-and-pepper hair, his grey eyes concerned. 'I think this calls for another round of drinks,' he said heavily.

Jenny, less circumspect, leaned forward, a bar of sun glinting in her tumbled red curls. 'You *can't* stay alone, Bryden—it's impossible!'

'It's my sight I've lost, not my brains!' Bryden snapped. 'Stop treating me as if I'm mentally retarded.'

'I'm *not*. You're so intelligent you scare the life out of me, I can't even balance my budget while you deal with three-dimensional equations and research so abstract I don't even know how you put it down on something as mundane as paper. But you *are* blind, Bryden—you'll go crazy at Ragged Island on your own for a year!'

'I'll go crazy if I stay here.'

Bryden's voice had been devoid of emotion. But Jenny's vision suddenly blurred with tears, for she was a warm-hearted woman and could guess the sterility and pain that lay behind his words. Allowing her feelings to override caution, she rested her hand on Bryden's wrist, enveloping him in a wave of expensive perfume and feminine concern.

His recoil was instant, almost instinctive; she could have anticipated it, for she had known him a long time. She dropped his wrist and said incoherently, 'Oh, Bryden, I'm so *sorry*...'

'You'll have another Scotch, Bryden?' Matthew said with ponderous tact.

'No, thanks. I'm meeting the rental agent in half an hour to sign the final papers; I'll have to be going.'

'You mean it isn't final yet?' Jenny asked, hope brightening her jade-green eyes.

'Jenny, I'm spending the next year at Ragged Island—that's final,' Bryden replied.

She ignored her husband's gesture towards her glass. 'You're running away,' she announced. 'You're going to bury yourself in the country and pretend——'

'Jenny!' Matthew exclaimed.

Bryden reached for his long white cane and got to his feet. 'I'm doing what I think is best,' he said tightly. Then he nodded in Matthew's direction. 'Thanks for the Chivas Regal, Matt, it sure beats the rest of them, doesn't it?'

He had long been familiar with the layout of the Sibleys' living-room. His movements unhurried, full of assurance, he crossed the room and headed for the front door. Jenny scurried after him. 'You're not cross with me, are you, Bryden?' she wailed. 'Please don't be!'

His face softened, his eyes the same smoke-blue they had always been. 'You're forgiven,' he said lightly. 'I won't be leaving for three or four days, you must both come over and have a drink before I go. Just as long as you don't try and make me change my mind.'

'No chance of that,' Jenny responded tartly. 'Although I could tell your rental agent that the neighbours are terrible.'

'I've already warned him,' was the bland reply. 'See you later.'

The oak door with its swirls of leaded glass, which dated from Jenny's Olde English period, closed behind him. Matthew said drily, 'You excelled yourself today, sweetheart.'

'Do you know what absolutely *kills* me?' she gulped, blinking back more tears and ignoring his statement. 'The way he uses words like look and see just as if he still can... Matthew, what are we going to *do*?'

'I'm going to give you a hug and take you out for lunch,' Matthew said promptly.

Jenny flung her arms around her husband's rather too considerable girth, her brow furrowed in thought. She adored Matthew, but did not consider him infallible. 'We can't just let him disappear into the wilds of Nova Scotia,' she mumbled. 'For a whole *year*.'

'Darling, Bryden is twenty-nine years old and has always been what you might call a man of strong will, to put it mildly. If he says he's going to spend the winter at the cottage, then he will. And who knows, it might be the best thing for him?'

Jenny raised her head. 'How can you even *think* that, let alone say it? He'll *die* of loneliness down there, Matthew. He *hates* being blind, and he's far too proud to ask for help, so he'll end up stuck in the house day after day, I know he will.'

'If he gets lonely enough, he'll do something about it. Don't scowl like that, Jen, it doesn't become you.'

'He's always been a loner,' Jenny grumbled. 'Ever since we've known him. How many women have I thrust under his nose in the last five years? And not one of them took. Not one!'

'He had affairs with a couple of them.'

'But nothing permanent,' she said crossly.

'Bryden's protracted bachelorhood is scarcely your concern, my love. Hurry up and change your dress and I'll take you to Michelle's.'

Michelle made desserts that normally could deflect Jenny from any of her concerns; it was a measure of her fondness for Bryden that she rubbed her nose on her husband's shirt-front and went on thoughtfully, 'His problem isn't really that dreadful accident that left him blind. Even though it must be *awful*. His problem goes a lot further back... I met his mother once, she would be enough to put you off women, certainly. But there must be more to it than that.'

'He's a self-sufficient, rational, cold-blooded scientist, who finds duality theorems more interesting than the curves of the opposite sex,' Matthew said. 'I'm sure you're the nearest he has to a female friend. Even so, Jenny, there's nothing you can do. So why don't——'

She was not listening. A brilliant smile suddenly lit up her face and her eyes glowed like emeralds. 'Matthew, I've just had a brainwave! Do your remember that charming young woman we met at Susan and Peter Drapers' last party? In April? What was her name? Casey! Casey Landrigan. I remember thinking Casey wasn't the right name for her at all—far too tomboyish. You must remember her, she was *very* beautiful.'

Matthew said cautiously, 'I believe I do remember her, now that you mention it. She was a distant cousin of Susan's, wasn't she?'

'That's right.' Jenny paused triumphantly. 'Guess what she does?'

With commendable patience Matthew said, 'I have no idea.'

'She trains guide-dogs. For the blind. How's that for coincidence?'

'You've just finished saying Bryden's main problem isn't his blindness. Anyway, I'm quite sure he doesn't want a dog.'

'She'll change his mind.'

'How can she? She doesn't know him—he wasn't at that party.'

'She will,' Jenny said confidently. 'Because I'm going to arrange it. You see, at the end of each class that she teaches, she gets a holiday. And she's teaching a class this month, she told me that, because she was worried about the effects of the heat on the dogs and the students.'

'Jenny, you cannot coerce an unknown young woman to spend her holidays with a complete stranger.'

'Not *with* him. Next door to him. Because who owns the cottage next to his?'

Matthew groaned. 'Susan and Peter Draper,' he supplied obediently. 'Seven years ago Peter mentioned that the cottage next door to theirs was for sale and we told Bryden because we knew he was looking for seashore property in Nova Scotia. So he bought it.'

'Exactly! I'll call Susan and tell her to offer the cottage to Casey in September. It's perfect!'

Matthew took a deep breath. Clasping his wife's shoulders, he said with the utmost seriousness, 'Jenny, you can't interfere in people's lives like that. It's immoral.'

A shadow of doubt crossed her face; Matthew did not often speak to her in that tone of voice. 'Truly?' she quavered.

'First of all, Bryden has to come to his own terms with his blindness—it's only been four months, after all. Secondly, if he has cut himself off from marriage, or even from long-term relationships, his reasons must be sufficient, powerful and private. And finally, a guide-dog trainer on holiday would not appreciate your throwing her at a man who happens to be blind.'

'But she was so *lovely*!'

'So were a good number of the other women you introduced Bryden to over the years. Drop it, Jenny.'

Jenny looked him in the eye and said without a trace of affection, 'I'm afraid for him, Matthew. Oh, not that he'll do anything foolish like swimming straight out to sea and not coming back, I don't mean that. But I'm afraid his...his courage will fail him. His inner strength. This self-sufficiency you talked about. I can't imagine anywhere more desolate than Ragged Island in February.'

Matthew had been to Ragged Island and agreed with her; its wild beauty could be lonely enough at the height of summer. Furthermore, over twelve years of marriage he had learned to trust in what he called Jenny's intuition. 'You could be right—he might turn into a real recluse.' He frowned. 'I still don't see what this Casey Landrigan can do.'

'In all honesty, neither do I. Because I agree with you, a dog isn't the issue at all. But she impressed me very strongly, and I don't just mean her looks.'

His frown deepened. 'There's nothing to lose by trying, I suppose,' he said reluctantly. 'Although she's probably got other plans for her vacation.'

'She's probably got a six-foot fiancé,' Jenny said gloomily.

'Cheer up, darling. At least you'll know you tried.'

'Bryden would be furious if he found out.'

'We won't tell him,' Matthew rejoined.

'Matthew Sibley, I love you.'

He kissed her very thoroughly. 'You just want me to treat you to raspberry cheesecake.'

'That, too,' Jenny said.

CHAPTER ONE

CASEY LANDRIGAN was standing at the bedroom window in the Drapers' cottage. The sun was shining, a fresh sea breeze was billowing the curtains against her body, and the gulls that drifted across the sky over the spruce trees and the granite cliffs were a dazzling white. An island offshore, rocky, spray-swept, took the brunt of tides and currents that had crossed the cold Atlantic unimpeded. Ragged Island. She had been here less than twenty-four hours and she was already in love with the place. Three weeks ago, she marvelled, she had not even known it existed. But for her cousin Susan, she still would not. But what better place to spend the precious eight days of her holiday?

She closed her eyes, savouring the cool, salt-laden wind. The last month in Ottawa had been unbearable. Hot, humid, the dogs listless, one of her students homesick, the other afflicted with hay fever. Even Douglas, the head trainer who was supervising the final months of her apprenticeship and who was normally the most even-tempered of men, had been short with her. She herself had come as close to doubting her vocation as she ever had.

She needed a holiday, she thought ruefully. She had caught sight of herself in a washroom mirror at the airport yesterday: shadows under her eyes, the skin pulled tight across her cheekbones, even her hair lustreless. Not all of it could be blamed on fluorescent lighting.

A gull flapped down to land on the crown of the spruce tree nearest the cottage; after an ungainly lurch or two, it settled its wings and presented Casey with a profile of hooked yellow beak and cold yellow eye. Its landing reminded her of the rather bumpy descent of the aircraft the day before; she was terrified of flying. But she had not wanted to waste four days of her vacation on the road.

What she did want was peace and quiet and no demands on her time. And this, she thought ecstatically, looked like the perfect place to find all three.

It certainly had privacy. Behind the cottage the driveway wound through fragrant pines to the main road and the village of Ragged Harbour, hidden in a dip in the land. The only other habitation in sight was the shingled roof of the next-door cottage, which Susan had vaguely intimated was occupied only in the summer.

Casey did not mind that it was empty. The last month had been inordinately full of people and their demands, and she had as usual given unstintingly of herself; to get away from the whole world for several days had seemed a wonderful idea. And a good way to start her vacation, she decided, was to spend the morning lying on the beach. Quickly she gathered up her gear, ran downstairs to the kitchen and ate some cereal and fruit, then dropped her book in her canvas tote bag. She would probably fall asleep before she read more than three or four pages. But that was all right—she was on holiday!

After pulling the door shut behind her, Casey stood on the veranda and took a deep breath of the clean, sweet air. The murmur of the waves soothed her ears. The sun fell warm on her bare arms and legs. Perfection, she thought. Sheer perfection. Could anyone be luckier than she?

She walked down the steps and across the grass, admiring the pansies and marigolds in the flower-beds. The gate squeaked as she pushed it open, and she stopped beside her rented car to get her bearings. Cut across the neighbour's property to go to the beach, Susan had told her; it was far quicker than skirting the cliffs that surrounded the cottage.

So Casey took the path on the other side of the driveway that led inland through the trees, whose needled boughs were swaying lazily in the breeze. The path soon doubled back towards the sea again, giving her tantalising glimpses of the curve of sand below. The beach would be sheltered, she thought smugly. Sheltered and private.

There was no noticeable boundary between the Drapers' property and that of their neighbour. Casey was rather pleased by this. There were far too many 'No Trespassing' signs in the world, she mused, her feet sinking in the carpet of fallen needles. Wars were fought over boundaries. Feuds erupted over the placing of fences. But who, in any real sense, could own the shimmering pattern of sunlight on the forest floor or the fragments of blue sky that pierced the swaying green boughs?

The woods suddenly ended, thrusting her on to a neatly mowed lawn. Stretched out on the lawn, face up, was a man.

Casey gave a strangled yelp that expressed surprise, shock and fear. The man's body, absolutely still, was clad in skimpy blue swimming-trunks; his eyes were hidden behind a type of sunglass that she particularly disliked, the kind that in two miniature mirrors reflected the face of the beholder. She could not even tell if he was awake or asleep. Or dead, she thought with a twinge of sheer terror, her eyes flicking round the empty clearing.

'I'm sorry!' she gasped idiotically. 'I didn't know anyone was here... are you all right?'

A shudder ran through the man's body as though he had woken too abruptly from a nightmare. Rubbing at his face with one hand, almost as if he had to reassure himself he was real, he reared up on one elbow, the glasses rendering his face blank of expression. 'Who are you?' he said harshly. 'What are you doing here?'

'I'm sorry I woke you,' Casey stumbled, although inwardly she was so grateful that he was alive that she did not sound as sorry as she might have. 'I didn't realise anyone was staying in this cottage.'

'I own it,' he answered, an unpleasant edge to his voice. 'Why shouldn't I be staying in it?'

'No reason whatsoever,' Casey said, wishing he did not sound so irritable. 'It's just that I was led to believe it would be empty.'

'By whom?'

Wishing he would take off his glasses so she could see his face, wondering if it could possibly match the muscled perfection of his body, Casey said politely, 'By the Drapers. Who were kind enough to lend me their cottage for the next few days.'

His breath hissed between his teeth; she did not need to see his face to sense an anger out of all proportion to anything she had said. 'Who *are* you?' he demanded.

She was beginning to grow angry herself; there was no need for him to be so unfriendly. Drawing herself to her full five feet nine, wishing her shorts and bikini top were not quite so brief, she answered with exaggerated courtesy, 'My name is Cassandra Elizabeth Landrigan, I am more commonly known as Casey, Susan Draper is my second cousin, I'm from Ontario and I'm here on holiday. Susan told me it was easier to get to the beach across your property... so that's what I was doing. I didn't mean to disturb you.' But I'm darned if I'm apologising again, she added inwardly.

He did not reciprocate by telling her his name. Instead he said grimly, 'I see. Well, I'm sorry to undo Susan's instructions, Miss Landrigan, but I would much prefer you not to use this path to the beach.' He gave her a curt nod. 'You might as well continue along it now that you're this far. But kindly go back along the cliffs.'

Her jaw dropped. Paradise had been invaded by the snake, and the perfection of the morning marred. 'It's a lot longer to go that way, isn't it?'

'I suppose so. However, you're on holiday, you said—you must have lots of time.'

She flushed. The 'No Trespassing' signs had been posted with a vengeance. 'I don't even know where the cliff path is,' she retorted.

'Go east from the beach around the headland. You'll see the steps up the cliff.' Another curt nod. 'Goodbye, Miss Landrigan.'

Casey tilted her chin. She said with a demureness that would have alerted someone like Douglas, 'Goodbye, Mr... but you haven't told me your name.'

Inexplicably his anger was very much in evidence again. 'You mean Susan didn't tell you?'

'I would scarcely be asking you if she had.'

'There's no need for you to know my name—we won't be meeting again... I'm sorry if I sound rude, but I guard my privacy very jealously.' As if to signal that the conversation was over, he turned on his stomach.

The muscles rippled along his spine. His skin, taut across his ribs, was tanned a light gold; a great deal of it seemed to be exposed. Dragging her eyes away, Casey said stiffly, 'I came here to get away from everyone, too. So I most certainly will not be bothering a neighbour as unwelcoming as you... and I don't think you're the least bit sorry that you sounded rude.'

Knowing her last remark had been childish in the extreme, she stalked past the man's recumbent form. Behind him the lawn sloped up to his cottage. Although to call it a cottage was a form of reverse snobbery, Casey thought crossly, taking a moment to study it. An architect must have designed its subtle blending of cedar, stone and glass that made it an integral part of the evergreens that shaded its slanting roof. Wisely the garden had been left in its natural state, with a brook meandering through the maples on the far side of the clearing, its soft plashing in counterpoint to the sigh of the wind. The beauty of the place caught at her throat, making her even angrier.

She found the break in the trees that marked the path to the beach and headed across the grass towards it. When she reached it, she risked a backward look. The man was still lying on his stomach, his head buried in his arms. Asleep already, she thought. She'd meant no more to him than a fly he would brush from his shoulder.

As she was enveloped by the trees again, she found herself wondering what colour his eyes were. His hair was a darker brown than her own, unruly hair rather in need of cutting. Perhaps it would compromise his privacy to go to the barber's, she thought nastily. With that colour hair his eyes could be any colour: blue or grey or brown. Grey would be her bet. Grey like stone. Or storm-clouds. Or steel.

Casey suddenly realised she was tramping through the woods as though she were on her way to a fire. She was even breathing hard. Trying to be amused by this, but not really succeeding, she consciously focused on the rhythm of the surf and the glimpses of sand that filtered through the trees, and slowed her steps. She did not want her first view of the beach to be spoiled by a temper tantrum.

A minute or two later she came to wooden stairs, cedar-stained, that led down to the sand. The beach was V-shaped, sheltered from the wind by the cliffs and the trees, and again something in her responded instantly to the seclusion and beauty of the scene. She was the only person in sight. Had it not been for that unpleasant incident with her neighbour, she would have been perfectly happy.

She spread her towel on the sand, anointed herself with sun-screen, and determinedly began to read. But the man's face, shuttered behind the glasses, kept intruding itself between her and the page, until finally she gave up and stared out to sea, where the island guarded the shore and broke the force of the waves. Why had he affected her so strongly?

She found that she could recall every detail of the man's body, the dark hair that curled on his chest and legs, the narrow hips, the smooth play of muscle in his shoulders. Even his voice, resonant with authority, rang in her ears. Yet she did not know his name, and if he had his way they would never see each other again. For her to feel disappointment as acute as any she had ever known was ridiculous.

She was not used to men being rude to her. Her father was a man very much in touch with his feelings, capable of expressing his rare anger in a constructive way, and while her three brothers had been guilty of the normal horseplay in a growing family there had never been real animosity behind it. She had had her fair share of dates, tending to pick young men who most reminded her of her father. Douglas reminded her of her father. Douglas, she was almost sure, would be seriously in pursuit of her once her apprenticeship was finished and he no longer had a supervisory role over her. She was in no hurry. But she liked him very much.

This man was not like her father. Or Douglas. So why was she allowing him to ruin the first day of her holiday? After all, she had come here for privacy. She could scarcely deny him his.

Eventually Casey got up from her towel and wandered down to the edge of the sea, then picked her way among the tide pools in the rocks, until slowly sun and surf worked their spell and she regained most of the carefree happiness of early morning. Not even the discovery later in the day that the cliff path was both long and arduous could destroy her peace of mind. This was her holiday. She was going to enjoy it.

Casey went jogging later in the afternoon, discovering a network of dirt roads near the cottage; she slept peacefully for nearly ten hours, and woke to the patter of rain on the roof. So she spent most of the next day in the cottage, reading, baking biscuits, and listening to records in front of the fire.

The following day, her third at Ragged Island, dawned clear and bright. There was no wind; the sea gleamed like a mirror. Like her neighbour's glasses, thought Casey as she stood at the bedroom window, and found that the memory still had the power to hurt. She would go to the beach after breakfast, but she would go by the cliff path. She would not risk another confrontation.

The news on the radio warned of an approaching low-pressure system with high winds and heavy rain; incredible though this seemed on so peaceful a morning, Casey must have believed it, because she found herself hurrying through her breakfast to spend as much time as possible on the beach. So it was early when she rounded the headland and saw the curve of pale sand in front of her.

But not early enough. Her misanthropic neighbour was there before her.

LOVE AT FIRST SIGHT

Casey stopped in dismay. He was sitting hunched on the sand, staring out to sea, his body angled away from her. He had not seen her, nor could he have heard her approach; she could turn tail and he would be none the wiser.

For a moment she was tempted to do so. The beach was small—too small for the two of them. She could lie on the grass in front of the cottage instead.

But then something in his pose struck her: a rigidity, an absolute stillness that was almost frightening. What was he thinking about, this tall stranger with his lean, beautiful body and his obsessive need to be alone? Why was he so tangibly unhappy?

And, more to the point, why should she allow him to drive her off a strip of sand that below the high-tide line was public property?

Gripping her tote bag a little more tightly than was necessary, Casey marched across the beach. A seagull screamed overhead and a flock of sandpipers skittered away from her on legs like tiny twigs. About fifty feet from the hunched figure on the sand, she put down her bag and spread out her towel. He was still gazing at the horizon.

She stripped to her bikini and sat down. He paid her no attention. She took out her book, a fat historical romance whose heroine, spirited, dashing and seductive, would have made mincemeat out of the stranger. He ignored her. She made rather a production of rubbing on her sun-screen. No reaction.

Casey discovered that her serenity had vanished, to be replaced by the slow boil of rage. The glitter of sun on the waves seemed to mock her, while the cries of the gulls were derisive. Privacy was all very well, she fumed, but it would not hurt him to at least say hello.

She forced her attention back to her book. Her heroine in less than two pages managed to free herself from the bonds around her wrists, confront her captor—who bore a strong resemblance to the stranger on the beach—and shoot him with a pistol, then steal a horse to make good her escape. Casey stood up. Enough was enough.

The sand was hot on the soles of her feet. When she was within twenty feet of the man, she called out in a carrying voice, 'Good morning! Isn't it a lovely day?'

He gave an overdone start, his head swinging in her direction. He was wearing the same dark glasses. She added kindly, 'You're getting a touch of sunburn on your shoulders; you really should use sun-screen.'

He said slowly, 'Miss Cassandra Elizabeth Landrigan.'

'So you remember my name—I'm flattered.'

'Don't be. I rarely forget facts.'

'How useful,' Casey said smoothly. 'I wish I were more like that. But if you were to tell me your name, I promise I'd do my best to remember it.'

He replied just as smoothly, 'It would be unkind of me to tax your mental capacity.'

She could feel her temper rising again. Determined to be pleasant, she said, 'Are you going for a swim?'

'No.'

'I'm a bit nervous of swimming alone, even though Susan said it was quite safe here—no undertow. Do you mind keeping an eye on me?'

'I'm about to leave,' he said brusquely.

Casey took a deep breath. 'You really don't want anything to do with me, do you?'

'I thought I'd made that clear the other day.'

'I was giving you the benefit of the doubt... we all have days when we get out of bed the wrong side.' She added, 'I do wish you'd take those glasses off—I feel as though I'm talking to a plate-glass window.'

'Whereas,' he said with dangerous quietness, 'I feel as though I'm talking to a thick-skinned young woman who's incapable of taking a hint.'

Casey flinched, aware of the salt sting of tears. She said furiously, 'Very well! Since I have as much right to be on this beach as you, I suggest you stick to this half and I'll stick to the other, and I promise I shall not repeat my mistake of acting like a reasonably polite human being—it's obviously wasted on you!'

She whirled and ran back to her towel. She had had the last word, but it was a hollow victory. Grabbing her book, she tried to read, but the words swam together on the page and the heroine's feisty manner, rather than behaviour to be emulated, now seemed merely silly. Real life was not like that. Real life was the most attractive man she'd ever met in her life being quite abominably rude to her for no reason that made any sense.

She sneaked a sideways glance through her lashes. He was still sitting there, still contemplating the horizon. So his excuse that he was leaving and therefore could not watch her swim had been a lie; he simply didn't want to be bothered.

It would serve him right if she drowned under his nose, she thought darkly. However, she did not think she would attempt this as a tactic to gain his attention. He would be quite capable of letting her sink to the bottom of the sea.

She then discovered she was blinking back tears again. What was wrong with her? At the school she was frequently commended for her disposition: kind, calm, unruffled Casey, who could be counted on to keep her head in any situation. Who never let the students get to her. Who had infinite patience with the dogs. Yet this one man, whose name she did not even know, had the capacity to arouse her to anger, disappointment and—she lowered her eyes to her book—desire.

She had wanted to sit down beside him on the beach; she had wanted to touch him; she had wanted to smooth the tension from his shoulders with her palms and run her fingers through his hair.

Her movements jerky and hurried, Casey shoved her book back in her bag, picked up her towel and got to her feet. Turning her back on the seated man, she walked with as much dignity as she could muster towards the headland, where the incoming tide swirled around the rocks. Picking her way among them, wincing at the initial chill of the water, she was soon beneath the channelled grey cliffs, the complaints of the gulls loud in her ears. She was also out of sight of the man on the beach, and was aware of an almost palpable relief. She kept going, clambering over the larger boulders, walking on the sand whenever possible, and finally climbing the steep flight of steps that belonged to the Drapers. Although she was out of breath at the top, she did not stop until she came to the lawn in front of the cottage. The sun was warmer here than on the beach. Spreading out her towel, Casey lay down on the grass.

She must not talk to the man again. No more hellos on the beach, no more requests that he watch her swim. She would treat him just as if he were a chunk of granite on the sand, a part of the scenery to be ignored, of no more interest than a gull or a passing ship. She would not allow him to spoil her holiday; she had worked too hard for it and needed it too much. He meant nothing to her. Nothing.

For the first time since she had arrived at Ragged Island, Casey wished she had company. Specifically, Douglas's company; he would make her forget the stranger on the beach. But Douglas took his professional ethics very seriously, and would not contemplate spending a vacation with her while she was still his apprentice.

Casey heaved a sigh, feeling definitely out of sympathy with professional ethics, and went in the cottage to get some fruit juice. Life, at times, was hard to fathom.

By afternoon the horizon wore a ruff of purple-edged clouds and the wind had freshened; dusk came early, for the clouds now hung low over the sky and gusts of rain drove against the window-panes. Casey was glad to be indoors. She drew the curtains, lit a fire in the stone hearth, and took out the pullover she was knitting for her niece Leeanne, daughter of her elder sister Anne. She liked to knit. But she went to bed early, for it was a day she somehow wanted to put behind her. Tomorrow would be better, she thought sleepily. Tomorrow she would explore the village; and she would stay away from the beach.

However, four hours later Casey was wide awake. The news broadcaster had been all too accurate in his forecast, for the wind was howling around the cottage, rattling the windows and carrying with it the deeper roar of the sea. She tried burying her head under the pillow to dull the noise, not sure whether she should be afraid or exhilarated. One thing was certain: she could not go back to sleep. Eventually she got out of bed and went to the window.

In the eerie glow cast by the moon, which appeared and reappeared between the ragged-edged clouds, the branches of the pines were tossing in the wind like frail ships adrift in a riptide; the island offshore had vanished behind sheets of driven foam.

Another adjective frequently used to describe Casey at the school was 'sensible'. She discovered the storm did not make her feel in the least sensible. She wanted to be out in it, a part of it; she wanted to stand near the edge of the cliffs and fill her ears with the rage of the surf and feel the salt spray trickle down her cheeks.

Why not? It was no longer raining. And she was certainly not likely to meet anyone else at this hour of the night.

Before she could change her mind—one part of which was sure Douglas would not approve of her crashing through the woods in the middle of the night at the height of a storm—she got dressed in jeans, a sweater and a wind-cheater, and went downstairs. The wind almost ripped the front door from her hand; she slammed it shut and headed for the cliff path.

Douglas, she thought as she struggled down the path, could have been right. The trees creaked and groaned, the gale keened, the ocean's roar grew louder. Bent forward, she scurried through the woods, her eyes adjusting to the half-light of the moon. She'd look silly if she tripped over a root and fell. Sillier still if a branch crashed on her head.

But the scene that met Casey's gaze at the end of the path was worth every step of the way. At the foot of the cliffs among the churn of foam and the rearing waves the blunt-nosed boulders stood firm, like primitive sealions; the noise was deafening. She took shelter under a tree, searching out the tiny strip of beach, now piled high with seaweed and driftwood. Beyond it was the property of her neighbour. Although the cliffs were less sheer over there, they seemed more exposed to the ocean's fury. Even as she watched, a great cloud of spray exploded into the air with a loud thump that overrode the cacophony of the storm.

A blowhole, she thought, her eyes gleaming. Thirty seconds later the water erupted again with a thud like distant dynamite.

Anyone as disagreeable as her neighbour would not be out on a night like this, Casey was sure. He'd be asleep in bed. She was going to trespass on his property and get a closer look.

She hurried back up to her cottage, then took the trail to the beach. She could remember a fork in the trail before it came to the steps that led down to the sand; she'd be willing to bet that that fork led to the blowhole.

The house next door—she refused to call it a cottage—was in total darkness. She pulled a face at the upstairs windows and fought her way across the grass. When she re-entered the forest, the trees offered almost no shelter from the wind. A branch slapped her face. A pine-cone whisked past her cheek.

She had to wait a minute for the moon to reappear before she could locate the trail that led away from the beach to the cliffs. The undergrowth was thicker here and the trees crowded more closely together, the trunks black as pitch against the moonlit sky, the boughs flapping like the wings of crows. Twigs, finger-like, plucked at her sleeves. Aware of a sudden unease as strong as it was irrational, Casey battled onward.

Whump! went the blowhole, and the driven spray wet her cheeks and made her blink. Into the sudden lull, like a gunshot, a branch cracked in two.

She froze, her heart pounding, but the moon chose that moment to disappear behind a cloud, so she could see nothing through the tangled black branches. That's because there's nothing there to see, she told herself firmly. Don't let your imagination get the better of you.

The clouds parted. In the pale, ghostly light she distinctly saw movement, a huddled black shape near the edge of the cliff. Then the wind lashed the boughs of the spruce trees and the shape vanished among all the other shapes.

A figment of your imagination, Casey. There's nothing there.

But she found she was rooted to the spot, the blowhole no longer the lure it had been. She was crazy to be out in the woods in a gale. Out of her mind. Under the ceaseless roar of the ocean anything could creep up on her and she would never hear it. Never even see it. She should be home in her bed.

But as she turned to leave her eyes flickered nervously towards the cliff and she saw it again: the dark bulk of a body blundering among the trees. Terrified, she dug her nails into the trunk of the nearest tree. What was it? A bear? But there weren't any bears in Nova Scotia... were there?

Casey was not sure she wanted an answer to that question. Her imagination, fed by the wildness of the night and the fitful pallor of the moon, took another leap forward. It was a deer. A deer that had injured itself on the rocks.

She'd better go and see, she couldn't just leave it there to suffer. Nor would she be able to sleep for the rest of the night if she didn't satisfy her curiosity. Carefully noting the position of the path so she could find it again, she gathered all her courage and began threading her way through the trees, ducking to avoid low-hanging branches, every sense alert.

Her imagination had not created the figure among the rocks. It was real. It also seemed to be moving closer to the edge of the cliff. Then it suddenly straightened, and with a pang of sheer terror Casey realised it was a human being, its arms flailing the air. It staggered into the angled trunk of a fallen poplar and rebounded against the rocks. Rocks that made an unstable wall between the forest floor and the sheer drop to the sea below.

She yelled as loudly as she could, 'Don't move—stay still!' The wind tore the words from her lips and the night swallowed them. She began to run.

CHAPTER TWO

BOUGHS, wet from rain and spray, dashed water in Casey's face as she dodged between the trees. Her jacket caught on a snag; she yanked at the sleeve, not caring that it tore. Stumbling over the rough ground, she shouted again, 'Stay where you are!' She could see now that the figure was that of a man, crouched among the rocks.

Casey cleared the fallen poplar trunk in a leap she would never have attempted in daylight, got her balance and thrust herself between the man and the edge of the cliff. 'Are you trying to *kill* yourself?' she gasped. 'You're only ten feet from the edge!'

Then the ground shuddered. A curtain of spray burst from the blowhole and, whipped by the wind, drenched them both in cold salt water. Casey grabbed at his arm and heard herself scream, 'I don't even know your name!'

For the man was her neighbour. His face was ghastly in the pale grey light, the eye sockets like black pits, his hair streaking his forehead. He had cut himself, so that mingled blood and water trickled down his cheek. He also seemed to have lost his voice.

Casey shook his arm; he was wearing a dark shirt that clung damply to his skin. 'What in God's name are you doing here?' she demanded, she who never swore. 'You frightened the life out of me! I thought you were going over the edge.'

He muttered something in a low, choked voice. Her body stilled as a cold fist seemed to clutch her heart.

She did not know what he had said, and was afraid to ask him to repeat it. She did know she had to get him away from here, up to the house, to warmth and light and the shelter of four walls. His face was only inches from hers, the deep-set eyes staring fixedly over her head. She said with a compassion so fierce that it shook her to the roots of her being, 'Come on—let's go up to the house.'

Awkwardly, because she was still clutching his sleeve, he stood upright; he was four or five inches taller than she. His body was shaking as if he had a fever. 'I don't know the way,' he said in a low voice.

For a horrified moment she wondered if she was alone in the woods with a madman. 'But you live here,' she faltered. 'We're not that far from the house.'

The muscles clenched under her fingers. He said harshly, 'I'm blind... hadn't you guessed?'

For a moment Casey was paralysed with shock. Then, swift as lightning, all the tiny indications that she, of all people, should not have missed dropped into place. The dark glasses. His start when she had spoken to him on the beach. His refusal to watch her swim. Even his obsessive need for privacy. But before she could say anything the dull thud of trapped water again reverberated under her feet. 'Duck!' she said urgently, and pulled his head down into the shelter of her shoulder.

The spray, driven by the gale, stung her cheek and dribbled down her neck. She released him, remembering with startling clarity the hard line of bone under his wet hair, and said with a calmness that was quite false, 'No, I hadn't guessed. Come on, we'll go up to the house together.'

But he did not move. 'Susan didn't tell you?'

'All Susan said was that the cottage next door was only used in summer—she was far too busy telling me about bedding and the switches for the power and water, and what to do if squirrels had got into the pantry.' A frown creased Casey's forehead. 'If you're blind, where's your cane? Don't tell me you came down here without it.'

'I lost it back there in the woods,' he said so tonelessly that she had to strain to hear him. Then the words came pouring out. 'I've always loved storms, even as a kid. Ever since I bought this place I've been fascinated by the blowhole—the locals call it the Devil's Ear, and the tides and the wind have to be just right for it to work. Tonight I figured I could find my way down here without any trouble, I've been here a hundred times, and even if I couldn't see the spray I could hear it and get some sense of the ocean and the storm.' His body was racked by a spasm that had nothing to do with the cold. 'I can't even manage that! After I dropped my cane I panicked...lost my bearings, couldn't find the path, didn't know where the cliff was...lost in the woods like a four-year-old.'

His voice was caustic with self-disgust. It would have been all too easy for Casey to have given him sympathy; her heart ached for him. Instead she said what a few moments ago she had been afraid to say. 'So you didn't come down here to throw yourself over the cliff?'

'God, no! I don't think I ever contemplated that, not even right after the accident.' His face set in grim lines, he muttered, 'I must have looked like a fool, floundering around in all those rocks...a goddamned fool.'

She could imagine all too well his humiliation. A grown man lost in the woods and rescued by a woman to whom he had been exceedingly rude was not an enviable role. She said crisply, 'You'd have been fine if you hadn't lost your cane. And it's little wonder you lost your bearings——'

Once again the thunder of confined water shook the earth beneath their feet. But this time it was he who abruptly turned her about and pressed her face to his chest to protect her from the spray, taking its lash on his back.

Casey stood very still. He was holding her impersonally, she was sure, his motives nothing more than belated good manners; no reason for her to feel as though heaven had opened its doors and beckoned her in. Certainly no reason to feel she could spend the rest of the night in his arms among the wind-tossed trees.

He pushed her away and said roughly, 'Let's get the hell out of here.'

With an actual physical effort Casey made herself sound natural and relaxed. 'Take my elbow,' she said, 'and I'll lead the way. We'll have to keep our heads down until we find the path.'

She set off up the slope, warning him of rocks, holding up boughs that might have struck him in the face, and all the time she was acutely aware of the strong grip of his fingers at her elbow. He resented having to trail behind her, she would swear, and asked without any of her usual tact, 'How long have you been blind?'

'Five months.'

His clipped voice discouraged further questions. Casey said with transparent relief, 'Here's the path again—but I can't see your cane. If we don't find it tonight, I'll look for it in the morning.'

'No need—I've got another one in the house.'

He could not have said more clearly that he did not want her wandering around his property in the morning: did not want to be further indebted to her. Furious with him for rebuffing her, furious with herself for caring, Casey marched up the path, her arm rigid in his clasp. 'You might at least introduce yourself,' she said frostily.

'If you'd slow down a bit I would.'

She stopped dead, so that he almost cannoned into her. 'So now your lack of courtesy is *my* fault?'

The moonlight filtering through the trees showed her that he was smiling; a smile that looked as if it had not been exercised very much lately, but was nevertheless a smile. 'You have a temper, Cassandra Elizabeth Landrigan,' he said.

'Casey,' she spat. 'Casey will do just fine.'

He raised one brow. 'And I'd guess you're about sixteen?'

Even over the shrill of the wind he must have heard her indrawn breath. 'You have to be the most insulting man I have ever met!'

He brought his free hand up and unerringly traced the line of her jaw. 'You're not a day over thirty. No sag.'

'I am twenty-three years old, and I will have you know that women do not sag, as you so delicately put it, until they're in their fifties. So I could be considerably older than thirty!'

'You're forgetting I had my arms around you back there by the cliff,' he said with an intonation that made her blush fierily in the darkness. 'Anyway, I knew from your voice the first time I heard you speak that you were young.'

'But not as young as sixteen!' Consciously unclenching her fists, she added coldly, 'Now it's my turn—your name, please. And you might as well tell me your age, too. Just to keep things equal.'

Any remnants of his smile vanished. 'Equal?' he snarled. 'That's a laugh.'

Deliberately misunderstanding him, she said, 'It is rather—I've never met anyone as overpowering as you.'

With cruel strength his fingers tightened their hold. 'So you don't think blindness is a barrier to any kind of a normal relationship?' he demanded.

'No, I don't.'

He dropped her arm with a smothered curse. 'Then you don't know anything about it.'

He had given her the perfect opportunity to say that she knew a great deal about it. But something kept her silent. 'Your name?' she repeated gently.

'Bryden. Bryden Moore. With two "o"s and an "e". Aged twenty-nine.'

Casey said, mischief warming her voice, 'Now that we've been formally introduced we could continue this conversation in the house—I'm soaking wet.'

He said stiffly, 'I'd appreciate it if you'd take me as far as the house.'

The moon was behind a cloud, so his face was in shadow. But the message was clear: he still wanted nothing to do with her. We'll see about that, thought Casey, and held out her elbow. 'Let's go,' she said.

The rest of the journey was accomplished in silence, with the wind at their backs and the sound of the surf gradually diminishing. She led him round a rock wall to the side of the house, said evenly, 'The door's straight ahead of you,' and waited.

He said with a formal inclination of his head, 'Thank you for your help. I won't ask you in—it's late.'

'You'll have to do better than that,' Casey said clearly. 'The fact that it's three in the morning has nothing to do with why you're not asking me in—at least pay me the compliment of telling the truth.'

His lips thinned. 'I'm tired and cold and I don't feel like company—is that better?'

'*My* company,' she said with real hurt. 'You've made that clear from the beginning.'

'Anyone's company!'

'So who are you hiding from?' she flashed. 'The whole world? Because you're blind?'

'I can't stand people feeling sorry for me!'

'At the moment I'm so angry with you that the only person I feel sorry for is myself for having you as a neighbour,' Casey cried incoherently. 'We're *neighbours*! I'm only here another five days; it wouldn't hurt you to ask me in and make hot chocolate and I could wash that cut over your eye and put on a band-aid. It would be a friendly thing to do and I wouldn't want to do it any more or any less if you had your sight, that's got nothing to do with it.'

There could be no mistaking her sincerity. The lines of Bryden's mouth relaxed and for a moment she thought she had won. He said, a note in his voice she had not heard before, 'That's nice of you, Casey Landrigan... but I'm still not going to ask you in. My reasons are personal and private and I know you don't——'

'There's someone with you—a woman!' Casey gasped, her whole body suddenly bathed in cold sweat. 'I never thought of that! I'm sorry, I didn't mean to intrude.' She should have realised he would not be alone; every woman in the countryside must be after him.

Clipping off his words, Bryden said, 'There's no one with me, woman or otherwise. It's very simple, Casey— we have nothing to say to each other. As you mentioned, you're only here a few more days. You go your way and I'll go mine... it's better that way.'

He might just as well have slammed the door in her face. Wanting to burst into loud and undignified tears, knowing she would die rather than do so, Casey said flatly, 'I get the message—finally. I'm sorry I was such a slow learner, but where I grew up we treat the word neighbour very differently. I promise I won't bother you again, Mr Moore. Goodbye.'

It was one of the hardest things she had ever done in her life to turn on her heel and walk away from him; but she did it. She had no choice. Nor did he call her back, or even say goodbye. When she reached the edge of the woods, where the path led to her cottage, she looked back over her shoulder. Bryden had gone inside and the door was closed, its blank brown face mocking her.

The next day Casey did not go near the beach; she could not have swum anyway, for the sea was generously spattered with whitecaps. Instead she drove into the village, where she bought some groceries, had lunch at a café and poked around in the antique shops. Then, after a five-mile jog along the back roads, she cooked fish for supper and read in front of the fireplace. The other thing she did was try very hard not to think about her neighbour.

She did not altogether succeed. She carried with her all day a steady ache in the vicinity of her heart, a nagging pain that neither reason nor activity could dispel. Casey was not used to being rebuffed by members of the opposite sex. Without vanity, she knew she was an attractive woman who enjoyed the company of men; men, in consequence, seemed to enjoy her company. This was not true, however, of Bryden Moore: he had evinced a positive distaste for her company.

But there was more to it than that. She liked Douglas very much, and for some time had sensed that he more than liked her; she was perfectly content to wait the last eight months of her apprenticeship to see if indeed he did. No impatience. No hurry. Whereas Bryden, with whom she had had three brief and highly unsatisfactory encounters, aroused in her a fury of impatience and frustration. She had only a few days of her holidays left. She wanted to march over to his house and throw herself at the door and pound on it until he had no choice but to let her in.

And then what? Be ordered off the premises, like a love-struck teenager?

Why, Casey? she asked herself, abandoning the book to gaze into the dying fire. Why are you even contemplating a course of action so foreign to your nature?

As if Aunt Bridget, her mother's elder sister, were in the room, she could hear the echo of her voice. Casey's such a nice girl. So thoughtful. So kind... Bryden did not make her feel nice, or thoughtful, or kind. Bryden brought out another Casey, a young woman who was wild and hungry and restless as the sea; a Casey she herself had never known existed.

This new Casey frightened her. Another dimension to her personality had been revealed by an inadvertent meeting with a stranger. A man who happened to be, by a supreme irony of fate, blind.

The last little flame collapsed upon itself into an orange glow of heat; sparks like miniature fireworks were eclipsed by the blackness of the chimney. With a heavy sigh Casey got to her feet and went to bed.

The following morning the sea was as smooth as glass, reflecting the cloudless blue of the sky. The trees were still, and the strip of sand a dazzling white in the sun. Going into the other bedroom, the one that overlooked Bryden's house, Casey subjected his property to a close scrutiny. She was sure she could see someone moving around in the front garden. If Bryden was in the garden he was not at the beach. So she would go to the beach.

LOVE AT FIRST SIGHT

Carrying her portable radio, which dispelled a loneliness she was not ready to admit to, Casey headed for the wooden steps at the far boundary of the Drapers' property. She had no trouble rounding the headland today due to the low tide; because she knew she was alone, she was singing quite loudly, assisting John Denver and Placido Domingo with a soprano more noteworthy for enthusiasm than pitch. Then, in mid-phrase, she broke off.

Bryden *was* on the beach. He had heard her coming—who would not have? she thought in a mixture of mortification and panic—and had got to his feet, facing her. He began crossing the beach towards her. 'Casey?' he said.

Her feet felt as heavy as rocks in the warm sand. 'No! Yes!' she gasped. 'I'm leaving—right away. I only came down here because I saw someone around your house so I thought I'd have the beach to myself. Bryden, go away! You're *ruining* my vacation.' In a cracked voice she heard herself add, 'And why is it that whenever you come within twenty feet of me I *sound* like a sixteen-year-old?'

He was much nearer than twenty feet now, walking at a steady pace straight towards her. Ten feet. Five feet. Two feet. Then he stopped. He was wearing the glasses she hated so much, and this gave her the courage to say with asperity, 'There's nothing wrong with your hearing, that's for sure.'

'John Denver will never know what he's missed.'

'I was not referring to my singing,' she said haughtily.

'Ah... if you mean how I can walk across a beach to within touching distance of you,' he reached out one hand and brushed the bare skin of her arm, 'that's not just the sound of your voice. I can smell your perfume, too.'

Struck dumb, her eyes darkening with involuntary emotion, Casey gazed up at him, and saw in his glasses her own twin image, wisps of hair about her face, her lips unsmiling. He went on calmly, 'You probably saw Simon in the garden. Simon McIver. He used to be the lightkeeper on Ragged Island until they put in an automatic light. Now he does a little fishing and looks after the grounds of some of the summer places. In fact, I think he looks after Susan's in the spring and the fall.'

'Oh. I think Susan did mention his name.'

Bryden had approached her this time, not the reverse; and in comparison to their other meetings he looked positively friendly. Somehow this gave Casey courage. Searching for the right words, she went on quietly, 'Bryden, I hate talking to you when you're hiding behind those glasses. I don't know what kind of an accident cost you your sight... but even if your eyes are—are deformed in some way, I'd rather see them as they really are. Please?'

She had no idea how he would react. She waited, her heart hammering so loudly that she was afraid he would hear it, and saw him reach up and take off his glasses.

His eyes were blue, an indigo-blue, smoky, full of mysterious depths; around them was a network of tiny white scars, and over one brow the cut, already healing, from the night of the storm. Had his eyes not been focused an inch or two below the level of her own, she would never have known he was blind. Her throat tight, she stepped closer to him, took his hand and brought it to her forehead. 'I'm taller than the average female,' she said huskily.

He said in a low voice, 'I wish to God I could see you.'

He was stroking the hair back from her forehead, although she was not sure that he was aware of what he was doing. Because it did not seem to her to be a time for false modesty, she said, 'I've been told I'm beautiful. Certainly you're the first man who's ever given me the brush-off quite so consistently.'

His hand slid down her cheek and the slender line of her neck to her shoulder. 'I was convinced I was doing the right thing,' he said, his face so bleak that she had to fight against the impulse to put her arms around him.

Instead she asked the obvious question. 'So why did you speak to me today?'

His hand fell to his side. 'I don't know—I couldn't help myself. You sounded so happy, singing away as you came round the rocks... Did you mean what you said the other night, about it making no difference that I'm blind?'

'Yes. I meant it.'

'Blindness is a terrible handicap!'

'Yes, it is,' she said steadily. 'But you—the essential you, the person who is Bryden—you're the same.'

'I've always been a loner.' Then he gave his head a little shake. 'There's something about you—I always end up saying far more than I intended.'

Intuitively she knew better than to pursue this. She said pertly, 'So if I suggest we go for a swim, will you bite my head off?'

She had taken him by surprise. 'Swim? Now?'

'Why not? It's a perfect day.'

There was naked longing in his face. 'I haven't been swimming since last summer.'

'I'm sure you haven't forgotten how,' Casey teased. 'By the look of those biceps, you're probably Olympic class.'

This time he did smile, a smile that literally took her breath away. 'Flattery, Cassandra?'

'Whatever works,' she answered airily.

'Can I leave my shirt and glasses with your stuff?'

'Sure.'

As Bryden hauled his T-shirt over his head, Casey took a step backwards in sheer self-defence. She had grown up with three brothers and had been to the beach with several young men over the years, but nothing had prepared her for the surge of primitive desire that seized her at the closeness of Bryden's body. She had never felt like this in her life, she thought frantically, and the self-image she had always taken for granted of placid, level-headed Casey took a step backwards as well.

'What's the matter?' Bryden said sharply.

'Nothing!' she sputtered, adding with complete illogicality, 'How do you know something's the matter?'

'I... just seem able to sense whatever you're feeling,' he said slowly.

With admirable insouciance Casey replied, 'You're what my younger sister Kathy, who's the baby of the family, would call a hunk. It's nothing a dip in the cold Atlantic won't fix—come along.'

But he resisted the tug of her hand. 'What colour's your hair, Casey?'

'Brown.'

'Your eyes?'

'Blue. Although not nearly such a beautiful blue as yours.'

He grimaced. 'It's so damned frustrating... if only I could see you, just for a split second.'

'We're going for a swim, Bryden.'

His sudden grin was vibrant with life. 'You have the temper of a wildcat and you're used to getting your own way with the opposite sex. Correct me if I'm wrong.'

'Whereas you're stubborn and strong-willed. No corrections permitted.'

'You got it.'

They were standing a couple of feet apart, their hands loosely linked. Casey said matter-of-factly, as she began leading him towards the water's edge, 'The rocks are well to your left, so if you head straight out you can't come to any harm. I'll stay nearer to shore—I'll yell if you should get way off course.'

The sand was damp now underfoot, and then the first chill ripples broke over her toes. She gave an exaggerated shiver. 'This was my idea, wasn't it? I must have been crazy.'

But Bryden was not listening. The profile he had turned to her, as strongly carved as the cliffs behind him, was immobile; had she not known better, she would have sworn he was staring at the horizon. He gave her fingers a quick squeeze. 'Thanks, Casey,' he muttered. Then he let go and ran headlong into the water. When he was waist-deep he plunged under the surface, emerging in the trough between two breakers, his hair slicked to his skull. In a strong overarm crawl he started swimming out to sea.

He swam with a fierce energy, like an animal that had been cooped up too long in a cage. Every now and then he dived under the waves as though they were his natural element, the place where he was at home, then burst into the air again as playfully as a porpoise.

Slowly Casey waded out into the water. There was a lump in her throat, for she was seeing a Bryden she had not seen before: this was the real man, a man of power and vigour exulting in his freedom; a man as different from the crouched and defeated figure among the rocks as day was from night. Afraid of the intensity of her emotions, she began to swim, letting the waves buffet her body, her eyes never leaving the swimmer churning tirelessly through the water.

Bryden swam for a long time. Then he lay on his back, floating aimlessly, and although Casey would not have disturbed him for the world, she could not help wondering what he was thinking about, with his face turned to the sky and the waves rocking his body. Eventually he let the incoming tide carry him towards the shore; he was doing a lazy breast-stroke, as though reluctant to give up the buoyancy of the ocean for the ungiving solidity of land.

She called out to him as he drew closer, and he changed course, reaching her in half a dozen long strokes. Lightly she touched his wet shoulder. 'Did you have a good swim?'

He stood up, shaking the spray from his hair like a puppy, the darker hair on his chest sleek as a pelt. Encircling her waist with his hands, he lifted her high over his head and held her there, his face alive with laughter, his white teeth gleaming. 'Wonderful!' he exclaimed.

Casey gave a breathless laugh. 'I'm heavy—put me down!'

'I could lift ten of you,' he boasted.

With a delightful chuckle she responded, 'But how fortunate you don't have to prove it.'

'Are you calling my bluff?'

'I do believe I am,' she said demurely.

Abruptly he lowered her into the water, and as he did so a breaker, white-crested, thrust her against his chest. He tightened his grip automatically. Casey stood very still, her face raised to his, feeling as though time itself had stopped, leaving her in a place where she had always, without knowing it, wanted to be.

'Casey?' Bryden said. 'Casey...'

As he lowered his head, she met him halfway, her lips unashamedly hungry, her body trembling lightly in his embrace. He kissed her as though it were years since he had held and kissed a woman, as though only she existed to him in the whole wide world. She responded with reckless generosity, and in so doing crossed into a territory where she had never been before.

The tide was flowing more strongly now, and the wave that struck Casey's back made her stagger in Bryden's arms. He shifted his weight to keep his own balance, and somehow the spell was broken. Holding her away from him, the indigo eyes fastened on her face, he said hoarsely, 'I didn't mean that to happen... I'm sorry.'

Casey found she was staring at the pulse at the base of his throat, a pulse which was pounding as rapidly as her heart. 'S-sorry?' she faltered.

'I haven't touched a woman in a long time—I lost my head.'

'If you lost yours, I certainly lost mine,' Casey said wildly, and then, as his expression hardened, added with sudden fierceness, 'and don't you dare say it's because I feel sorry for you!'

Another wave rudely shoved her towards him. Bryden said tersely, 'Look, can we continue this on dry land? I left my towel over by the rocks.'

Her emotions in a turmoil, Casey led the way across the beach. Bryden shook the sand from his towel and began rubbing his chest in short, hard strokes. 'It was because of the swim,' he said. 'I haven't been able to let go like that for months—that was why I kissed you. I shouldn't have... I'm sorry.'

'I do wish you'd stop saying you're sorry! Because I'm not. I liked it.'

'That's not the point.'

'So what is the point, Bryden?' Casey asked, her eyes glittering. 'That you might risk turning into a real human being?'

'Lay off, Casey.'

She wanted to bang her fists against his chest; paradoxically she also wanted to make him laugh again. But the iron wall of his will beat her back from either course of action. She said with a courage born of desperation, 'What if tomorrow I want to come to the beach your way, Bryden? Am I still forbidden to do that?'

'Of course not—how could I be so churlish after what you did for me today? Hell, Casey, I know I've handled this all wrong... I promise if we swim again I won't fall on you like a starving man.' He draped his towel over one shoulder and gave her a crooked smile. 'And in the meantime we'd better go our separate ways.'

It was, rather more politely, another brush-off. Shivering, her flesh covered in goose-bumps, Casey said with a valiant attempt at normality, 'Can you find your way home?'

'Yes. I always put my towel the same distance from the rocks.'

'Goodbye, then.'

'Goodbye, Casey.'

There was something horribly final about the way he said those words. She stumbled across the sand, picked up her belongings and headed for the promontory. In a few short minutes she had gone from an ecstasy she could not have imagined to a pain like the stabbing of a dull knife. And another Casey had emerged: a wanton Casey who would have coupled in the sea with a man she scarcely knew.

CHAPTER THREE

THAT afternoon, when Casey was listlessly washing an accumulation of dishes in the sink, someone knocked on the back door. In a flare of hope she was sure it must be Bryden, for who else did she know in Ragged Island? But when she opened the back door an old man stood on her step. He had flowing white hair, a beard worthy of the Old Testament, and far-seeing grey eyes under brows like crests of foam. 'Simon McIver,' he said economically. 'Come to do the lawn.'

His denim shirt and trousers, faded from many washings, were spotlessly clean; however, his tan would never fade, for it was the kind of tan that came from a lifetime spent outdoors. 'Can I help out?' Casey asked. 'I don't have anything to do this afternoon.'

'You c'n clip.'

And clip she did, hard-pressed to keep up with him as he zipped around the shrubs and trees with the lawn mower. Then she raked while he weeded some of the flower-beds. He would not allow her near the compost pile. 'You got to know how to handle compost,' he said seriously. 'It's temperamental. Like a woman, I guess. If you don't treat it right, you don't get no heat.'

She had to smother a smile, for Simon was in deadly earnest, and the fact that she was a woman did not seem to have occurred to him. 'Have you ever been married, Simon?' she asked.

'Nope.' His eyes sought the jagged rocks of the island offshore, as if it were a loadstone. 'Women want to talk more'n I care for. Never could think of enough things to say to them.'

She watched in dutiful silence while he carefully layered weeds, grass clippings and earth in the compost bin. Then he gave her a sober nod. 'You tell Mrs Draper I'll look after the pruning in a month or so.'

She, Casey, would be long gone by then. 'Is Mr Moore going to stay all winter, Simon?' she blurted.

If he thought her question out of place, he gave no sign. 'Guess so. Yep.'

Hoping she could induce Simon to gossip, she remarked, 'He's like you—he's a loner.'

'Don't talk much, Mr Moore don't. That's true. Well, must be off.' Simon raised his hand in salute with the definite air of a man fleeing a too-curious female, and climbed in his battered old truck. It roared up the driveway, the garden tools rattling in the back like percussion instruments in a band.

Casey went back indoors.

The next morning it rained, a gentle misty rain that under other circumstances she would have enjoyed. But she could not go over to Bryden's in her swimsuit in the rain, and she had no other excuse for going there. She wrote three letters, then walked to the post office to mail them, and on the way back, as though a magnet were dragging her, she turned into Bryden's driveway, her footsteps leaving a silvery trail on the grass verge.

Simon's truck was parked near the house beside the tall cedar hedges. Behind the hedge she could hear the sound of voices, Bryden's deep tones interspersed with Simon's laconic comments. She was about to call out a greeting when she heard Simon say, 'Went to the Drapers' yesterday after I left your place.'

'Oh?' said Bryden. 'Did you meet the young woman who's staying there?'

'Yep.'

'What did you think of her?'

'Good worker,' Simon replied. 'Knew enough to stay away from the compost.'

'High praise indeed,' Bryden commented drily. Then his voice changed. 'Simon, what does she look like?'

There was a puzzled silence. 'OK, I guess. Kinda tall.'

'What colour is her hair? Her eyes?' Bryden persisted.

'Brown 'n' blue,' Simon said promptly.

Through the thick hedge Casey could hear Bryden's exasperated sigh. 'You can do better than that, Simon. Brown like garden soil or brown like the shingles on the house?'

'Oh.' Another silence, during which Casey could picture Simon knitting his brows in unaccustomed thought. 'Well, now, you know that table in your living-room, the one you can see through the window? Mahogany, ain't it? That's what her hair's like. Sort of smooth and polished-lookin'. Shiny, like.'

'And her eyes?'

The silence was shorter this time. 'Her eyes, now that's dead easy. Off Ragged Island, where the water drops to four fathoms, that's what her eyes are like. That green-blue colour, deep, kinda mysterious.' Simon was warming to his task. 'I just figured out what else she reminds me of. My first boat. She was a beauty, that boat, the cleanest lines you ever saw. A proud boat, with a life of her own on the sea. Yet you could trust her in a storm like no other boat I ever had.' Simon sighed. 'It was a sad day, the day I had my last sight o' her. *Lisa-Jane*, I called her.'

'What happened to her, Simon?'

'Lobsters were scarce two seasons in a row. Couldn't keep up the payments.'

'You were never able to buy her back?'

'Guy who bought her sank her a year later in a storm... you see, you had to know how to handle her. Mettlesome, she was. Not the boat for everyone.'

'You should have called her *Cassandra-Elizabeth*,' Bryden said.

Casey's cheeks were pink; eavesdropping was not a pastime to be recommended. She crept back along the grass verge, glad of the thickness of the cedars, and heaved a sigh of relief when she reached the end of the driveway. But despite some moral qualms, her heart was singing. Bryden was no more a man to make idle conversation than was Simon. So he must be very interested in her to coax Simon into speech; he had really wanted to know what she looked like. And had got, she thought wryly, remembering *Lisa-Jane*, rather more than he had bargained for.

But the conversation she had overheard gave her the courage that afternoon to take the short cut to Bryden's property. The mist was thicker now, shrouding the trees and muffling the sound of the surf; the prying of its chill fingers around the collar of her jacket made the prospect of swimming out of the question. Perhaps she and Bryden could just talk, she thought optimistically. Around the fire.

However, when she reached the boundary of the trees below his house she discovered that Bryden was not sitting in his living-room in front of the fireplace. Rather, he was jogging in the back garden. Round and round, like a convict in the yard of a prison. He must have been doing it for some time, for the grass was beaten down in a rough square around the circumference of the lawn. Twenty-six paces one way, thirty-three the other, Casey counted, knowing with a sick sensation in the pit of her stomach that he would not want her watching him. This was a private ritual, yet another limitation brought on by his blindness.

But as she turned to go her heel caught in a twig, which snapped with a crack like a whip. Bryden stopped in his tracks and his head turned her way. 'Who's there?' he said sharply.

It never occurred to her to creep away without answering. 'Casey,' she replied, wishing the ground would swallow both the twig and herself.

He walked towards her, his mouth a grim line; he was wearing nylon shorts and a sleeveless mesh shirt, and looked formidably angry. 'You sure have a penchant for spying on me. Do you get your kicks that way?'

'*No!*'

'Don't tell me you're going swimming,' he added with heavy sarcasm.

He was breathing hard from the exercise, beads of sweat trickling down his chest. Casey said vigorously, 'Bryden, I'm *sorry*. I came over to see if you'd offer me a cup of tea on such a wet day, I had no intention of spying on you. Anyway,' she finished in a spurt of temper, 'that's a horrible word to use, and what are you doing running round and round the garden when you could be jogging properly along one of the back roads? There are miles of dirt roads around here—you don't have to skulk behind your house!'

His own temper flared to meet hers. 'You seem to be forgetting that I have this small problem—I can't see where I'm going. First of all I'd have to find the dirt road, and secondly I'd have to stay between the ditches and out from under the wheels of passing cars. Get real, Casey.'

'You get real,' she retorted. 'I'm not so naïve that I'm suggesting you go alone! Have you made any enquiries thing these days—I know you could find someone to run with you. But have you even tried, Bryden?'

'No,' he said tightly.

Her temper died. Desperately wanting to touch him, keeping her hands firmly at her sides, Casey said, 'Just the other day I read about a blind man who runs in marathons. He has a regular partner who runs with him.'

As though the words were being dragged from him one by one, Bryden said, 'I used to run in marathons.'

Somehow she was not surprised that he had competed in a sport so individual, and, at a deep level, so lonely; not for Bryden the camaraderie of the baseball team. She said gently, 'You could run in them again.'

He rubbed the sweat from his forehead with the back of his hand, his smoke-blue eyes focused above her head. 'Did the partner train with him as well?'

'That's right. As I recall, the blind man was the faster runner, so it was a challenge for his partner to keep up with him... Bryden, if the worst comes to the worst, you pay someone to run with you. I don't think you'll have to. But it's better to pay someone than to run in circles around the garden.'

In an expressionless voice he said, 'You sure say it like it is, don't you?'

'Freedom is what's important,' she answered with passionate intensity. 'I never go to zoos because I can't stand seeing the animals run round and round their cages.'

'So can you run, Casey?'

She gaped at him. 'I jog every other day—but six or seven miles is my limit. I couldn't run a marathon.'

'Will you take me? Now?'

It was the first favour he had asked of her. Recognising in an instant that she could refuse him nothing, instantly burying this knowledge deep in her subconscious, Casey said with a radiant smile, 'Sure. Give me ten minutes to go home and change.'

'You have such an expressive voice,' Bryden said quietly. 'It's one of the first things I noticed about you... you're smiling, aren't you?'

'I'm blushing,' she gasped, added, 'Back in ten minutes,' and fled.

It took her no time to change into her shorts and a tank-top, and lace up her running shoes. But then she had to rummage in the back porch for a dog leash she had noticed a couple of days ago: she would use it today to keep her and Bryden together while they ran. She soon found it on a hook beside a raincoat, and for a moment stood smoothing the worn leather in her hands.

Inevitably it reminded her of her job. She had not told Bryden what she did to earn her living; partly because he had not asked, partly because she was afraid that if she did he would interpret her interest in him as professional, himself as just an extension of that job.

Nothing could be further from the truth, she thought unhappily. Bryden interested her simply by existing. And explain that one, Casey Landrigan.

She could not. So she left the cottage, and a few minutes later was back in the clearing. Bryden was stretching out his calf muscles against the side of the house. She went to join him, leaning her palms flat on the cedar shingles, bending first one knee, then the other. 'I love running in the rain,' she said conversationally.

He grunted; he looked as if he was already regretting his impulse. So Casey went through her regular stretching routine in silence, then said, 'I'm ready when you are. I brought an old leash of Susan's—if you hold one end and I take the other, that should keep us close enough.'

She should tell him now, she thought. It was a logical

knew she was incapable of saying brightly, Oh, by the way, did I ever tell you that I train guide-dogs? I didn't? How silly of me!

Bryden would not be impressed. One thing at a time, Casey, she adjured herself, and passed him the loop of the leash. He took it without comment.

They went round the corner of the house to the driveway, which was hedged in by the concealing cedars. 'Let's go,' Casey said.

'I'll let you set the pace.'

After they had jogged up the drive, they turned left on to the main highway. Making another effort at conversation, Casey said, 'There's a dirt road we can take a quarter of a mile from here—it goes through a stand of pines and then some open fields, it's very pretty.'

'I know the road,' Bryden said repressively. 'This is my seventh summer at Ragged Island.'

Feeling like a child that had had its knuckles rapped, Casey bit her lip and concentrated on running. She was in good shape, so that once they had turned on to the dirt road her stride lengthened. Bryden adjusted his, and they loped along in silence. Birds chirped in the pines; a tractor growled in one of the fields; a car passed them, the driver plainly noticing nothing out of the ordinary in a pair of joggers on a country road. Insensibly Casey began to relax; it was hard to stay angry and run an eight-minute mile simultaneously.

She glanced over at her companion. He was running easily, his body loose, the tension smoothed from his face. Into her head, perfectly formed, the thought dropped that there was nowhere else in the world she would rather be than here with Bryden.

She increased her pace, not sure how else to cope with this realisation. Smoothly Bryden increased his. They house and the ruins of a barn. Twenty minutes later, breathing hard, Casey said, 'I'm not very smart—I figure we've already gone five miles, and we still have to get home.'

Bryden laughed. 'Want to walk for a while?'

'Great idea.' She added, puffing theatrically as they turned around, '*You* could go another ten miles.'

'Seven or eight.'

'Such modesty. Oh, Bryden, don't the woods smell heavenly in September?'

'Tell me what they look like.'

She stood still, marshalling her thoughts. 'Goldenrod and tiny purple asters in the ditches, with scarlet rose-hips tangled among them. Straight ahead of us there's a birch with a silver trunk and lots of gold leaves... like little heaps of coins. Then behind that there's a maple that's starting to turn, its leaves all mottled orange and green.'

'Van Gogh would have loved all those colours, wouldn't he?' Bryden said softly, resting his hands on her shoulders. 'I'm sorry I was rude to you when we started out, Casey. I guess I'm still fighting how dependent I am on others.'

She did not want to be lumped in with anonymous others. 'If you consider it dependency, maybe that's what it turns into. Look at it another way, Bryden—each of us has had an enjoyable run.'

'And it hasn't cost me a cent,' he said fliply.

She flinched away from him. 'Why do you have to spoil everything? Did you think I was going to hold out my hand for ten dollars when we got home? Is that what you thought?'

'No—I'm sorry.' When he tried to pull her closer, he must have felt her resistance. He said harshly, 'I say

'Afraid?' Casey repeated blankly. 'Of *me*?'

'Yes. Of you. Cassandra Elizabeth Landrigan. Five feet nine, with hair like polished mahogany and eyes like the depths of the sea—and if you're wondering how I know, I asked Simon.'

Remembering what else Simon had said, Casey stared down at the ground. 'Why did you do that? I didn't even think you liked me.'

'I had to know.' He was smoothing the bare skin of her shoulder with his thumb in a slow, mesmerising rhythm. 'That's what frightens me... there's no element of choice.'

She scuffed at the dirt with her toe. 'That's the way I feel, too,' she confessed.

'I don't believe you! Why in hell would you feel that way?' he said in violent repudiation.

She raised her head, conscious of the cool air on her overheated body. 'Bryden, if we're going to spend any time together at all—and you're committed to being with me for at least the next half-hour—let's get something straight. In a very real way your blindness is irrelevant to me. You just happen to be the most attractive man I have ever met.'

Bryden's expression was inscrutable; she waited for his reply, her breathing still faster than normal. 'Attractive?' he said finally.

'It's not much of a word, is it?' Recklessly, Casey decided to go for broke. 'You're gorgeous. You turn me on. You're the sexiest man east of Ontario.'

Another protracted silence, during which she wondered what on earth had possessed her to speak her mind so plainly. With a strange note in his voice Bryden said, 'You really mean that, don't you?'

'Every word of it.' She gave him an impish grin. 'Once

Another nod, her forehead moving against his mesh shirt. He said suggestively, 'I could make love to you under a spruce tree. Although it might be a little damp.'

'Very damp,' Casey muttered. 'There's swamp on both sides of the road.'

The laughter rumbled in his chest. 'Can I trust you? Real swamp, with water, peat and mosquitoes? It's not that you've changed your mind?'

'You can trust me, Bryden,' she said soberly.

'Yeah...' With subdued violence he went on, 'You make it all seem so easy, Casey—swimming, jogging, laughing, even making love. All summer I've been like a squirrel on a treadmill, running faster and faster and getting absolutely nowhere. And then you come along... hot-tempered, bossy and so very beautiful.' He stroked her hair with a hand that was not quite steady. 'You're sure Simon didn't lie to me? Your hair's not red?'

'Dark brown,' she insisted, her eyes brimming with happiness.

'Just being able to swim yesterday and run today—I feel like a new man.'

'I noticed,' Casey said pertly.

Throwing back his head, Bryden laughed out loud, the tendons in his neck as strong as rope. 'Despite the fact that we didn't make love in the road, I feel wonderful,' he proclaimed. 'We could get rid of our frustrations by running home.'

'Or we could run to Halifax. It's only sixty miles.'

'You're very good for my ego.'

'Bryden,' she blurted, the words appearing from nowhere she had openly acknowledged, 'are you married?'

'No.'

'Divorced?'

'I've never been married.'

'We haven't talked much about personal things,' she stumbled.

'No.' A shiver ran through his body, as though he was cold. He said restlessly, 'Let's run for a mile or two and walk the rest of the way.'

He had not asked if she was married. Cursing her unruly tongue, for she had totally shattered the closeness between them, Casey led the way across the road so they would face the traffic, and began to run. And, whether it was from sexual frustration or from fear of all the other emotions that were rampaging in her breast, she was able to jog the whole way home. When they finally reached Bryden's house, she passed him the leash. 'You might as well keep this for now,' she gasped.

He took it, slapping it against his palm. 'The weather's supposed to clear tomorrow,' he said abruptly. 'Do you want to swim in the afternoon?'

Casey had been afraid he would not suggest another meeting. Wishing it were today, for she had only two more days left at the cottage, and hoping he could sense neither her relief nor her impatience, she said with assumed casualness, 'Sure.'

'Come to the house, if you like. We'll go down to the beach together. Around two?'

She would have come at five in the morning. Somehow humiliated by this knowledge, she said crisply, 'Fine. See you then.'

'Thank you, Casey,' Bryden said.

She did not want his gratitude. She mumbled something and turned on her heel, wishing she had the energy to run back to the cottage. To run away from Bryden.

The cottage, now familiar to her, welcomed her back. She showered, lay down on the bed and fell asleep.

CHAPTER FOUR

WHEN Casey awoke, she felt out of sorts and extremely tired. She had been crazy to run the better part of ten miles, she thought grumpily. And even more crazy to indulge in lovemaking with a man who was not even interested enough in her to ask if she was married. He probably just wanted an affair, she decided cynically, shutting her mind to the all-too-real emotion Bryden had exhibited. After all, he knew she was only here for another two days. What could be better? Lovemaking, on or off the road, and no commitments. Perfect.

She threw together an omelette for supper, and managed to burn the onions and overdo the eggs. Afterwards she lit a fire in the living-room and picked up her book. But the heroine's very strenuous activities, far too many of which were in bed, did nothing to soothe Casey's nerves. She went back into the kitchen and made a pan of brownies with lots of nuts, covered them with thick chocolate icing and ate half a dozen; she then had a cup of coffee. She read another chapter. She ate two more brownies. At ten o'clock, thoroughly disgruntled and suffering from indigestion, she went to bed.

She must have fallen asleep, for the next thing she knew she was sitting bolt upright in bed with her heart racing. Something had woken her. A noise?

The cottage was wrapped in silence. Slowly Casey relaxed. The noise had probably been part of a nightmare brought on by too much chocolate. She plumped up the pillow and lay down again.

A loud crash came from downstairs, followed by a series of smaller rattles and thuds. Casey sat up again. Her eyes wide, she stared into the darkness. No number of brownies could have made her imagine that. Someone was downstairs.

She had not locked the door when she went to bed. She had not locked a door since she had arrived at the cottage. Wishing frantically that she had, now that it was too late, she wondered what to do. The only telephone in the cottage was downstairs, and no power on earth was going to get her down there.

As if to underline this decision, she heard a sound like breaking glass. More than one person, she thought sickly. A second must have broken one of the windows.

She slithered out of bed, crept to the front window and raised the sash with exquisite care. Then she eased her body through the opening, bruising both elbows as she did so, and crawled out on to the roof of the veranda. The shingles were as rough as sandpaper under her bare feet. Crouched low, she tiptoed to the edge of the roof and peered over.

No one was in sight and the railing on the porch was not that far below. Once she was down, she could run through the woods to Bryden's.

The thought of Bryden gave her courage. Wincing as the edge of the shingles dug into her stomach, she lowered her legs and sought for the railing with her toes, terrified that any moment a shout from downstairs would herald her rather undignified escape. Then her feet felt the smoothness of wood; she rested her weight on the railing, got her balance and leaped to the ground. Bent low, she ran for the trees.

Her brief nightshirt was pale blue, a horribly obvious target. But the thieves must have been busy inside the cottage, for no one yelled at her or burst from the cottage in pursuit of her. Panting with fear, she reached the woods and pushed herself between two young fir trees. The boughs were wet with dew, plastering her shirt to her body. Casey did not care. She stumbled through the woods, making a wide circle of the cottage before daring to emerge on the driveway.

The stones hurt her feet as she scurried along the road, her ears alert for the sound of a vehicle following her; near the highway she cut through the trees to Bryden's driveway, with its tall cedar hedges. Not stopping to think, because if she had she probably would not have had the nerve to go on, she banged on his door and pushed the bell for good measure. If he was a sound sleeper he might not hear her... and then what would she do?

With startling suddenness the door swung open and she saw Bryden standing there, clad in a pair of jeans and nothing else. She ran straight at him, flung her arms around his waist and cried, 'Oh, Bryden, someone's broken into the cottage, or maybe there are two of them. I was so s-scared.'

In an automatic reflex his arms had gone around her. She snuggled into his bare chest and mumbled, 'You feel so solid. And safe. I was afraid you'd be asleep and maybe you wouldn't hear me.'

'I couldn't sleep. Casey, you're shaking like a leaf and you're soaking wet.'

'The trees were wet. So was the grass. Dew, I suppose.'

'You'd better tell me what happened.'

She described the brownies, the mysterious and terrifying noises from downstairs, and her precipitate flight via the veranda, by which time Bryden was grinning. 'It wasn't funny!' she said indignantly. 'I was scared out of my wits.'

'I'm sure you were,' he said, trying to wipe the smile from his lips and not really succeeding. 'You got out of a nasty situation very neatly and I'm glad you came here—even if you are in some kind of a nightgown that's far too abbreviated for my peace of mind. But tell me something else... why the eight brownies?'

She said sweetly, 'To take my mind off you, of course. Why couldn't *you* sleep, Bryden?'

'None of your business.' Very firmly he pushed her away. 'In the closet in my bedroom you'll find some sweatsuits hanging up. Put one on and then we'll go over to your place and see what's going on.'

'By ourselves?' she squeaked.

'We'll case the joint,' he said with another grin.

'You and John Wayne.'

He laughed outright. 'With you as the beautiful heroine who rescued herself rather than waiting for the hero. Off you go, Casey.'

'And what happens if they're still there?'

'We'll call the police. Unless one of them just happens to get in my way. In which case I'll slug him.'

For a moment he looked extremely dangerous. 'You would, wouldn't you?' she said slowly.

'I don't like people who break into houses and scare young women. Particularly if the young woman happens to be you.'

Casey was quite pleased by this last sentiment. 'We should hurry,' she said, 'in case they're vandals.'

'I'm not crawling through the woods with you unless you're properly dressed,' he said inflexibly. 'So move it.'

'Yessir,' said Casey, running for the stairs.

By the time she came down, Bryden had collected a torch, a stout stick, and a shirt, which he was pulling on. He looked very happy. Said Casey, 'You're enjoying this.'

LOVE AT FIRST SIGHT

'Are you respectably covered?'

She was inelegantly clad in a sweatsuit five sizes too big. 'I would inspire no one to lust—trust me.'

'It's not you I can't trust. Let's go.'

The journey back to the cottage did not seem nearly as threatening with Bryden at her side, large and imperturbable in the gloom. When they approached the cottage from the rear, it was in darkness and utterly quiet. 'We'll circle it,' Bryden whispered. 'Try not to make any noise.'

Casey had no intention of making any noise. As they came around the side of the house she breathed, 'The door's open... they must have gotten in that way.' Then she stopped in dismay.

Across the grass, leading to the front door, were two separate trails of footprints in the dew. But they were not human footprints. They were far too small and narrow for that. She followed them to their end, saw where they disappeared under a low-hanging juniper shrub, and said in a choked voice, 'Bryden, I've made a complete fool of myself. There are animal tracks in the grass. One set going to the door and one set leaving.'

In swift comprehension Bryden said, 'Perhaps you only partially latched the door last night?'

Her brow furrowed. 'I could have, I suppose.'

'Racoons,' he said, and again an irrepressible grin tugged at his lips.

She scowled at him. 'Racoons,' she repeated. 'Four-legged fur-bearing animals that live in the woods.'

'And sport black masks worthy of any burglar,' Bryden supplied, now openly laughing. 'I bet he got into your garbage.'

She wailed. 'Will you ever forgive me for hauling you over here in the middle of the night?'

'Let's go in and see if he ate the brownies. If he didn't, you can offer me one and I'll consider the matter.'

They went up the steps, through the open door into the cottage, and then into the kitchen. The metal rubbish bin was tipped on its side, its contents very thoroughly scattered over the floor. Although a glass had been knocked off the counter, the brownies were intact.

'Sit down,' Casey said, 'while I clean up the mess and make you a cup of tea.'

Ten minutes later Bryden was licking chocolate icing from his fingers. 'You're forgiven,' he said blandly. 'Can I have another one?'

She pushed over the plate and wondered why sitting in a disordered kitchen eating brownies should make her feel so wondrously happy. Because Bryden seemed happy too? Was that it? Thoughtfully she took her ninth brownie of the night.

When he had finished his tea, Bryden scraped back his chair. 'I'd better be going,' he said. 'Unless you'd like me to stay, Casey?'

Not sure what he meant, she stammered, 'Oh, I don't think I'll be nervous. Now that I know it was only a racoon.'

'I wasn't thinking about your nerves,' he said.

The width of two chairs was between them and he was making no attempt to touch her. But she now knew exactly what he meant. She blushed, stood up and said, her voice not quite under control, 'I ... I don't think I'm ready for that, Bryden.'

'Then would you mind walking with me to the end of my driveway?'

There was neither surprise not disappointment in his voice: no emotion at all. Not for the first time Casey had no idea what he was thinking. Had he been hurt by her refusal? Or did he even care? 'Just let me get my sneakers,' she muttered and hurried upstairs.

LOVE AT FIRST SIGHT

They walked in silence to his house. At the door Bryden said, 'Two o'clock for a swim?'

'I'm looking forward to it. And, Bryden—thanks.'

'The Great Racoon Rescue,' he murmured. 'It was fun, Casey. See you tomorrow.' And he walked up the steps.

She would have liked a kiss. As she tramped home, she reflected that Casey the intrepid escapee across the veranda roof was not all that brave: she had lacked the courage to kiss Bryden goodnight.

Or did she lack the courage for any consequences of that kiss?

The weather was perfect the next day. Casey and Bryden swam, sunbathed on the sand, and swam again. Then Bryden said, giving her his rare, singularly sweet smile, 'Let's go up to the house. I'll make you a tall, cool drink and we can sit on the patio.'

This sounded like a fine plan to Casey. A few minutes later she was settled on a chaise-longue on Bryden's porch, which overlooked Ragged Island and the ocean; the distant sigh of the waves and the nearer chuckling of the brook fell soothingly on her ears. She took a second sip of the delicious, fruit-laden drink he had made for her and said dreamily, 'It's so beautiful here. I feel very lazy.'

Bryden was sitting beside her in a matching chair. 'No wonder, after chasing burglars all night.'

'It'll be a long time before I make brownies again ... you won't be insulted if I fall asleep, will you?'

He stretched out; he was still in his swimming trunks. 'I may do the same. Hard work being John Wayne.'

Casey lay back, the sun caressing her bare arms and legs. Happiness was something she could very easily get used to, she decided just before she fell asleep.

She slept for the better part of an hour. When she woke, she glanced over at the neighbouring recliner. Bryden was still asleep.

She studied his face thoughtfully. With the indigo eyes closed, those eyes that tragically could not see, the rest of his features came into prominence: the dark brows, the decided chin, the slightly crooked nose that gave his face character. Her mother would have thought his hair needed cutting; she, Casey, loved the way it curled around his ears and flopped over his forehead in a thick wave.

A mosquito landed on his cheek. She reached over and brushed it away. Bryden's eyes flew open; he was instantly awake. 'Did you sleep well?'

'You were about to be bitten by a bloodthirsty mosquito,' she explained. 'And yes, I feel wonderful.'

He was smiling at her again, which made her feel even more wonderful. Then her eyes narrowed. 'Hold still,' she said, 'there's that mosquito again.'

She slapped at it, missed, and hit Bryden's ear. He captured her hand, bringing it to his lips. 'Into attacking me, are you?' he murmured, kissing her fingertips one by one.

'If you keep that up, I might.'

'Promises, promises...'

Then he had taken her by the shoulders and was easing her on top of him on the chaise-longue. It creaked alarmingly. Casey said with a breathless giggle, 'We'll fall off.'

'You talk too much,' he said, and stopped her lips with his own.

It was a slow, gentle and infinitely sensual kiss. Achingly conscious of his sun-warmed skin and of the rasp of his body hair against her belly, she kissed him back.

From a long way away she heard him whisper against her mouth, 'Casey, I think you'd better go home.'

'I don't want to.'

'If you don't, we'll end up in bed...will you go to bed with me, Casey?'

She raised her head, pushing back her hair, her eyes searching his face. 'I want to. More than anything. But——'

The chair creaked again. Bryden said, laughter warming his voice, 'We'd better get up. When there's a perfectly good bed available, why make love on a cedar floor?'

Not very gracefully, Casey scrambled to her feet. Bryden stood up too. He let his hands drift up her arms to her shoulders, then bent his head, his mouth trailing kisses along the hollow of her collarbone before dropping lower to discover the warm valley between her breasts. Her body quivered as a poplar leaf quivered at the lightest touch of the wind; she rested her cheek on the silky thickness of his hair, enveloped in sensations all the more powerful for being new to her.

'Come to bed with me,' he said again.

Desperately Casey tried to gather some remnants of common sense. 'Bryden, I—I'm not prepared,' she stammered, unable to be more direct, her cheeks scarlet. 'But quite apart from that, I don't know how I feel about you——'

He said forcefully, 'You want me. I want you. I'll look after the other.'

Feeling as though she were being torn in two, for the Casey of the last twenty-three years had collided head-on with the wild, seductive creature she had become at Ragged Island, she faltered. 'I want you, yes. But there's got to be more to sex than just desire...my mother always said that to go to bed with a man you didn't love with all your heart was to betray something very precious in yourself.'

His face hardened. 'If that's your answer, then you'd better go home.'

His sudden change of mood terrified her. 'Are there no other choices?' she pleaded. 'Why can't we sit here in the sun and talk? Get to know each other better. Or go for a walk on the beach?'

'Because I can't keep my hands off you—that's why! You drive me crazy.'

'I'm not sure that's altogether a compliment, Bryden,' Casey answered, her heart thumping in her breast as she sought to understand the abyss that was suddenly yawning in front of them. 'Maybe it's a cop-out—seduce me so you don't have to treat me like a real human being, so you don't have to talk to me and maybe reveal something of yourself, of your own emotions.' His hiss of indrawn breath told her she was near the mark. 'You're not really afraid of me,' she added in sudden inspiration, 'you're afraid of yourself. And I don't think it's anything to do with your blindness.'

'Since you're so clever, why don't you tell me what I'm afraid of?' he demanded, holding her at arm's length with fingers like claws.

'I can't—I don't know what it is. Although I do know a woman has to be more than just someone you take to bed!'

'You're a born romantic,' he sneered.

Casey was very near tears; from the man who had kissed her so tenderly, he had turned into a cynical stranger. 'If by that you mean that I believe in love—lasting, committed love—then I guess you're right, I am a romantic.'

'You want the world wrapped up in tinsel and pink ribbon, don't you?' he taunted. 'You can't deal with honest lust—you want it prettified, strewn with red roses, enshrouded in love.' He gave an ugly laugh. 'Love...that has to be the most abused word in the English language.'

'Love is important!' Casey cried defiantly.

His words like the flick of a whip, he said, 'So were you lastingly in love with each man you've gone to bed with, Casey?'

Her body seemed to shrink in the cruel grip of his fingers. She had never been to bed with anyone, for the simple reason that she had never been lastingly in love. 'That's a horrible thing to say. I'm not like——'

'Or perhaps you're married and out for a little summer fling?'

Her body dissolving in pain, she tore herself free, knowing she had to get away from his mockery and his ugly accusations that were so far from the truth. 'I'm going home,' she said jaggedly. 'I hate it when you behave like this, Bryden. I hate *you*!'

In her bare feet she ran across the patio. The stairs were a blur; then there was grass underfoot and the welcome shade of the trees. She raced along the path until she came to the cottage, took the steps in two bounds and slammed the door shut behind her, her breath sobbing in her ears. For the first time since she had come to Ragged Island, she turned the key in the lock.

Her last day at the cottage. Casey stood at the upstairs window, remembering how the wind had billowed the curtains on her first day here. There was no wind today. Only a mockingly perfect morning, calm, pristine, exquisitely beautiful.

Inwardly she gave thanks for her rented car. She would leave the cottage right after breakfast and stay away all day. No trips to the beach, no jogging along the dirt roads. No Bryden.

To her surprise she had slept solidly, a leaden sleep that had passed the long hours of the night, even if it had not refreshed her. Nor had it altered in any way her stark view of what had happened yesterday. Bryden was not the man for her: he despised her for believing in love. Bryden thought women were for taking to bed, sexual objects to whom one did not relate in any emotional way; it was so blatantly the classic male chauvinist position that it was almost funny. Almost.

Who are you kidding, Casey? she jeered. It's not funny at all. Meeting Bryden has turned your world upside-down. And do you know why? Because he's made you see yourself as you really are—someone whose sexuality has never been sufficiently aroused to call her moral standards into question. Now that you've met him you'll never be the same again, because through him you've found out you're not at all the person you, and everyone else, thought you were. Calm, even-tempered Casey. Dispassionate, level-headed Casey. Patient, placid Casey.

Her mouth twisted in an unhappy smile. Bryden, certainly, would not apply any of those adjectives to her. Why should he? She had behaved in a way exactly opposite to them ever since she had met him.

And she still had no idea why. He was as far from her image of an ideal man as he could be, for after her father Douglas was her ideal, and Douglas and Bryden were poles apart. Douglas was kind and calm and caring, a man who knew himself and had his life in order. Unlike Bryden.

What was Bryden like? she wondered, gazing unseeingly at the crisp line of the horizon as she recalled all the clues of the past week. A man of passion, who only rarely allowed his passion an outlet; a man of fierce energy and drive, now trammelled by blindness; an independent man, sufficient unto himself, apparently immune to loneliness. Also, she admitted with reluctance, a man afraid of his feelings. Or maybe she was glossing over the unpleasant truth that he had no feelings.

What else did she know about him? He was unmarried. He had had no visitors since she had been here, apart from Simon. He had pushed her away at every opportunity, yet she would swear that from the beginning he had been attracted to her.

As a sum total this did not seem very significant compared with all the blanks in her knowledge. She did not know how he had lost his sight, or how he had earned his living before he had been blinded. Nor did she know where he came from, whether he had family, or why he had never married. These were important facts, she thought sombrely. The basic coinage of human interchange.

The other side of that coin was that he knew almost nothing about her personal life, and had shown very little curiosity. When she left tomorrow she would at least know his address and telephone number. He did not even know where she was from.

The message was clear. He did not care.

Suddenly unable to bear her own thoughts, Casey whirled around the bedroom gathering her camera and swimsuit and book, and ran downstairs. The first thing she did was take the phone off the hook. Then she ate a quick breakfast, packed a picnic lunch and left the house.

The garden smelled sweetly of pansies. Not lingering, Casey closed the gate behind her, got in her car and drove off. She turned right so she would not have to pass Bryden's driveway, drove a mile or so, then pulled up and studied the map, soon deciding to take the road along the shore; there were some interesting peninsulas and coves.

The shoreline was both interesting and extremely beautiful, sprinkled with antique and craft shops, and interspersed with charming fishing villages and small, stout white churches. But for all Casey's determination to enjoy herself on this, the last day of her vacation, she was forced to admit by the afternoon that she was only going through the motions. She had found a beach, where she had swum and then eaten her picnic. But it was Saturday, she now realised, and she was the only unaccompanied female on the entire stretch of sand. Beaches were for families and groups and couples.

Especially couples.

She buried her face in her arm, swept by a wave of despair and hopeless longing. I'm going back to the cottage, she thought. I've got to—I have no choice. I'll reconnect the phone and pray that Bryden calls me. And if he doesn't, I'll go and see him this evening. To say goodbye. I suppose I'm being spineless and accommodating and weak-kneed. But I can't leave tomorrow without seeing him again.

She felt minimally better for this decision. After picking up her gear, she went back to the car and headed home; forty-five minutes later she pulled into the driveway and parked in the shade near the cottage. Carrying the picnic basket, she fumbled with the latch on the gate and pushed it open; the hinges squealed.

'Casey?' said a man's voice.

Her head jerked up. Bryden was sitting on the bottom step.

CHAPTER FIVE

CASEY'S first reaction when she saw Bryden sitting on her steps was pure, uncomplicated joy. He had sought her out. She would not have to leave Ragged Island without seeing him again. But fast on the heels of joy came the memory of how they had parted the day before, of the depth and importance of their misunderstanding.

'Is that you, Casey?' Bryden repeated, getting to his feet.

Clutching the picnic basket to her chest as if it were a shield, her heart thudding like a drum, she slowly closed the gate behind her. 'Yes, it's me,' she said. 'How long have you been here?'

'Ten o'clock this morning.'

It was now four in the afternoon. 'Have you had lunch?'

'I brought some fruit with me and ate that.'

She had been walking towards him. 'You'd better come inside.'

He followed her up the steps and closed the door. Casey put the basket on the counter, heard the low, impersonal hum of the telephone and reached over to put the receiver back on the hook.

Bryden said with no discernible emotion, 'I started calling you at nine this morning. By ten I figured you'd taken the phone off the hook so I came over here. If you hadn't left the door unlocked, I'd have been worried that you'd left for good.'

He could not see her; so why should she be so conscious that all she was wearing was an unbuttoned cotton shirt over her bikini? Her body felt lethargic from the sun; her skin was flaked with salt. She said noncommittally, 'I'd gone by nine.'

'When do you go home, Casey?'

'Early tomorrow morning.' Her flight left at eight, so she would have to leave the cottage by five-thirty.

'I don't even know where you live.'

'You haven't asked,' she replied with false calm. They were like two boxers circling each other, she thought fancifully, neither prepared to make the first move.

'I haven't asked anything about you.'

And what was she supposed to say to that? She knew what her Aunt Bridget would say; and with rather overdone politeness said it. 'Would you like to sit down? May I get you a cup of tea?'

'No, thanks. You're not being any help, Casey, are you?'

The first feint. 'I don't see why I should be, Bryden.'

'I suppose not...I came over to apologise.'

'I see,' she said untruthfully.

He took an impetuous step towards her. 'I feel as if I'm talking to a robot. Or one of those dummies in a window display.'

Casey held her ground with an actual effort of will. 'That's because I have no idea what to say to you. Whatever I say seems to be wrong.' With treacherous speed her equanimity deserted her. 'I've never fought with anyone as much as I have with you the last week!'

Two more steps. '*That's* entirely mutual.' With no change in tone he added, 'What are you wearing, Casey? I need to have a picture of you in my mind.'

Her nostrils flared. 'A blue cotton shirt over a bikini. My hair's a mess and I've got sand between my toes. Is there anything else you'd like to know?'

'Now you sound more like the real you,' he said drily.

'I don't know who the real me is any more!' Briefly she closed her eyes, struggling to moderate her voice. 'Bryden, we're getting off topic—you did mention an apology.'

He said flatly, 'Give me your hands.'

She scowled at him in perplexity. His indigo eyes were fastened on her face as if he could actually see her sun-flushed cheeks and tangled curls, and with a pain that pierced her to the core she realised that tomorrow he would vanish from her life.

It seemed more than she could bear. Silently she held out both hands.

He took them in his, enveloping her fingers in his own with a strength he was possibly unaware of. 'I had a long speech prepared,' he said wryly, 'which I had lots of time to rehearse while I was waiting for you. But all I have to do is touch you and it's gone.'

'I don't want long speeches,' she answered with painful honesty. 'I only want to know what you're feeling. Why you're here.'

He said, choosing his words with care, 'You know me well enough, I'm sure, to understand that that's the hardest thing you could ask of me, Casey. Because that's the whole problem—I don't know what my feelings are towards you. Yesterday afternoon it seemed as though the only way to handle them was to take you to bed. I didn't like it when you turned me down—didn't like it at all. I'm sorry for the way I treated you and the things I said to you... although I'd be dishonest to say that I've changed my mind. I still want to take you to bed. My God, how I want to!'

He suddenly brought her hands up to his face, kissing her palms, his head bowed. 'You've been swimming,' he muttered. 'I can taste the salt.'

'I went to the beach at Blandford.' Casey bit her lip. 'I wasn't telling the truth yesterday when I said I hated you, Bryden. I don't hate you. Although I hated the things you said. But I don't understand you, I don't see why you're so afraid of me.' She gave an unconvincing laugh. 'I've never thought of myself as intimidating.'

He let go of her hands, moving his shoulders restlessly. 'I've been alone since I was a boy,' he said. 'You challenge that. You've gotten through my defences, just by being yourself.' His voice roughened with emotion. 'I—I don't even worry much about being blind when I'm with you—it doesn't seem to matter. Heaven knows how you've done that.'

His admission touched her to the heart. Her eyes wet with tears, Casey whispered, 'Bryden, that's the nicest thing you could have said to me.'

He touched her cheek and said huskily, 'You're crying.'

'I guess I am...'

Her tears seemed to loosen his tongue. 'Somehow you seem to understand what it's like to be blind, while at the same time you force me out there into the world to do the things I always used to do. Then the other night when I came over here to punch out the burglars I realised *I* was helping *you*, and not the reverse. You don't know how good it felt, to be of use to someone else—I'd figured my days for that were over.'

He was stroking her salt-tangled hair, each touch of his hand quivering along her nerves. In a small voice she said, 'But yesterday I felt you despised me. Just because I said that love was important.'

'I was angry,' he said slowly. 'Angry and hurt. I'd thought you wanted me just as much as I wanted you. So I wasn't prepared for you to say no.'

In anguish and confusion Casey cried, 'Maybe I was a fool to say no—relying on what my mother said rather than my own feelings.'

He said flatly, 'Whatever is between us is both powerful and elemental, Casey. But it's not love.'

She shivered, pulling away from him. Had she in her heart of hearts hoped he was falling in love with her? 'Let's forget the whole thing,' she said in desperation. 'Because we can't resolve it—we're too different.'

She could see him making a visible effort to follow her lead. 'OK,' he said. 'OK. Which, I guess, brings up the other reason I came here. It's your last evening...will you have dinner with me? Fresh lobster courtesy of Simon, candle-light and wine.'

A potent combination, thought Casey. 'I accept.'

The line of his shoulders relaxed infinitesimally. He hesitated, 'You've already been to the beach. Do you want to go for a run?'

He had spent most of the day sitting in the sun on her step. 'I'd rather go for a swim,' she said quickly.

He smiled at her. 'Great! Why don't you come with me now and I'll change at my place?'

It did not take much to make Bryden happy, Casey thought humbly, following him out of the door. As for herself, she had wasted a whole day when she could have been with him. She must not waste another minute of the little time that was left.

As they descended the steps to the beach, the late afternoon sun was slanting across the sand, the clefts in the headland deeply shadowed, the waves chuckling to themselves. Casey spread out her towel beside Bryden's and grabbed his hand. 'Last one in's a chicken,' she chanted.

LOVE AT FIRST SIGHT

'When I was a kid, we used stronger words than chicken.'

'You were a boy,' she said primly, and ran with him into the silvery wash of water on the sand. Again, he soon left her far behind, swimming straight as an arrow towards the horizon; when he returned his face was peaceful, drained of the tension that seemed so integral a part of him.

Casey had been diving for shells. After she had presented him with a rather battered horse mussel, she led the way back up the sand, wringing the water from her pigtail. But when she leaned down for her towel, Bryden reached for his at the same time, and his elbow struck her hard in the ribs. Her gasp of pain was lost in his, 'Casey, I'm sorry! I didn't——' He broke off, then finished bitterly, 'I didn't see you.'

Rubbing her side, Casey said spiritedly, 'People with perfectly good eyesight bump into each other, Bryden. You know that as well as I do.'

'I suppose they do.' He managed a smile. 'Do we need an ambulance?'

'For two broken ribs? Heavens, no.'

He gently squeezed her ribcage. 'I know when you're faking,' he said. Then his voice changed. 'Casey, I'm going to miss you. The beach will be empty without you...'

When he bent his head to kiss her, she responded with a kind of desperation, for in less than twelve hours she would be gone from here and what did her mother's strictures mean in the face of that? His hunger leaped to meet her own; he pulled her against the length of his body, clasping her waist, and in their wet swimsuits they might as well have been naked.

With every nerve in her body Casey felt his hands roam the long curve of her spine and the swell of her hips, and felt, too, his instant arousal. Drowning in a bittersweet longing, she kissed him with fierce possessiveness, setting her seal on him, for he belonged to her and she to him, and so it had been from the first moment she had seen him.

She did not resist when he pulled her down to lie with him on the crumpled towels, the sting of sand on her shoulders, her wet hair coiled about her throat. His thigh was thrown over hers; one hand found the fullness of her breast, pushing aside the thin fabric of her bikini to cup her bare flesh.

His body stilled. He said with passionate intensity, 'You're so beautiful, Casey. Your skin is so smooth—like the inside of a seashell.' He raised his head, his eyes a deeper blue than the ocean. 'When I accused you yesterday of coming here for a fling, I knew it was wrong as soon as I said it. You wouldn't do anything like that—cheat or lie. You're too honest.'

Impetuously he buried his face in the hollow between her breasts. She held him to her, and said with careful truth, 'I've never been married or fallen in love with anyone, Bryden. So I've never made love with anyone, either... because I've always believed that love and commitment would have to be part of making love.' He was changing that, but she could not tell him so. 'Unfashionable sentiments, I know, but that was the way I was brought up.'

He raised his head. 'We come from different worlds, Casey. I've always steered clear of women who want commitment. Then, since I was blinded, I wondered if I'd ever make love again... how could I, when I couldn't even see the woman?'

She held him more tightly. 'You can't see me... but does it really matter, Bryden?'

With exquisite sensibility he drew his hand the length of her body, tracing all its curves and concavities. 'It's as though I can see you,' he said huskily. 'As though I know you in a way I never knew a woman before.'

Then, deliberately, he rested his palm on her hip and lay still beside her, dropping his cheek into the hollow of her elbow, tension in the line of his shoulders, his breathing carefully under control. Casey understood immediately that, whatever the cost to him, he would not force her into anything she might regret, even if he was not in sympathy with her reasons. Her heart overflowed with tenderness. Was this the love she had talked about a few moments ago? she wondered. This upwelling of joy mingled with the ache of desire? This absolute certainty that Bryden was the man whom, unbeknown to her, she had been waiting for?

She suddenly felt coolness blanket her skin, and with a thrill of superstitious fear saw that the sun had fallen below the jagged line of spruce trees high on the cliff; their shadows, elongated, sinister, stabbed the sand like black icicles. She had been in danger of forgetting something: Bryden was not in love with her. Did not want to be in love with her.

'You're shivering,' he said in quick concern. Leaving a trail of kisses from her breast to her throat, he gave her a fierce, hard hug, then pulled her to her feet. 'The sun must have gone down.'

'It went behind the trees,' she replied, trying to anchor herself once again in reality. The next sunset she saw would be in Ontario, from her apartment window; a long way from this lonely little beach.

He still had an arm around her, and together they began walking towards the steps. 'Why don't you go to your cottage and have a shower, and then, whenever you're ready, come back to my place?' Bryden said prosaically.

'All right,' she answered in a small voice.

He turned her to face him. 'What's wrong, Casey?'

'You sound so—so ordinary,' she muttered. 'As though nothing's happened.'

'Then I'm a damned good actor,' he said grimly. 'The reason I came to Ragged Island last month was to try and come to grips with the whole issue of my blindness, to figure out what I'd do next. I planned to learn braille. I was going to get on my feet again. Time out. Space to make some decisions.' He gave a short laugh. 'The best laid plans of mice and men... because then you arrived, and in just over a week shifted the entire scenario. When I'm with you, I'm not fighting blindness. I'm fighting something else altogether, something much deeper-rooted. Hell, I don't even know what weapons to use.'

'Won't you tell me what you're fighting?' She was almost sure she knew: Bryden the loner had collided with the demands of intimacy. But she also knew he had to share this with her.

He hesitated. 'I don't think I can, Casey—not yet.'

But we have no more time, she wanted to cry. Only tonight and then I'll be gone. 'You can trust me,' she said with a touch of desperation.

'It's not that.' Obviously seeking a change of subject, he patted her arm. 'You're cold, let's go up to the house.'

She had to half run to keep up with him as they crossed the sand. Against the golden sky the tops of the spruce trees looked like witches' hats, harbingers of darkness; there was not a breath of wind, and even the gulls were silent. Fighting for patience, she who was normally never impatient, striving to keep back the questions that wanted to burst from her lips, Casey trotted up the steps and felt the spikiness of grass under her feet. 'Is the dinner burning?' she puffed.

'Sorry,' Bryden slowed down. 'It's my problem, that's what I was trying to say. Something I have to work out on my own.'

'Maybe you do too much on your own.'

'You might have been brought up to believe in all the old-fashioned virtues—but I wasn't,' he answered shortly. 'I was brought up to sort things out by myself. Different strokes for different folks, Casey.'

They had reached the house. The tension was back in his face, she saw with a pang of apprehension. 'I understand,' she said, not altogether truthfully, and gave him a quick kiss on the cheek. 'I'll be back in an hour—I have to wash my hair and it takes a while to dry. Can I bring anything?'

'Yourself,' he answered promptly.

She laughed. 'That's easy! Won't be long.'

Bending down, she pulled on her flip-flops, then padded across the grass. At the edge of the woods she looked back. He was still standing by the back door, his face a pale circle in the evening light. She called clearly, 'See you soon,' and disappeared into the trees.

An hour later Casey was tapping on Bryden's door. She was carrying a bunch of pansies, and the fluttering of her heart was more like that of an adolescent on her first date than a young woman of twenty-three.

The door opened. 'Come in,' Bryden said.

She stepped past him into a large living-room whose windows overlooked the ocean; woven Tibetan mats were scattered on the polished pine floor and Navaho hangings glowed against the stark white walls. The furniture was grouped around a stone fireplace that reached all the way to the cathedral ceiling.

Casey said spontaneously, 'What a beautiful room!' Then, rather breathlessly, 'This is the first time I've seen you formally dressed.'

His shirt was raw silk, full-sleeved with a Cossack collar, tucked into lean-fitting dark trousers; he looked much different from the tousled man on the beach. Hurriedly she added, 'I've brought you some pansies from the garden.'

He took the flowers from her, inhaling their delicate scent before putting them on the plain mahogany coffee-table. A thread of laughter in his voice, he said, 'My turn. So stand still, Casey—I assure you this is purely platonic. I just want to know what you look like.'

She stood very still as he rested his hands on her shoulders. 'You're taller,' he commented. 'High heels?'

'Yes. Turquoise sandals.'

He ran his hands lightly over her body. 'A dress...full skirt, tight at the waist, and——' his voice deepened '—a low neckline.'

'Bryden...'

He kissed the hollow at the base of her throat. 'Your heart-rate's dangerously fast,' he murmured.

'It doesn't know the meaning of the word platonic,' she whispered. 'Nor, I think, do you.'

'Not when I'm within fifty feet of you.' He straightened, his own breathing more rapid, and brushed her earrings. 'Pretty. Gold?'

'Silver and turquoise. My dress has flowers all over it, mostly turquoise, but pink and silver and green as well. My father says I look like a walking rainbow in this dress.'

His touch as delicate as a butterfly's wings, he was exploring her hair; she had piled it high on her crown. 'How do you keep it there?' he asked with genuine amusement.

'Pins and prayer. It's dreadful hair, too fine, so it's always falling all over the place. I had it cut short once, but my brothers said I looked like little Orphan Annie.'

'It feels like satin to me,' Bryden said. 'But I suppose brothers are allowed to make those sorts of remarks.'

'Do you have any brothers or sisters, Bryden?'

'No. Would you like a drink, Casey? Dry sherry or sweet?'

'Dry, please,' she replied, her chin tilting rebelliously. 'I have three brothers, two sisters, four nieces and one nephew, my parents are flourishing after thirty-two years of marriage and I live not far from Ottawa. Where do you come from, Bryden?'

As he passed her a glass of the pale gold sherry, he said evenly, 'Ottawa.'

The liquid rocked in her glass. *'Really?'*

'Really.' He held up his own glass. 'Should we drink to coincidence, Casey?'

'Indeed,' she said warmly, took a sip of sherry, and sat down on the chesterfield; inwardly she was marvelling that in the vastness that was Canada she and Bryden should come from the same city. Destiny, her heart sang. They were meant to be together. 'How long are you planning to stay here?'

'All winter.'

A little of her euphoria evaporated, for this was only September, and Canadian winters were long. 'By yourself?' she asked.

'That's the idea.'

'But you'll be living in a vacuum!'

He located the chair nearest the fire and sat down himself. 'I'll have lots to do. I have a computer with a braille keyboard, and a machine that transcribes the print in books to either a tape or braille... and I'm paying someone in Ottawa to tape the articles that would interest me in the latest journals. I'm a mathematician, you see, so most of my work is head stuff.'

Knowing she was being far too persistent, but unable to help herself, she said, 'Couldn't you do all that in Ottawa?'

'I needed to get away, Casey. Anyway, I've rented my Ottawa house out for a year.'

This conversation was like a game of draughts, she thought. One gain, two losses. 'Did you lose your sight in Ottawa?'

He nodded. 'The stupidest accident you could imagine,' he said emotionlessly. 'I worked for a think-tank, a mixture of academics, government types and freelance researchers like myself...a good friend of mine is a chemist there. He wanted my advice on some statistical computations, and while we were talking he was showing me some new equipment he'd got.' Bryden tossed back his sherry. 'There was a flaw in a distillation flask. It exploded and I got acid in my eyes. Five seconds either way and I'd have been in the clear.'

Casey could think of nothing to say; the ten feet between Bryden's chair and her own felt like a hundred miles. Or the thousand miles that would be between them by this time tomorrow, she thought wretchedly.

A log tumbled in the fire, shooting sparks up the chimney. Glad to have something to do, she got up and pushed it back with the poker. Bryden said matter-of-factly, 'Enough doom and gloom. I want to know more about you, Casey. Who's your favourite actor, do you read poetry or eat Thai food, what do you think of rock music...that'll do for a start?'

Gamely she rose to the occasion, pushing all thoughts of tomorrow from her mind, and soon she began to relax. Bryden was an imaginative cook, and privately she was impressed by his deftness in the kitchen, which was extremely well organised, with all the ingredients labelled in a raised code. He served a cream of spinach soup he had made the day before, followed by lobster in a brandy cream sauce, salad, and bottled fruit marinated in liqueur. He was an equally accomplished conversationalist, and to her delight she found they had several interests in common.

She carried the coffee into the living-room, and they sat together in front of the fire. 'That was wonderful, Bryden,' Casey said lazily. 'If you ever get tired of mathematics, you could get a job as a chef.'

He laughed. 'I don't think it would be as much fun if I had to earn my living at it... speaking of which, I've never asked you what you do, Casey.'

The moment of truth. Casey had rather hoped the subject would not come up; in a vague way she had visualised herself telling him over the phone at some future date. She said with a careful lack of emphasis, 'I'm an apprentice trainer at a guide-dog school near Ottawa.'

There were five seconds of absolute silence. Then Bryden banged his cup down on the table. Coffee slopped into the saucer. 'Guide-dogs? For the blind, you mean?'

'Yes. In eight months I'll be fully qualified.'

His features were taut with anger. 'Why didn't you tell me this before?' he demanded.

'There really wasn't the opportunity——'

'For God's sake, Casey—you should have told me as soon as you knew I was blind!'

'I suppose I should have. But you weren't——'

Again he ruthlessly interrupted her. 'No wonder you understood so well what it's like to be blind; it's your job, after all. So all along I was just an extension of your profession, wasn't I?'

'No!'

He ignored her frantic denial. 'Although if you were on holiday I wouldn't have thought you'd want to spend your time with a blind man. A busman's holiday—isn't that what they call that?'

'Bryden, stop!' she cried, her fists clenched in her lap. 'You're acting as if I were admitting to being a prostitute, for goodness' sake! All right, so I should have told you. But you were as rude as you could be when we first met, and you never did encourage any kind of personal exchange—stop treating me as though I've committed a crime.'

'I thought your interest in me was personal,' he grated. 'Stupid of me, wasn't it? It wasn't personal at all—I was just another opportunity for you to do good. Poor Bryden, I'd better take him swimming and jogging, can't have him sitting around feeling sorry for himself, that's bad psychology—what are you, a kind of Florence Nightingale for the blind? An off-duty Pollyanna?'

Casey stood up in a flurry of skirts. 'You're twisting everything,' she said furiously. 'It *wasn't* like that. I really liked you. For yourself.'

'Oh, sure,' he sneered. 'I'm just surprised you didn't put the move on me to get a guide-dog. Shouldn't you be out drumming up some business?'

'I don't have to stand here and listen to this,' Casey blazed. 'I'm leaving and I——'

In a flash of movement he grabbed her wrist, his fingers wrapping around it like a manacle. 'You're not going anywhere until we have this out,' he said grimly. 'Because I'm beginning to realise something else. This was all arranged, wasn't it? Not coincidence at all.'

'What *are* you talking about?' she said, futilely trying to tug free.

LOVE AT FIRST SIGHT

'Susan Draper is a cousin of yours. She's also a friend of my next-door neighbours in Ottawa—Jenny and Matthew Sibley. Do you know the Sibleys?'

Puzzled, Casey searched her memory. 'I know who they are, yes. I met them some time last spring, at a party at Susan's house. Although I talked to Jenny more than her husband. So what, Bryden?'

'So this *was* a set-up. I can hear it all now—you and Jenny and Susan sitting around having a cosy cup of coffee and thinking what a great chance to improve Bryden's life—get him involved with a guide-dog trainer. A pretty one into the bargain. Jenny always was thrusting stray females under my nose.'

With dangerous calm Casey said, 'Are you suggesting I deliberately came down here to get to know you?'

'That's exactly what I'm suggesting.'

'Do you realise what that implies,' she seethed. 'It implies I lied to you right from the start.'

'I never did have much faith in coincidence.'

Casey fought for breath, angrier than she had ever been in her life, and at a deeper level terrified out of her wits. Through gritted teeth she said, 'Susan phoned me and offered me her cottage. I had a week's holiday coming up and jumped at the opportunity. Your name was at no time mentioned.'

'And then you just sort of forgot to tell me that you work with blind people all year round,' Bryden jeered. 'Forgive me if I have trouble with that story, Casey.'

'It's not a story—it's the truth,' she cried. 'And please let go of my wrist, you're hurting it.'

He dropped it as if it were a poisonous snake. 'Why don't you get the hell out of here?' he snarled. 'And when you get home, tell Jenny and Susan to mind their own business. I don't need a woman any more than I need a dog.'

The world lay in ruins around her feet. Casey said flatly, 'I doubt very much if you'd get one—a dog, that is. You have to be capable of loving a guide-dog, of bonding to it...I don't think you're capable of loving anything or anyone, Bryden, you're too busy protecting yourself. You've got all your emotions safely under lock and key and that's where they're going to stay.'

'So that's what you think, is it?' With that swiftness of movement that was so unexpected, he seized her by the elbows, hauled her towards him, and kissed her with bruising strength on the lips. It was a kiss compounded of fury and frustration, and when it was over he pushed her away so violently that she staggered. 'Get out of here, Casey, before I do something I'll regret.'

'Like listen to me?' she flashed.

'Like take you to bed.'

Unconsciously she backed off a step. With raw truth she said, 'I wouldn't go.'

'Then what are you waiting for?'

What *was* she waiting for? A miracle, she thought frantically. 'Bryden, we can't part like this——'

The words burst from him. 'I was starting to trust you. To believe you represented something new in my life, something other people seem to take for granted that has always been out of my reach.' He laughed, a laugh that shivered along her nerves. 'So much for trust. So much for emotion. I was a blind fool, Casey—which has nothing to do with the fact that I can't see you.'

Grasping at straws, she said, 'I'll get Susan to write to you, to explain. Or Jenny.'

'Please don't bother. Just go, will you?'

Out of sheer desperation she made one last stand. Gathering the remnants of her dignity, she said, 'This is wrong, Bryden. What we're doing is wrong.'

He said nothing, simply standing statue-still waiting for her to leave; there were lines carved in his face like the crevices in the cliffs. Her throat raw, she whispered, 'A couple of hours ago you told me I was honest, that I wouldn't cheat or lie.'

'I was wrong.'

Casey made a tiny, pleading gesture with one hand, then let it fall helplessly to her side. 'There's nothing more to say then, is there? I—take care of yourself.'

She could not bear to say goodbye. Rounding the end of the mahogany table, the table that was like the colour of her hair, she walked steadily to the door, her heels clicking on the floor. She opened it, passed through, and closed it quietly behind her. Only then did she start to run.

The woods enveloped her. With the agility of a deer Casey raced along the path, her breath sobbing in her throat, her skirts swirling about her legs. She knew exactly what she was going to do. She was going to pack her things, clean up the cottage, and drive to the airport tonight. She would rather spend the night on a bench in the terminal than next door to Bryden. Bryden, who believed her capable of deliberate deceit. Bryden, who had not believed her when she had spoken the truth... she never wanted to see him again, she thought, almost falling up the steps of the cottage.

You never will, Casey, a mocking voice whispered in her ear.

She stumbled upstairs and threw her suitcase on the bed. But then something drew her to the window that overlooked the cedar and stone house of her next-door neighbour. She stared across the tops of the trees, which stood unmoving like sentinels around his property. The beauty of the starlit night caught at her heart.

The house was in darkness. The darkness that Bryden had chosen...

At the first opportunity after she got home, Casey phoned Susan and arranged to return the key of the cottage. She wanted it out of her possession, for it was too tangible a reminder of Bryden. Once she was rid of it she would start to forget him, she thought, as she rang Susan's doorbell. She had to. Because remembering him hurt too much.

Susan, who had long black hair and a tranquil disposition, ushered her indoors. 'The coffee-pot's on,' she said, leading Casey into the kitchen.

Jenny Sibley was sitting at the round maple table.

Casey stopped in her tracks and said levelly, 'So Bryden was right—it *was* a set-up.'

Jenny's lashes flickered. 'Hello, Casey. Good to see you again.'

Casey had only met Jenny once, but she was not in the mood for social niceties. 'You're the one who suggested to Susan that she lend me the cottage,' she accused. 'Knowing Bryden would be next door.'

Jenny tossed her head and said defiantly, 'Yes, I did—I thought you were just the person Bryden needed. So today, when Susan mentioned you were bringing the key back, I invited myself over to find out how you got along.'

Susan passed Casey a mug of coffee and said pacifically, 'Did you like the cottage, Casey?'

'Oh, I loved the cottage,' Casey replied, her eyes pools of brilliant turquoise as she threw the key on the table. 'But you might at least have told me you had a neighbour who was blind.'

LOVE AT FIRST SIGHT

'Jenny persuaded me not to. She thought it would be more natural if you didn't know. Here's the cream, Casey—do you take sugar?'

Casey, perforce, pulled out a chair and accepted the cream jug. She said with painful accuracy, 'Bryden thinks the three of us sat down just like this and plotted my holiday. All for his own good, of course.'

Jenny scowled. 'You mean he was angry?'

'You might say so.'

'But you straightened it out before you left,' Jenny said hopefully.

'We parted on the mutual understanding that we would never see each other again.'

'You didn't *like* each other?' Jenny cried.

'I didn't say that.' Casey picked up her mug with both hands so no one would see that they were trembling; meanly, she was rather pleased that Jenny was suffering a little.

'We should have been straightforward, Jenny,' Susan put in.

'But then Casey wouldn't have gone... would you, Casey?'

'Probably not!' Casey snapped. 'And we'd all have been better off.'

Susan said with genuine concern, 'You certainly don't look very rested.'

As Casey knew all too well, she looked dreadful; a lavish amount of make-up had not been able to hide the circles under her eyes. 'You fell in love with him!' Jenny exclaimed, with a lack of tact excessive even for her.

'I did *not*,' Casey retorted, and stared hard into her coffee so she would not cry.

'You're really angry with me, aren't you?' Jenny moaned. 'But I acted for the best, Casey. I was *worried* about him all alone there in the middle of nowhere and

I hoped you'd at least bring him back to Ottawa where he belongs, and I really liked you that one time I met you, so I thought *he* would too.' She bit into one of Susan's muffins, looking on the verge of tears herself; Jenny liked to be liked. 'Matthew warned me not to interfere,' she finished dolefully.

Casey gulped down her coffee, wishing Jenny had paid more attention to her husband. 'Well, it's done now,' she said. 'Over and done with,' and heard the words like a knell on her heart.

'I'll phone him and explain!'

'Please don't. He wouldn't believe you.' With an immense effort Casey managed to pull herself together. 'Your cottage is beautiful, Susan. By the way, Simon cut the grass while I was there and said he'd look after the pruning.'

'Simon's a gem,' Susan responded, patently glad to discuss someone other than Bryden, and rambling on long enough for Casey to finish her coffee.

Casey stood up. 'I can't stay, I've got the school van and several more errands to run. I'm sorry if I was rude, Jenny... and thanks again for the cottage, Susan.' With a falsely bright smile that included them both, she headed for the door. And as she drove to the school she told herself, over the rattle of dog cages in the back, that the episode at the cottage was now finished. All that remained was to forget the man with the indigo eyes who, in bringing her body to life, had also become entangled in her emotions.

He was in the past. He had no place in her future.

CHAPTER SIX

ON A cold March night, with a light snow drifting past her windows, Casey dreamed about Bryden.

She was lost in the woods behind his house at Ragged Island, snow squalls whirling round her like dervishes, ice coating the trunks of the spruce trees and weighing their branches to the ground. Slipping and stumbling, she blundered through the trees. And then she suddenly saw the house through the shifting curtains of snow; Bryden was standing at the bedroom window, his figure silhouetted in a dim yellow light. With a great surge of relief she shouted his name and staggered towards him, waving her arms. But he did not see her. Immobile, he stared over her head. As the light faded away and the house disappeared in the swirling snow, she screamed his name in terror and longing and woke to hear her voice echoing in the dark bedroom.

Casey lay still, her heart hammering. She had dreamed of Bryden many times over the long winter months, and all the dreams were variations of this one: he did not see her, or he turned away from her, and she was left alone.

Shivering, she climbed out of bed and got a drink of water. Ever since September she had fought against her memories of Bryden, forcing herself to forget him. Had anyone asked she would have said she had succeeded; that she had relegated her brief acquaintance with him to the back of her mind as one of those experiences that caused one, uncomfortably, to mature.

It was always the nights that betrayed her. She would wake aching for his kisses and the touch of his hands on her body; or she would wake, trembling, from a dream like the one she had had tonight.

Getting back into bed, Casey picked up the book on the table beside her and began to read, and eventually the words blurred in front of her eyes and she fell asleep again. The electronic beep of the alarm clock came much too soon, and her regular Monday morning chores seemed to take twice as long as usual, so she was late when she parked her car at work and scurried across the quadrangle, head down against the biting wind.

The guide-dog school was housed on an estate that once had belonged to the richest man in the country; giant oaks protected the Tudor-style house from the road, while behind it were twenty acres of fields and woods. After running inside, Casey hurried upstairs to the conference-room, shedding her coat and gloves as she went, and at least outwardly her bright-eyed daytime self was in full control.

The meeting this morning was to match students and dogs for the last class she would teach before her qualifying exams. Nothing must go wrong with this class, she thought. But she was confident that nothing would. She was looking forward to it.

She just had time to slide into her seat and smile at Douglas before the director of the school wandered into the room, his half-glasses sliding down his nose, the knot of his tie skewed under his right ear. David Canning was that anomaly, a man who never raised his voice or moved fast, yet who had the respect of all his staff and could accomplish the work of two men in a day. He sat down at the head of the table and said mildly, 'Last class before your exams, Casey. Let's hope the weather improves.'

LOVE AT FIRST SIGHT

March was at its worst, loud, blustery and importunate. The windows of the conference-room looked over the kennels, behind which were fields where dirty snow lay in the furrows and the maples stretched their frozen limbs to a leaden sky. Casey laughed. 'It can only get better,' she said.

The glasses slipped a little further on the director's long nose. 'Douglas, who have you got lined up for us?'

Douglas shuffled his papers; his eyes, grey as the sky, were lit with enthusiasm. 'Four students, two from the west coast near Vancouver, and two from the east, one from New Brunswick and one from Nova Scotia. On the basis of the interviews I've tentatively matched them with the dogs: two for Casey and two for me. Here's the sheet.' He passed one to David Canning and one to Casey.

All prospective students were interviewed in their homes; Douglas had done all the interviews for this class because Casey had been tied up training dogs and doing some publicity work around the province. Without the slightest premonition that any of the names on the list would mean anything to her, she scanned it, wondering which dogs Douglas had chosen. At least three that she had been training for the last six months were ready for a client; she ran her eyes down the page.

The name of the fourth person leaped out from the paper. Bryden Moore.

Totally unprepared, she dropped the paper. It skidded off the table on to the floor. Douglas leaned over to retrieve it, passing it to her with one of his good-natured grins. Then his brow creased with concern. 'What's wrong, Casey? Don't you feel well?'

The colour had drained from her face and her eyes were blank with shock. The sight of Bryden's name on a piece of paper, the knowledge that he would be arriving here in just over a week, had horrified her. 'I'm fine,' she said shakily, and knew she would have to tell the truth, or, at least, an edited version of the truth. 'I've met Bryden Moore. Last September. We didn't exactly hit it off.'

David Canning frowned. 'That's unfortunate. I notice, though, that he's matched with one of Douglas's dogs. Did you know about this, Douglas?'

'No,' said Douglas. He too was frowning at her.

Casey had told no one other than Jenny and Susan about the débâcle of her holiday at the cottage. She said defensively, 'You were away when I came back to work last fall, Douglas. Anyway, I never expected to see him again—why would I mention him?'

'What do you mean by not hitting it off?' Douglas asked in an unfriendly voice.

'His house was next door to Susan's cottage. We just . . . argued a lot,' she finished weakly.

'You know the rules, Casey,' David Canning said evenly. 'Absolutely no involvements of a personal nature between students and staff.'

'This happened six months ago. There's been no contact since then,' she said defensively. Nor had there been. At first every telephone call and mail delivery had caused her heart to beat faster in the hope that she would hear from Bryden; but as autumn had faded into winter and Christmas had passed she had gradually given up hope.

The director nodded. 'Fine. I'll depend on you to treat him the same as you treat the other three students. Now, Douglas, you've put Bryden Moore with Caesar and the other man with Maggie . . . what's the rationale?'

The conversation became technical, revolving as much around canine psychology as human, and Casey knew the subject of her relationship with Bryden would not be referred to again. Providing, she thought with a quiver of fear, she obeyed the rules.

She forced herself to pay attention. Her two dogs, Bess and Dan, had been allocated to the two female students, Marsha and Carole; she listened carefully, because the matching of the dogs to the students was a critical part of the process. The meeting did not last long, for David Canning put a lot of faith in the judgement of his trainers and rarely questioned their decisions. Pushing back his chair, he said, 'All four people arrive Monday afternoon, then. The usual briefing that evening in the lounge,' gave them his deceptively vague smile and ambled out of the room.

Quickly Casey stood up. But before she could follow him, Douglas said, 'I still think it's funny you didn't tell me about meeting Bryden Moore. He is blind, after all.'

'When you interviewed him, did he tell you about meeting me?' she retorted.

His eyes narrowed. 'No. So am I supposed to believe it's coincidence that he's turning up at the school where you happen to teach?'

Coincidence. She hated that word. 'I have no idea what's going on in his head,' she said shortly. 'All I know is that I have had no contact with him whatsoever since last September.'

Douglas also stood up, making rather a business of gathering his notes. 'This puts me in an awkward position,' he said gruffly. 'I'm sure you know how I feel about you, Casey. But you also know I can't do anything about that until your apprenticeship is over; it would be highly unprofessional.'

Since last September Casey had not been so sanguine that she and Douglas would drift into any kind of relationship, particularly the one she had always envisaged: comfortable, friendly, adding a dimension to her life without in any way disturbing its tenor. Bryden had killed that dream. With Bryden she had discovered the meaning of passion, and the lesson could not be unlearned.

She fumbled for words, for how did one refuse a proposal that had not been made? 'I don't know what I want, Douglas,' she said as honestly as she could. 'Can't we just leave it for now?'

'We don't have much choice, do we?' he said with a glimmer of the smile she so much liked. 'What are you up to today?'

'I thought I'd take Dan, Bess and Barney into the city and do some on-kerb obstacle work.' She was having a slight problem with Barney; she began to discuss it as they went downstairs, and the day slipped into its normal routine.

Because Casey's job was demanding, the week before the arrival of the students passed more quickly than she wished. She was delegated to meet the two students from the west, who were arriving on the same plane; Douglas connected with the flights from the maritimes later in the day. So Casey was in the student lounge at the school chatting to Carole and Hartley and trying very hard to ignore her watch when Douglas finally ushered two people in the door. Determined that none of her inner turmoil would show, Casey calmly finished her sentence and stood up.

'Marsha, this is Casey Landrigan,' Douglas said. 'Casey's our other instructor...Marsha McMillan, Casey.' Casey shook hands, murmuring commonplaces. 'And Bryden Moore...I believe you two already know each other.'

Bryden looked fit and handsome, his face tanned, his bearing relaxed; he did not look as if he had been pining for her all winter in the way she had pined for him. 'How

LOVE AT FIRST SIGHT 105

are you, Bryden?' Casey said politely. 'You certainly look well.'

Holding out his hand, he said in the deep voice she remembered so well, 'I took your advice and found someone to run with. We're training for a marathon in July.'

When she took the proffered hand in her own, she discovered instantly that nothing had changed: the strong clasp of his fingers brought back memories that had lain dormant for months. Furious with herself and very much aware of Douglas listening to every word, she said, 'I was surprised to find out you were coming here—I hadn't expected to meet you again.'

He said casually, 'Hadn't you? But you're the one who initially gave me the idea of a guide-dog.'

Remembering with embarrassing clarity the very words she had used, Casey took refuge in formality. 'Welcome to the school... Marsha, how was your journey?'

She was never to remember what she said or did for the rest of that day; somehow she got through it without singling out Bryden in any way and thereby disgracing herself. After dinner, served in the oak-panelled diningroom, they all moved back to the lounge, where in front of a cheerful log fire David Canning described the daily routine for the next month. 'Two days of harness work before you get your dogs,' he finished. 'I know you're all anxious to meet your dogs, but we have to satisfy ourselves that we've made the best match possible. Any questions?'

Inevitably there were. But by nine-thirty Casey was driving home to her apartment in the nearby village of Humbertsville, more tired than she had been for months. She was also suffering from an acute sense of anticlimax: she had met Bryden again after nearly seven months and absolutely nothing had happened.

What did you expect, Casey? she jeered. That he'd fall on you in front of everyone? That *would* finish your prospects at the school. Just be grateful he's not one of your students and stop thinking about him.

Like most advice, this was easier said than done. She watered her plants, wrote cheques out for a couple of bills and went to bed.

For the next two days Casey worked extremely hard with Marsha and Carole; then she, Douglas and the director had an early morning meeting in the conference-room. Douglas said soberly, 'There's a problem. I don't think Bryden's suited to Caesar. The man's got a lot more sensitivity of touch than I'd realised—he'd be much better with a dog like Bess.'

With a horrible sense of inevitability Casey said, 'Marsha's too heavy-handed for Bess.'

'Easy,' said David Canning. 'Switch them.'

For several minutes they discussed the consequences of this. Then the director said, 'You'll be all right with that change, Casey? You don't seem to be having any problem with Bryden.'

'I'll be fine,' she said fatalistically. She had to be. The job that she loved depended on it.

'I'll tell him,' Douglas said.

'Good. Give them the dogs this morning, let them spend an hour or so together in their rooms, and then start the training this afternoon,' David Canning said, pushing his glasses towards the bridge of his nose. Promptly they slid down again. 'I'm off then. Good luck.'

She would need it, thought Casey with grim humour as she vanished into her little office to look after the necessary paperwork. Then she went to the kennels and led Dan, a blunt-nosed Labrador retriever, to Carole's room, where she introduced the dog to her and stayed a few minutes to make sure they were comfortable together. Carole had waited a long time for this moment, and as always Casey was touched by the initial meeting of the dog and its blind human partner.

She walked back to the kennels, hunched in her jacket. Bess was a favourite of hers, and as she clipped on the white leather harness Casey said her private farewell to the dog, for from now on she must back away so that the all-important bond between Bryden and Bess developed as it should. She and the dog walked briskly to the house and down the corridor where the student rooms were located. She tapped on Bryden's door. 'It's Casey.'

'Come in.'

Bryden was sitting on the bed, dressed in grey cords and a blue sweater. Casey said, 'I've brought your dog, Bryden. Her name's Bess—she's a golden retriever who's almost two years old. She'll need firm handling, because she can be strong-willed, but on the other hand she also needs a lot of affection because she's very sensitive... I'm sure you'll get along well together.'

When she led the dog over to him Bess sniffed his hand, her tail wagging. Bryden rubbed the dog's forehead, his face set. 'Thank you,' he said.

Clearly he wanted her to be gone. Casey said with a serenity she was far from feeling, 'Her coat is beautiful, all shades of gold and chestnut... after lunch, we'll go out for the first walk.'

She left his bedroom and marched to the grooming-room, where she checked some supplies, making rather a lot of noise about it. This month could be a definite test of character; if she could maintain her equanimity with Bryden, she could work with anyone.

Her equanimity was put to the test that very afternoon. The first walk was along the pavement from the school to the village and back again. Casey took Bryden and Bess first, adjusting Bryden's gloved hand on the harness, explaining to him how the dog had been trained to walk in a straight line. As soon as she had finished, he said, 'Is there anyone else here?'

'Douglas and Marsha are just ahead of us.'

The wind ruffled his hair. 'When will I get the chance to talk to you alone?'

'You won't.'

'A month is a long time, Casey. We'll be alone sooner or later.'

'This isn't Ragged Island, Bryden,' she said steadily. 'Here, I'm your instructor, and any conversation between us relates only to the course.'

'We'll see about that,' he said in a steel voice. 'Now, where are we going?'

Casey bit her lip. What had he wanted to say to her? And why did he have to be alone with her to say it? 'We'll walk to the village,' she said, and carefully went over the commands he might need.

Casey's character was tested more than once during the next week. But she was calm, friendly and supportive with both Carole and Bryden as she took them and the dogs through their paces in straight-line walks, right and left turns, kerb work and obstacles; her voice, she was proud to notice, was no different whether she was with one or the other.

When they worked together Bryden listened carefully to everything she said and rarely forgot any of her instructions, and he was unfailingly polite. There was only one area in which Casey could fault his efficiency: at least twice a day she would have to remind him to praise Bess, to pat her and tell her she was a good dog. He would immediately do so. But it was at best a mechanical performance; his heart was not in it.

LOVE AT FIRST SIGHT

Casey could not help remembering the words she had flung at him about love and bonding, words that were proving more accurate than she cared for. However, she did not yet share her concern with Douglas, for there were three weeks left in the course and most problems surfaced in the early days. Neither did she share with him or with anyone else how much it was costing her in terms of emotional energy to spend so much time with Bryden. He, apart from that initial outburst, did not seem the slightest bit affected by her.

That this was not the case Casey found out one crisp morning the second week of the course, when a free run was scheduled. To the right of the kennels was a fenced paddock; she and Bryden went there alone half an hour before lunch. She described the latch on the gate and waited until he had locked it behind them. Then she said matter-of-factly, 'There's no one else here, so there aren't any distractions for Bess. Next time we have a free run Carole and Dan will be here, too, which will make it much more of a challenge. The idea is——'

Bryden interrupted her. 'Are you telling me we're alone?'

'Yes. But——'

Again he ruthlessly overrode her. 'No one in sight?'

'That's correct,' she said frostily. 'It's best for the dog to——'

'The dog can wait. Do you realise this is the first time in ten days that you and I have had five minutes to ourselves?'

She did. All too much. She said disagreeably, 'The object of this course is not for you and me to exchange pleasantries.'

'Are you engaged to Douglas?'

Her jaw dropped. 'No!'

'Then what the hell's wrong with you? Ever since I came here you've been acting as if we'd never met before. Let alone nearly made love in the middle of a dirt road... you hadn't forgotten that, had you, Casey?'

'That's in the past, Bryden. *You* were the one who kicked me out of your house—or have you forgotten that?'

'I made a mistake,' he said stiffly.

'And it took you six months to realise it?'

'No. A great deal less than six months.'

'Too bad you hadn't bothered to let me know.'

'I applied to the school instead.'

It was not the answer she had wanted. Casey cast caution to the wind. 'So are you here to get a guide-dog or to pester me? Because if it's to pester me, you've come to the wrong place!'

'To get a dog, of course—I need to be more independent. But I also had to see you again, Casey. It's been hell the last ten days—I can't even stop dreaming about you, for God's sake!'

He looked more angry than loving. But he had grabbed her sleeve, and she had no idea what he might do next. Horribly aware that the old Tudor house had at least twelve windows overlooking the paddock, and that it would only take David Canning looking through one of them to ruin her reputation, Casey took a deep breath and said with icy calm, 'Let's get something straight right now, Bryden. My job's at stake here. There's one inviolable rule at this school—no personal involvement of any kind between students and staff. I'm almost at the end of my apprenticeship... three years of hard work. I'm not going to jeopardise that just so you can kiss me in the paddock.'

His jaw taut, Bryden demanded, 'Is that why you've been treating me like a complete stranger?'

'You are a stranger to me, Bryden... September was a long time ago and is better forgotten. But you're also one of my students, and in case you hadn't noticed I've been passing on a lot of hard-earned knowledge so that you and Bess will be a successful unit. That's my job. That's what I'm paid to do.'

'So to you I'm one half of a unit? No different from Carole or Marsha or Hartley?'

'That's right, Bryden,' she said, and knew that she was lying.

'I see.' He let go of her arm, his face an inscrutable mask. 'Then we'd better get on with this free run, hadn't we? As that's the only reason we're here.'

By a monumental effort of will Casey voiced none of the questions beating in her brain. Are you sorry you kicked me out? Do you still believe the whole visit was a set-up and that I wilfully deceived you? Instead she said in a colourless voice, 'We use a different collar for free runs, one with two bells on it so you can hear where Bess is. You call her back with this whistle.'

The lesson proceeded. Bess had a marvellous run, and Bryden, on the third attempt, coaxed her back to him. But afterwards, when they went to the dining-room for lunch, Bess was the only one who looked happy.

Even Bess did not look happy the following day. The lesson was on near and far traffic; Douglas, driving his car, purposely set up situations in which Bess, trained to step out into the road at Bryden's command, was now required to disobey in order to protect her master. It was a difficult lesson; Bryden was tense and Bess balky. To make matters worse, the weather seemed in conspiracy against them, the wind raw and a fine, freezing rain stinging their faces.

Eventually Casey said, 'OK, let's call it quits. This session is hard on the dog, Bryden, because she has to go against the rules. So she needs lots of praise. She can feel your tension too—try and relax.'

Bryden blew on his cold fingers rather than bending down to pat the dog. Casey sighed. She was increasingly afraid that she and Douglas had not made the right match after all, for Bess needed far more affection than Bryden seemed capable of giving. You can't legislate love, she thought unhappily, walking twenty feet behind Bryden as he and Bess started back along the suburban street towards the van.

Because the ground was uneven, the paved driveways that led from the pavement to the neat brick houses were on a steep upward slope; as Bryden approached one of these driveways, a long blue car came rolling down it in neutral, its engine silent. Bess stopped, sitting down.

'Forward!' Bryden ordered.

The car was no more than four feet away from them. Bess stayed where she was. 'Hup-up!' Bryden said even more sharply, giving an exaggerated hand signal, his whole bearing fraught with tamped-down anger.

The engine roared into life. With a screech of tyres the car pulled out on to the street. Bryden's head swung to the left to follow the sound, the colour seeping from his face. Casey said quietly from behind him, 'Bess stopped because she saw the car coming. Otherwise you would have walked right in front of it.' And then she waited to see what he would do.

He closed his eyes, his shoulders sagging. 'That car was for real—nothing to do with Douglas?'

'Douglas went back to the van five minutes ago.'

'I'd have gone right into it.'

She said nothing. His face still very pale under his wind-tangled hair, his red ski-jacket a bright patch of colour, Bryden knelt down on the wet pavement. Awkwardly he put his arms around the dog. 'Thanks, Bess,' he said huskily. 'Good girl... good dog.'

Bess wagged her tail and licked his nose. For a moment Bryden rested his cheek on her silky hair, his face convulsed with an emotion so strong that Casey averted her eyes. Then he stood up, picked up the harness handle again and said, 'Forward, Bess.'

A lump in her throat, her mind full of questions, Casey trudged along behind them to the van, where Carole was waiting her turn. When they eventually arrived back at the school everyone was tired. The students and dogs headed for the grooming-room; Casey got herself a coffee in the kitchen, drank it staring out of the window at the stripped oak trees, then walked down the hall to the grooming-room herself to see how the feed was holding out. The room was not, as she had expected, empty; Bryden was sitting on one of the wide benches, Bess beside him. He was brushing the long golden hair on the dog's flanks, an expression on his face Casey had never seen before.

'I'm sorry—I didn't realise you were still here,' she said.

'Casey?'

The expression was gone, the face closed. 'Bryden,' she said, 'did you ever have a dog before?'

As he got to his feet Bess jumped to the floor, shaking herself. 'What business is that of yours?' he said curtly.

'I wondered. That's all.'

He picked up the brush and comb. 'I had a puppy once.'

Casey stared at him, all her senses alert. 'What happened to it?' she said softly.

'My father thought I was growing too fond of it. He had it destroyed.'

In a shocked whisper she said, 'That's terrible, Bryden!'

'The puppy was really the housekeeper's. She smuggled it into the house and I used to play with it after school.'

'I don't understand how he could do that!'

'He believed in all the Ernest Hemingway stuff, the macho virtues, the strong silent men who had no use for women or the gentler emotions. Animals, according to my father, were to be hunted. Not kept as pets.'

'It must have broken your heart,' Casey said, entirely without hyperbole.

His mouth thinned. 'I was only six, but I already knew better than to cry in front of my father.'

It was the kind of story that revealed far more than it described. Casey rested her hand on his sleeve. 'Is that why it's been so difficult for you to give Bess any affection?'

He shrugged free and said irritably, 'Quit psychoanalysing me, Casey.'

She was sure she was right. She was also sure she would get no more confidences out of Bryden today. 'It's nearly suppertime,' she said casually. 'So I'd better check the feed in case I have to get more from the kennels. Excuse me, will you?'

As she turned away he put the brush and comb in his locker and left the room. Gazing at the heaped sacks of dog food, her face very thoughtful, Casey knew she had been given her first real clue to the mystery that was Bryden.

CHAPTER SEVEN

BECAUSE the weather was still bitterly cold the following day, Douglas decreed they would do some inside work in one of the Ottawa malls. Casey took Carole and Dan first, putting in an hour and a half's intensive work with them, finishing with a short bus ride back to the van; then she said cheerfully, 'Your turn, Bryden. Got your gloves? You're going to need them.'

They left the van, which was parked on a quiet sidestreet, and turned on to Rideau Street. Pneumatic drills clattered from a construction site; buses roared around the corners; horns blared and pedestrians jockeyed for position at the traffic lights. Bryden, Casey was pleased to notice, took his time at the lights, listening carefully to the direction of the traffic before ordering Bess to leave the kerb. As they threaded their way along the wide pavement, she kept up a soft-voiced commentary. 'Bess took you to the left there to avoid a display rack... she's hesitating because three women are blocking the way... the door straight ahead of you opens towards you...'

A bunch of teenagers, their ghetto blaster at full volume, jostled Bryden as he passed through the doors into the mall. The air smelled warm and stale. Muzak assailed their ears. They negotiated two flights of steps; they went down on a crowded escalator; they went into a shop so Bryden could purchase some razor-blades; and through all this noise and confusion Bess threaded her way, head up, ears pricked.

When he had walked out of the shop, Bryden stood for a moment, a tall, commanding figure in his ski-jacket and cords. 'I need to go left to find the stairs again, don't I, Casey?'

'Correct! You've got a fabulous sense of direction,' she teased. 'I often get lost in here.'

But he was not listening. A strange expression on his face, he said, 'And then Bess will show me where the first stair is, and she'll find the exit doors, and when the bus arrives she'll guide me up the steps...'

Puzzled, Casey said, 'That's what she's been trained to do.'

'Until yesterday I'd been fighting this whole process,' Bryden said with subdued violence. 'Fighting Bess—and indirectly, you, I suppose. But do you know what I'm beginning to realise, Casey? I can go anywhere with her. Into shops and on buses and across city streets...I don't have to walk slowly with a white cane held out in front of me, and ask for help at every turn.'

Intent on their own business, supremely incurious, the shoppers and businessmen eddied around Casey and Bryden, granting them as much privacy as if they had been standing alone in a field. Casey said fairly, 'Sometimes you'll have to ask for help. And you always have to know where you're going.'

'Just think of what I'm gaining, though. Freedom, Casey. Independence.' His voice changed. 'Give me your hand.'

Even if David Canning had been standing right beside her, Casey could not have refused. Bryden took her fingers and squeezed them between his own; the contact seared every nerve in her body. 'I have you to thank,' he said. 'I know how hard you've worked the last two weeks—you put everything you've got into your job, don't you?'

His intensity had brought tears to her eyes. Trying to be flip, she gulped, 'So does Bess.'

His smile was twisted. 'I promise that in a minute I will pat Bess and tell her she's the most wonderful dog in the world. But right now it's your turn.' He leaned forward and kissed her on the cheek; and, when he did so, felt the wetness of her tears. He said fiercely, 'I didn't mean to make you cry...don't cry, please.'

She spoke a small part of the truth. 'I've been afraid for you and Bess. Afraid you weren't going to make it.'

'You don't need to be. Not any more.' His lips brushed her cheek again. 'Thank you, Casey.'

The floor of the mall rocked and settled. 'You're welcome,' Casey mumbled.

When Bryden stooped to praise Bess, just as if nothing had happened, Casey had to thrust her hands into her pockets so she would not lace her fingers in his thick dark hair. It was just as well that Douglas was nowhere in sight. Her scarlet face would be no advertisement for a cool, detached instructor.

'Shall we go?' Bryden suggested, his smile crackling with vitality. 'Forward, Bess.'

The trip on the bus was accomplished without incident, and Douglas was already waiting for them in the van. Perhaps inwardly Casey had worried that Bryden might repeat his gesture in some way, and thereby cause her embarrassment. She need not have worried. He did not then, nor did he as the April days passed one by one. Instead he worked with a ferocious concentration that she could only applaud, as if determined to learn everything he could; and day by day the bond between him and the golden-haired dog grew stronger.

Some kind of barrier deep within him had fallen, Casey knew; and acknowledged with a rather desperate attempt at humour that she had never thought to find herself jealous of a dog. At a much deeper level of her psyche she was beginning to acknowledge something else: the nightmare prospect that Bryden, at the end of the course, would disappear from her life as thoroughly as he had eight months ago.

She took what comfort she could from the fact that both David Canning and Douglas were well pleased with her work and had certainly observed nothing untoward between her and Bryden. What, after all, had there been to observe? A brief clash in the paddock, when she had told Bryden he meant nothing to her. A couple of kisses that had by no means been impassioned and that she now construed as gratitude.

It did not seem much for nineteen days.

On the last weekend of the course it was Casey's custom to take her students to her parents' home for Sunday afternoon tea, where the warm welcome Bill and Marion Landrigan always extended helped to dispel the homesickness that had often accumulated by the final few days. This time Casey was careful to offer the invitation when both Carole and Bryden were there. However, Carole had other plans, that included Hartley. One romance at the school was flourishing, thought Casey, hesitating a fraction too long before saying, 'Bryden? Will you come?'

His face had that shuttered look that she so dreaded. 'Thank you, I'd like to,' he said in a precise voice that masked any trace of feeling.

'We'll leave around one-thirty,' she said quickly, and fled from the room, not sure whether to be appalled or ecstatic at the prospect of an afternoon in his company. But when the time came she found herself dressing with unusual care in a full skirt of forest-green, an off-white mohair sweater and gleaming leather boots, her hair in a thick braid, her make-up impeccable. The final touch was a fringed green scarf flung artistically over one shoulder. Unfortunately she could do nothing about the state of her nerves.

Bryden was waiting for her outside the school. She drew up beside him, wondering with a sickening lurch of her heart what she was going to talk about all the way to her parents'. It was a forty-minute drive. She had to say something. Her mind a blank, she reached over to open the door.

Bryden solved the problem for her. Once he was settled, with Bess at his feet, he said, 'I don't know why you're doing this.'

He had not bothered with any more conventional greeting. Casey drove on to the highway, heading south. 'Because my parents invited you for tea,' she said.

'As they invite all your students.'

'That's right.'

'Nothing special about me,' he persisted.

'You didn't have to come! But now that you're committed, I hope you'll at least be polite.'

'Oh, my manners are excellent,' he replied ironically.

They then drove in silence for twenty minutes, a silence that seemed to beat against Casey's ears. Bryden was the one to break it. 'Where are we?' he asked.

'On a country road east of the school.'

'Would you mind pulling over for a minute?'

She glanced at him, caught by something in his tone. 'Are you all right?'

'Pull over, Casey.'

She did so; this was a back road and there was little traffic. As the car came to a stop, Bryden reached over, turned off the ignition and pocketed the key. She gave a squawk of indignation. 'What are you doing?'

He favoured her with the smile that had always had the power to weaken her knees and said, 'Is Douglas following in a ten-ton tank with all the guns trained on us?'

'He is not.'

'Is Mr Canning peering at us through the shrubbery?'

'Mr Canning spends every Sunday in the bosom of his family,' Casey replied. 'Bryden, what are you up to?'

'You still wear the same perfume,' he said.

Although she had not really expected he would remember, she had chosen the perfume on purpose. Wondering if she had been altogether wise, she said severely, 'Give me the key.'

'When I'm ready,' he replied with another lazy smile. 'There's something I want to find out first.'

Reprehensibly, part of her was enjoying this. 'We'll be late for tea,' she said.

'I'll leave you to explain why.' Then he put his arms around her in a comprehensive hug, tilted her chin with one hand and kissed her with great thoroughness and very little regard for her lipstick. His quickened breathing fanning her cheek, he said, 'I've been wanting to do that for three weeks.' Releasing her, he sat back, looking undeniably pleased with himself.

Feeling as though the whole world had tilted on its axis, Casey said faintly, 'You've got lipstick on your chin.'

'Unless you want your mother to know you've been misbehaving with a student—and on the Sabbath, no less—you'd better wipe it off.'

She undid her shoulder-bag and extract a Kleenex, with which she scrubbed at his mouth. 'You shouldn't have kissed me,' she muttered, secretly admiring the sculpted line of his upper lip.

'I wanted to find out if you're as indifferent to me as you keep saying you are.' He extracted the key from his pocket and held it out to her, his teeth gleaming as he smiled at her. 'Shouldn't we go? I wouldn't want to disappoint your parents.'

Casey jammed the key in the ignition and checked the rear-view mirror, seeing the bright-eyed reflection and overly pink cheeks of a woman who had been far from indifferent. 'My father has eyes in the back of his head,' she said despairingly, pulling out into the road.

'I promise I shall not ravish your lily-white body on the hall carpet.'

Struck dumb, Casey glared at the highway, her hands gripping the wheel as if she were steering a very small boat in a very rough sea, and conspicously said nothing.

'Would you like me to?' Bryden asked.

'That's a ridiculous and totally unfair question!'

'Because it might jeopardise your job?'

'Nothing to do with my job,' she fumed.

'Good.'

'All right then,' Casey suddenly snorted. 'Now it's my turn to ask a question. Do you still think I deliberately lied to you last September, Bryden? That I went to the cottage knowing you were blind and set out to get your attention? Because if you do, I'm not particularly flattered by any suggestions you make concerning the hall carpet!'

For a long moment he was silent. She stole a glance at his profile, remembering with a wrench at her heartstrings the stark granite cliffs that edged the beach. Finally he said, 'No. I think Jenny was behind it. But not you.'

Discovering she was still furiously angry, Casey snapped, 'When did you come to the conclusion that I'd been telling the truth?'

'Oh, the day after you left the cottage,' he said bitterly.

She remembered all the times she had hoped for a phone call or a letter, and with answering bitterness cried, 'Why did you never *tell* me that?'

'I couldn't at the time—I wasn't ready. Later, of course, I wasn't sure it would matter to you.'

'You called me a liar, and now you say it wouldn't matter to me?'

'Casey, you told me in the paddock that I was no more to you than Hartley. I believed you. Was I then supposed to burst into an impassioned apology for something that happened last autumn?'

She did not want to talk about the paddock. Breathing hard, she said, 'I still don't understand why you didn't tell me last September. Did I mean so little to you that you couldn't even be bothered?'

In a low voice he said, 'You meant far too much to me... I couldn't handle it.'

Meant, he had said. Past tense. She slowed down to turn left to the village where her parents lived and said flatly, 'We're nearly there.'

Bryden ignored her. 'I was furious that night when I found out how you earned your living. Because it meant that all week you hadn't been interested in me for myself—I was just an extension of your job.'

'I seem to remember that line,' Casey said, and heard the hurt underlying her words.

'So the next logical step was that you'd set me up. It took me well over twenty-four hours to cool down and realise that the Casey I knew would not have lied to me. By which time you were gone.'

'You knew where I was!'

'I wasn't ready to get in touch with you, Casey! I don't expect you to understand that... I'm not sure I understood it myself.'

'I told you more than once that your blindness is irrelevant,' she said, so quietly that he had to strain to hear her over the sound of the engine.

'I remembered that, too,' he said harshly.

'I *don't* understand.'

He took a deep breath. 'Casey, I'm sorry if I caused you pain.'

It was something; but it was not enough. Not knowing what to say, Casey kept silent.

Bryden's face was bleak; he was absently rubbing Bess's head. 'When I arrived here, I felt as though you'd changed completely. You were the instructor and I was the student—you made that very clear. Serves me right, I guess, after six months of silence.' He gave her a forced and rueful smile. 'Now that the course is nearly over I understand the need for those roles, and I certainly don't want to jeopardise your job in any way, that would be totally wrong of me.' Briefly he rested his hand on hers. 'We're not stuck with them forever.'

As Casey well knew, it was the policy of the school to provide continued supervision and support after the course. 'We're stuck with those roles for at least eight years,' she said wildly. 'I go back to Ragged Island with you next week. In three months I visit you again, and then every year until Bess retires.'

'I swear on a stack of Bibles this discussion will resume before eight years are up,' Bryden said grimly.

Wishing her job had never been invented, Casey said with an air of fatality, 'The driveway's just around the corner.'

'Then slow down. Because there's one more thing I want to say to you.'

The driveway was a long curve between tall trees. Casey stopped beneath the bare branches of the old maple she used to climb as a child; she could see the blue wood-smoke rising from the chimney of the ranch-style bungalow her parents had lived in for thirty years.

Bryden's fist was banging repetitively on his knee, the knuckles white with strain. 'You say my blindness is irrelevant. I want you to think that over very carefully, Casey. Because, apart from any of the other implications, when you make love for the first time you might want to do so with a man who can at least see you.'

She put her foot on the accelerator, and the other trees, mountain ash and birch, began to slide past the car windows. She said without finesse, 'When I make love for the first time, Bryden, I want to do so with the man whom I love more than anyone else in the world. Any other considerations are, if you'll pardon my using the word again, irrelevant... ah, there's my mother. I bet she's checking to see how many of the bulbs survived the winter.' Winding down the window, Casey called, 'Hi, Mum!'

She jumped out of the car and hugged her mother, then led her round to meet Bryden. He was wearing his red ski-jacket and a lambswool sweater the same colour as his eyes, and looked, she thought, quite devastatingly handsome. Which did not mean he was the man she loved more than anyone else in the world. Did it?

Her manner a little over-animated, she made the introductions and explained Carole's absence. Her mother led Bryden over to admire the early crocuses; she had the gift of putting strangers immediately at ease. She looked wonderful, Casey thought affectionately, slim and vibrant, her cap of pewter-coloured hair shining in the sun. Then Casey's father, Bill Landrigan, joined them, his bluff welcome just as sincere. He insisted on taking Bryden on a tour of his beloved greenhouse, where he raised orchids and was attempting to create new strains of primroses and irises. 'I had thirty-five years in the classroom,' he said to Bryden, guiding his hand to the iridescent pink petals of a moth orchid. 'Isn't she a beauty? A grand total of one thousand, one hundred and forty-three eight-year-olds. Not to mention schoolboards and unions, which generally were far more trouble than the children. Do you wonder that I enjoy the peace and quiet of my greenhouse?'

'It smells like a tropical rain forest,' Bryden commented.

It was exactly the right reply. Bill approved of Bryden, Casey could see. 'I've installed a very complicated system of pumps—my next project is a fountain. *Ascocenda* loves running water.'

'And they all love the dirt floor,' Marion said with fastidious distaste.

Bill grinned. 'Bryden, the closest Marion and I have ever come to a divorce was when she decided to houseclean here one day—threw out all the seeds from my first-generation crosses of *Primula beesiana* and *Primula bulleyana*.'

'All I did was dust the counter,' Marion protested.

Bill gave his wife a hug. 'I must love you, my darling, if we survived that. The parts for the fountain should arrive on Tuesday, Casey.'

Casey had been watching Bryden. There were frown lines between his eyes, which she was almost certain were a reaction to her father's casually spoken words of love. She said lightly, 'You'll be serving dinner in here that night, Mum.'

'I won't be serving dinner at all—it's a class night,' her mother replied with rather touching pride.

'Mum's started a degree in philosophy at Carleton University,' Casey explained. Carleton was in Ottawa.

Marion said a little defensively, for this was a new venture for her, 'One day, after Bill had counted the number of students he'd had, *I* added up how many apple pies I'd made in the last thirty years. So I decided it was time for a change.'

'Plato would tend to put apple pies in their proper perspective,' Bryden said drily. 'Have you ever, for instance, baked the Ideal Apple Pie?'

Marion laughed, tucking his arm in hers. 'I have not. However, this morning I did make a chocolate cake that approaches perfection.' She smiled up at him, and, a little reluctantly, he smiled as well.

Casey, unaware that her heart was in her eyes, watched them leave the greenhouse. Bill said gruffly, 'I always knew sooner or later you'd fall in love.'

She gaped at him. 'I haven't!'

'I suppose you're worrying because you've only known him three weeks. I was in love with your mother five minutes after I met her.'

'I met Bryden once before,' Casey confessed, gazing absorbedly at the tawny petals of a slipper orchid. 'Last September when I was on holiday in Nova Scotia.'

'You didn't tell us.'

'He kicked me out.'

Her father laughed heartlessly. 'Good for him. You've always been able to wrap all your dates around your little finger, I'm glad to hear he's different.'

He was different in more ways than that. But there were limits to what she could share with her father. 'He's a loner who's scared of his own emotions,' she said.

Bill's gaze was both shrewd and kind. 'I would suspect that he has them, though. Come on, I'll pour you a sherry.'

Shortly afterwards Casey's sister Anne arrived complete with husband and two children. Anne wanted to go for a walk along the trail behind the house to look for wild violets, so eventually they all set off, Bryden letting Bess run free as he fell into conversation with Casey's father. Anne said softly, 'That has to be the best-looking man I've seen off a movie screen. And Dad likes him, you can tell.'

Casey had to agree with both these statements. Anne added provocatively, 'You like him, too.'

Anne, nine years older than Casey, blonde-haired and rather plump, was happily married and wanted the same fate for Casey. 'He's a student,' Casey said repressively.

'If the children weren't in earshot I'd say something very rude. Has he fallen in love with you yet?'

'No—and he has no intention of doing so!'

'Interesting... I'm going to test him out,' Anne said, and fell back before Casey could protest.

Casey's niece Leeanne seized her hand. 'Where are the violets, I can't find any, d'you think we're too early?'

The violets were located, tiny purple faces among the dead beech leaves, and Bess was restrained from tramping on them. Tea was served when they got back to the house; Casey's father and Anne's husband Jim got into their usual political discussion, one in which Bryden more than held his own, and the children got chocolate cake all over their faces. A normal Sunday afternoon, thought Casey, then knew she was guilty of self-deception. How could it be normal when Bryden was there?

She frowned, hoping he was enjoying himself. His manners were indeed excellent, and he was by no means standing on the sidelines; yet she, who knew him well, was certain he was holding something back. He was not truly a part of the gathering, for all his seeming participation. He was...she sought for the right word. Watchful.

Anne whispered in her ear, 'You can't take your eyes off the man.'

Casey pulled a face and went to start on the dishes. Anne and Jim left. Casey finished cleaning up the kitchen, then said without enthusiasm, 'We should get back, Bryden.'

He stood up and in his deep voice said to Bill and Marion, 'Having met Casey's parents, I understand more clearly her qualities of honesty, warmth and kindness... thank you both for your hospitality.'

Marion gave him a spontaneous hug, Bill shook his hand, and Casey blushed. Avoiding her father's eyes, she kissed both her parents and got out of the house as quickly as she could. As she started down the road, Bess fell asleep at Bryden's feet and Bryden seemed disinclined to talk, so she concentrated on her driving and tried not to think about the man at her side.

She managed this for maybe five minutes. Then she stole a glance at him, wondering what he was thinking about. His eyes were closed, his chin set. She blurted, 'Didn't you like my father and mother, Bryden?'

'They're wonderful people—you're very fortunate.'

He had bitten off the words as if they hurt. She ventured, 'You haven't told me much about your parents.'

'One reason I left Ottawa was because my mother was weeping and howling all over me, while my father thought I was making far too much fuss over a minor inconvenience like blindness.'

Casey digested this in silence. 'I know I'm fortunate—I grew up surrounded by love. Taking it for granted, perhaps.'

'Don't. It's rarer than you think.'

He leaned his head against the back of the seat. No more revelations about his parents, she thought, absently counting the crows flying across a field of winter rye, and giving an unconsciously heavy sigh. Seven crows a secret. Bryden was full of those...

Almost as though she had spoken aloud, Bryden said, 'Your sister Anne got a great deal of information out of me—I'm not quite sure how. She's afraid you'll marry Douglas. Douglas, according to her, is nice, but dull.'

'She thinks you're better-looking,' Casey rejoined with a lightness she did not feel.

He raised one brow. 'She extended an open invitation for me to visit her and Jim.'

'She's been throwing me at various men since I was eighteen, Bryden.'

'But none of them took. I wonder why.'

'That will give you something to think about when you get back to the school,' Casey said waspishly.

'So it will... I didn't tell Anne everything, though.'

After a brief struggle Casey's curiosity got the better of her. 'What didn't you tell her?'

'She was extolling your virtues, among which honesty figured large. I didn't tell her that I thought you'd been dishonest with me at least once, Casey—that day in the paddock.'

His voice was casual. But the skin was tight across his knuckles, and she sensed that her reply was of overwhelming importance to him. With startling clarity she suddenly knew she wanted this man, wanted him in ways she had never wanted a man before. Ways perhaps beyond her imagining. The ways of intimacy, she thought soberly. She did not understand his defensiveness and his silences any more than she understood his fear of emotion; yet surely the very least gift she could give him was that of honesty?

She said calmly, 'I wasn't telling the truth that day—I suppose I was trying to protect myself.'

Something in his face relaxed. 'So I'm more to you than Hartley, and I'm not just half a unit.'

Her words must have rankled. 'Right,' she said drily.

Stretching his long limbs, he drawled, 'I think it would now be advisable for us to go back to our roles as student and instructor. In the interests of professional ethics.'

Casey had wanted him to pursue that conversation in the paddock, to precipitate her into admitting the way she felt about him. Her emotions in a turmoil, she said nastily, 'Only eight more years, Bryden,' and snapped her mouth shut.

CHAPTER EIGHT

THE last four days of the course flew by. Because of the constraints of geography, it had been decided Casey would fly to Halifax with Bryden on Friday, spend a couple of days with him, and then drive to Marsha's home in New Brunswick; Douglas would look after Hartley and Carole, who lived within a hundred miles of each other on the west coast.

There was the usual Thursday evening party, which came to an end around nine-thirty. Douglas and Casey left the school together, walking across the pavement in the cool, starlit darkness to Casey's car. As she threw her bag on the back seat, Douglas said, 'I was discussing your appraisal today with David—we're both very pleased with your participation in this course, Casey. I'm particularly pleased about the way you've worked with Bryden—there was some concern about that at the beginning of the class, if you remember.'

She could scarcely have forgotten. 'That's good,' she said lightly. 'I'm wiped, though, are you?'

Douglas ignored this undoubted red herring and ploughed on. 'Any worries I might have had on my own account have certainly been allayed. I can see there's nothing of a personal nature between you and Bryden.'

Casey stared at him in silence. It was not the moment to realise, with absolute certainty, that she was in love with Bryden. Had been, probably, since the first time she had seen him, stretched out half naked on the grass. Trying to subdue the mingling of terror and exaltation that this knowledge aroused in her, wishing Douglas were a million miles away, she stammered, 'I-I've got to go home, Douglas, I haven't packed yet and yesterday's dishes are still in the sink.'

Douglas, normally the most sensitive of men, was frowning to himself. 'I will admit I'd rather I was travelling with Bryden tomorrow—no aspersions on you, of course, Casey,' he added hastily. 'I have total trust in you.'

Which was more than she had in herself. Guilt now adding itself to all her other emotions, she edged the car door open and said with a sprightliness that grated on her nerves. 'You just don't want to chaperone Carole and Hartley.'

'Nice to see them happy together,' Douglas said with a meaningful look. 'By the way, David and I were also discussing some future scheduling today. Looks as if I'll be doing interviews in Nova Scotia in July, so I can look after the three-month visit with Bryden.'

He was smiling at her indulgently, and obviously expected her to be delighted with this decision. Casey fought down a wave of fury, said crisply, 'As his instructor I would have thought I'd have been included in that decision, Douglas,' and got in the car. 'See you in the morning. Goodnight.'

She backed out, leaving him standing with a perplexed frown on his face, and drove home; and all her emotions drove home with her. Not until she was unlocking the door of her apartment did she acknowledge that she should have waited a week to discover she was in love with Bryden: her timing was atrocious. For the next two days her role was to be his instructor and the official representative of the school. For some reason it seemed more important to preserve this role when she would be a thousand miles from the school than when she was right under David Canning's nose.

She must, therefore, maintain a dignified distance between herself and Bryden and not even let the word love into her mind.

How? whispered a little voice in her ear.

I don't know, she admitted in despair, and began to wash the dishes.

Casey was very much on her dignity when she loaded Bryden's suitcase in her car the next morning. She was wearing her green skirt, the fringed scarf now elegantly draped in the neckline of a brown leather jacket. Her make-up was generous, in an effort to hide the fact that she had had almost no sleep the night before, and her manner was as impersonal as Douglas could have wished.

Bryden, in a grey suit and navy overcoat, looked both sophisticated and handsome, and appeared not to notice any change in her. Bess was groomed to perfection.

They drove to the airport, making only desultory conversation, walked from the car park to the terminal, and crossed the floor to the ticket counters. They attracted quite a lot of attention, Casey noticed. Bryden was the kind of man who would always draw a second glance, particularly from the female half of the population, while the sleek golden dog at his left side evoked everything from interest to outright sentimentality. That she, on his other side, looked composed and beautiful would have surprised her; make-up, she would have thought, could accomplish only so much, and the prospect of flying, as always, terrified her.

Their seats were in the first-class section against the bulkhead so there would be room for Bess. 'Why don't you take the window-seat?' Bryden suggested.

'No, thanks,' Casey answered hastily. Watching the ground tilt and the clouds envelop her made her feel worse, not better.

The stewardess, who was obviously smitten with Bryden, offered them drinks. Casey shook her head, for she had learned long ago that alcohol did nothing to settle her nerves when she was thirty thousand feet above the ground; Bryden was served a Scotch and water.

The other passengers filtered on. The door was closed. The plane taxied away from the terminal, and while it was awaiting clearance from the tower the stewardess went through the safety regulations. Casey hated this routine almost as much as she hated take-off, for phrases like 'should an incident occur in flight' had always seemed to her the ultimate in euphemism.

They manoeuvred on to the runway, the engines roared into full power and the plane surged forward. Casey closed her eyes and gripped the armrests.

Bryden said casually, 'What is it, a two-hour flight to Halifax, Casey?'

But Casey was concentrating on willing the plane up into the air, and did not answer. He turned his head, touched her lightly on the wrist, and felt the tendons as taut as if she were physically trying to lift the plane herself. 'Casey?' he said sharply. 'What's wrong?'

In a muffled voice she said, 'I'm a little frightened of flying. Ignore me.'

The wheels were no longer bouncing on the tarmac. Tilted at an angle, the aircraft rose into the sky. With some difficulty Bryden detached Casey's left hand from the armrest and chafed it within his own. 'A little frightened?' he said sceptically. 'Wouldn't terrified be more accurate? You should have told me.'

'No point.' She winced as the undercarriage was retracted, her fingers convulsively clutching his.

LOVE AT FIRST SIGHT

She was very grateful that he made no attempt to rationalise her fears away; instead he said comfortingly, 'It's lousy when you're really afraid of something, isn't it? Particularly when the rest of the world takes it in its stride.'

'I fly quite often—I have to, because of my job,' she said in a staccato voice. 'I've never told Douglas.'

'Once we level off and the seat-belt sign goes off, you can put your head on my shoulder and go to sleep.'

'But *I'm* supposed to be looking after *you*!' And preserving my dignity, she thought helplessly.

'Look on it this way,' Bryden replied, laughter warming his voice. 'You're giving me the chance to prove what a big strong man I am.'

For a moment her fear receded. She said spontaneously, 'Bryden, I really like you.'

'I like you, too,' he replied, and fumbled for the latch on the armrest.

Fortunately the seats across the aisle were unoccupied. Casey rested her cheek chastely on Bryden's broad shoulder and closed her eyes. She would recapture her dignity once they were on the ground again, and she would hold on to it firmly for the next forty-eight hours.

The engines had settled into a dull drone, and Casey was extremely tired. Her head drooped and her breathing deepened.

The officious voice of the stewardess wakened her. 'The armrest must go up for landing, madam.'

'Why are we landing so soon?' Casey gasped. 'What's wrong?'

Bryden said easily, 'We're coming into Halifax.'

She sat up. His arm was around her, and she had the fleeting remembrance of his heartbeat against her cheek.

'I wish she hadn't woken me up,' she gulped. 'Because I hate landing worse than taking off.'

He gave her shoulders a quick squeeze. 'I have a favour to ask you—do you mind if we drive into the city and do a couple of routes with Bess in the business section and around the university before we head to Ragged Island? I go to Halifax once a month at least...if you've got a piece of paper I can describe the areas I'd need to know.'

As he began listing streets and office complexes her pencil flew over the page, although her ears stayed alert for the lowering of the flaps. 'We could pick up a map at the car rental,' she suggested, then gave a yelp of alarm as the wheels hit the runway. The flaps screamed. The plane slowed down, and gradually her pulse did the same. 'I've dropped the pencil,' she confessed.

'It accomplished its purpose,' Bryden said wryly. 'What's the weather like here?'

She peered through the window. 'Patches of dirty snow and a bad-tempered sky.'

The sky more than lived up to its description as Casey, Bryden and Bess walked the downtown streets of Halifax. The wind from the harbour, tunnelled between the tall buildings, threw grit in their eyes and penetrated every chink in their clothing; the snow in the gutters was more black than white, while the pedestrians looked pale and hunched and out of sorts. 'This is the season they call spring,' Bryden grunted. 'If you can just find the Xerox Building we'll call it quits and head uptown.'

The university area was more pleasant to look at, but no less cold. After they left there, they went to a grocery shop in one of the malls and stocked up on food for Bryden and for Bess; then Casey battled the late afternoon traffic out of the city.

LOVE AT FIRST SIGHT

It was almost dark when they turned into Bryden's driveway, the house a stark black outline among the trees. 'Well, Bess,' Bryden said softly, 'this is your new home.'

Bess, predictably, wagged her tail. Casey said, 'Be careful when you get out, Bryden, there are patches of ice between here and the house. Shall I unlock the door?'

He passed her the key. 'I'll let Bess have a run in the garden.'

The house was cold, and Casey's footsteps made the floorboards creak. She flicked on some lights, turned up the furnace and went back to get the groceries. If she had any sense she would leave right away for the bed and breakfast where she had a reservation. But there was no family to welcome Bryden home, no hot meal ready for him, no fire blazing in the hearth; she did not want him to be alone on his first evening home. Anyway, she thought with a toss of her head, she was hungry and restaurants were few and far between along the shore at this time of year. She had been lucky to find a place to stay.

While Bess sniffed in all the corners, Bryden helped Casey with the luggage and the groceries. Then he said, 'I bought two fillets, Casey... you'll stay for dinner?'

'I'd love to,' she said.

He was standing by the counter in the kitchen, a lettuce in one hand and a bag of tomatoes in the other; he gave her a smile that melted her heart and said huskily, 'There were lots of nights last winter when I never thought you'd be here again.'

'There were lots of nights when I never thought I would be, either.'

'I was a fool not to get in touch with you—I'm sorry.'

'You're forgiven,' she said, and discovered it was true. Then belatedly she remembered she was on duty, that this evening was as much a part of her job as the supervised lessons at the school, and added with a touch of severity, 'Do you want me to make the salad?'

'It's OK, Casey, I'm not going to jump on you,' Bryden said shortly. 'But we can be friendly, can't we?'

Only five minutes ago she had carried his suitcase up to his bedroom, whose tall windows overlooked the ocean. He had a king-size bed heaped with silk cushions that glowed like jewels, and she had been stabbed by a desire so sharp as to cause her pain. Friendly, he had said. 'I guess so,' she replied.

'All right, then. Why don't you pour each of us a drink? I keep the alcohol in the corner cupboard in the living-room.'

She had survived the plane trip, and she would be gone from here right after supper. She mixed a Scotch and water for Bryden and a rum and coke for herself, passed him his glass and clinked hers with his. She said seriously, 'To you and Bess, Bryden—a good partnership.'

He said just as seriously, 'You made it so, Casey. I learned such a lot about you the last month...you never once lost your patience, and your encouragement of me was steadfast, rock-solid, never faltering even on the worst of days—because you believe in what you do.' He took a long pull at his drink. 'You were always there when you were needed, yet in four weeks Bess and I have become an independent unit. That takes skill. Skill and caring.'

Although Casey had been praised for her work before, she knew she would cherish Bryden's words to the end of her days. 'Thank you,' she said, and cleared her throat. 'You worked hard, too. So did Bess.'

He was standing on the far side of the counter, gripping its edge. 'You're changing my life...you know that, don't you?'

Suddenly panic-stricken—for what if he only meant that she was increasing his ability to deal with his blindness by making him more independent?—Casey said flippantly, 'You could change my life right now by cooking me dinner—I'm starving.'

'I've never thought you were a coward, Casey.'

Nor had she. But then she had never been in love before. She said with frantic truth, 'I don't think we should have any conversations we wouldn't want Douglas to hear.'

Bryden said pithily, 'To hell with Douglas.'

'I *am* on duty, Bryden,' Casey replied, and winced at her own pomposity.

'Thanks for reminding me.'

He had unquestionably snarled at her. 'I don't have to stay for supper,' she said haughtily.

'Dammit, Casey, will you stop acting as if Douglas were sitting on your shoulder?'

'Why don't *you* stop yelling?'

'You're the first woman I've ever yelled at in my life!'

'Is that supposed to be a compliment?'

'I think perhaps it is,' Bryden said with undoubted menace. 'Because with any of the other women you wouldn't see me for dust if I thought my emotions were in danger of getting involved. I'd run. Run as fast as I knew how. But I don't want to run away from you, Casey. I want to shake you until your teeth rattle. I want to kiss you until you melt in my arms. I want to haul you up to bed. But run—no, thanks.'

Trying to ignore the last part of this all-inclusive speech, Casey said spiritedly, 'And just how many other women were there, Bryden?'

'Jealous, Casey?'

Horribly. 'I would be being dishonest if I were to say no,' she answered, a quiver of laughter in her voice.

'I find your rare urges to dishonesty as interesting as your rectitude,' Bryden said, tossing back his drink. 'Unfortunately the word rectitude reminds me of the shade of Douglas. I shall feed the dog if you would care to start the salad, Casey.'

'You're not the only one whose teeth could do with rattling,' she said breathlessly. 'Vinaigrette or mayonnaise?'

'Your choice.' He gave her a grin that drove every recipe she knew out of her head. 'I discover in myself a person I never thought existed when I'm with you.'

She said slowly, 'I felt that way about myself when I met you last September.'

'Sooner or later we're going to have to give Douglas—and the director—the boot, Casey.'

Again she felt that flicker of panic. 'We can't when I'm here on business.'

'If I can deal with elliptic equations I should be able to work around that. Now, Bess, where did I put your food?'

'In the cupboard to the right of the sink,' said Casey, and tried to focus her brain on the ingredients for salad dressing.

Between them, and perhaps to the surprise of each, they produced a delicious meal, which they ate by candlelight at the pine table in the kitchen alcove. Bryden, who seemed to have forgotten his outburst, was a charming host, while Casey sparkled in conversation; and not one of the topics they covered would have caused Douglas disquiet. Afterwards they cleaned up the kitchen. Then Casey said with a regretful sigh, 'Bryden, I've got to go—I'm dead on my feet. I'll be back around nine-thirty tomorrow morning.'

He said gently, 'The other thing I learned about you the past month is how hard you work—you must be tired. Be careful on the ice outside, won't you? And sleep well, Casey.' He made no attempt to touch her as he held the door open.

Casey had wondered if she might have to drag in professional ethics again; obviously not. 'Goodnight,' she said, went down the steps and crossed the driveway to the rented car, absently noticing that the ice was the worst between the high cedar hedges where the sun could not penetrate. Tomorrow she must spread some sand there.

When she started the car its tyres whined as they sought traction, then the vehicle jerked dramatically as the wheels dug into the dirt. She backed out of the driveway and turned towards the village.

She had made her reservation at Ragged Harbour's only bed and breakfast two weeks ago, and had said she would probably be late checking in. As she approached the village the lights twinkled cheerfully through the trees, and she kept her eye out for the signpost: at the far end of the village, the owner, a Miss Elvira Worthington, had said. Casey pictured her as tall and rather forbidding, her furniture and moral standards as being of the Victorian era.

The sign was attractive, hand-carved and gilded; the house had gables and rigidly pruned yew bushes. It was also, Casey noticed with faint unease, in darkness apart from a light over the front door. She parked the car, ran up the brick path to the door and pressed the bell. It jangled inside.

The house remained in darkness. No Miss Elvira Worthington to chide her for lateness; no sounds at all. Casey pressed the bell again, and for good measure banged the ornate, cast-iron knocker.

A car slowed up on the highway. A man's voice called, 'You lookin' for Elvira?' Casey nodded vigorously, walking across the cropped grass towards the road. 'She's in hospital,' the man said; although bearded like Simon, he was as talkative as Simon was silent. 'Took a turn last Tuesday. Today's the first day she's been herself at all. C'n I help?'

'I've got a reservation to stay the night,' Casey said unhappily.

'Well, now...' The man frowned prodigiously. 'You might try the Havestock Motel in Martin's Cove. Although I'm of the opinion they don't open until late in May. Nothin' else short of Halifax or Millerton.'

Millerton was as far west as Halifax was east. Casey said, 'I'll go to the phone booth and try the motel. Thanks for your help.'

The motel's phone rang unanswered. Casey tried two other motels in the area with the same lack of success, by which time she had run out of quarters. The tourist season was not under way in late April in Nova Scotia; why should it be, when there was still ice in the ditches and snow on the hills? Nevertheless, she drove to the little variety shop at the other end of the village to get some more quarters.

The shop had closed five minutes before she'd got there. She stood outside in the chill, damp air, wondering what to do.

The choices were not many. She could drive to Halifax or Millerton, which would take over an hour; or she could go back to Bryden's. Encased in professional ethics, she thought dourly. And what would she tell David Canning when she could not produce a receipt for her two nights in Ragged Island?

Halifax was the logical destination; it was a big enough city that she would have no trouble finding a place to stay. But even as she reached this conclusion, she felt a dead weight of exhaustion descend on her. She could not face the drive back to the city.

She would go to Bryden's.

CHAPTER NINE

FIVE minutes later Casey was turning into Bryden's driveway again. She parked nearer the road this time, not wanting to skid on the ice, and through the flat cedar fronds saw that he had switched off the outside light. She reached for her overnight bag in the back seat, hoping he had not gone to bed.

Her scarf caught in the door-handle as she shut it; it was a measure of Casey's tiredness that this added mishap brought tears to her eyes. She blinked them back, took off her gloves, freed the fringe of the scarf, which now had grease on it, and picked up her bag again. Trudging down the driveway, she searched the upstairs windows for any signs of life. Bryden, of course, would not need lights. Surely he wouldn't be asleep already?

She was almost at the steps when the leather heel of her boot slipped on a patch of ice and her feet went out from under her. Her bag threw her further off balance; she crashed to the ground, her shoulder striking the edge of the steps, her hand bent under her. Inside the house Bess began barking.

Casey lay very still, temporarily stunned. The door opened. Bryden said loudly, 'Who's there? Steady, Bess, *steady*!'

'It's me,' Casey mumbled, and added with professional accuracy and a slightly hysterical giggle, 'at the bottom of your steps. On your left.'

'*Casey!* Sweetheart, are you all right? Don't move... Bess, down!'

Casey was not sure she wanted to move. Sweetheart, he had called her. Sweetheart, she thought muzzily, was a beautiful word.

Bryden hurried down the steps, Bess at his heels, and knelt at her side. As he ran his hands over her body, the dog licked her ear. Bryden said urgently, 'Where does it hurt? Did you fall on the ice? I thought of throwing some salt down, but I didn't bother—I wasn't expecting you back. Casey, say something!'

'Why did you call me sweetheart?' she whispered.

She had taken him aback; for a full five seconds he was silent. 'I did, didn't I?' he said slowly. 'I suppose because you scared me half to death.'

'So you didn't mean it?'

'Casey, this is no time for a discussion on Freudian slips of the tongue,' he said impatiently. 'It doesn't feel as though you've broken anything...can you stand up?' He put his arm around her waist. 'Here, lean on me.'

Through his sweater his arm had the tensile strength of steel. After he had pulled her to her feet, she stumbled up the steps and into the house. Bryden kicked the door shut behind him and guided her towards the chesterfield, where he eased her down with exquisite care. 'I have no idea what the medical journals would say, but I'm going to get you a brandy,' he said. 'Stay there.'

Casey could not have done otherwise. Shock was wearing off and pain replacing it. Her shoulder felt as if someone had kindled a fire inside it, while her wrist was being rhythmically stabbed with a pick. She felt very cold. When Bryden returned with the brandy in a tumbler, he had to wrap her fingers round the glass and hold them in place; she was shivering.

The first mouthful made her choke; the second burned a trail down her throat and at least supplied a counterirritant to all her other woes. 'The bed and breakfast was closed,' she sputtered. 'The owner is in hospital.'

'No reason for you to try and join her.'

She took another gulp of brandy. 'I shouldn't have come back here. But I was t-too tired to drive back to Halifax.'

'I'd have been furious with you if you had. For heaven's sake, Casey, all this professional ethics stuff is well and good, but you can carry it too far. You're going to finish that brandy, you're going to have a hot bath, and then you'll sleep in the spare room.' Clipping off his words, he went on, 'If it'll make you feel better, I personally will call Mr Canning and explain that the only accommodation in thirty miles was shut and that just for good measure you almost broke your neck on my back steps.'

Rather pleased that Bryden sounded so angry, Casey said meekly, 'Very well.'

'What, no fight?'

'Fighting takes energy,' she replied with a suppressed giggle; the brandy seemed to have surrounded her in a rose-coloured aura.

Bryden raised his brow. 'I suppose your bag is outside at the bottom of the steps.'

'Oh.' Less than convincingly Casey said, 'I'll get it.'

'You will not. And no more brandy, or I'll be carrying you up the stairs.'

'How romantic,' she said dreamily.

'How unprofessional,' was the dry response. 'Hold Bess, will you, while I go outside?'

Cold air wafted around Casey's ankles from the open door; the brandy did not seem to have extended as far as her ankles. Carefully she put the glass on the mahogany table and patted the dog. When Bryden came back carrying her case she pushed herself upright with her good hand and followed him up the stairs. Then she saw that he was carrying her bag into his bedroom, not the spare room.

In a confused rush of emotion Casey wondered what she should do. Scream for help? Make love to Bryden? Much as she might want to do the latter, the time was not right. She hesitated in the doorway, feeling gauche and unhappy, wishing he had not put her in this position.

Bryden said casually, putting her bag down on the floor, 'You can sleep in here rather than the spare room, Casey—it's warmer and the bed's already made up. I'll take the other room.' Then he must have sensed something in the quality of her silence. He scowled at her. 'I see—you were afraid I was setting you up for the big seduction scene.'

'I didn't know what to think,' she faltered.

Her reply had angered him further. 'You can quit worrying,' he rapped. 'I've already said I'm not going to jump on you... apart from all the other considerations, and there are many, the timing's lousy.' He nodded behind him, still frowning. 'The bathroom's through there. Towels in the closet.' He turned on his heel to leave the room.

Casey burst into tears.

It would have been difficult to say who was the more surprised by her action, she or Bryden. As she sat down hard on the bed and buried her face in her hands, sobbing noisily, Bryden uttered an expletive under his breath, sat down beside her and put an arm around her shoulders.

She flinched. 'That hurts,' she hiccupped. 'I banged my shoulder on your step.'

He shifted his arm to her waist and said strongly, 'Listen to me, Cassandra Elizabeth Landrigan. I'm going to turn on the water, then I'll go downstairs and make some hot cocoa. By the time that's ready, you'll be in bed. You will drink it and go to sleep and tomorrow will be a whole new day.'

She snuggled her cheek into his shoulder, thinking she was making a habit of this. 'It couldn't be a worse day than today,' she sighed. 'I was planning to be so dignified and proper and correct. Casey, the perfect instructor... oh, Bryden, you do feel warm.'

He detached himself from her and stood up. 'I'm only flesh and blood,' he said drily. 'I can be tempted. I'll be back in a few minutes with the cocoa.'

He had forgotten to turn on the bath water. Casey did so herself, poured in a generous amount of bubble bath, and with difficulty, because her wrist was very sore, found her nightdress and housecoat in her bag. Her nightdress would not tempt him. It was made of fleecy cotton, reached to her feet and had ruffles at wrist and throat. Not that she had any intention of tempting him, she told herself hastily, and closed the bathroom door.

The gravel in the driveway had scraped her wrist raw, an ominous red blotch on her shoulder would no doubt turn purple by tomorrow, and her face looked like that of a woman who had just cried copiously.

However, fifteen minutes later when Casey lay down in Bryden's bed with the covers pulled up to her chin she was both feeling and looking much better. The curtains were open, so she could see the light flashing on Ragged Island: a solitary light in a blackness that stretched for thousands of miles... her eyelids drooped shut.

A hand was stroking her cheek. 'I'm not really asleep,' she mumbled.

'How do you feel now?'

'Much better.' Bryden was sitting on the edge of the bed. His eyes looked almost black, depthless like the ocean, his hair was tousled, and she was very conscious of the reality of his body beneath his shirt and trousers. It was a good thing he could not read her thoughts.

'Cocoa,' he said.

'Oh, good,' Casey said brightly, and took one of the steaming mugs from the tray that was balanced on his lap. The cocoa was too hot to drink fast. She racked her brains for something innocuous to say. 'Do you have a bed for Bess?'

'When Douglas was here for the interview, he suggested foam rubber with a removable cover. So I had one made.'

'What a good idea.' It was, she thought, just as well that Douglas could not read her thoughts either.

She swallowed the cocoa as fast as she could, and all the while the restraint in the room thickened, palpable as a blanket. 'I'm sure I'll fall right to sleep now,' she said finally, putting her mug back on the tray.

Bryden took the tray and stood up. 'I'd better go.'

'Thank you, Bryden,' Casey said, and in exasperation decided she sounded like a wind-up toy.

But Bryden did not move. His face a mask, he said deliberately, 'I've adjusted reasonably well to my blindness by now. I no longer contemplate cutting my throat. I don't want to break the chairs that I trip over into smithereens, and my hide's getting a little tougher for dealing with those members of the public who want to help me over streets that I don't want to cross. But right now I'd give my fancy braille computer to be able to see the expression on your face—you have no idea how frustrating it is to be second-guessing all the time! You *sound* so sweet and polite—yes, Bryden, no, Bryden, as if you don't give a damn that you're lying in my bed... but what the hell are you thinking?' As she made a strangled sound, he added in disgust, 'I know—I'm an insensitive boor, and you're exhausted.'

LOVE AT FIRST SIGHT

Casey found her voice. 'I'm sounding as sugary as Pollyanna so that I *won't* tell you what I'm thinking!'

'Which is?'

If it had been a hard month for her, it had been more difficult for him; she was not the only one who must be exhausted. She said, taking her courage in her hands, 'Bryden, I hope some day we'll be together in your bed. I'd like that. But even though we both know it can't be now, that doesn't mean I'm not capable of being tempted, too.'

The light on Ragged Island flashed and vanished, flashed and vanished. Bryden said quietly, 'You shake my heart with your honesty, Casey.'

Casey said in a small voice, 'You could kiss me goodnight.'

He put the tray down on the bedside table, sat down beside her and braced his hands on the pillow on either side of her head. Then he bent to find her mouth, touching her only with his lips. His kiss made no physical demands; it had more the nature of a pledge, a secret inner promise not yet ready to be put into words. And when it was over he dropped his face into the curve of her shoulder, resting his weight on her and closing his eyes.

With infinite tenderness Casey wrapped her arms around him and held him to her, her cheek against his hair, and allowed the love that she had suppressed all day to wash over her. Perhaps it would reach him, she thought humbly, and bring him whatever comfort he sought.

His breathing was so deep and slow that she wondered if he had fallen asleep. But eventually he raised his head, pushing himself away from her with his palms flat on the bed. Then with one finger he traced the delicate bones of her face, his own face intent. He said softly, 'I don't need to see your expression now... I don't understand how or why, Casey, but you heal me. Heal wounds I'd never acknowledged were there.' Briefly he laid his cheek against hers again. Then he got up from the bed, picked up the tray and strode out of the room.

As Casey lay back on the pillow she caught the faint fragrance of his aftershave, and, more elusively, the scent of his body. Wrapped in happiness, she closed her eyes and fell asleep.

It was pouring with rain when Casey woke up. Getting out of bed was an act of physical courage, because she was sore in places she had not known existed. Walking to the bathroom was comparable to a marathon. Her shoulder, she saw when she stripped for another hot bath, resembled a very lurid sunset, and bruises like small purple clouds were scattered over the rest of her body.

The bath helped. She dressed in jeans and a blue sweater and descended the stairs with great care. Bryden was in the kitchen. She sniffed the air appreciatively and said, 'A man after my own heart—the coffee's brewed.'

'Have you looked out of the window?'

'It's going to be a long walk to the village,' she said philosophically.

She, Bryden and Bess worked extremely hard that day. They walked to the village and traced routes there that Bryden would be likely to use. They walked home and had lunch. Then they drove to Martin's Cove, the nearest town of any size, where they located the various shops Bryden might need, and tracked from one to the next in the teeming rain. Because Bryden had a phenomenal memory they were able to accomplish a lot; but all three were soaked to the skin when they finished at four-thirty.

They trailed up the steps of Bryden's house. His first concern was to dry Bess, so Casey went upstairs and had her third hot bath. She put on a pale pink tracksuit, her feet bare, her hair loose; when she went downstairs Bess was lying on the rug in front of the fireplace, where Bryden had been brushing her. 'I think she wants you to light the fire,' Casey said.

Bryden straightened, his wet hair still clinging to his scalp. 'I'd planned to take you out for dinner tonight,' he said. 'But it would mean driving into Halifax again.'

She said sincerely, 'I'd much rather have pizza in front of the fire.'

Bryden's rare smile lit his face. 'So would I.'

'I'll make the pizza if you'll light the fire. I like making pizza—lots of room for creativity.'

He laughed. 'There are only two things I can't eat—squid and maraschino cherries.'

That left Casey with plenty of scope. An hour later she and Bryden were sitting side by side on the chesterfield munching thick wedges of pizza, while Bryden tried to list all the ingredients. Casey felt warm and relaxed and happy; she chattered on about her family and about the qualifying exams she would write early in June. 'I'll be glad when they're over,' she admitted, licking her fingers. 'I've got a lot of studying to do.'

'Have you always liked dogs, Casey?'

She was off again, describing the stray cats and dogs her father was always bringing home. 'Unfailingly, the cats were female and pregnant,' she said with a reminiscent smile as she got up to put another log on the fire.

They had not bothered to switch on any lights; at their backs, through the tall windows, was the black of ocean and sky and the beat of rain, with only the small circle of orange and yellow light at their faces. Casey sat down again. 'Did you ever have another pet, Bryden—after the puppy?'

'No. I was sent off to boarding school soon afterwards.'

At the age of six. Casey swallowed a flash of pure rage. 'Was I the first person you ever told about that?'

'Yes.'

'I'm glad you told me,' she said, adding fiercely, 'Not all fathers are like yours.'

'And I can't live the rest of my life in his shadow...I'm starting to understand that.' He drained the last of the wine from his glass and changed the subject. 'What will you do once exams are over? You're due down here in July.'

She said baldly, 'Douglas will be coming. Not me. He had interviews in this area, so it's the logical thing to happen. I was going to tell you before I left.'

Bryden gave an unamused bark of laughter. 'Douglas doesn't have to worry—you've stuck to your role admirably. Casey the virginal instructor will be returning to the school exactly as she left it.'

'You don't have to be crude!'

'I'm sorry!' he snapped. He got up, picking his way between the furniture to stand facing the window, where the rain trickled down the glass in tiny, intermingling rivers. He said heavily, 'Casey, forget the school. Forget everyone else's expectations. If circumstances were otherwise, would you want to keep on seeing me?'

'I told you I hoped we'd make love.'

'Not just that,' he said roughly. 'More than that.'

'Yes,' she whispered.

If she had then expected to be swept into his arms, she was soon disappointed. Turning to face her, he said violently, 'I hope you know what you're saying.'

'It isn't easy—you tell me very little, Bryden.'

'I know I'm asking a lot of you, Casey. But I've been locked up inside myself for so long...finding you is

LOVE AT FIRST SIGHT

forcing me to change in ways that are new for me.' He raked his fingers through his hair. 'And every minute I'm with you, I'm fighting to keep my hands off you.'

Trying to make a joke of it, she said, 'We've managed very well in that respect the last twenty-four hours.'

'We're fools,' he said savagely. 'You'll be leaving tomorrow, and God knows when we'll see each other again.' He raked his fingers through his hair and added with an abruptness that was characteristic of him. 'Do you mind if I go into my study for a while? I need a break from all this.'

So he needed to be alone. He had spent a great deal of his life alone, Casey thought, suddenly afraid. Could she change that? Could anyone? 'Please don't shut me out, Bryden!' she begged.

He was banging on the window-frame with his fist, the small repetitive thuds jarring her nerves. He asked, 'What time do you have to leave tomorrow?'

'Eight-thirty at the latest. It's a five-hour drive.'

'I'll be up.' He called Bess and left the room.

She remembered the dreams she had had all winter, dreams where he had turned his back on her and left her alone. The rain rattling against the tall windows was now a threat, and the dying flames brought her no comfort. She placed the screen in front of the fire and went upstairs.

The door to the study was closed. She went into Bryden's room and closed that door as well.

At eight-twenty the next morning Casey was standing by her car. She and Bryden had eaten breakfast together, making small talk as if they were two strangers, and then she had loaded her case in the back seat. She bent and hugged Bess. 'Be a good girl, won't you?' Then she looked up at Bryden.

His navy blue sweatshirt darkened his eyes. The wind, damp from the sea, played with his hair. 'Bryden?' she said. 'Is this goodbye?'

He clasped her by the sleeves of her leather jacket. 'No,' he said hoarsely. 'I'll see you before summer. I don't know how yet, but I'll work something out...I hate for you to leave, Casey.'

'I'll miss you,' she said helplessly.

His answer was to wrap his arms around her, one hand moulding the line of her spine, the other seeking the fullness of her breast under her jacket. His kiss was another desperate searching. She clung to him, kissing him back with passionate abandon, a surge of desire overwhelming her, blinding her to anything but the present moment.

When he eventually released her, his chest was rising and falling as if he had been running. But all he said was, 'I'll phone you.'

She had wanted a declaration of love, an outpouring of his need for her. She bit her lip, praying she would not cry. 'I'll look forward to that.'

He produced a semblance of a smile. 'We shouldn't have congratulated ourselves last night. One kiss under the cedar hedge and we're in trouble.'

Her heart was still hammering against her ribs from that one kiss. Knowing she could not bear to prolong this scene, Casey whispered, 'Take care of yourself, Bryden.' Then she quickly kissed his cheek, got in the car and backed out of the driveway; the ice had melted in the rain. Her last view was of a tall, blue-eyed man with one hand raised in salute, a golden-haired dog at his side.

LOVE AT FIRST SIGHT

She did not know when she would see him again; she did not know if he would ever love her as she craved to be loved. All she knew was that leaving him was the most painful thing she had ever done.

CHAPTER TEN

CASEY put down her pen with a tired sigh. She had written the three essay questions as fully as she could, then she had edited them and checked for spelling mistakes. There was nothing more she could do.

This was her final exam. She looked out of the upstairs window of the office where she had been writing; it was a beautiful day, the oak trees decked in the fresh green of early summer, sun and shade waltzing among the branches.

It was also June, she thought, watching a tiny yellow bird flit through the leaves, and Bryden had promised he would see her before summer. He had phoned her three times, stilted phone calls full of things unsaid that always left Casey on edge and irritable, even while simultaneously she longed for the next one. He had said nothing, for instance, about a visit. And she, intimidated by the distance between them and by the silences that hummed along the line, had been too proud to ask.

Back in April he had sworn it was not goodbye. She had to trust those words, for she really had no other choice. But waiting, she was finding, was very difficult, and her prediction that she would miss him had proved horribly true. She ached for him and longed for him, and she would never again say 'I'll miss you' without realising the inadequacy of the words.

She dragged her thoughts back to the present. In one way she was sorry her exams were over, for they had kept her mind occupied; although this was not something she would tell her parents tonight when she went there for dinner to celebrate the end of the exams. Neatly she arranged the answer booklet inside the question folder and left the office.

David Canning was talking to Brenda, the secretary whose desk was across the hall. He eyed Casey over his glasses. 'How was it?'

'Two or three of the multiple-choice questions had me stymied, but the essay topics were fine.'

'You'll do well, I'm sure.' He smiled at her. 'Going on a pub crawl tonight?'

'Going to have dinner with my parents,' she rejoined with a grin.

'Douglas is away until Friday noon...once he's back I want you to take a couple of days off. Come back next Wednesday, say. You've worked hard the last month, Casey.'

With or without his half-glasses, David Canning missed very little. Casey said ruefully, 'Do I look that bad?'

'You look fine. Together with the weekend, that would give you four days—go away somewhere and forget about the lot of us.'

Her eyes clouded; away meant Ragged Island. Realising the director was still watching her, she smiled determinedly. 'Thanks, David,' she said. 'I'll probably stay home and sleep.'

'You can do better than that,' he said. 'In fact, I'm sure you will.' He picked up some papers from the desk and drifted down the hall. Casey pulled a face which made Brenda giggle, and ran downstairs to her car.

The bungalow looked very peaceful, late daffodils blooming in big clumps like sunbursts among the birches, and the air full of birdsong. Casey parked by the house, tapped on the back door and stepped inside.

Her mother hurried down the steps from the kitchen, wiping her hands on a towel; she looked unusually flustered, as if she had just discovered the head of the philosophy department on her back steps rather than her middle daughter. 'Darling! How did it go today?' She offered her cheek for a kiss. 'Before you get settled, will you do me a favour? Pick a big bunch of pansies for the table from the back borders, would you mind?'

'Have you got the best silver out?' Casey asked in comical dismay. 'I didn't bother going home to change.'

'You look lovely,' Marion said firmly. 'Off you go.'

Casey loved the garden, for her father's untidiness was in full spate in the rampaging perennials and massed bulbs. The pansies were growing wild at the very back, where the garden joined the trees; she knelt and began picking them, charmed as always by their velvet-complexioned faces.

To her right a thrush was singing, its plangent notes cupped in the deep silence of the woods. The fragrance of the flowers in her hand reminded her of the pansies she had picked at the cottage and given to Bryden, so many months ago...

In a loud rustling of last year's leaves, the peace of the garden was disrupted. Casey looked up, startled. A dog was racing through the birches towards her, trampling daffodils as it came. A dog that was as familiar to her as her own face. Bess.

As the dog skidded to a halt, her tail thrashing the air, Casey flung her arms around her. 'Bess, what are you doing here? Yes, it's lovely to see you—but I don't understand!' She pushed Bess away, looking all around her. The thrush was still singing in the woods, and the sun slanting through the birches made silver wands of their trunks. There was no sign of movement. She said slowly, 'Is Bryden here? Bess, is your master here?'

Bess panted sympathetically, and the little bells on her collar jingled. Said Casey, 'Find Bryden, Bess. Find Bryden.'

The dog set off through the daffodils again, purpose in every step. Casey followed, scarcely daring to hope, quite unable to understand. Bryden couldn't be here...here, at her parents' house, on the day she finished exams. Clutching the pansies so hard that their stems were bruised, she threaded her way through the birch trees, and heard in her ears the thudding of her heart.

Bess had come out on the path where last April they had searched for violets, and was trotting along it, looking back over her shoulder to see if Casey was following. Casey was almost running, her turquoise eyes wide open. Although she desperately wanted to believe in this miracle, she was afraid to.

Then she came round a curve in the path, and saw, a hundred feet ahead of her, a man waiting under a tree. A tall man in trousers and a smoke-blue sweater, whose head was turned towards the sound of their approach. Every line of his body was tense.

Bryden.

Casey slowed down, not knowing whether to sing or dance or cry. All her senses heightened, she heard her shoe scrape on a rock, saw the sun glance off the polished surface of a beech leaf, felt the lightest of breezes lift her hair. 'Am I dreaming?' she said softly. 'Am I going to wake up and you'll have vanished? Or are you real, Bryden?'

'Come here, Casey...because I need to know that you're real, as well.'

Like a woman in a trance she closed the distance between them, her eyes seeking out every loved and remembered detail of his appearance. The indigo eyes and broad shoulders were the same, as was the air of holding back, the reserve that he always seemed to carry with him. She said with incredulous joy, 'I can't believe you're here!'

Her voice rang with that joy. Bryden threw his arms around her, almost lifting her off the ground, and kissed her as if his life depended on convincing her she was wanted. She strained into him, kissing him back with generosity and passion, her whole being consumed with a hunger that she could not have hidden from him had she wanted to.

His hands were roaming her body in frantic rediscovery. He breathed against her mouth, 'You're real—my God, you're real! You wouldn't believe how I've waited for this.'

He was dropping quick, hard kisses all over her face. 'Yes, I would,' she said, clasping her hands around his waist and feeling the pounding of his heart against her breast. 'Because I've been waiting, too.'

He kissed her with an explicitness that left her trembling. 'So *this* hasn't changed,' he said.

'Were you afraid it would?'

'When you're not with me, I'm afraid you don't exist,' he said huskily. 'You're the angel on top of the tree, Casey—the miraculous gift I have no right to be given, and very little knowledge of how to receive.'

As always, he had the capacity to reduce her to tears. She whispered, 'That's the most beautiful thing anyone has ever said to me.'

His hug drove the breath from her lungs, and for a long moment they stayed locked in each other's arms. Then Bess whined at their feet, and with a catch of laughter in her voice Casey said, 'The ear that you were kissing Bess kissed first.'

'That tells me where your priorities lie.'

'Furthermore, we're standing in a sea of pansies. Mum sent me out to pick some, and I must have dropped them when you kissed me.' She added in sudden enlightenment, 'Of course, Mum knew you were here—that's why she wouldn't let me in. Have you been in cahoots with my parents, Bryden Moore?'

'Yes,' he said.

'You're not supposed to confess that easily!'

'I've been in Ottawa for the last week, staying with Jenny and Matthew. I had some business to look after and I didn't want to disturb you while you were studying, so when I was talking to your father one day last week he invited me out this evening.'

'That nice little speech is exactly like your phone calls—it doesn't say nearly enough,' Casey announced, and was no longer joking.

With all the force of his personality Bryden replied, 'I know you don't understand. But in two more days I'll have a lot more answers... can you bear with me until then?'

The thrush's song was so far away now that she could scarcely hear it. She said slowly, 'You're shutting me out again, Bryden. Just as you did all last winter.'

'What do you mean?'

For a moment she was silent, for although what she had to say was of crucial importance, it might also drive him away. 'Part of any relationship has to be sharing. It's easy to share the good times—but it's much more difficult to share things like decisions and failures and worries. If you don't, though, the relationship isn't a relationship at all, it's just two separate people. Unconnected. Not real to each other.'

'I've always carried everything alone, Casey.'

'Then you must change,' she said. 'Because it hurts when you shut me out.'

'I don't want to hurt you!'

She clasped his hands in hers, needing their strength and warmth, and said steadily, 'Tell me what answers you might have in two more days, Bryden.'

Because she loved him, she could sense the inner struggle before he spoke. 'I decided last winter I didn't want to go back to my old job, so I applied to Carleton University for a teaching position. They're to phone me Friday morning with the verdict.'

A new job would mean a great deal to him in terms of independence and self-worth. 'Thank you for telling me,' she said quietly. 'I do hope you get it.'

'I'd be based in Ottawa again. Not that far from the school,' he said, and suddenly smiled at her with the vitality that always drove coherent thought from her brain. 'Speaking of which, how did the exams go?'

Knowing that she and Bryden had crossed a major hurdle, Casey bent down and began gathering the pansies, some of which Bess had sat on; she chattered on about the traumas of examinations on whose results depended her three-year apprenticeship while Bryden put Bess's harness back on. By the time they set off for the house the raw emotion of their meeting had receded sufficiently that Casey felt able to face her father's eagle eye.

That evening was one of the happiest of Casey's life, although outwardly nothing out of the ordinary occurred; it was a normal family dinner complete with dissertations on orchids and Aristotle. Yet Casey felt like a child on Christmas morning. She did not have to search far for the reason—he was sitting across from her at the table, laughing at some joke of her father's. Part of the family, she thought, in a way he had not allowed himself to be the first time he was here. That was why she was so happy.

She and Bryden left at about ten o'clock. As they turned on to the highway he said, 'Are you free tomorrow evening, Casey?'

Had she had ten dates, she would have cancelled every one. 'I was planning to clean the apartment. But I could be distracted from that,' she said jauntily.

'Jenny and Matthew are having a party, and would like you to come.'

Casey had not seen Jenny since last September. 'You'll be there, of course,' she said, more as statement than as question. 'Sure, I'll go. What time?'

'Any time after eight. She's calling it a dessert party, so don't eat too much for dinner...she's hired a catering firm known for their cheesecakes and tortes.'

'That'll be fun, I haven't been to a party in ages.'

'None with the estimable Douglas?'

'He's given up on me,' she said. Some time in May Douglas had dropped one of his rather ponderous hints about the change in their relationship once her apprenticeship was over; she had told him as kindly as she could that she did not want any changes, that she was content with the friendship they shared during working hours and wanted nothing more. He had been hurt, as she had known he would be, and she had hated causing him pain. But she had also known that Bryden was the man she wanted, and no other would do.

She could explain none of this to Bryden. She said, 'What should I wear tomorrow night?' and the conversation moved into safer channels.

When she pulled up in front of the Sibleys' house, Bryden said, 'Will you come in?'

'I'd better not—I have to be up at seven.'

He did not insist. 'Thanks for the drive, Casey. I'll see you tomorrow night,' he said, kissed her cheek with all the passion of a maiden aunt, and got out of the car with Bess. Casey watched until he had unlocked the front door. Then she drove off.

Bryden was looking for a new job in Ottawa. Did that mean he wanted to share more of his life with her?

* * *

At eight-thirty on Thursday evening Casey was ringing the doorbell of the big brick house where the Sibleys lived. Her white silk blouse, brief green leather skirt and patterned tights made her look slender and leggy and provocative, a look which her hair, gathered in a demure green velvet bow at the nape of her neck, should have ameliorated and did not.

She had hoped that Bryden would open the door. But it was Matthew who ushered her in. 'Casey!' he said hospitably. 'How nice to see you again, do come in. Would you like to take your jacket upstairs, the room on the right? Then we'll get you a drink.'

The curved staircase had a partial view of the livingroom, from which emanated the convivial hum of a party well under way. Short of standing part way up and staring, Casey could not see Bryden. She left her jacket on the bed in company with several others, all more expensive than hers, and checked her appearance in the bevelled mirror; her hair was smooth as satin, while her brilliant eyes and flushed cheeks scarcely needed the make-up she had so carefully applied. She took a couple of deep breaths and went downstairs.

Jenny, in a dress of royal blue Thai silk that co-existed rather edgily with her vivid red curls, was waiting for her at the bottom of the stairs. 'Matthew told me you'd arrived; I'm so *delighted* you could come. I'll introduce you to a few people, and then I'll get you a drink. How are you?'

She led Casey into the living-room, which was furnished with extreme eclecticism, yet had a haphazard charm. Bryden was taller than most; Casey still could not see him. Swallowing a panic that seemed out of all proportion—what did she expect, that he had gone back to Ragged Island?—she said with an attempt at casualness that would not have deceived a child, 'Isn't Bryden here?'

'He was meeting a couple of business acquaintances for dinner; he should be along soon,' Jenny said vaguely, her eyes searching the room. 'Ah, there's a couple you'd like to meet.' And she led Casey across the room to an older man and woman who appeared to be having an argument in front of the bookshelves. There was something tantalisingly familiar about the man. Wondering whom he resembled, Casey heard Jenny say, 'Cressida, Harold, I'd like you to meet a friend of Bryden's...Casey Landrigan. Casey is a guide-dog trainer at the school where Bryden got his dog. Casey, these are Bryden's parents, Cressida and Harold Moore.' She gave Casey the smile of a woman who had achieved her purpose. 'Tell me what you'd like to drink.'

Harold Moore was glaring dyspeptically at Casey. 'A double rum and Coke,' Casey said, and smiled at his wife.

But before she could say anything, Cressida Moore had draped her chiffon-clad sleeve over Casey's arm and, leaning forward as if Casey was deaf, was breathing, 'What miracles you must accomplish! To give the blind sight, to move them from a world of darkness and despair into the light of freedom, to guide their every step and teach them anew the glory of life...ah, if only I were younger, I could embrace such work with all my heart.'

Casey blinked, not sure how to respond to such a confusion of prejudice and misinformation. Cressida Moore's eyes, hedged with mascara, were swimming in sentimental tears that she began dabbing at ineffectually with a lace-bordered handkerchief. Casey said carefully, 'I don't think——'

'You're too modest, my dear, too modest.' Cressida's voice had a tremolo worthy of any soprano. 'Your task is so admirable—giving the blind the appearance of normality. So they seem the same as the rest of us.'

'Those who have lost their sight are normal in every respect but that——' Casey began, her eyes blazing.

But Harold Moore interrupted. 'Far too much fuss being made,' he snorted. 'A waste of the taxpayers' money.'

'The school operates almost entirely on donations,' Casey said pleasantly.

'Lot of hogwash. Bryden was managing fine without a dog.'

'But it's such a beautiful dog,' Cressida cried. 'Those big brown eyes... I don't know how you can bear to discipline the dogs, Miss Landry, if they're all as sweet as Bess.'

'Landrigan,' said Casey. 'A dog should always——'

'Sweet?' Harold Moore retorted. 'That's the problem with you, Cressida, you wear rose-tinted glasses. That dog is a semi-domesticated carnivore who happens to have been taught a few cute tricks. Bryden did not need a dog. It's just another way for him to gain attention and sympathy.'

Perhaps fortunately at this juncture a white-jacketed waiter brought Casey's drink on a silver tray. She took a hefty swallow and tried to change the subject. 'Do you live in Ottawa, Mr Moore?'

Cressida, whose cheeks were patched with hectic colour, snapped, 'Bryden needs a great deal of attention and sympathy, Harold! Far more than you're prepared to give him. It's been such a terrible tragedy for me, Miss Landry, quite terrible, to suddenly find myself the mother of a blind man, to have to watch him struggling to do the simple little things we take for granted, to see him helpless, an object of pity. My heart aches for him. My poor Bryden——'

Casey fought to control any number of emotions, the chief of which was fury. She said crisply, 'Bryden does not need pity, Mrs Moore. He is an extremely intelligent man who is using all his skills to surmount what is certainly a terrible deprivation, but by no means an end to what you call normal life. A guide-dog is just one aspect of his struggle. The dog gives him greater freedom of movement and increased independence. That's all. Bryden does the rest.'

'That's sweet of you, dear,' quavered Cressida, who plainly did not believe a word Casey had said.

'I'm sick to death of all this modern psychological claptrap,' Harold announced. 'In my day we kept a stiff upper lip and didn't expect the rest of the world to come running to our rescue. We were the captains of our souls, Miss Landrigan, we were the masters of our fates. None of this sloppy-minded, wishy-washy liberalism!'

He gave Casey a militant nod. He had eyes only a shade lighter than his son's, but they were protruberant in a choleric complexion. Casey, who had not been aware she had been expressing either claptrap or liberalism, gave him her most dazzling smile and said smoothly, 'I deal in practicalities, Mr Moore. A guide-dog enlarges Bryden's sphere of activity and enables him to move more easily within that sphere. Makes him, if you like, more the captain of his soul.'

'You know you've always hated dogs, Harold,' Cressida put in with real malevolence. 'The puppy Bryden had all those years ago—you had it shot.'

'And I'd do so again,' he said pompously. 'It was nothing but an ill-bred mongrel.'

'He loved it,' Cressida protested. 'It was an adorable little thing.'

'Given a free rein you would have made a sissy out of our son, Cressida—crying all over him every time he skinned his knee, allowing him to sleep with a flea-ridden mongrel, wanting him to go to the local school rather than the boarding school where my father and grandfather had gone. *I* went away to school when I was six.

No reason why he should not.' He drew himself up to his full height. 'I chose to make a man of him.'

Casey, with some effort, had managed to keep her face expressionless during this tirade. She was beginning to understand much more clearly the forces that had shaped Bryden. Smothered by the shallow emotions of his mother, repelled by his father's rigidity: no wonder Bryden had trouble with love. His defence had been to become a loner, sufficient unto himself, and she was becoming increasingly sure that she was the first woman to storm those defences.

Cressida tossed back her drink and said spitefully, 'Well, darling, you succeeded—Bryden's twice the man you are.' Her eyes filled with easy tears. 'Or he was, before that dreadful accident ruined his life. Because what kind of a future does he face? He'll be all alone. No woman in her right mind will look at him now.'

Casey said clearly, 'I consider myself to be in my right mind, Mrs Moore, and I find your son the most attractive man I have ever met.'

'Darling!' Cressida Moore gushed. 'We were just talking about you.'

Casey nearly dropped her glass. Knowing exactly whom she was going to see, she turned around. Bryden, looking exceedingly handsome in a three-piece suit, was standing a foot away from her. 'Good evening, Bryden,' she said with immense dignity.

He rested one hand on her shoulder and kissed her unhurriedly on the cheek. 'I thought eavesdroppers were supposed to hear only ill of themselves.'

'She probably feels sorry for you, darling,' said his mother.

Casey's breath hissed between her teeth. Imperturbably Bryden remarked, 'Hello, Mother. No, she doesn't feel sorry for me. We had that one out several months ago.'

'Oh? So you've known each other quite a while?'

'September,' Casey said, with a brevity that probably sounded rude and for which she did not apologise.

With a puzzled frown, as if Casey had just admitted to an unmentionable disease, Cressida said, 'How strange! You're a very lovely young woman...but I suppose because you work with blind people all the time, it doesn't bother you being around Bryden.' She gave an affected little shudder. 'I'm terribly sensitive, you see, so I feel things more than the average person.' Then she turned to Bryden and cried, 'Oh, darling, I've done it again—why do I use words like see and look around you? I'm so sorry, I don't mean to be cruel!'

Casey had never met anyone with such a gift for unintended insult. Before Bryden could respond, she said strongly, 'I enjoy Bryden's company, that's why I choose to be with him.' And the only reason he bothers me is because I want to take him to bed, she thought, wishing for Bryden's sake she could say it out loud.

'I suppose he's like an extension of your job,' Cressida said kindly.

'We've had that one out too, Mother,' Bryden remarked.

Frantically Casey searched for something to say. 'We've strayed rather a long way from guide-dogs, haven't we?' she managed. 'You should visit our school, Mr Moore, you'd probably find it very interesting.'

Pointedly Harold Moore looked all around Bryden's feet. 'And where is this wonder dog? Don't tell me you can get along without it.'

'Bess is upstairs—she'd be in the way in a crowded room like this,' Bryden replied with praiseworthy restraint. 'How did your deal go with the computer company on Monday?'

'Now, Bryden, you know I dislike talking business in front of your mother,' Harold said huffily. 'Although actually I do have to admit it was finalised very much to my advantage.' He preened his moustache. 'It's a good thing I'm making some money—you seem to show no signs of going back to work.'

Casey saw Bryden's jaw tighten, and knew she had had enough. She took his hand and pressed it between her arm and her body, hoping he could feel the swell of her breast, and said limpidly, 'Will you excuse both of us? Some friends of ours have just arrived... it's been so nice meeting you.'

Informative would have been a more accurate word than nice, she thought, as she led Bryden away. So much for her much-vaunted honesty. Then Bryden said in a low voice, 'What friends?'

'The Drapers. Whose cottage began all this.'

'As long as you still consider them friends... by the way, you might want to lower my hand by six inches. Unless you're trying to drive me mad with lust in the middle of this rather sedate party.'

'I wanted to take your mind off your parents,' Casey retorted. 'Whom you and Jenny engineered that I meet. You're shutting me out again, Bryden.'

'If we're going to have a fight, I suggest we do it somewhere other than in front of the Drapers.'

'In that case I'll save it until later,' Casey promised. Then she donned a bright social smile. 'Hello, Susan, how are you?'

The party continued. The desserts were both delicious and calorie-laden, and, having disposed of rather more than her share, Casey found herself and Bryden temporarily separated from the rest of the crowd. She said, 'Why don't we disappear for a few minutes—no one will miss us.'

'There's a sun-room leading off the kitchen.'

The caterers were in efficient control of the kitchen. Casey complimented the chef on the hazelnut torte before leading the way into the solarium and closing the door. She let out her breath in a long sigh, tried to wriggle the tension from her neck and said, 'What wonderful plants!'

A profusion of hibiscus, amaryllis and begonias flaunted their showy blossoms in every corner. 'We didn't come here to admire the plants, Casey,' Bryden said drily. 'We came to have a fight.'

She glowered at him. 'This evening was another set-up, wasn't it? You wanted me to meet your parents and you didn't want to be around when I did.'

He made no attempt at denial. 'Jenny wasn't responsible this time, though—I was the one who suggested it. She just helped out.'

'With something less than subtlety.' Casey added carefully, 'Are you trying to warn me off?'

His face guarded, he said, 'My parents go along with me, Casey... and they're a far cry from yours.'

She thought of the love and support that had surrounded her since she was a baby, and which she had tended to take for granted, and said frankly, 'You must have had the personality of an ox not to have been driven mad by the age of two.'

He said with a faint smile, 'I took the coward's way out—I ran away. Only the place I ran was inside myself, where they couldn't touch me.'

'It's called survival, not cowardice,' Casey said shortly. 'Did you think *I'd* run away once I'd met your parents? That they'd scare me off?'

'I wanted you to be free to run if you so chose,' he said in a tight voice.

'I'm still here,' she said quietly.

'They made me what I am,' he said, slamming one fist against the other with a violence that made her jump. 'It's only since I met you that I've understood I don't have to stay that way for the rest of my days—that love and happiness can be mine in a way I never thought possible. You're so alive, Casey, so overflowing with warmth and generosity and laughter...'

'You can trust me,' she whispered. 'I won't go away.'

He brought a hand up to her cheek. 'Promise?'

'Promise,' she said, and all her love was in the single word.

As he found her mouth and kissed her with fierce dedication, cupping her face in his hands, she rested her palms against his chest, feeling the heat of his skin seep through his shirt, searching for the heavy beat of his heart. Between short, hard kisses he was muttering her name. His hands drifted down her throat, his fingertips as delicate as the brush of feathers on her flesh. Then he traced the rise of her breast under the silk fabric.

She swayed towards him, pliant as the pine boughs in the sea winds at the cottage. He said hoarsely, 'I won't rest until I have you in my bed. I——'

Light streamed into the room and Jenny said, 'This is the solarium, which we only finished a year ago... oh, I didn't know anyone was in here.'

Casey sprang away from Bryden, her cheeks as red as the hibiscus that nodded at her side. 'We were just leaving,' she babbled.

Bryden said with considerable panache, 'Casey has been admiring your green thumb, Jenny.'

Whatever Casey had been admiring had been quite unrelated to any part of Jenny. She said valiantly, 'That pink and white amaryllis is absolutely gorgeous.'

'Isn't it?' Jenny said complacently. She introduced the couple that was with her, whose names Casey could never afterwards recall, and somehow Casey contributed with reasonable intelligence to a discussion on the care of tropical blooms. Then they all joined the party in the living-room again, where she had a cup of very strong coffee. When she had finished it, she said, 'Bryden, I've got to go, I have to work tomorrow.'

They were near the front door, surrounded by people whose noise level indicated a very successful party. Bryden said, 'Can I call you at work tomorrow morning when I hear about the job?'

'Of course!'

In the same even voice he said, 'Thanks for not running away.'

Someone bumped into her and apologised profusely. 'I'll never do that,' Casey vowed.

'Just remember that I want you more than I have ever wanted anything or anyone in my entire life.'

She wanted to kiss him; she wanted to cry. As two more people jostled her, she said acerbically, 'You do choose your moments, Bryden Moore.'

'I'll learn to do better in the future...did you have a coat?'

'Upstairs.'

'I'll wait for you here.'

Her jacket was submerged under a mound of suede. Casey threw it round her shoulders and ran downstairs. Bryden was talking to Matthew and Jenny; she thanked them for a lovely party, kissed Bryden full on the mouth, and left.

CHAPTER ELEVEN

AT A quarter to ten the next morning Casey was loading a Labrador retriever into the van when Charlene, who managed the kennels, called through the window, 'Telephone, Casey!'

Casey latched the cage, climbed down from the van, and ran for the telephone, which was located outside the feed-room near the long row of pens. The three nearest dogs started to bark. 'Hello?' she gasped.

'This is Professor Bryden Moore speaking, of the mathematics department of Carleton University.'

'Bryden, you got the job!' she said warmly. 'I'm so happy for you, congratulations.'

'I'll have to acquire an air of absent-mindedness and a tweed jacket with leather elbow patches,' he joked. 'But before I do that, I'm planning a kidnapping... what the devil's that noise?'

'I'm in the kennels. Who do you want to kidnap?'

'You, of course.'

She tried to erase the silly grin from her face and said succinctly, 'When and why?'

'Five-fifteen at the airport. Bring enough old clothes for four days, plus that very sexy outfit you wore last night.'

She had not told Bryden or her parents that she had Monday and Tuesday off. 'How do you know I don't have to be back to work until Wednesday?' she demanded.

'David Canning told me. Two weeks ago.'

She scowled into the phone and said, 'Come clean, Bryden.'

'You're a very strong-willed woman,' he said plaintively. 'Not to say bossy. Maybe I should reconsider.'

'You're too late—I accept. Now tell me why you were talking to my boss.'

'With all due respect to your professional ethics, I felt eight years was too long to wait. Because what if I then wanted another dog? That would be another eight years. So I decided—are you listening, Casey?'

Wait for what? she wondered, in a turmoil of hope and panic. She said, only half joking, 'You're taking a very long time to get to the point.'

'I told David Canning my intentions towards you were highly honourable, that I was doing my best to get a job in Ottawa, and that our student-instructor role was not advancing my cause... what did you say, Casey?'

'N-nothing,' she spluttered.

'He was most sympathetic,' Bryden said blandly. 'From now on if there are any problems with Bess, I'll deal with Douglas rather than you. Which means we can be ourselves. Bryden and Casey.'

'I see,' Casey croaked.

'He also told me he was giving you a couple of days off after your exams, which he was quite sure you would pass with flying colours.' Abruptly Bryden dropped his bantering manner. 'That was when I took the risk of booking two seats to Halifax. Hoping that you would spend the four days with me at Ragged Island, Casey. But please don't think I took your answer for granted, because I didn't. *Will* you go with me?'

'There's nothing I'd like better,' she said.

There was a small silence. 'Thank God. I thought of going somewhere closer so you wouldn't have to fly, but I have this quite irrational urge to go back to the place where we met. Could you be at the airport by four-thirty?'

'If I'm going to be at the airport at four-thirty I'll have to stop talking on the phone—I've got a million things to do!'

'I'll meet you at the Air Canada ticket counter. Goodbye, Casey.'

He had rung off. She replaced the receiver and in a daze walked past the pens to get the other dog she would be working with that morning. She had asked Bryden why he was kidnapping her and he had not answered. Did honourable intentions mean marriage? Or was that only in Victorian novels? And would she and Bryden be sharing the big bed in his room? She remembered the heaped-up cushions whose colours glowed like jewels and discovered she was trembling.

But dawdling in the kennels would not answer any of her questions. Nor would it get her to the airport on time.

She must simply wait and see.

As it turned out, Casey had very little time to think about Bryden's proposal, honourable or otherwise. Brutus, the second dog she worked with that morning, seemed bent on breaking every rule of his training in the space of an hour. He gobbled some popcorn that had been spilled on the pavement, he tried to tree a big grey squirrel, and he hauled Casey halfway across the pavement when he sighted a black cat washing itself on a fence. With all the patience at her command Casey took him through his paces again and again until she was sure he was getting the message; which meant she was late for lunch and did not have the time to go to her apartment as she had hoped.

She worked with two other dogs that afternoon, both of whom behaved perfectly. At three-thirty she unloaded them from the van and ran the keys inside. David

Canning was crossing the hall. 'Haven't you left yet?' he demanded.

She considered a number of replies, shook her head and blushed.

'Off you go. And I don't want to see you before Wednesday morning.' His glasses slid a little further down his nose. 'Although I do expect an invitation to the wedding.'

'I haven't been asked to marry anyone yet,' Casey said.

'I'm sure you will be.' He waved her towards the door. 'Off with you!'

Casey had hoped to have time for a leisurely soak in the tub with lots of her favourite bath oil; instead she threw the bath oil in her travelling kit along with her other toilet articles. Jeans, sweaters, socks, shorts... mentally she ticked things off one by one, meanwhile carefully folding her white silk blouse in tissue paper and leaving the leather skirt to lie on top of everything else. She opened her lingerie drawer, packed her prettiest underwear and, after hesitating for a moment, added a nightdress her sister Anne had bought her a year ago: the kind of nightdress one wore on one's honeymoon. Then she changed out of her work clothes into a green three-piece linen suit whose loose, casual lines were very becoming.

It was ten minutes past four and it took twenty-five minutes to drive to the airport. She grabbed her suitcase, locked the apartment and ran down the stairs.

Half the population of Ottawa also seemed to be heading to the airport. There were delays at every traffic light and much of Casey's view was blocked by the transport truck that was ahead of her. The hand on her watch crept slowly towards the thirty-minute mark.

At twenty to five she drove into the car park, where she spent five minutes crawling along the lanes searching for an empty spot. She glimpsed one two lanes over, but by the time she got there it had been taken by a big black Cadillac. Then she saw another only three spaces away. She drove in and turned off the ignition.

The vehicle ahead of her, a flashy yellow sports car that had been backed into its space, was just leaving. The driver, who was young and male, gunned the motor and gave her a cheerful wave; too late she saw that his reverse lights were still on. She had time to brace herself before he reversed into the front of her car.

He leaped out, full of apologies and, when she got out of the car in her smart green suit, of admiration. The damage to her bumper was such that they had to exchange names; he would, she was sure, have asked her for a date if she had not said with frantic truth, 'I'm going to miss my plane—I've got to go!'

Grabbing her bag, she ran across the tarmac in her high heels; and in one of those sudden tricks of memory realised she had left her leather skirt hanging in the wardrobe. All she needed now, she thought desperately as the automatic doors swung open to admit her, was for Bryden to have gone on without her.

It was one minute after five. She searched the length of the Air Canada counters and saw him standing under the first class signs with Bess lying at his feet. His face was set in grim lines. Her heels clicking on the floor, she ran towards him.

'Bryden, I'm sorry!' she gasped. 'Everything's gone wrong from the minute you phoned. Have we missed the plane?'

He said harshly, 'I thought you'd changed your mind.'

'I told you I'd never do that. *I* was afraid you'd have gone on without me.'

'No fear of that, Casey.' Roughly he took her in his arms, expressing in his kiss all his pent-up fear and frustration.

The ticket agent said courteously, 'They're boarding your flight now, sir. You should proceed to gate twenty-one.'

'First things first,' Bryden growled and kissed Casey again.

They were the last passengers to get on board; by the time they were settled in their seats, the plane was taxiing away from the terminal. Casey was busy rattling off the disasters of her day; she reached the admiring young man in the yellow sports car just as they took off, and somehow managed not to mind the lift-off as much as usual. 'So that's why I was late,' she finished in a rush, releasing her clutch on Bryden's sleeve.

The aircraft was levelling off. She had survived again.

'It was the longest thirty minutes of my life,' Bryden said. 'But, in view of all you've told me, you're forgiven.'

As the steward brought them drinks, Casey requested, 'Tell me more about your job.'

He grinned boyishly. 'I'll be teaching mathematics to postgraduates and co-ordinating several research projects. So it's a big change from my other job, which was pure research and where I worked almost totally alone. This one involves a lot of contact with students and other professors.'

'You're coming out of the closet,' she said slowly.

'One of the reasons I holed up at Ragged Island was so I could work on the computer and find out what my limitations were.'

'I wasn't referring to your blindness,' Casey said even more slowly. 'I meant in terms of other people.'

'I can't fool you, can I, Casey? Of course that's at the root of the change—I want a job where I deal with people.'

'You won't be a lone wolf any more.'

He gave her a crooked grin. 'I never was much of a wolf.'

The pilot's voice came over the intercom, mentioning the cruising height and speed and describing the Nova Scotia weather as mild with coastal fog. Casey was so busy listening to Bryden's impressions of the university that she paid little attention to the weather; although the Halifax airport was wreathed in fog when they arrived there an hour later, the pilot made a faultless landing.

While she waited for the luggage Bryden took Bess for a walk; perhaps because she had been so late arriving at the airport in Ottawa, her suitcase was not among the baggage spewed on to the carousel. With a resigned sigh she went to the counter and entered a claim for it, and was told by the bored middle-aged clerk that it would be delivered the next morning. Then she and Bryden picked up the rental car, bought some groceries in the outskirts of Halifax and had a quick meal in a little restaurant in Bedford.

When they finally set off for Ragged Island it was dark, the fog thick enough that Casey had to concentrate on the guide line along the shoulder to keep herself on the road. Leaning forward in her seat, her hands gripping the wheel, she strained to penetrate the thick curls of mist. Bryden wisely kept silent, although he did say once, his voice full of frustration, 'This is when I hate being blind—everything falls on you.'

In this instance, at least, he was right. Casey said briefly, 'We should be there in half an hour.'

But as they got nearer to the sea the fog worsened, the headlights making such a small circle of yellow light that she was forced to drive even slower. So it was midnight before she turned into Bryden's driveway between the cedar hedges. She coasted down to the door, turned off the ignition and said with heartfelt relief, 'We're here. Thank goodness!'

'Let's get the stuff inside,' Bryden said shortly.

They unloaded groceries and suitcases and turned on the furnace to take the dampness from the house. Wishing she could dispel the tension in the air as easily, Casey said, 'Tea, cocoa, or a Scotch on the rocks?'

Bryden put his hand on her shoulder; it was the first time he had touched her since the airport in Ottawa. 'You've had a long day, Casey,' he said. 'You must be worn out. Why don't you go to bed... the last time the cleaning woman was here she made up the bed in the spare room. I'm going to take Bess for a walk on the beach, she's been cooped up all day and I need to stretch my legs as well.'

Nonplussed, Casey stared up at him. Although it had been a very long day and she was tired, she would have liked to walk on the beach in the fog; but she had not been invited. And from the first part of his speech, it looked as though Bryden's intentions were nothing if not honourable. In fact, she thought painfully, he looked as if he could not be rid of her soon enough.

Bess had heard her name and was sitting expectantly, her tail swishing on the pine floor. Bryden added with a reasonableness that Casey found intensely irritating, 'After all, you're here for four days, we've got lots of time.'

Time for what? she wondered, watching him take Bess's collar out of his kit bag. Not sure she could trust her voice, she said flatly, 'Have a nice walk,' and headed for the stairs.

Under other circumstances Casey would have been delighted to stay in the guest bedroom with its attractive rock maple furniture and peach-coloured carpet. But she had passed beyond tiredness to a kind of hypersensitivity, her nerves twitching, her brain racing, her eyelids scratchy. She kicked off her shoes, childishly pleased with the thunk they made as they hit the wall. Had she put up with balky dogs, forgotten skirts, crumpled bumpers and smooth-voiced pilots just to be sent to bed like a naughty child?

She marched downstairs. Bryden and Bess had gone.

How dared he leave her alone? she thought vengefully. Dragging her all the way from Ontario to sleep in the spare room...it was intolerable! If he was that much of a loner, he'd got the wrong woman. And she was going down to the beach right now to tell him so.

She stormed through the kitchen to the back porch, where she pulled on an old raincoat and a pair of Bryden's rubber boots and let herself out of the side door, slamming it shut behind her. The mist, redolent of the salt tang of the sea, bathed her face in coolness. The boom of the foghorn sounded very close. She stalked round the house to the back lawn and crossed it in the light from the living-room windows.

Bryden's boots were far too big for her, and her hands were lost in the sleeves of his coat. Clomping along, Casey found the path into the woods, which gathered her into their silent, damp darkness. In miniature rainshowers drops fell from the boughs on to her face as the foghorn, lonely voice of the sea, beckoned her forward. Stoutly telling herself she could not possibly get lost, Casey pushed onward. She could not go very fast, because of the boots; it was with a distinct feeling of relief that she found the cedar steps to the beach.

The sand was damp, and even in the darkness she could see the imprint of Bryden's steps and the miniature craters where Bess had been running. The sigh of the waves caressed her ears, and for a moment she forgot that she was furious with Bryden. There was no wind and the air was not cold; she let the boots fall from her feet and stripped off her tights, leaving them at the foot of the steps and wriggling her toes in the sand as she headed purposefully towards the ocean.

LOVE AT FIRST SIGHT

The tide was low. There was a stretch of smooth, unmarked sand, much cooler, then the wash of ice-cold water over her bare feet. With a tiny shriek of dismay Casey backed up.

The foghorn moaned through the mist. The white curl of water advanced, retreated, advanced again, and suddenly she was aware of how the darkness and fog were pressing in on her, encircling her, surrounding her. The house could have been a thousand miles away, and she the only person in the world... attacked by a paralysing loneliness of spirit, she felt the last vestige of her anger slip away like a retreating wave, and fear advance in its place.

Bryden had left the house without her. Instead of gathering her into his arms and making love to her, he had sent her to the spare room and gone for a walk alone. His parents have won, she thought in utter terror. Sure, he had a new job and he was running in marathons and getting his life in order after the loss of his sight. But he was still afraid to love. Harold and Cressida had won. She, Casey, had lost.

She shoved the back of her hand against her mouth to prevent herself from crying out, whirled, and staggered across the sand. The foghorn pursued her, mocking her, and she ran faster, wanting only the comfort and security of the house.

Her foot struck a rock. She stopped dead, and felt panic add itself to loneliness and pain, for as she peered through the mist she saw the humped shapes of boulders, and knew she had run towards the headland instead of the steps. Behind her the waves sucked and gurgled among the rocks, long strands of seaweed stirring lazily in the water like the hair of the drowned. Her skin crawled. She screamed Bryden's name into the darkness.

The fog smothered the sound of her voice. 'Bryden!' she cried again, but only the hollow boom of the foghorn answered her. He had vanished, she thought with another pang of terror. Insubstantial as the mist, he had gone from her life.

Thrusting her cold hands in her pockets, she tried to calm the battering of her heart against her ribs. Maybe this was a nightmare, like the ones she had had all last winter, and any minute she would wake and find herself in the maple bed in the spare room...

Then, like a nightmare, she heard something behind her, something that was not the splash of the waves. Frozen to the spot, straining her eyes, she glimpsed a dark shape emerging from the mist and gave a whimper of dread.

Bess barked. Bryden's voice said, 'Casey—is that you?'

Her body sagged. She stumbled towards him and threw herself into his arms, sobbing his name over and over again, burrowing her face into the wet nylon of his jacket. Bryden's arms went hard around her and he said, 'Thank God I've found you!'

As Bess sniffed at her bare ankles, his words penetrated her distress. 'What do you mean? *You* weren't looking for *me*. It was the other way round.'

'I certainly was looking for you! Five minutes after I came down here I realised I'd been a damn fool to leave you alone. So I was heading back to the house as fast as I could when Bess found the boots at the foot of the steps. That's how I knew you were down here, too.'

Casey raised her chin, all her anger rushing back. 'You flatter yourself when you say you were a damn fool! After all I've gone through today, I do not appreciate being sent to bed like a seven-year-old. If you want to be a loner, Bryden Moore, you go ahead—but you can count me out. *I'm* getting the first flight back to Ottawa tomorrow morning.' She finished with a defiant sniff.

He seized her by the elbows. 'I don't want to be a loner any more——'

LOVE AT FIRST SIGHT 185

'You have a funny way of showing it.' Her voice shook. 'You wouldn't even take me to bed!'

'Sweetheart, I had the best of motives for that... I wanted everything to be right. It's the first time for you, and you were tired and tense... so I thought we should wait until tomorrow.'

She drew a deep, hiccupping breath. 'You might at least have asked me how I felt about it.'

'That's the conclusion I came to down here in the fog, that of course I should have asked you. I'd been guilty of shutting you out again, making decisions on my own the way I always have.'

'Oh,' Casey said. 'I thought you didn't want me. At all.'

'Nothing could be further from the truth. The reason I came down to the beach was to work off some of my—er—energy.'

She said in a small voice, 'That's the second time you've called me sweetheart.'

As the foghorn echoed through the mist, Bess sat down on the sand and began to scratch herself. Bryden said quietly, 'I called you that because I love you, Casey.'

'I—*what* did you say?'

'Darling Casey, I love you with all my heart.'

They were the words she had waited for for months, spoken with all the passion she could have wished. With a sigh of utter contentment she rested her cheek on his jacket. 'Thank goodness,' she said.

'Is that all you've got to say?'

'I'm happier than I've ever been in my life.'

'Casey,' he said urgently, 'do you love me?'

In genuine surprise she said, 'Of course I do—didn't you know that?'

'Five minutes ago you were going to get the first flight back to Ottawa. No, Casey, I did not know that.'

She wrapped her arms around him. 'Bryden, dearest Bryden, I love you. With all my heart and soul I love you.' Then she reached up and kissed him.

He kissed her back with love and pent-up desire and with deep joy. 'I think we should go up to the house,' he said.

'Bess is getting wet and my feet are cold,' she said agreeably, taking his arm as the three of them walked across the sand. At the foot of the steps she put on his boots again, and together they threaded their way through the dark trees and across the lawn. She hung up her borrowed jacket in the back porch; by now she was feeling both shy and frightened, for she had never made love before and had no idea how they were to make the transition from the cluttered porch to the bedroom.

As if he sensed her diffidence, Bryden said easily, 'Do you want a quick shower to get rid of the sand, Casey? I'll lock up.'

'OK,' she mumbled and fled for the stairs.

The shower got rid of the sand and warmed her feet, although it did nothing for her nervousness. Her seductive nightgown, which might have helped, was in her suitcase somewhere between Ottawa and Halifax; she pulled on a robe of Bryden's that was hanging on the bathroom door and padded into the hall. Bryden's door was ajar.

The carpet muffling her footsteps, she crossed the hall and edged around his door. Although the covers had been pulled back, the bed was empty. Bryden was standing by the window; through an open louvre wafted the quiet rhythm of the waves. He was naked.

For a moment she gazed at him in simple pleasure, for the planes of his body from the broad shoulders and narrow hips to the long, lean legs were very beautiful to her. Then, with an ache in her heart, she wished fervently that he could see her as she was now seeing him.

He could not. He would never be able to.

But the desire that throbbed in her veins and dispelled her nervousness by its very insistence also told her what to do: she walked into his room, shedding the robe so that it fell in a tiny swish of sound to the floor. 'Bryden?' she whispered.

He had heard the soft fall of her steps. His body swung round. 'Come here, sweetheart.'

She walked right up to him, slid her arms up his hair-rough chest and kissed him. His hands went out to her; she felt the shock run through him as he discovered she also was naked. He groaned deep in his throat and pulled her against the length of his body.

When she felt the warmth and hardness, the muscle and bone that were the essence of him, the last of her fears vanished, for Bryden wanted her as passionately as she wanted him. The sound of the waves receded as they clung to each other, mouths devouring, hands frantically searching. Then he swung her into his arms and carried her over to the bed, laying her on her back, falling on top of her in his haste.

Glorying in his weight, Casey laced her fingers in his hair and kissed him again, their tongues dancing, their lips hungry for more. He rained kisses on her face, her throat, the soft hollows beneath her collarbones; he found the firm, ivory swell of her breast and traced it to its tip.

An arrow of sweetness pierced her to the core. Immersed in sensations new to her, utterly overwhelming in their intensity, Casey heard his hoarse whisper from a long way away. 'Casey, I love you. I love you so much, I can never have enough of you...tell me you'll marry me.'

She raised herself on one elbow, clutching his smooth, bare shoulder. 'Are you sure you want to marry me? Marriage is the opposite of being alone.'

He reached up and kissed her, then murmured against her mouth, 'More sure than I've ever been of anything in my life.'

In the dim light she searched his features, finding tension and love equally mingled. Holding his head to her breast, she dropped her cheek to his silky hair and cried joyfully, 'Yes...oh, yes. Because I love you so much.'

'I never thought I'd hear you say those words.'

'I've been wanting to say them for months. I was so afraid your parents would win, Bryden, that you'd stay a loner for the rest of your days.'

He eased her down on the pillows. 'How could I, when you've taught me how to share? Casey, I'll never shut you out again, I swear.'

With complete trust she opened her arms to him and whispered, 'Show me how much you love me, Bryden.'

He began caressing her with slow, sensual movements, seeking out one by one the places where she had never been touched before, and not until she was whimpering with pleasure and begging for more did he enter her. She felt no pain, only wonderment and a driving hunger that broke the last of her restraint. Through the gathering storm they travelled together, and together were flung into the waves and the wind's cry and the rhythms that could not be denied, and there Casey found the wild creature that Bryden had always made of her and joined that creature to him, woman to his man.

They were silent for a long time afterwards, resting in the storm's aftermath. Finally Casey said softly, running her finger along his upper lip, 'Thank you—that was wonderful.'

'For me, too.' He drew a strand of her hair gently through his fingers. 'I have the rest of my life to learn what you look like. To picture your beauty in my mind...to hold your love in my soul.'

It was not the first time Bryden had almost reduced her to tears. She nuzzled her face into his shoulder. 'I'm so glad we came here, where it all began.'

'I fell in love with you here.'

'You were very rude to me here!'

'That was because you scared me to death and entranced me at one and the same time. Little wonder that I tried to get rid of you.'

'I'm glad you didn't succeed,' Casey said with a contented sigh, threading her fingers through the hair on his chest.

'I'm glad I didn't, too.' He stroked the curve of her hip. 'And we have four more days... maybe we should spend them in bed, Casey.'

She gave a rich chuckle. 'Until my suitcase arrives, I don't have any proper clothes.'

'Fate,' he said solemnly. 'In the guise of an airline.'

Certainly, when a taxi delivered Casey's luggage at noon the next day, she and Bryden were still in bed.

EMMA DARCY

at her most daring with an unforgettable tale of ruthless sacrifice and single-minded seduction

THE SECRETS WITHIN

When Tamara Vandlier learns that her mother is dying she is elated—and returns to the family estate to destroy her mother's few remaining months, in return for her own ruined childhood. Loyalty turns to open rivalry in this novel that explores the dark, hidden secrets of two branches of a powerful Australian family.

AVAILABLE IN PAPERBACK FROM AUGUST 1997

MIRA

DEBBIE MACOMBER

THIS MATTER OF MARRIAGE

Hallie McCarthy gives herself a year to find Mr Right. Meanwhile, her handsome neighbour is busy trying to win his ex-wife back. As the two compare notes on their disastrous campaigns, each finds the perfect partner lives right next door!

"In the vein of When Harry Met Sally, Ms Macomber will delight."

—**Romantic Times**

AVAILABLE IN PAPERBACK FROM SEPTEMBER 1997

JAYNE ANN KRENTZ

Joy

When a couple win a mysterious emerald bracelet in a poker game, their peaceful Caribbean holiday becomes a rollercoaster of adventure, desire...and deadly peril.

"Jayne Ann Krentz is one of the hottest writers in romance today." —USA Today

AVAILABLE IN PAPERBACK FROM SEPTEMBER 1997

CAROLE MORTIMER

Gypsy

She'd always been his one temptation...

Shay Flannagan was the raven-haired beauty the Falconer brothers called Gypsy. They each found her irresistible, but it was Lyon Falconer who claimed her—when he didn't have the right—and sealed her fate.

MIRA®

AVAILABLE IN PAPERBACK FROM SEPTEMBER 1997

Elizabeth Lowell

Tell me no Lies

An international crisis is about to explode unless a desperate trap to catch a thief succeeds. Lindsay Danner is the perfect pawn in a deadly game. Now it's up to ex-CIA agent Jacob MacArthur Catlin to make sure Lindsay succeeds—and survives.

"For smouldering sensuality and exceptional storytelling, Elizabeth Lowell is incomparable."
—Romantic Times

AVAILABLE IN PAPERBACK FROM OCTOBER 1997

LAST NIGHT IN RIO

JANICE KAISER

Michael Hamline could never resist his ex-wife. This time she'd conned him to help clear her brother, languishing in a Brazilian jail. But they got more than they bargained for in sultry, dangerous Rio. This time, it could cost them their lives.

"...this one has big screen written all over it"
—Publishers Weekly

AVAILABLE IN PAPERBACK FROM OCTOBER 1997

RISING *Tides*

EMILIE RICHARDS

The reading of a woman's will threatens to destroy her family

As a hurricane gathers strength, the reading of Aurore Gerritsen's will threatens to expose dark secrets and destroy her family. Emilie Richards continues the saga of a troubled family with *Rising Tides*, the explosive sequel to the critically acclaimed *Iron Lace*.

MIRA

AVAILABLE IN PAPERBACK FROM OCTOBER 1997

The prequel to *Rising Tides*—where the foundations of the Gerritsen family are carefully crafted.

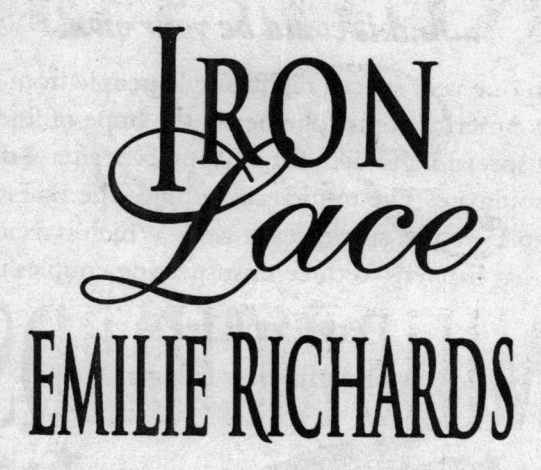

IRON Lace

EMILIE RICHARDS

Behind the iron lace gates of wealthy New Orleans, and beneath the veneer of her society name, lingers truths that Aurore Gerritsen has hidden for a lifetime—truths that threaten to change forever the lives of her unsuspecting family. Now, as Aurore faces her own mortality, she needs to reveal the secrets that have haunted her for so many years.

"...vividly drawn characters...brilliantly complex work"
—Affaire de Coeur

MIRA® AVAILABLE NOW IN PAPERBACK

Mills & Boon® invite you to a wedding...

...And it could be your own!

On one very special night, single people from all over America come together in the hope of finding that special ingredient for a happy ever after—their soulmate. The inspiration behind The Ball is simple—come single, leave wed. Which is exactly what happens to three unsuspecting couples in

Day Leclaire's
wonderful new trilogy:

FAIRYTALE WEDDINGS

Look out for the following books:

December: ACCIDENTAL WIFE
January 1998: SHOTGUN MARRIAGE

"Day Leclaire ensures a good time will be had by all."
—*Romantic Times*

Enchanted™

MILLS & BOON

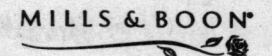

Christmas Treats

A sparkling new anthology
—the perfect Christmas gift!

Celebrate the season with a taste of love in this delightful collection of brand-new short stories combining the pleasures of food and love.

Figgy Pudding
by PENNY JORDAN
All the Trimmings
by LINDSAY ARMSTRONG
A Man For All Seasonings
by DAY LECLAIRE

And, as an extra treat, we've included the authors' own recipe ideas in this collection—because no yuletide would be complete without...Christmas Dinner!

MILLS & BOON

Season's Greetings To all our readers!

The Season's Greetings Gift Pack brings you four fabulous romances from star-studded authors including Betty Neels.

And as an extra special Christmas treat we're offering the pack at a discounted price of just £6.60--that's 4 books for the price of 3.

The Mistletoe Kiss by Betty Neels
Merry Christmas by Emma Darcy
The Faithful Wife by Diana Hamilton
Home for Christmas by Ellen James

Available: November 1997